A Time to See

Chapter 1

Evan raised his hat and wiped the sweat from his brow. He stared at the pale blue sky, searching for any sign of rain. Not a single cloud, just the constant haze that hung like a veil over the valley. He walked to the next row and took a knee by a mound of dirt. Reaching down, he dug out the drip line which had been buried by the silt from the latest flash flood.

"If it's not enough water, it's too much water," Evan muttered to himself.

He scraped the mud off the hose to ensure the line was working and repeated the process every few feet. One of his sheep, a dirty, white ewe with a black face, ambled up behind him and nudged him under his armpit.

"Not now, Stasia," he told her, "I've got to finish before noon, or I'll bake in this sun." The ewe nudged him again and let out a soft bleat. "I hear you, but you're gonna have to wait." As if she understood, Anastasia wandered back to join the rest of the herd. "I don't know why I'm doing this," Evan chastised himself. "I make twice as much selling wool, yet I spend all my time digging up these weeds and trying to get these fickle plants to grow."

Evan grew up on the farm, third generation on the same plot of land. He preferred to be called a rancher, though. That's what he really enjoyed doing. Raising his sheep and cows. Sheering, milking, shoveling manure. Any of that was better than trying to get mother earth to cooperate with him.

"If it wasn't for Liz …."

His voice trailed off before he said anything else. He would never disparage the woman that owned his heart

1

even though she wasn't around to hear him anymore. She had saved him. Saved him from his past and brought him out here, far away from the killing fields.

A low rumble, half-absorbed by the ancient mountains that surrounded the valley, made its way across the plain.

"*Sounds like thunder,*" Evan thought.

He scanned the horizon. Towards the east, a small black dot rose into the mid-morning sky. It hung over the patch of land that belonged to his neighbors on the other side of the ridge.

"Looks like the Carsens will be getting some rain," he noted. "Good for them."

A parliament of ravens, the largest group he had ever seen, flew out of the still rising sun. They passed directly overhead and spun in a large circle above him, blocking out the light for almost a minute.

"Never bring anything but bad luck, them birds. I should take a couple of them out now." He reached down for his revolver but thought better of it. "What'll I get? One? Two at most? That's if I even manage to hit them."

It was times like this he wished he hadn't sold the shotgun. But desperate times. Liz needed the medicine. And no one would buy his Mosin-Nagent bolt-action from him. Told him it was an old piece of junk.

"I can hit a coyote's eye from a thousand yards with it. In a cross wind. Old piece of junk. They have no idea what they're talking about."

The ravens headed towards the river and made a sharp left when they reached the edge of the forest at the end of the farm. Oak trees that stood tall when Evan's grandfather was a young boy guarded the beech trees which grew in their shade. The groves were thick on the banks of the Carmel River but thinned out as they scaled the slopes on either side. Halfway up the nearest ridge, the pine trees asserted their dominance, and only a few lonely oaks survived among them.

Evan headed back to the truck, kicking at rocks he found on his way. A couple of cows strode over to him to voice their displeasure. They could smell the bags of feed in the bed of the pickup and demanded their share. Ignoring them, he sat down in the driver's seat.

As he rested, a shadow passed over the truck and blocked the sun, sending a chill down his spine. He pulled his feet inside and reached behind the worn-out seat of his pickup to pull out a blanket he hadn't needed since late February. It was a family heirloom, at least two hundred years old, that his great-great – he couldn't remember how many – grandfather had bought at a Navajo trading post on his travels around the country. Over the years it had been passed down to the first-born male as a legacy, but by now it had lost most of its inherent as well as sentimental value.

Evan wrapped himself in the dusty, ragged threads and felt the chill dissipate. Feeling the blanket around his shoulders, he began to think about his connection to the past. The world had changed. At a pace that made him feel uncomfortable, heading in a direction he wished it wasn't. But what could be done about it? More importantly, what could he do?

"Nothing right now," he said out loud. He reclined as best he could, leaning his head in the corner. "Just a quick nap. Five minutes, no more," he promised himself. From his position, Evan could see the cloud traverse the northern boundary and pass over his house. "Well, maybe a bit longer. It looks like it'll rain a while."

Evan fell asleep as soon as he closed his eyes. He snored softly and dreamed of sunny days and blue skies, thoughts of simpler, happier times. His dog Zoe. His little sister Cate.

3

Her soft blonde hair flying back and forth as she ran up to hug him.

She was six years old in his dreams. She was always six years old just like the last time he saw her. He felt her frail arms wrap around his neck and heard her laugh as he picked her up and swung her around and around. Her eyes were dark emeralds that flashed sparks of light when she smiled. He missed her. Oh, how he missed her. But here she was, and his sadness eased for a moment.

Evan set her down and looked away. When he turned back, a young woman stood in front of him. A mask covered her entire face. Clumps of blonde stuck out from between the charcoal hair of the mask. Only her eyes shone through, green and empty.

"Save me," she said.

Evan wrinkled his brow in confusion.

"Save me," she repeated and pointed to the sky.

He looked up to see a cloud hovering above his truck. It was black. Unnaturally black like the deepest cavern on the darkest night. A light behind the darkness fought to make its way through, but it couldn't. Or wouldn't.

The cloud shifted shape and took the form of a dragon. Its jaws opened wide, and black figures spewed from its mouth. Shadows without form floated and danced in front of Evan's eyes. Shadows which appeared beautiful, enticing on first glance, like they held some splendid secret hidden away in their darkness. A mystery Evan had to learn.

He called out to them to come tell him their secret, but they didn't answer. So, he watched and delighted in their movement as they danced an ethereal ballet, rolling and twisting but ever beautiful. Evan felt himself caught up in the music of motion and whirled around with the shadows, inebriated by their dance. His head spun, and he collapsed to the ground, content but empty at the same time. Wanting more, needing more, he cried out to the shadows, begging to be filled.

They began to move again but not as before, jerking and stretching into dark blobs. Mutated, misshapen bodies without faces. Creatures which were neither human nor animal. A pair of wings sprouted from their twisted bodies only to be torn off by a pair of unseen hands, and they fell towards the earth, their screams a raging fire.

A host of winged horses spilled out of the dragon's mouth and raced to catch the falling creatures. Evan heard their hooves thunder as they galloped across the sky and felt the blast of the air from their beating wings shake the truck in a violent storm. A terror gripped him. There was no longer any rational thought. Only fear. His mind shut down and his body took over.

Evan threw open the door and ran. A shallow ditch reached out and tripped him, throwing him headlong into a ditch. He tried to pick himself up, but his feet had become stuck in the mud. In a moment, the shadows were upon him, swooping down in waves, clawing at him with crooked talons, swinging at him with clubs they carried in their deformed arms.

A terrible noise came from inside the shadows. High-pitched, banshee-like wails full of anger, loss, and revenge. Evan curled into a ball and covered his ears with his hands. He rocked back and forth and sang a song his mother had sung to him when he was afraid, but their screams overpowered his song.

The light from the sun had all but disappeared. Only a single ray shone through the middle of the dragon's head, illuminating Evan's face. As if summoned by an unspoken command, the black army returned to the sky and descended on the far side of the field. From there, it split in two, heading in opposite directions. One headed north towards the horizon. The other advanced towards Evan again, tearing through the valley.

In a matter of seconds, the shadows were on him. Without thinking, he drew his revolver and squeezed off five shots. The bullets struck the creatures but didn't do them any harm, didn't even slow them down. He braced himself, waiting to be torn apart, and stood there like a helpless child, impotent, afraid.

But nothing happened. He felt the creatures as they passed through him. They had no substance. Just shadows. Of what used to be men. Or something that looked like men. He felt their cold inside him. The cold of nothingness, of emptiness, of meaninglessness. But not regret. An icy determination. Unwavering in their single-mindedness.

The last one disappeared around the bend of the river that led towards the sea. Evan waited for a moment and wandered back towards the pickup, stopping every few moments to see if the shadows were following.

As he continued walking, he heard a rush of wind. He jerked his head to the left but saw nothing. To the right, but there was nothing there either. He felt the wind push at his back, and he spun around. Rising above the earth, a formless mass cloaked in a black mist towered over him. No face, no distinguishing features. Just a shadow. It stood in front of him, beckoning him, inviting him. For some reason, he felt no fear and simply listened as the shadow spoke to him. As it spoke his name.

"I have what you have been looking for, Evan," it whispered to him. "Come and take. Have your fill."

It didn't try to force him. This shadow offered him something. Something he wanted but hadn't been able to attain. He walked towards the shadow, towards the gift it held in its outstretched arms.

"Come and take," the shadow repeated. "It's for you."

Evan reached out to take hold, to accept the offer. It was what he desired, more than anything else, and it was in his grasp for the first time in as long as he could remember.

The happiness that filled his heart distracted him from noticing the shadow's arms as they became chains, coiling around him and locking him in their grip. In an instant, he felt himself wrenched from his fantasy and pulled into the shadow, the darkness wrapping around Evan and blocking his view of the world outside. Like a serpent caught in the mouth of a predator, he twisted and flailed, attempting to break the chains that held him in place. He screamed, but no words emerged.

Then, he stopped fighting. Out of the middle of the shadow, a face appeared. The face of a beast. A face with narrow slits for eyes and a mouth that spilled out blasphemies with every breath, speaking a name over and over. A name from the darkest nights of his past.

A thud on the passenger door woke him up. The blanket had wrapped around his shoulders and held him tight. Evan looked out the window and saw the beautiful, blue, sky above, streaks of red and orange beginning to appear.

"A dream?" he asked out loud but to no one in particular. He shook his head and breathed a sigh of relief. "A dream."

He stepped outside and planted both feet on the ground. Raising his arms into the sky, he stretched his shoulders and back.

"That felt good," he said to a ram grazing by the back tire.

The sheep looked up when he heard his master's voice. He lowered his head into the fresh herbs and took another mouthful, his jaw grinding back and forth, his front teeth showing through with each bite. Evan went up to the sheep and patted him on the head.

"Well, Franklin. You might not have much of a life, but, honestly, sometimes I envy you. No worries other than filling your belly with green grass and clear water." He paused. "And no dreams."

Evan climbed into the bed of the pickup. One by one, he threw bags of feed over the side. The sheep gathered around when they recognized the thump of the food hitting the ground. Two rams pushed their way through the mass of white and speckled wool to take up their positions in the front and chewed the bags in order to get at the treat which lay inside.

"Hold on, Dmitri. It's not all for you," Evan cajoled his favorite sheep as he leaned over the side of the truck. "There's plenty to go around, and most of it is for the cattle anyway."

He let out a loud, "Heee yaaahhh," and then another. One large cow a hundred yards away lifted her great black head and looked at him. A second later, she was trotting towards the truck. She arrived as Evan sliced into the last bag of pellets. He picked up the bag by one end and dumped the food on the ground, backing away from the pile and leaving a wide trail for the cattle to eat.

"Hi Olga," he said to the cow. "Good to see you made it. I'm sure your brood will be here shortly."

He patted the cow on the shoulder and scratched her ear for a few seconds. She pushed her face against his hands as if to indicate that she wanted more and let out a soft *moooo* when he started again.

Climbing back aboard the pickup, he sat down to watch his herds. The cows looked like they were dressed for a formal occasion. Black faces and shoulders, a white band around the middle, and a black rump and rear legs. His little girl, Laney, four years old and the spitting image of her Aunt Cate, called them vest cows.

"I want to go see the vest cows," she would say to her father when he headed off to the valley. She danced up and down unable to control her excitement whenever he said yes. That day two years ago, he had told her no. "OK, daddy," she had said before giving him a giant squeeze and letting out a final, "I love you."

He sat against the rear window of the pickup and felt the breeze as it swept down from the mountains. He leaned his head back and took a deep breath. The cool air filled his lungs and restored his energy. For half an hour he sat there, breathing in and out, not a care in the world.

"This is how it's supposed to be, Olga," he told the cow as he gave her a smile.

He stood up to stretch and threw himself over the side of the pickup. As he hit the ground, he heard a noise like a rush of wind. He jerked his head around but saw nothing. Without thinking, he drew the gun from its holster. It felt light. Lighter than it should have been. He opened the cylinder of the revolver and looked inside. One bullet. Five empty shells. He closed the cylinder and held it in front of him, looking to his left and then to his right. When he turned to his left again, it was there. The face from his nightmares, towering over him and clothed in darkness.

"It's time," it hissed. "I have come to collect."

"No. No more," Evan said.

"You owe me," it demanded.

"I've paid in full." Evan trembled as he spoke.

The shadow's face contorted in rage. "Fool!" it said. "You are mine."

Evan's heart began to pound as he raised the pistol to his temple. The shadow's eyes narrowed, small slits in its face staring through Evan as if it knew him better than he knew himself.

"If that's the way you want it," it said.

It watched the battle in his mind, saw his finger start to pull the trigger but stop, knew it had won again.

"Just a few more," it said. "I promise and then you will be free. She will be free."

"Just a few more," he said, "and then it's all over." His words were a command that he knew wouldn't be obeyed.

It smiled a bitter, mocking smile.

"When?" he asked.

"Soon," it replied. "Soon."

Chapter 2

Ryah sat in his usual spot. The bartender gave him a nod and poured a draught. A couple of regulars, friends from his days at Braxis Industries, sat in a booth, ignoring the fights on the screens above the bar. "Talking politics, I'm sure," Ryah said to himself.

"Hey, Ryah. Come over and join us."

"Give me a minute, Dare," Ryah answered.

Taking a sip from the frosted mug, he allowed the aroma to float up through the foam and into his sinuses. A wide grin spread across his face.

"Perfection," he said.

The bartender chuckled.

"Go ahead and laugh, Trev," Ryah said to him. He took another sip. "But this is the closest I'm going to get to heaven."

"I'll drink to that," a man on Ryah's left replied, and he raised his glass in a toast. Ryah returned the gesture and set his beer down.

A cheer erupted from the screen. The challenger had dodged the first swing of the sabat, but he failed to account for the backswing. The metal studded club slammed into his head, and he went down, stiff, lifeless, oblivious to the spectators' bloodthirsty screams for more. The victor obliged and raised his club.

Ryah had been on the receiving end of the sabat once. That was enough. He had also laid out more than a few people during his fighting days. It had been years, though, since he had entered the ring.

A waitress made her way across the packed room. Her red skirt reached the middle of her thigh while a white t-shirt hugged her body. Suggestive but with an air of modesty. Ten pairs of hands groped her as she passed by. Two of the patrons propositioned her, offering her the best night of her life.

"Not tonight, gentlemen," she told them. "I've got a flare up, so I'll have to take a rain check."

"Seems like that's been happening a lot recently," a guy retorted.

She winked and blew him a kiss. Ryah studied her face as she walked. She wasn't ugly, but she wasn't pretty either. There was a quality about her, though, that was attractive. An old-world femininity which cut through the modern androgyny. A gentleness at odds with a society which worshiped strength and power.

A man noticed Ryah and gave him a light shove on his shoulder. "She's lookin' pretty good tonight, don't ya' think?"

"Whatever you say, buddy. Just watch where you put your hands."

"Sorry, friend. I didn't mean any harm."

Ryah gave him a glare but didn't reply. The man either didn't notice or didn't care and continued on.

"She your girl, or one of your girls?" He gave Ryah a knowing nod. "You're a good-looking guy. I bet you have a bunch of women … or do you have trouble making it with the ladies?"

"You have a point?"

"I'm just saying, if you ever need someone to hook you up, I'm the one for you. I've got blondes, brunettes … girls from Asia, Africa, America. Good prices, no diseases. I check them myself. And they'll give you anything you want."

"No thanks," Ryah said.

"You into guys then? I got them too. They cost a little extra, of course."

Ryah's face showed his annoyance. "I'll pass."

The man looked left then right, checking to make sure no one else could hear. He spoke in a hushed voice. "The young ones, huh? That's your thing. It's alright with me. I've got them as young as six. You'll have to follow me if you want them. Boys, girls. Don't matter. Younger than that, I can hook you up with a friend of mine. It'll cost you a finder's fee, though."

All of Ryah's six foot four, two-hundred twenty pounds was ready to send the pimp to his maker, but he scurried out the door before Ryah got the chance. Ryah took one last drink as if to wash the bad taste out of his mouth. As he got up to join his friends, he bumped into the waitress and knocked her serving tray to the floor.

"Sorry, Bren. I wasn't watching where I was going," he said as he handed her a cup.

"It's alright, Ry. I always enjoy running into you."

She wore a grin as she walked behind the bar. Ryah returned her smile.

"Ryah!" Darius yelled out when he reached the table. "Glad you could join us. What're you drinking tonight?"

"Just a coffee. I reached my limit already."

Darius called out to the waitress. "Hey Brenda. Come on over when you can."

Brenda held up one finger to let him know it would be a minute and went back to her conversation with the bartender.

Darius was a bit older than Ryah. He was mid-management. Got his job, never having spent a day in the military, because he knew the right person. Normally, Ryah despised this type, but Darius was a good guy. He worked hard, didn't have an inferiority complex trying to prove he was as tough as the former soldiers that filled the ranks at Braxis.

Connor, the other guy at the table, was one of the best programmers at the company despite having lost his right hand when his armored vehicle hit a land mine in The War. He was always upbeat, even after the land mine, and never lost his sense of humor. Ryah didn't have the opportunity to work with them often, only on certain missions that required their particular expertise. One day, they hung out at lunch, starting a routine that lasted almost three years. They became as close to Ryah as he would allow anyone to get. Even after he left the company, he would see them a few times a year, usually in the same spot he saw them now.

"You still working for Representative Cruze?" Darius asked Ryah.

Ryah nodded his head. "Yep."

"How's that going?"

"I'm livin' the dream," Ryah replied.

"Yeah, well, we miss you at Braxis," Darius said. "Wish you could have stayed on, but when the Council calls…." He didn't finish the sentence. Everybody knew what happened when the Council made a 'request'.

Brenda's cheery voice interrupted the reunion. "Alright, boys. What can I get you?"

"I'll take another Wild Turkey on the rocks," Connor said. "Darius, you need anything else? On me this time."

"No. I'm good," Darius answered.

"And you, Ryah?"

"Coffee."

"Black. One sugar, right?"

"You know me well," Ryah replied.

Brenda acted like she was going to leave but hesitated and turned back to Ryah. "So, how's the Council? You liking it?"

"It's alright, Bren. They say it's good for my career, but I miss the action."

"You went there for your career, huh?" Brenda gave him a knowing nod.

"That's what I tell myself. By the way, how's your mom? Is she getting any better?"

Brenda's ever-present smile faded, and a profound sadness crossed her face. "No. It spread to her pancreas. They said it's too far advanced to operate." She wiped a tear from her eye. "You know, with all the advances we have, you'd figure they'd have found a cure by now."

Ryah didn't reply but squeezed Brenda's fingers. She returned the gesture, and Ryah felt the warmth of her hand in his own. He held on as she wept silently for a few seconds. Regaining her composure, she withdrew her hand and placed it on Ryah's shoulder.

"Thanks for asking," she said. "Now, about those drinks." She turned and walked off through the gauntlet of paws.

Darius raised his eyebrows and grinned. "You really need to go for it."

"No man. She's like my sister. It would feel weird. Besides, there're too many women wanting this," he said pointing at his body. "The Ry-man can't be tied down."

"Mm hmm," was Darius's reply. "If you say so." He took a drink from his glass. "So, what are you hearing on your end?"

"About what?" Ryah asked.

"About the Chinese Republic. Any word from the Council about how they're going to respond."

"No. I'm pretty much in the dark. Representative Cruze isn't on any of the military or strategy committees, so I'm not privy to the details of what they're planning. I mean, I've heard a couple rumors, but I have no idea if there's any truth to them. You two probably have a much better idea of what's going on."

"We've known for a couple of years that something like this was coming," Connor injected. "When China invaded Japan and the UN slapped the Chinese with meaningless sanctions, you knew they'd go after more territory."

"Yep," Ryah said. "The UN gave China everything they asked for in hopes of keeping them happy. 'Prevent them from doing anything worse', they said. Didn't work out the way they expected, now did it?"

"Nope," Connor replied. "By the way, weren't you there on an undercover around the time the Chinese landed in Japan?"

"You know I can't talk about those missions whether or not I went," Ryah replied. "Even with you guys."

"Of course," Connor said. "Anyway, it happened with Chamberlain and Hitler, us and the Persian-Ottoman Empire. How many other times, I couldn't count. Appeasement has never worked. It seems to me that history repeats itself regardless of what we remember. I guess people were so tired of war that they didn't have the stomach or the heart to do anything."

"The Chinese knew what they were doing," Darius said. "Their timing was intentional ... and well planned, might I add. They stayed out of the war and let everyone else wear each other out, bleed each other's resources. We couldn't have fought back even if we wanted to. We thought they were going to stop when they took half of India. Maybe it was just wishful thinking. I figured there might have been a chance that they would have continued on down to the Philippines. But Russia?" He shook his head in a mix of disgust and amazement. "How many soldiers did they send across the border?"

"Fifty-thousand, give or take, is what I heard," Connor replied. "It took the Russians by surprise. Maybe the Chinese were just looking to see how the Russkies would respond."

"It won't be pretty," Darius said. "Russia doesn't mess around. I expect a swift, harsh response. Remember what they did when the Persians landed at Rostov? That was the beginning of the end for the Empire."

"True," Connor said, "but according to our intelligence, the Chinese have as many as three times the number of troops that the Persians did and possibly twice as many as the Russians. It'll be a mess. I just hope this stays conventional."

"I hope so too. But you know, even as big as their army is, the Chinese are stretched thin. Got a few too many fronts. Besides, one thing I know is that you should never underestimate the Russians." Darius raised his glass to his lips and drained the final drops out of it. "So Ryah, the rumors you heard, any indication which side we're going to take?"

"Not really," Ryah answered. "I get the feeling the Council doesn't want to align itself with either of them. I'm not sure we'll have that option though. I figure we'll end up having to choose the lesser of two evils."

"That's gotta be the Russians," Darius said. "I'm not a big fan of theirs, but that's who we should go with."

"You're out of your mind," Connor argued. "There's no way we should ever align ourselves with the Russians."

Ryah sat quietly with his hands on the table, his fingers interlocked. "*Here they go,*" he thought.

Connor continued. "You can't trust them. They'll tell you lies, half-truths, whatever you want to hear, and then turn around and do whatever they want. Get you looking one direction and then hit you from another. At least the Chinese are honest about their intentions."

"Yeah. They'll tell you they're gonna take over your country, steal your resources, rape the women, and then they'll do it," Darius retorted. "That's the kind of honesty I can get behind."

"At least they're staying over in Asia. They don't have any desire to rule the world. Just become a dominant economic power. That's all they really care about. For all their talk about communism and such, they don't care about ideologies. They just want the power. They're basically isolationists. Isolationists who want to be rich and flex their muscle. Always have been. But those Russians. You give them a chance, and they'll be sweeping down through your land, driving you out. Killing you. They're a bunch of remorseless killers, and you know it."

"Remorseless killers, huh?" Darius responded. "Try thirty million of their own people. The Chinese killed thirty million of their own people. And what do you think they've done to the people they conquered?"

"Make that fifty million of their own plus countless others, and you got the Russians," Connor said.

"Well," Darius replied, "now that the Russkies have control of most of oil fields in Persia and access to the Red Sea, they have what they want. The Chinese still don't have … actually, I have no idea what their end game is."

"C'mon now. You don't think the Russians are done, do you?" Connor asked. "They spared the Saudis, but that's only for now. And Israel… how is it still around? They're the cause for all the problems in that region anyway. I mean, that's how all this mess started in the first place. If the UN had rid the world of that blight like they said they would, none of this would have happened."

"That I can agree on," Darius said.

"Hey guys. Still talking shop?" Brenda asked, drinks in hand. "Don't you ever take any time off?" She smiled at them and handed Ryah his coffee. "I put a little extra something in there for you," she said and blew him a kiss. She gave Connor his whiskey and spun around, her hair flipping across Ryah's face.

"Mm hmm," Darius repeated. "Just like your sister."

18

Ryah blushed and blew across the top of his coffee. A sudden chill overtook him, and he wrapped his hands around the sides of the cup to capture its warmth. From the bar, a cheer rose as a sabat crushed a man's jaw.

Chapter 3

Ryah took another sip of coffee and felt someone tap his arm. He turned to find a man, considerably taller than average, with dark, brown hair and a sparse moustache that couldn't make up its mind whether or not it wanted to grow. A tailored suit, gray with light pinstripes, floated as he moved, creating the illusion that nothing held it up. Dark eyes sat in a pleasant enough face, but the more Ryah stared at it, the more uneasy he became.

"I couldn't help overhearing what you were talking about," he said. "The Russia-China mess. Do you mind if I join you?" His voice was deep but with strange high-pitched undertones.

"Not at all," Connor said. "Ryah, slide on down so he can sit by you."

"He can pull up a chair and sit on the end." Ryah said. "Or even better, he can keep moving."

The stranger wasn't fazed and grabbed a chair from the table behind him. "My name is Abbad."

He reached out to shake Ryah's hand. Ryah just stared at him. Abbad withdrew his arm and stretched it out towards Darius, who returned his handshake.

"I'm Darius, and this is Connor," he said indicating to his left. "Never mind our friend Ryah over there. He doesn't like strangers. What brings you here tonight?"

"I'm in town on official business. Staying up the road at the Watermere and decided to come down here for a drink," Abbad said.

"Business, huh?" Darius said. "What business are you in?"

"I work for an ambassador to the UN. That's why your conversation caught my attention."

"UN," Ryah interrupted, now even more annoyed by the intrusion. "That's one organization I never had any use for. Worthless from the beginning. Kicking them out was the best thing we ever did."

"C'mon Ry. Play nice," Darius said.

"That's alright," Abbad said. "I understand why he might feel that way, and I must admit, up until a couple of years ago, I would have agreed with him. But after I got to know Ambassador Tanas, I changed my mind. More accurately, he changed my mind. Do you know him?"

Darius shook his head.

"No matter," Abbad continued. "It wasn't long after I got transferred to our European Bureau that the UN moved their headquarters to Rome. It was there, in Rome, that I met Ambassador Tanas for the first time. It was at a cocktail party hosted by the Vatican. Wasn't sure what I was doing there, other than my supervisor handed me an invitation and said I had to be there that evening. As soon as I arrived, I was escorted to the VIP section where Tanas was chatting it up with some bishop or cardinal – I can never tell them apart – when the Ambassador called me over. He said, 'Abbad. It's good to see you could make it.' It shook me a little, because I didn't know who he was. I asked him how he knew me, and he said that he was the one who had sent the invitation. We spent the evening talking, and by the time I left, I had a new job working for him. You can't say no to this guy, I learned that early on. Anyway, he's on a mission to reform the UN, make it a worthwhile institution, you might say. Which is what brings me here now."

"To make the UN worthwhile? Good luck with that," Ryah scoffed.

Darius shot Ryah a look. "What are you planning to do?" he asked Abbad.

"We're here to ask for help from your country in negotiating a ... what should I call it ... a voluntary surrender of power."

"From who?" Connor asked. "From us?"

"Well. Sort of. But in the end, it's really about Russia and China. We all know what would happen if war broke out between them, so we're in discussions with your Council to broker an agreement."

"Why us?"

Abbad replied. "You're neutral and have connections in the governments of both Russia and China. Besides, if you were to give up a tiny bit of control to the UN, say a small territory or the right to command a battalion of your troops, some gesture like that, it would be a sign of good faith for the other nations to follow suit."

"Never going to happen," Ryah said. "Why in the world would you think we would ever consider giving up control to some outsiders?"

Abbad answered, doing his best to sound convincing. "If nations would submit themselves to a united government, there would be less conflict. Instead of taking matters into their own hands, the representatives at the UN, who can see the big picture, would determine a compromise that is in everyone's best interests."

Darius spoke up this time. "I doubt the Council will go for it. There doesn't seem like there's anything in it for us."

"It's like I said," Abbad responded, "Ambassador Tanas can be very persuasive."

A commotion from the front of the bar interrupted the conversation, and all four turned to find the source. A security guard held the arm of a man who had just entered. The man was yelling something unintelligible and, for someone of such small stature, was putting up a good fight. Another guard came to help, but the man slipped away and ran through the maze of tables and chairs towards the back where Ryah sat. The patrons stopped and a hush fell over the place.

Seizing the opportunity, the man climbed onto a table and screamed out, "Judgment day is coming! Judgment day is coming, and it's already here! Look around you. They're in your midst. Can't you see them? They're here and they want to destroy you. Turn! Turn back and change your ways. Judgment day is here! You fools. What did you think would happen? What did you think he would do? He has come to collect. It's judgment day for you all."

He looked around the room, pointing and gesturing until his eyes rested on Abbad. The man's face became ashen, and, in a voice barely more than a whisper, he said, "You …"

Before he could finish, the guards arrived, dragged him to the front, and tossed him into the street.

Darius didn't move during the entire scene. When the show ended, he said, "That Giordy is one crazy guy. At least he changed up his speech this time."

Ryah was focused on Abbad the entire time and didn't hear Darius. He noticed Abbad tense up and shudder the moment the commotion started and didn't calm down until Giordan was thrown out. There was a quality about Abbad that Ryah found untrustworthy when he first saw him, like an actor hidden behind a mask speaking well-rehearsed lines. Giordan's appearance had peeled back the veneer, at least, for a moment.

"Well, I better be going," Abbad said.

As he stood up, his eyes met Ryah's for the briefest of moments. In the reflection of those dark eyes, eyes into which light could not penetrate, a face stared back at Ryah. But it wasn't Ryah's face. Nor was it Abbad's.

Ryah jerked back, knocking his cup over and sending the last bit of coffee spilling across the table.

"You alright, Ryah?" Darius asked, wiping up the mess.

Ryah shook his head. "There's something wrong with that guy. I don't like him. He's hiding something, but I can't tell what."

"You don't like anyone," Darius said, teasing him a little.

"This is different."

"What do you mean?" Darius said.

"First off, the Watermere, where he says he's staying, has a bar where all the power players from the Council go for a drink after work. Why would he come down here? It seemed like he wanted to talk with us specifically. But that doesn't make sense if he really is who he says he is. Was he trying to convince us of his cause? Why would that matter? I'm a nobody." Ryah paused to ponder his own words. After a while, he added, "You know, he never had a drink in his hands the whole time he was here. There's definitely something not right about him."

"I don't know Ry. I don't know," was all Darius could say.

"I guess it doesn't really matter," Ryah said. He took a look out the window. "Well, nice chatting with you guys but I better get going. I've got an early day tomorrow."

He passed the bar, pausing to wave at Brenda, and stepped into the crisp evening air, wondering aloud how strange it was to have such cool weather this time of year. A dove cooed in agreement and tucked its head back under its wing.

Ryah took a quick glance around and headed down the road lost in his thoughts. Oblivious to the shadows which grew and dissipated each time he passed under a streetlight. Unaware that Giordan lay in an alley behind him gasping for air. Never hearing the shot which tore through his lungs.

Chapter 4

He arrived home after midnight, angry at himself that he had stayed out so late.

The previous night, he had been rousted from his sleep by a loud noise. He woke to find a thin beam of light slipping through the blinds, casting enough of a glow to see the outline of objects in the room. An uneasy sensation had overwhelmed him, an impression that someone else was inside his home. He walked through the apartment checking and double checking every corner before he could convince himself that he was alone. When he finally lay down again, his mind was racing, thinking about a hundred different things at once, none of which was worth losing sleep over. After a few hours, exhaustion finally had overtaken him.

"Tonight will be different," he thought.

It wasn't. For the longest time, he stared at the walls, thoughts of Abbad and Brenda drifting through his mind as fatigue waged war against the effects of the caffeine which lingered in his system. The last time he checked the clock before he slipped into unconsciousness, it was half past one.

A brilliant light blinded Ryah. He shielded his eyes and peered through his fingers as he tried to adjust to its intensity. It was as if the morning sun had risen in his room and was shining directly in his face, yet he didn't feel any heat. The light was white, but at the same time Ryah could distinguish all the colors of the spectrum. He struggled to see the closet door, a window, anything that he might recognize, but all he could make out were shapes and outlines.

He heard noises also. Water flowing down a small stream and splashing past rocks at the end of a gentle incline. A peaceful rustling of leaves blown by soft gusts of wind. They were followed by what appeared to be a song but with chords and notes that were foreign to his ears. A harmony would rise up and fall, allowing another even more beautiful one to take its place. Ryah had no idea what was happening, but he didn't care. The symphony of sounds stood in stark contrast to the usual cacophony which clattered outside his window, and he reveled in its beauty.

A hand touched his shoulder, and he spun around. He found himself standing in a field of grass, long and silky, blue-green in color but with a subtle purple hue. Perhaps it was the way the sunlight reflected off it that gave it this shade, or perhaps it was the field itself.

The light came from all sides as if he stood on a planet hidden in the sun's core, and he wondered why he was not being consumed by the flames. No shadows touched his feet or bent beneath the blades of grass. No sun stood in the sky to let him know if day had just begun or welcomed its end.

At last, he noticed the person who had touched him. Or was it a person? He was much taller than Ryah, a foot or more, with long slender legs and arms that nevertheless gave the impression that he possessed great strength. His shirt was bleached white and perfectly laundered, and it looked like it had never been worn before. He began speaking to Ryah in a language he hadn't ever heard but one which he could understand. The man held an arm out in front and moved it up and down, pointing at Ryah. Ryah looked at his own clothes. Wet with mud plastered from shoes to collar. Shame burned his neck. He tried to scrape off the sludge, but it clung to his clothes. Even that which he managed to remove would grow back thicker and stickier.

"Take these." The man held out a set of clothes to him. "You'll need to put them on."

As soon as he took hold, Ryah found himself dressed in the new clothes. They fit his body as though tailored for him, cut from a soft, breathable fabric which kept Ryah warm but cool at the same time.

"My name is Guriel," the man said. "Come with me."

"Where are we going?" Ryah asked.

Guriel didn't answer but turned and walked across the silken field, Ryah close behind. Beyond the grass lay a path made of clear granite climbing a long hill. The path felt cool on his bare feet. He wiggled his toes as he walked, letting them enjoy their newfound freedom.

A few others passed by as they ascended the hill. Each of them carried a tool, distinct and unlike any Ryah had ever seen.

"Where are they going?" Ryah asked.

Guriel smiled at him. "They're building a new city. Over there." He indicated a place off to their left. "We're expecting an influx of people soon."

"Where are we?" Ryah asked him.

"In due time," Guriel answered.

He started up again, striding along at a furious pace. Ryah was forced to move at a half walk, half jog and found himself tiring from the exertion. After what felt like an hour, the ridge at the top of the hill seemed just as far away as when they began.

"I'm a modern-day Sisyphus," Ryah said to himself, "being punished for something I did … but in a veritable paradise." He laughed to himself at the irony.

"We're almost there," Guriel said.

As soon as he spoke, they reached the summit. Below, a great plain stretched before them. A multitude of people

– that's how Ryah decided to describe the creatures he saw – entered and exited a city a few miles up ahead. The city was enormous, larger than any he had ever seen, and, even though a mountain rose directly in the center, Ryah could see all the way through to the other side as light appeared to bend around solid objects.

A palace rested on the top of the mountain, a castle straight out of a fairy tale. Ryah imagined a princess waiting for him in a room at the top of a tower, standing by the window out of which a red flag rode on a calm breeze.

"We're headed there," Guriel said, pointing at the palace. "But we're going to stop here and rest for a while."

He pointed off the path towards two houses. The one on the right had been sculpted out of solid marble and rose high above the plain. Ryah marveled at the designs which covered the face. Vines, branches, and flowers curled around in intricate patterns, intertwining and connecting with each other in a display of spring and new life. Precious metals covered the flowers with hues of gold, crimson, and blue. Emeralds and brown sapphires inlaid the vines and branches, the crystals reflecting light at just the right angles to bring the carvings to life. Inside, three people talked around a table.

A small, wooden building sat on the left, an oval window resting in the middle of the front door. Guriel guided Ryah towards the door and rapped on the frame beside the window. A woman with pale blue eyes opened at the sound of the knocking and invited the two to enter. As Guriel passed, the woman kissed him once on each cheek, greeting Ryah in the same manner. A bowl of fruit sat on a table next to a cup filled with water. He took a drink and set it down. As soon as it touched the table, the cup refilled itself almost to the point of overflowing. He reached out to try a piece of fruit but swallowed only one bite, becoming full as soon as the food settled in his stomach. In a moment, his eyes grew heavy as if he had been awake for days, and he laid his head on the table.

When he woke up, he was lying in a bed, and Guriel and the woman were nowhere to be found. He opened the door and walked out, expecting it to be late in the afternoon, but the sky was the same as when he first arrived.

"That's strange," he wondered. "Either I didn't sleep much at all, or I slept an entire day."

"Neither," a voice spoke from behind him. Ryah turned around to see Guriel standing there. "It's always like this here."

"Don't you get tired of it?" Ryah asked. "Come to think of it, do you ever get tired?"

"It's time to go," Guriel replied.

"Not much for small talk, huh?" Ryah asked, the annoyance starting to show.

"You're a peculiar creature," Guriel said. "I wonder what the king wants with you. No matter. We need to hurry. Everyone is waiting for you." He took off with Ryah struggling once again to keep up.

They arrived at the edge of the city and crossed over a river whose source was somewhere in the mountain. The water was deep and so clear that Ryah could see to the bottom. Gems and jewels of many colors littered the bed, the same as those used to decorate the house. The city itself was spectacular, as if it had been designed to the last detail by a master engineer of immense talent. People walked down wide roads, talking among themselves, laughing, smiling, enjoying their lives.

Soon, a crowd of hundreds surrounded Ryah. Some reached out to touch him, drawing their hands back as soon as they did like a child learning to pet a dog. Even though they towered over him, they all seemed to marvel at his presence. A few of the smaller ones walked beside Ryah and tried to mirror his gait. Their long arms and legs, which normally had a smooth, fluid movement, flailed like a newborn when they tried to emulate him. They laughed at themselves and ran in front to get a better look. He smiled back at them and played with them, even grabbing onto one of their arms when they reached out to touch him, beginning a tug of war that lasted a few steps. At the bottom of a long flight of stairs, the crowd dissipated, leaving Ryah alone with Guriel.

"Up there. All the way to the top. Take a right and then a quick left. Walk through the doors you see. I will be waiting for you when you return." Guriel made as if he was going to walk off. He paused, and said, "Make sure you bow when the prince enters," then turned and left Ryah by himself.

"*So, there is a prince*," he thought to himself. "*Probably a princess too.*"

At the top of the stairs, he took a right and then a quick left and found a set of double doors, which reached to the ceiling, carved out of a type of wood he had never seen before. Perfectly preserved, they looked as if they had been cut that very day and were adorned only by their natural beauty. He pushed against them, expecting their weight to push back, but they swung open with ease.

He entered a great hall with white walls, alabaster with rainbow streaks as though cut from a gigantic pearl. Flags flew at regular intervals, but no other ornamentation covered the walls. No coat of arms. No paintings. No tapestries or anything else to indicate who the king was.

At the end of the hall, an entryway led to another room. Instead of doors a huge curtain hung on the wall to the side of the entrance. Two guards, one on each side of the door, stood in front of the entrance, while a third man waited by the drawstring.

Inside, incense rose through the floor and imbued the room with a sweet aroma not unlike a mixture of fresh bread and a fine Moscadello. Twenty-four chairs guarded the edges of the semi-circular room. Twenty-four men sat in the chairs and watched as Ryah entered. At the apex of the semi-circle, another chair, larger than the rest, more ornate, and made of white gold faced the entranceway. In it sat a man dressed in white. A sword, sharpened to a razor's edge, lay across his lap. Ryah bowed to the man in the chair, who acknowledged him with a subtle nod of his head.

"Welcome, Ryah," he said.

"How do you know who I am?" Ryah asked.

"You have been chosen by the king."

"For what?"

"You have been chosen to see," the prince said.

The prince nodded his head again. Guriel came inside and led Ryah down the long hallway to the top of the stairs. He pointed off into the distance over the vast plain that surrounded the city.

"Look out there," Guriel said.

From his vantage point near the top of the mountain, Ryah could see for hundreds of miles. At the edge of the horizon, a cloud of dust rose above the expanse and bore down on the city at an alarming rate. A single trumpet blast sounded from the highest parapet of the palace, followed by another and then another in a chain reaction that echoed throughout the land. The hustle of the city stopped, and the people stepped inside their homes. A few moments later, tens, perhaps hundreds of thousands of riders on horseback charged from a cavern at the base of the mountain and tore off across the plain towards the cloud of dust. Leading the cavalry was a man with a sword in his right hand, exhorting his followers. A shield with the same markings as the flags in the hallway hung by the saddle and bounced up and down with each stride the horse took.

"Who is that?" Ryah asked.

"General Chael," came Guriel's reply.

31

General Chael's horse was the most magnificent creature Ryah had ever seen. It was larger than a Clydesdale but ran with the grace of a thoroughbred. Its coat was red-brown, striped with bands of dark grey, giving it a brindled appearance, and it strained against the bridle, not waiting for its rider to urge it on but wanting to arrive at the fray before the rest. The thousands of riders who followed each held a sword and a similar shield, prepared to engage in a battle which dwarfed any Ryah had ever witnessed. Even with such a great distance between him and the armies, he could see everything in perfect detail.

At the head of the invading force was a handsome man riding a pitch-black horse, beautiful and ferocious in its own right. The man wore a smug look on his face as he called down curses on the king, the prince, and all their subjects, swearing on his life that he would drive them from the kingdom and reign in their place. The attackers, clearly outnumbered, fought with a ferocity Ryah thought would guarantee their victory, yet the clash raged back and forth for hours as neither side was able to control the field of battle. Soon, the two armies became intertwined to the point where Ryah could not distinguish which was which.

After another hour of battle, a brigade broke away from the main group and charged towards the palace. Unsure of which side they were on, his answer came in the form of a volley of arrows aimed directly at him.

He tried to run, to escape the arrows' path, but his feet wouldn't move. Stone, which had held him firm, had now swallowed his legs up to his shin. He pulled against the stone, legs burning under the strain. The flaming arrows drew ever closer. Ryah screamed for help, but no one answered. The first arrows whistled past his head. The second wave bore down on him. He threw his arms up to shield his head.

Ryah opened his eyes. His heart was beating through his chest, and sweat poured down his face. It was pitch dark. The streetlights outside his window had turned off, and he couldn't see anything except for the clock beside his bed which read 2:00 am.

The vision replayed in his mind. Not a single detail had vanished from the dream as they normally do. He thought of Guriel and the field of silky grass. The children in the city who danced around him. General Chael on horseback. The prince. The prince seemed familiar. Or maybe it was his voice. Had he heard it somewhere else? And the prideful one who rode against the city. Ryah had seen him before. But it wasn't him. Yet it was him. From where did he know him? Where had he seen him?

"*It must have been a movie,*" he thought. "*I think I saw them in a movie. Many years ago when I was a kid. That must have been where I saw them.*"

He continued searching his memory, repeating the scenes in his mind until he had gone over them from every possible angle. When there was nothing left to think about, he checked the time.

"Five o'clock?" he asked with exasperation as he looked at the clock. "Already? In less than two hours, I've got to be on the transit."

He rubbed his face in frustration. The sleep he desperately needed wouldn't come that night. At least not enough for what waited.

Chapter 5

The lack of sleep had taken its toll. Ryah closed his eyes and tried to rest, but every time he nodded off, a sharp turn of the subway tracks would jolt him awake.

"It's not going to happen," he told himself, rubbing his eyes to focus them. "Eight years military, top of my class in grad school, and this is my life."

He surveyed the scene. Gray walls once white. Posters announcing a concert for a metal band which broke up two years ago. Graffiti that was worth dying over, covering everything except for the propaganda posters for the People's Governing Party. And the smell. It floated towards his sinuses and deluded him into breathing it in. Dust and human waste mixed with life and decay. He was surprised what he had become used to and wondered how it all came to be.

The back door of the car opened with a loud rush. An unwelcome and all too familiar sound, Ryah chastised himself for not going through his normal preparations when he boarded. There were three of them this time, dressed in their unofficial uniforms – black pants and shirts, steel-toed boots like the kind worn by paramilitary units, and a red bandana covering the lower part of their faces, indicating the gang to which they swore allegiance.

"Not today," Ryah muttered.

A man sitting near the back of the car looked up at the three and then back down at the floor. In his hands, he carried some official looking papers. The tallest of the three intruders called out to a middle-aged woman who was sitting near the back door.

"Hey, momma. You looking for a good time?" he said.

He laughed and blew her a kiss. She made no response but stared straight ahead, the expression on her face a perfect blend of fear and hate, one which Ryah had seen a thousand times before.

He slithered up to her and sat down beside her. "Come on, now. Don't tell me you don't want this."

She refused to look at him. Reaching behind the woman's head, he stroked her short, black hair, looking at it as he curled a lock in his abnormally long fingers. His caress was light, almost tender, like a man comforting his wife.

"Alright, baby." He looked back at his partners and winked. "I'll get us started, then my friends here can go next. What d'ya say?"

The woman said nothing, but her eyes told the story. Scared, angry, despondent. It wouldn't be her first time. It wouldn't be any woman's first time.

The man continued running his fingers up and down, back and forth while his other hand went to the woman's thigh. "That's right. Just like that. I know you want it."

She wanted to resist. She tried to resist, but all she could do was place her hand on his to stop him from going any further.

"Don't fight it now," he whispered. "Look at me. C'mon baby. Look at me. I said, look at me."

He grabbed a handful of her short, black hair and jerked her head back. A knife creeped down the woman's face, delaying for a few seconds below her right eye before it found its home next to the jugular. The point of the blade pushed into her neck, enough to make a dent but not enough to draw blood.

The attacker placed his face an inch away from hers. She dug her knuckles into the armrest, preparing for the assault, unable or unwilling to respond. He gave her a quick kiss, then another, before he sucked her bottom lip into his mouth. The woman let out a slight squeal, and her chest heaved forward. Her spine arched, and she dug her shoulders into the seatback, pressing her feet into the floor in an involuntary spasm.

The man let out a muffled groan and reached for his face. A few drops of blood trickled out of his lip. He wiped his mouth, looked down at his hand, and saw the small crimson streak across the tips of his fingers. Before the woman could react, a slap threw her tumbling to the ground. The leader laughed again and motioned for the two to follow him.

"She's not my type," he said, checking his mouth once more. "At least not today."

He moved forward, his knife swinging from a strap on his arm, his two partners trailing behind like a pair of unwholesome shadows as they stalked their next prey.

Their short stroll ended in front of the man with the official papers. Perspiration began to condense on his sparse, Hitleresque moustache, and a small puddle formed by his right shoe. He tried to maneuver his left hand back into its sleeve to hide the gold Rolex which wrapped around his wrist.

One of the shadows saw the motion. "What you got there?"

The man's shaking hands betrayed his attempt to appear calm. "Nothing. I'm not sure what you're talking about," he said.

"Sure, you do," the shadow replied. "Right there. On your left wrist."

"Oh. Th ... that. It's just an old watch I found. I guess someone had tossed it away. It was just lying there in the street. I picked it up. Just a piece of junk."

The shadow gave a nod of understanding. "I see." He paused. "But you know what? I've been looking to get me a watch, and I think I'm liking that one. It's just like the kind my daddy used to own." He grabbed the wrist of the government man to take a closer look. "Come to think of it, this looks exactly like the one he was wearing the day he was gunned down in the streets. I was just a little boy and the preacher comes up to me and says, 'Son, I'm sorry but your daddy was gunned down today by some man in a suit.'" He looked the government man up and down. "Yeah, by some man in a suit... just like the one you're wearing." He glared at the man. "You're the s.o.b. who killed him, aren't you?"

"I ... I work for the Council," the government man stammered, the puddle by his shoe ever widening, "so I suggest you go away and find someone else to play your games with, or else h ... h ... holy hell will rain down on you."

Ryah pitied him. He could tell the man didn't work for the Council, and he was sure the gang knew it as well. A blow from a sabat to the side of the man's forehead gave Ryah his confirmation. Papers spilled all around as the man fell to the floor. The henchman kneeled down to remove the man's watch and whatever else he could find in the man's pockets. Finding nothing of value, he spit on the unconscious man and turned to his partners.

"This worthless piece ain't got nothing. I guess he'll have to pay another way."

"What're you gonna do this time, Kane?" The taller of the shadows asked. "Same old, or you been working on something new?"

Kane turned around, and Ryah's eyes met his for a moment. There was something dark, lifeless in them, as if they held nothing. As if they stared into the abyss. Kane turned back and grabbed the knife from the leader. The blade whispered as it slashed the air, twisting and twirling in an unholy dance, blood flowing out of wounds until the man's shirt had drunk its fill.

When Kane finished, he lifted the unconscious man's head and cursed the sky. Taking the spiked club he used to knock the man out, he struck the man once more for good measure. The smell of blood, urine, and sweat hung in the air. A man two rows back vomited and passed out. Kane raised his head and howled at the sky.

As the gang renewed its descent through the car, a flood of adrenaline dumped into Ryah's system, helping his body fight back against the exhaustion which overwhelmed him. On any other day, he would have stared them down and dared them to come after him, but today he didn't want to take the chance.

"That dream," he mumbled to himself. The dream that roused him at 2:00 am had concerned him enough that he spent the next three hours trying to understand what it meant. He finally fell back into a restless sleep and ended when the alarm sounded its heartless, trumpet-like tone. That dream was the cause of his fatigue this morning and made it difficult to assess what was happening with the clarity he would have preferred.

As the three approached his seat, Ryah inflated his body to make himself seem as large and dangerous as possible. He slid his hand inside his jacket and grabbed the wooden handle of the kitchen knife he carried for protection. When they came to power, the People's Governing Party had banned the public from owning personal weapons, so Ryah improvised, knowing the punishment for being caught with the knife but fearing the repercussions more if he was trapped without it. The leader glanced at Ryah. His instincts told him to keep walking. Ryah exhaled as they passed by and turned his head to follow the three in their path of destruction.

The gang found their next plaything at the far end of the car. A woman around Ryah's age, with blonde hair braided by inexperienced hands, sat in the far corner of the transit, her back at an angle so that she could watch the approach. The cheap makeup she wore couldn't cover the four-inch scar which sliced neatly down the left side of her face.

"*Probably from a previous encounter with these animals*," Ryah thought.

Instead of being afraid, though, the woman had a look of defiance on her face.

"Oh man. What do we have here?"

The tall one plopped down beside her.

"That's a nasty little scar you got," he taunted as he caressed her face. "Is it my handiwork? Nah. I'd remember doing you. Well, I guess today is your lucky day." He lifted her skirt with the tip of his blade and looked down to take a peek. "Mmm," he purred. "I'll be having some of that today."

She enticed him to come closer. "You want me?" she whispered in his ear. "You're going to have to make it worth my while."

"A feisty one," he said. "I like those the best."

She smiled at him and jerked his collar, bringing him down to her own level in a playful sign of dominance. Her thin, red lips spread apart as she prepared to receive his tongue. He complied, and she stood him up, their mouths locked in a passionate kiss as she began to pull his unbuttoned shirt off his shoulders. She stopped when his sleeves were halfway down his arms, holding him in an impromptu straight jacket, and rammed a knife into his face.

He jumped back. A hand reached to a bloody cheek.

"You witch. You worthless whore. I'm going to kill you."

The animals descended on her, attacking with the fury of a pack of wolves. She swung at Kane, but he blocked the thrust, causing the knife to fall from her hands. Grabbing

39

her arms, they dragged her into the middle of the aisle and launched her against the sliding doors with enough force to crack a window.

All the passengers on the car except for Ryah kept their sights on the space in front of their feet, not wanting to see the carnage that was bound to follow and not willing to take a stand to help a stranger. Even Ryah sat motionless as the leader tore at the woman's blouse while the other two held her arms.

The woman flailed wildly, managing to strike the leader in the groin and causing him to double over. But the assault didn't stop. The pain only increased the leader's rage, and he swung his blade at the woman, ripping through her top and causing a gash under her right clavicle. Still, the woman fought, cursing and spitting at her tormentors in a vain attempt at retribution.

"*Why did she fight back?*" Ryah thought to himself. "*It's almost as if she wants to die,*" he reasoned, "*or maybe she actually thought she could fight them off.*"

At that moment, he saw the answer to his question. Standing behind the woman was a young girl, probably less than ten years old, who had the same blonde hair and same facial features as the woman, only with a look of terror on her face as she struggled to make sense of what was happening. A scream finally forced itself out of the young girl's mouth as one of the shadows struck the woman in the head, knocking her unconscious.

The girl's scream awakened something primal deep inside Ryah, and he flew out of his seat, hurling himself towards the attackers. Before they could react, Ryah had grabbed the leader from behind, lifting him into the air and slamming him to the ground. The impact with the floor knocked the knife out of his hand. Ryah kicked it away. Using the thick heel of his boot, he stomped on the downed man's face. Teeth and nose went flying in all directions.

In his fury, Ryah threw himself on the other two shadows, evading a strike from a sabat before gaining control of it and using it to club both of them into a bloody, submissive heap. Even after they were down, Ryah continued to pound on all three until the sweat flowed down his forehead, a guttural roar, the only sound emanating from his lips. It wasn't until the transit jerked to a stop that Ryah's rampage ended.

The doors opened and six members of the city's security forces entered. None of them said anything to Ryah, and in under a minute, they had dragged the bodies off the train. Kane moaned as they lifted him, but the others had already made their last sounds. Darwin's Law was the order of the day, and Ryah had come out on top this time.

One of the riders on the train approached the woman, who had revived by this time, and tried to offer his assistance. She drove him off and walked to the young girl. The woman wrapped her arm around the girl's frail shoulders and bent over to whisper something in her ear and then turned around to pick up her belongings which had fallen on the floor.

As the woman stood up, the young girl tugged on her sleeve, pointed at Ryah, and whispered something back at her. A look of disbelief mixed with gratitude and residual anger crossed her face as she tried to make sense of what the girl said. The woman walked towards Ryah, her blouse partially ripped open, allowing him to see that the knife had made only a shallow wound which had already stopped bleeding.

When she reached him, she stared at him for a while without saying a word, studying his face as if she was trying to figure him out. Ryah stared back at her dark, almost emerald-green eyes which looked even fiercer up close. He wanted to ask her what kind of fool she was for bringing the girl on the train and yell at her for being so stupid. He wanted to tell her that she deserved everything she got, but he knew the truth was more complicated.

As if the woman were able to read the words crossing Ryah's mind, she opened her mouth to speak. "I didn't have a choice today," she said.

The transit approached the city center and stopped. The woman turned towards the girl and made a motion to let her know they would be getting off. She looked back at Ryah and said, "Thank you. You're a good man."

One more quick glance and the woman stepped onto the platform, made a left, and disappeared into the crowd.

Chapter 6

Maryam grasped her daughter Kaliya by the hand and dragged her out of the transit station. The city was a giant oval, not quite perfectly circular as the designers had planned, and had nine main arteries leading in and out of the center so that the layout had the appearance of a large, slightly oblong wheel with spokes. After walking a few blocks towards the southeast, Maryam took off down one of the narrow alleys which branched off from the main street. With her free hand, she closed the rip in her shirt to hide the wound from the eyes of curious strangers. Her head and her chest throbbed from the beating she had just received.

"Come on, Kalli. We need to keep going."

The young girl sobbed. "Mama, my legs hurt," she said.

Maryam softened her tone to allay Kaliya's fears. "I know, Leeya, but we're almost there."

As she walked through the alley, she passed by people that could be her. Gaunt, malnourished. Desperate, hollow eyes without light. Souls in need of redemption. Discarded. Unwanted. Forgotten.

"*They brought it on themselves.*" Maryam could hear the phrase echoing in her ears. "*You brought it on yourself. This is what you deserve. You made your choice. It's too late now.*"

She no longer wrestled with her conscience. She knew it was right. She *was* worthless. This had been here life as far back as she could remember. Even the few childhood memories she held on to, the innocent memories of growing up with her brother and her mother and father, laughing, always laughing, had died. All that was left was a future without meaning. Until Kaliya came. She would not let them take Kaliya away from her no matter the cost.

The addicts and the beggars heard Maryam's footsteps and called out to her. Bodies offered for a few crumbs or the next fix. Threatening, demanding, pleading to be satisfied for a moment, not caring about anything beyond the here and now. Their clothes were rags, soiled and stained. Their bodies reeked of urine and sweat and decay.

Maryam was one of them. The difference was people thought she was beautiful. After all she had endured, she was still beautiful. But she didn't feel that way. When she looked in the mirror, the darkness inside her reflected back, and what she saw repulsed her. There was light in Kaliya's eyes, though, and Maryam clung to that as if it were life itself.

Yet a doubt haunted Maryam each day. "*Is it too late for her too?*"

A voice answered back. It taunted her in her dreams. It whispered to her when she was awake. "*It is too late. What's the point? She'll end up just like you, so just let her go.*"

Maryam heard that voice again as she thought back to what brought her to this place.

Kaliya's condition had deteriorated again, the seizures destroying her already fragile body. Maryam had used up her savings taking Kaliya to every specialist she could, but none of the doctors could find either the cause or a cure. Or maybe they didn't want to. They always looked at her in the same way. They knew who she was, and they wanted her and her daughter out of their offices as soon as possible. The only hope one doctor offered was that Kaliya would probably not survive the summer. 'So Maryam wouldn't have to worry about her anymore.' Digging her hands into her sides so as not to claw that doctor's eyes out, she hurried out of the office and collided with a lady, causing her to

44

drop a package she had been carrying. The lady stooped over to pick it up and began apologizing to Maryam.

"No, no. It was my fault," Maryam replied, trying to hold back the hot, bitter tears.

Seeing the anguish on Maryam's face, the lady placed her hand on Maryam's elbow and gave it a gentle squeeze. When she did, her sleeve slid up her arm revealing a tattoo on her wrist. Maryam recoiled and jerked away from the stranger. She had heard many stories about those with the tattoo.

"It's OK. I'm not going to hurt you," the lady said.

The tone, the expression put Maryam at ease, and she forgot her own troubles for a moment. She looked in the lady's eyes expecting to see hatred, but she found an unexpected and unwarranted serenity instead.

"What's the matter, dear? Is there anything I can do for you?" the woman asked.

"No." Maryam replied, dismissing the woman. "I don't need anything from you." She turned to her daughter and said, "Let's go Kaliya."

"Are you sure you're OK?" The woman looked genuinely concerned.

There was something vaguely familiar about her that made Maryam pause. "No." She hesitated this time. "No, we'll be fine. And I'm sorry about the package. I hope I didn't break it."

"It's not a problem." She smiled at Maryam. "Look. I don't want to be nosy, and it's really none of my business, but …." She stopped. "Hey. Why don't you join me for a cup of coffee and a piece of cake?"

The last part was directed at Kaliya. Maryam opened her mouth to decline, but before she could, the woman spoke up. "I insist." There was no way to resist that smile. "It's just a few doors down. My treat," she added.

At the café, they found a table near the window. The lady pulled down the end of her cuff to make sure her tattoo was hidden before the waitress came to take their order.

"I'm Allison, by the way," the woman said.

"I'm Maryam, and this is my daughter Kaliya."

"Tell me about you two. What brings you to this part of town?" Allison asked.

It was a simple question, but it awakened something inside Maryam. She wanted someone to talk to. To listen. To care.

When Maryam had finished her story, Allison put her arm on Maryam's shoulder like a mother would do for her own daughter. She turned her head to the side and quietly whispered something Maryam did not understand. Turning back to Maryam, the lady handed her a small piece of paper with an address on it.

"Come by next Tuesday morning at eight. There are some people I would like you to meet. Perhaps we can do something for your daughter."

They finished their coffees and said goodbye. Allison ordered two cookies to go and placed them in a small brown bag for Kaliya. She hugged the young girl and watched as Maryam and Kaliya left the bakery.

As soon as they were out of sight, Maryam crumpled the paper. She thought about throwing it away. An impulse, a mother's instinct, who knows what, told her to hang on to it. Regardless, she had no intention of visiting this strange woman.

"She's one of them," Maryam said to herself. "They can't be trusted. That's why the Council outlawed them. But why did she show me the tattoo? Was it an accident?"

An incident a few days later made her change her mind.

"Ms. Maryam! Ms. Maryam! Hurry!"

"What is it?"

"Kaliya fell."

"What do you mean 'fell', Savanna?"

"Kaliya fell in the water."

"Where? Where did she fall, Savanna?"

"By the big tree where we like to count."

Maryam dropped the rice on the counter and rushed outside without bothering to put on her shoes. A small stream ran past the apartments and fed into the Carmel River. It was shallow most of the year, but during the rainy season, flash floods would tear through the creek and create a current with fierce undertows that could drown even the strongest swimmers. Maryam feared the worst, and her heart raced as she flung herself down the steps towards the field out back, not noticing the cold seep into her socks as she ran through the wet grass. It was in that field that Kaliya and Savanna liked to play hide and seek, counting behind the large oak that threatened to tumble over at any minute.

Maryam ran towards the edge of the stream thinking, hoping her daughter had slid down the bank and lay at the water's edge.

"Kaliya!" she called out. "Kaliya? Are you OK?"

There was no reply from Kaliya and no sign of her by the tree.

"Kaliya!" Maryam's anguished cry reverberated off the small cliff on the far side of the stream, sounding arrogant and pitiable at the same time as if the echo were mocking her. She ran down the banks, plowing through the forsythia and giant silver grass which fought back, slashing at her arms and legs and leaving long thin welts wherever they touched skin. On a shallow, gravel island three feet from the shore, she found Kaliya. The current had pushed the little girl's body almost fifty yards downstream until it found a place to dump it. She lay there with her shoulders on land and her face half submerged, her feet batted at by the water.

The twitching brought on by that infernal seizure the only indication she was still alive.

Maryam ran to her daughter and bent over to scoop her up. She felt the spasms wrench Kaliya's body as she carried her up the embankment and placed her on the cold earth which anticipated Kaliya as payment for Maryam's sins. She rolled her daughter over on her side and held her down as the seizure continued to shake her young body. Kaliya battled back, struggling to catch a breath, her mouth foaming like a racehorse at the end of a long sprint. Maryam's heart broke as she watched her daughter suffer, unable to help. When the tremors stopped, Maryam looked at her daughter's face and knew something was different as if this should have been the end.

That was what brought her here today. That was what made the ride on the transit necessary, why she would risk an assault she knew would probably come. As Maryam continued down the street, she let go of her blouse and touched the wound on her chest. It hurt. Just like the day he slashed her face. She looked down at Kaliya and smiled as they walked to the address on the wrinkled piece of paper in her pocket.

Maryam stopped as she approached a sign on the corner. "This is it, Kalli. We found the street."

They arrived at Riverplace and took a right down a straight, narrow alley towards a large, interconnected series of warehouses on the perimeter of a former Naval base. Most of the Naval offices had been torn down years ago to create an open plaza designed to attract tourists to the city center. In the middle of the plaza, a fountain fed by the waters of the Carmel River directed the eye of the visitor towards a sculpture of Poseidon riding two dolphins, which used to sit in the middle of the fountain. The god's face was upturned, water flowing from his trident and his mouth and pouring down on both sides of the dolphins, creating the illusion that they were skimming through the water. When the great earthquake hit Carmel, the plaza was one of the few places that was spared total destruction. The buildings remained intact, but the statue had broken and fallen over. It rested with its head on the ground, Poseidon's crown shattered and lying in pieces beside it. The rest of the city had been restored, but Riverplace remained deserted, save for a few families that lived as squatters in the vacant warehouses as well as the increasing number of homeless and destitute that sought shelter wherever they could.

Maryam double-checked the address on the wrinkled paper and stood in front of an old wooden door, turned a strange shade of gray by the salty mist which crept up the river from the sea. She tapped the door with her index finger. It was hesitant, anxious. Remembering why she was there, she tried again, this time with her hand clenched into a ball. The pounding resounded throughout the house and returned to her as a muffled sigh. The door creaked open, and Maryam saw the lady who had invited her to come.

"Hi, Maryam! Come on in. I'm so glad you and Kaliya made it. Did I remember your names right?" She noticed the rip in her blouse and the blood which had created an oblong stain down the front of her shirt. A look of concern spread across her face. "Are you OK, dear?"

"I'm fine. Just another run in on the transit, and yes, you got our names right," Maryam replied.

Allison motioned for the two to come in, but Maryam hesitated a little as if unsure she had made the right decision. The room they entered was small, no more than ten by fifteen feet, and had almost no furnishings other than a small but well-kept sofa and a lamp on a table in the corner that emitted a warm, bluish light.

"Well, I'm surprised I didn't get your names wrong. At my age, I find myself forgetting more things than I

49

remember. Please have a seat here. I have to go into the back room for a moment and let the others know you're here." Allison grabbed Kaliya by the hand before continuing. "And I'll bring you back something I hope you'll like."

Allison left through a back door. Maryam and Kaliya sat down on the sofa to wait. The house was aged but clean. Freshly cut flowers sent a gentle scent of lilac drifting through the air and brought a homey feel to the otherwise industrial architecture. The table was metallic of the cheaply mass-produced kind and stood in contrast to the sofa, which was handmade by a craftsman of immense skill. The front had been designed to resemble a large branch, and from it, vines extended and wrapped around the legs. Delicate and intricate carvings of clusters of grapes formed the feet, which appeared to float above the floor in the soft light.

Through the walls, Maryam could hear a muffled conversation between three people who seemed to be trying to talk over each other. She recognized Allison's voice and could tell that the other two were men. The voices stopped for a few moments and then began again. This time there were five discernible voices, the two new ones being distinctly feminine. Each one spoke in turn for a minute, but then all conversation stopped. The silence persisted for a few minutes, until it was broken by a single word.

Maryam grew more and more uncomfortable and swore at herself for making the trip. In her desperation to help her daughter, she had put them both in more danger, and now she was at the mercy of a company of peculiar, if not, treacherous strangers.

"Let's go, Kalli. I think it would be best if we left now."

"But mommy! The lady said she was bringing me something."

"I know Leeya, but this probably isn't …"

50

Before she could finish, Allison came back through the door holding a stuffed panda and a piece of candy wrapped in a light golden paper.

"Here you go, Kaliya. I know you're probably too old for toy animals, but this was my daughter's favorite toy when she was your age."

Allison handed Kaliya the doll and continued. "Also, I hope you like caramels. My husband always tells me not to eat them because of my condition, but they're so good, I can't stop. Whenever he finds them around the house, he throws them out and scolds me, but I found a good hiding place that he doesn't know about. I don't mind sharing them with a girl as beautiful as you are, though."

Maryam found Allison even more eccentric after this. No one married anymore, not that she knew of anyway, but something about Allison's warm demeanor put Maryam at ease.

"I also brought this for you," Allison said handing Maryam a cream. "This will take away the pain and help your skin heal up more quickly."

"Thank you." Maryam took the balm and put some on her wound. She paused before starting again. "I heard you speaking through the walls with a bunch of other people, and then you started …. I guess it's none of my business. It's just that I hope I'm not interrupting something."

"No dear. We were expecting you, but you got here a bit early. We needed to finish up before we brought you in. And we certainly don't mind you getting into our business." She laughed a delightful yet wistful laugh.

"If you don't mind me asking, then, what were you doing? It was," she hesitated a moment. "It was a little peculiar."

Allison grinned. "We were talking to someone," she explained. "Come on with me. I'd like you to meet the others."

Maryam and Kaliya followed Allison inside a bright room, slightly larger than the one they just exited. In the middle, two men and two women sat around an oval table in wooden chairs that were made in a better time. The lady closest to the door stood up and walked over to the two visitors.

"I'm Judith, but my friends call me Judy. You must be Kaliya," she said holding out her hand to the young girl.

"Yes, I am."

"Allison was correct. You are a beautiful young lady. Just like your mother." She looked up and smiled at Maryam. "Please take my seat. We have just a few questions to ask."

Maryam sat down in the wooden chair, and Kaliya came over beside her. Maryam put her arm around her daughter's waist and looked around the room into the faces of a group of odd strangers who were Kaliya's last hope.

One of the men spoke first. "Tell us about Kaliya. What seems to be the problem?"

Maryam repeated the story she had told Allison when she first met and added the details of her recent seizures. When she had finished, the other man spoke.

"Where do you live?"

"Outside of New Carmel on the North side, off of Highway 12."

"That's a lovely area, especially when the crape myrtles are blooming as they must be now. Tell us about Kaliya's father. What does he do?"

Maryam didn't know who Kaliya's father was nor did she care to know. She wanted the men in and out as fast as she could and often wouldn't even look at their faces. Their names were meaningless. By the look in her eyes, the man realized it was not a topic he should pursue.

"Never mind. That doesn't change anything here. The big question is what do you want?"

"I want my daughter to be well. Nothing more. Can you help me with that? I came here because Allison said you could do something. At least that's the impression I got."

Allison chimed in. "Well, we can't do anything ourselves, but there is someone who can. We just finished speaking with him before you came in."

"Who is he? Is he still here?"

"No, he left just as you were coming in."

"Why did he go? I thought you said you could help me." Maryam didn't try to contain her frustration. "Why would you bring me here to see someone just to have him slip out the back door when I show up."

Allison smiled, and the first man spoke up again. "That's all we need Maryam. Go home and wait. Someone will be coming to your home soon." He walked around the table to give Kaliya a hug. "It was a pleasure to meet you both. Allison will show you out now."

Allison led Maryam and Kaliya to the street and gave the girl another caramel from her personal collection.

"Thank you for coming by today."

"Is that it? What about my daughter?" Maryam felt her face begin to flush.

"There's nothing more to be done now, but please drop by any time you want." Allison bent over and kissed Kaliya on the forehead. "I hope you feel better soon, Kaliya. Actually, I know you will."

Allison turned around and went inside, leaving Maryam and Kaliya alone in the street. As the two made their way back to the station, Maryam felt her faith turn to hopelessness.

"Now I'm supposed to go home and wait for someone who doesn't even know where I live." For a moment, she considered turning back to give them her address but decided against it. *"What's the point?"*

She turned her head towards her daughter. Her heart broke as she looked at the frail body that could no longer fight off the malignancy inside. What a contrast it was to the powerful smile on Kaliya's face as she played with her new toy. Maryam walked to the station, holding Kaliya's hand and singing softly to her, unaware that the pain in her chest had completely disappeared.

Chapter 7

"The regular today?" Terrence called out to Ryah.

"Yep. You know it. How 'bout the breakfast special too? I'm sure you got a few ready to go."

"Sure thing," Terrence said as he finished pouring the coffee. "Black, one sugar."

He set the cup on the edge of his cart and opened the lid to a steam tank. Pulling out a hot dog, he placed it on a roll and wrapped it in a thin sheet of foil.

"Bit of a run in, this morning?" he asked as he handed Ryah his breakfast.

"That obvious, huh?" Ryah replied.

Terrence handed Ryah a few napkins to wipe off the blood caked onto his arms and face and went back to tidying up the cart. Ryah cleaned himself the best he could before taking a sip of the coffee. He felt the warmth as it slipped down his throat and traveled to his stomach. The adrenaline from the attack on the transit had worn off, and a steady drip of caffeine would be his only hope to make it through the day.

"You outdid yourself, T," Ryah said when he had finished eating. He took another drink and turned to leave. "Put this on my official account. We'll call this a business meeting."

He headed off and made his way to the stairs that led to the Council building. Thirty-two steps. Ryah counted them every time he ran up. He went through the large metallic doors which guarded the entrance to the administration building, where laws were passed and deals that were never intended to be honored were agreed upon. The representatives and administrators had a separate entrance which led directly to the secure offices and chambers where they would meet. Visitors and the rest of the staff were required to go through the main entrance through security. Ryah got in line and rummaged through his pockets for his badge. Finding it, he fastened it to his shirt pocket with his name and picture facing out.

"You should get one of the implants." A guard dressed in a dark gray uniform with the Council patch on his left shoulder spoke, not noticing or not caring about Ryah's appearance. "So you don't have to look for your badge every day. It doesn't hurt. Sits right there." He showed the back of his hand to Ryah. "You can use it to make purchases anywhere in the city too. Win win."

Ryah heard the same commentary every day and gave his stock reply. "Not a fan of them invading my body or my privacy."

"Another year or two and it'll be mandatory."

"I'll deal with it when the time comes," Ryah said.

The guard nodded and waved Ryah through, allowing him to bypass the line of visitors who required a more thorough vetting as well as the metal detectors which would have sounded if Ryah had passed through them. He reached inside his jacket and slid his finger along the blade of the knife inside the lining of his coat. It was cold from the morning air which had chilled him on his walk from the station. He removed his hand and patted the outside of his jacket where the knife would be, checking to see if it was noticeable to an outside observer. The last person they caught with a weapon received two years in a labor camp. He made it eight months before succumbing to malnutrition and exhaustion.

"*About time I ditched the knife*," Ryah thought. "*It doesn't look like I need it. Seems I've retained most of my training. Muscle memory was pretty good back there.*" He checked himself,

56

noticing a bit of arrogance in his self-analysis. *"I'm getting a little older though, so I probably should get back on a regular schedule."* He made a mental note to contact his former instructor to see if he would be available to work with him.

Beyond the checkpoint, there was a long, narrow corridor where portraits of current administrators and representatives kept a wary eye on all those who passed through. A man on a ladder blocked a part of the passageway and created a traffic jam as people pushed past each other in a hurry. A portrait had been taken down, exposing a year's worth of dirt and dust which had collected on the wall behind it. No communication had been sent out, but the removal of a name indicated only one thing. Being appointed for life was not a guarantee that the representative would have a long tenure on the Council.

Ryah continued down the hall and arrived at a bank of elevators. The last one had just left for the upper floors, and he prepared himself for a wait. In the polished metal of the doors, a reflection stared back at him. His face, stern yet thoughtful, held pale, hazel eyes speckled with copper flecks which glared out from within dark circles. A red spray coated his collar and displayed the aftermath of the morning's encounter. He made another mental note to change into the spare shirt he kept in his office for just such an occasion. Behind him, a man in a dark suit stared at the wall and waited for the elevator's arrival. He didn't say a word and kept his hands folded at his waist. A bell chimed, and Ryah saw the reflection of the man, his face hidden, walking towards the elevator as the doors began to open. Ryah entered and pressed the number 22.

"What floor?" he asked without looking up.

There was no reply.

"What floor are you going to?" Ryah asked again as he turned to face the stranger. Ryah looked around. He was alone. "I guess he decided to wait for the next car," he said to himself as he leaned back and rested on the glass. "Afraid of a little blood, I suppose. Probably gets someone to do the dirty work for him."

Ryah tried to concentrate, but his mind continued racing. It wasn't the attack this morning. He just had a feeling that he got sometimes, that something was not right. That's the way he explained it to himself. An uneasy, nauseating sensation he felt in his stomach like he was about to get sick. He started getting these feelings as a child. An intuition, almost a paranoia, that scared him when they occurred. A premonition of something terrible that waited for him. He would run to his room and hide under the blanket, peering out at an invisible evil.

When he was twelve, he woke up one night to find a man on top of him, his full weight pushing into his ribs so that he couldn't breathe. He struggled to get out from under the unknown assailant, fighting with all his effort to flip over onto his back like his grappling instinct told him to do. Writhing and twisting. Trying to curl up into a ball with his knees to his chest. But he couldn't. He had sunk down into the mattress and had no leverage to push himself out. Not that it mattered. The weight on top of him was too great. It pinned him down and held him tight, pressing, constricting, suffocating. His lungs burned as his diaphragm made a frantic attempt to contract and draw in some oxygen. He felt like he was drowning in his own bed.

A scream for help manifested itself as a muted groan. No one would come to help him. Desperation became surrender. A voice murmured in his ear, "Stop fighting. It will only hurt for a moment." He relaxed. "It won't hurt much longer," he agreed, and waited for nothingness to overtake him. Another voice spoke up. A different, softer voice. "One more try," it whispered. "Just one more." With a final burst of energy, Ryah shifted his hips and rolled onto his back to challenge his attacker. But no one was there. Just the outline of a face vanishing into the darkness. For the rest of the night, he lay there unable to go back to sleep, wondering if he had dreamt it or if it had been real. With nothing else to go on, he decided it must have been a nightmare and fell back asleep, hoping it wouldn't return. But that feeling in his stomach was there when he woke up, warning him, prodding him to be alert.

In the morning, Ryah took a walk through the woods running along the river. A chain link fence with razor wire on top cordoned off that part of the woods, but he had found a hole, dug by some creature which lived in the undergrowth, that he could squeeze through. Going down near the bank of the river, he would sit on the roots of a large oak tree. For hours, he would throw rocks at the sticks floating by, pretending they were enemy ships trying to land and that he was a missile team defending his nation from the invaders.

Up ahead, the sound of splashing caught his attention. Ryah snuck up to see what was happening, measuring each step so as not to alert anyone of his presence. At the edge of the river, a man lay face down, his head the only part in the water, his arms and legs flailing in desperation to lift his head out. He kicked and struggled with all his might to buck off a man who was sitting on top of him, succeeding for a moment to jerk his head out of the water and take a quick breath before being forced back under by the man on top.

His head popped back out and he looked towards Ryah. *"Did he see me? Can he see me?"* Ryah panicked.

It wasn't a man. Just a boy like himself, trying to scream. The cry for help was barely a gurgle, silt sliding down the corner of the boy's mouth, his body fighting to expel the buildup in his lungs. Back under, then out for a moment. Then again. One more time. The man on top cursing, sweat dripping off his hair and rolling down his shirt. Shoving him down. His own muscles burning. Sleeves wet up to the elbows. Pants muddy from kneeling on the bank.

"*Help him!*" Ryah screamed at himself. His feet where stuck in cement. "*Move!*" His mind thought a million things and nothing at once. He couldn't move. What could he do?

Again, the head came up. Turning purple. His eyes were bloodshot, his resistance fading.

"Stop fighting. It'll only hurt for a minute."

Ryah heard the voice. Was it meant for him? Panic overtook him, and he ran home, squeezing through the hole in the fence, vowing to never go back there, praying that he hadn't been seen. He was alone when he returned to the house and kept to himself the rest of the day, too afraid to go back outside, too ashamed to let anyone know of his cowardice.

As he got older, Ryah felt that fear again, many times. That particular, unsettling feeling in his stomach that warned him to watch out for something. For what? He didn't know until it happened. All he knew was that something was going to happen. There, on the elevator, he got the feeling again.

Trying his best to ignore the butterflies in his stomach and focus on the present, Ryah went over his schedule for the day. There were no pressing matters. Nothing out of the ordinary that would indicate a problem on the horizon. "I must have my wires crossed. Just tired from the insomnia," he convinced himself. "Think I'll take a nap to start my morning since I don't have anything to do."

The elevator jerked to a stop. The doors opened, allowing Ryah to pass into the corridor that looked like every other corridor in the back part of the building. Rows of neon tubes cast an insufficient glow on cement walls painted a hasty white. Not that anyone could tell in the half light of the halls. Here, everything looked gray. Like the days when the mist traveled up the Carmel River and veiled the city in a colorless haze.

As Ryah stepped into the corridor, the man in the dark suit with the folded hands brushed by him, his shadow lengthening and diminishing as he overtook each neon light. Ryah froze and followed the man's progress as he made his way down the hall. At the end where the passageway split, he turned and made a left, his footsteps echoing as he walked. Ryah saw his shadow linger, floating above the ground like a dark apparition, hanging there for a few seconds. As Ryah watched, a face emerged from the darkness and stared at Ryah before disappearing back into the shadow. It was just a fleeting glimpse, but it was enough. He recognized the face from a dream. From a twelve-year-old's dream. From the nightmare that returned even as he got older. An inhuman countenance without emotion. Except for hatred. Uninhibited, insatiable hatred.

Ryah leaned back against the wall. A cold sweat formed on his brow. His heart beat hard, pounding against his chest as it tried to escape its prison. His instincts told him to flee, to run and hide far away from what awaited him. But he was no longer a boy, and he had put aside the childish fears that terrorized him at night.

"Control your emotions," his drill sergeant would tell him. "Use the fear to propel yourself into battle. Attack your enemy head on. Take the fight to him and make him afraid."

Ryah had taken the advice to heart and was still alive. His enemies were not. And now, a new war threatened to break out. A war between Russia and China that promised to escalate and drag Ryah back into combat. But it wasn't that. A different war was already being fought, internally, externally, and Ryah couldn't wrap his mind around it, nor could he control it. It was intangible, but perhaps more real than the one where Connor lost his hand and Ryah lost half his company. And it was here now. Being fought in the halls of the Council building. Ryah was sure of that even though it made no sense. His instincts were always correct. Always, or so he believed.

Ryah took a few deep breaths and proceeded to the end of the hall. When he arrived, he looked to his right, half expecting to see the shadow waiting for him, but he found nothing. Just an endless line of buzzing, gray lights, emitting their inadequate glow.

He arrived at his office and held his badge to the electronic receiver affixed to the door frame. The audible click, which signaled that the magnetic lock had disengaged, never came, but the LED on the receiver was solid green. Fearing that someone was in the room, Ryah gave the door a gentle push and stood off to the side, letting it creak open to reveal the darkness inside. A faint odor of dust and mold escaped from the windowless room. The gray light from the hall illuminated the entrance but could only penetrate far enough to show the padded chair in front of Ryah's desk.

"Paranoia," Ryah proclaimed to himself and entered.

The automatic lights wavered, fighting their own battle to remain on or turn off and settling on a state somewhere in the middle. The room remained as Ryah had left it. A metal desk with a faux wood top and two drawers on each side, flanked by the padded chair for visitors, as well as Ryah's own rolling chair with a broken lift lever. A half-filled bottle of water, the liquid inside vibrating as air was pumped into the room by the force of an antiquated ventilation system.

The computer which doubled as the communication system collected dust and hadn't been cleaned in years. The only other objects in the room were a sofa, barely long enough to lie down on, with dirty, worn cushions, and a small wardrobe where Ryah kept his emergency change of clothes.

The room didn't have a window, so no one from the outside could see in. Not that it mattered as every room had a camera placed strategically so that it could view all that took place, feeding the information to an internal security force which monitored the activity of the Council building. Ryah had found a way to disable the link, sending in a half-hearted request to maintenance to "urgently look into this" but knowing that it would be months if not years before someone followed up and he was forced to find another way to evade the watchful eye.

Safe from the view of the outside world, he let his jacket slip off his shoulders. The knife, which he had forgotten about, clattered as it dropped on the floor. He pushed it under the desk with his foot, too tired to bend over and get it. He removed his shirt, straining to undo each button.

"I hope I didn't break it."

He opened and closed his left hand, looking at the palm first then flipping it over to look at the back. He gripped the injured hand with the other one, massaging it and checking for fractures.

"It seems OK. Probably just a sprain." A sigh of relief whistled through his lips.

After changing into the clean shirt, Ryah lay down on the sofa and sunk in, curling his legs a little so that they wouldn't dangle off the edge. The encounter that morning played through his mind. The three gang members. The one he left alive. The fake government official. The beautiful woman with the piercing green eyes and the scar. The little girl. Ryah didn't have time to worry about who they were or what might become of them. He had his own concerns which kept him awake at night. But he did wonder a little. Would he ever see her again? Hear her again? The words she spoke and the way she said them. One phrase. Soft. Firm. Anguished. Fierce. A few minutes on a train and one phrase, and he felt like he knew all he needed to know about her.

He stared at a tuft of dust that clung to the edge of a vent as gentle gusts of air blew past it. A spider lowered itself on a single thread and descended through the breeze, swinging back and forth. The movement was rhythmic, measured, like the pendulum on a grandfather clock. The spider landed and scurried across the floor only to climb back up the walls. Rappelling down and clambering up again. Over and over, patient and meticulous. Setting a trap for the unsuspecting. Invisible to the eye that wasn't looking for it.

Ryah wouldn't fall asleep and he knew it. He sat up, exhausted, almost catatonic, and watched the spider finish its web. The knife called out to him, but in his state, he didn't hear it. It spoke to him again, and he leaned forward to pick it up. The wooden handle was warm, dry, alive. He heard the knife a third time, and he walked towards the spider, holding the rusty blade by his side.

"Ryah." The computer screen flickered to life. It was Representative Cruze's assistant. "We need to see you down here in ten minutes."

The interruption broke the spell, restoring Ryah to his senses. He touched the monitor, and the assistant's face filled the screen. She was middle-aged and had been around since Ryah started there. Pleasant when she wanted to be. A bit acerbic at times but knew enough to keep her tongue in check.

"Sure thing, Kennedy." Ryah touched the screen again, and the image disappeared. "Wonder what this is about." His stomach turned at the thought of visiting Representative Cruze.

Ryah had never envisioned being assigned to the Council. The promotion had been presented to him as a stepping-stone in his career. A part of him believed it was a reward for his years of service and commitment to the cause. But at Braxis just like at the Council, it was hard to know what was true and what wasn't. Lies were the currency, half-truths the concealed weapons wielded against the unsuspecting who stood in the way of the ambitious or the amoral.

Solmon Cruze wasn't like most of the representatives. He knew his place and was content flying under the radar. He could grandstand with the best of them, making a show to his constituents whenever it was to his advantage. But his vote, for what it was worth, was offered to the highest bidder, a portion of the bribe being kicked back to whoever owned him at that moment. His office was in the left wing of the building on the tenth floor. Staff was supposed to be roomed close to the representative or administrator that they supported, but Ryah was an exception. Not that he complained. He preferred to be as far away as possible from the politicians and interact with them only when necessary.

Ten minutes later, exactly, Ryah entered the reception area where Representative Cruze's assistant sat.

"Hi, Ryah," she said. "Go on in. They're waiting for you."

"Thanks, Kenn. I trust this is about the raise I've been expecting."

She rolled her eyes and touched her screen. The door to the representative's office slid open. Inside the inner office, a man Ryah didn't recognize, dressed in the uniform of a ranking security official, talked with a gentleman in a hand-tailored suit, whose jet-black hair, just now starting to turn gray, was slicked back in the style preferred by the most powerful. Number three in the hierarchy of the Council, Administrator Klins now stood by Representative Cruze's desk. Ryah was so focused on the first two that he didn't notice a third individual sitting in the corner.

"Good morning," Ryah said. "Where's Representative Cruze?" If Ryah was concerned, it didn't show in his voice.

"How was your trip today?" Administrator Klins said.

"Just another day on the transit. I assume you know what happened. May I ask, is that why I'm here?"

"In part, but not for the reason that you think. I've actually been watching your career for a while, ever since I was a Representative and you started in the military systems division at Braxis."

Administrator Klins was charismatic, a naturally gifted speaker, and a born leader. He had a thin, strong face, with light brown eyes that would flash sparks of gray when he became animated. He would have been considered supremely attractive in any nation, in any culture, and in any time, but he never seemed to be aware of it, which only increased his appeal.

Klins continued. "I was surprised when you chose that path. You could have had the choice of doing anything – government, operations, tactics. I bet you would have made Representative by now."

"That wasn't for me. I prefer to be out of the spotlight, doing my job, protecting my nation."

"Hmm. So, how is it working for Representative Cruze?"

"I've had better assignments."

"That's the polite way of saying it. He was a bit on the incompetent side so I've heard." He stopped himself. "I'm sorry. I shouldn't be speaking ill of the dead."

Ryah's mind flashed back to the man on the ladder who was prying off the plaque. If he hadn't been so tired, he would have realized to whom the plaque belonged.

Klins went on. "Sometimes I speak before I think, which gets me in trouble. Probably why I haven't made High Administrator yet. But I've got to admit," he added with a satisfied smile, "I like it better this way. Life's more fun when you break the rules now and then."

Ryah returned his smile and relaxed.

"I admire what you did back at Braxis. Too bad they didn't see it that way. Personally, I would have promoted you. I guess some officials think it's more important to cover up their mistakes than to take responsibility, huh?"

Ryah raised his eyebrows and pursed his lips in agreement but didn't respond.

"But I can't afford to have people who are afraid to speak up working for me."

"Is that why I'm here?" Ryah asked again. "Am I being transferred?"

Klins ignored the question. "I have a good sense of your character, and the incident on the transit shows me you can handle yourself. I guess I knew that already, though." He opened a brown folder in his hands and flipped over a few pages. "Impressive." He nodded his head in approval. "Not many people have received the commendations you have. Every time I read it, I'm impressed." He closed the folder and looked Ryah dead in the eyes. "But I need to know a little more." He paused once more. "What are your feelings about the UN?"

"The truth?" Ryah asked.

"And nothing but," Klins replied.

"Worthless organization. Glad we got rid of them."

Klins looked past Ryah's shoulder and gave a slight nod. The man, who had been sitting in the corner, rose and walked to the desk. It was the first time Ryah had noticed him. By his appearance, Ryah would have guessed that he was the same age as himself, maybe a year or two older. He came up to Ryah and extended his hand.

"Ryah Olmen. It's very nice to meet you. My name is Lucio Romijn." Ryah held out his hand to shake Lucio's. "I am a Special Envoy to the UN, and I have asked the Council for your services. They have agreed."

Ryah remained silent.

Lucio Romijn continued. "Until further notice, you work for me."

Chapter 8

Ryah wasn't sure what to make of it. The UN was bad enough. Working there was worse. Being the lackey for some UN stooge was as bad as it got.

Klins read Ryah's thoughts. The stages of grief played across his face in fast forward. Denial. Anger. Bargaining. Depression. Acceptance. They were all there, and Klins couldn't help but let out a short laugh.

"I can see you're thrilled by the news," Klins said.

"Well, sir. I can't say I was expecting this. May I ask a question?" Ryah replied.

"Of course. Please speak freely." Klins seemed jovial, almost personable, not at all what Ryah would have expected from a man in his position.

"What exactly is my assignment?" Ryah asked.

It was Envoy Romijn who spoke up. "You will be part of my personal security detail with one other person. One of your gamma operators. You'll meet him in a few minutes."

"I'm sorry. I must be missing something. That's not my line of work. Are you sure you have the right person?" Ryah asked.

"You were requested specifically," Lucio said.

Ryah furrowed his brows and looked around the room as if the answer could be found on the walls. One phrase caused him the most confusion.

"I was requested … specifically." Ryah's words came out as a question as much as a statement. "By whom?"

"Ambassador Tanas," came Envoy Romijn's reply.

"*Tanas? Tanas?*" The thoughts echoed through Ryah's mind. The name sounded familiar. He was sure he had heard it before, but where?

Romijn answered Ryah's unspoken question. It seemed everyone could read Ryah's mind. "You met his assistant last night. Abbad. He came in to see you at the bar."

Ryah remembered. Tanas was an ambassador to the UN. Abbad that guy who Ryah immediately disliked when he met him. None of this made sense. He had never met Ambassador Tanas. Hadn't even heard of him before last night, and now he's specifically requesting him to be this envoy's bodyguard. Ryah couldn't care less if someone was out to get Romijn. The guy could eat a bullet for all he cared. Tanas could take one too. The world would be better off without them. They and all the other scum at the UN. Even more, why would Klins seem so eager to let him go?

"I think you have the wrong person." Ryah reiterated his comment in a half-hearted attempt to convince them.

"The deal is done," Romijn said. He hesitated for a moment. "We'll be leaving right away."

"Leaving?" Ryah wanted to ask where, but he didn't really care at this point. He was a good soldier, at least he used to be, and he knew when orders should be questioned and when they should be obeyed. He looked over at Klins. "If you approved this, then I'm ready to go. I just want to make sure this is coming from you."

Klins smiled. "It's been approved at the highest levels. You'll be leaving for Rome tonight." He turned his attention to Envoy Romijn. "If you don't mind, I'd like to speak with Ryah for a moment."

Romijn nodded and left the room. When the door closed, Klins turned back to Ryah. "I know this is a little unusual, but we would like you there."

"I'm still unsure as to why you want me," Ryah said. "To watch out for this UN creep? Let them find their own babysitters."

Klins let out a full-throated laugh. "That's exactly why we want *you* there."

"Sir?" Ryah said.

"Your cover is to protect Envoy Romijn," Klins said. "Let him believe that. He claims that he wants to represent our interests at the UN regarding the China-Russia conflict. I wouldn't put any stock in the claim, but we'll go along with it for now. Your actual purpose will be to gather intelligence, covertly of course, and report back to me. I'm sure you wouldn't mind doing that, now would you? That's something you're perfectly suited for, and I'm betting you'd like to get back into the game. Or am I wrong? Maybe you prefer the sedentary life."

Klins' last statement took on a menacing quality. How quickly his tone had changed from that of gentle persuasion to that of a ruthless autocrat who could dispatch a person with a single word. No wonder he was third in the chain of command.

"What kind of intelligence am I there to collect?" Ryah asked, knowing it was best to humor him but also excited by the opportunity.

"We'll be letting you know at a later time. For now, just poke your nose around and see what you can find," Klins said.

"I'm happy to do this," Ryah said, "but may I ask one last question?"

"Of course," Klins replied.

"Why do they want me? How do they even know about me?"

"We want you to figure that out as well."

The sick feeling in Ryah's stomach returned. He couldn't tell if Klins was more suspicious of Envoy Romijn or of him. This wasn't going to end well for somebody. But Ryah had been in worse circumstances, and he had always found a way out. Although, there were a few times when he had wondered how.

Like that time outside of Prague. He should have been dead. There was no way he should have made it. Lying under the brush he had pulled on top of himself in a feeble attempt at disguise. His ammo out. His radio broken. Surrounded by a platoon or more of furious Czech special forces who were searching for the assassin who had taken out their prime minister. It wasn't Ryah, but that didn't matter to them. They thought it was him, and that was what counted. Just as they were about to discover Ryah's position, they darted off in a different direction, firing and cursing in a combination of Czech and broken English. Ryah stayed there, not moving, for an hour before he dared to lift his head and look around. The Czechs were gone for good, and Ryah made his way to the pickup zone where the extraction team waited for him. As bad as that situation was, Ryah got the uneasy feeling this was even worse.

Administrator Klins dismissed Ryah and went back to speaking with the security official. Ryah stepped outside the inner office to where Kennedy had engaged in a conversation with Envoy Romijn. As soon as Romijn saw Ryah, the envoy stopped chatting and motioned for Ryah to follow him out of the office.

"Come with me. I'd like you to meet the person you'll be working with and brief you a little more on your assignment."

Lucio Romijn spoke in near perfect English, yet there was a hint of an accent that Ryah couldn't place.

"So. Bodyguard, huh?" Ryah said. "I guess you have a rather important position at the UN. Have you had any credible threats against your person? I assume that's why you need the protection."

"It's standard procedure. Two members of a security detail for anyone involved in negotiations. We figured that, if I would be representing your nation, your government would like a visible presence seeing as how you no longer have any direct representation there. This was the Council's way of showing they approved. It was that and common courtesy. Nothing more really. As far as credible threats, just the usual rumbling. Every one of us gets them and is used to it. We've learned not to make anything of it. If the rumbling increases, we tend to get a little nervous, but think about it. When was the last time you heard of anyone from the UN getting assassinated?"

Ryah thought about it and realized that he had never heard of a case. The envoy's use of 'assassinated' was curious though.

Lucio Romijn continued. "Besides, I'm a nobody. Certainly not anyone that needs to be made an example of." He flashed a warm, wry smile. It felt real, unrehearsed, not like the practiced smile of a seasoned politician, and it put Ryah at ease despite his natural reservations. "So, not what you were expecting today, I imagine?"

"No," Ryah said. "Not exactly. I was looking forward to shuffling papers across my desk for the next eight hours, but this is going to put a crimp in my plans."

Romijn laughed. "I get the feeling you like to speak your mind. I guess it's kind of hard to do in a place like this." He became pensive for a moment. "Yep. Kind of hard," he repeated and fell silent again. He finally spoke up. "Anything else you want to know about me? Ask whatever you want. Speak freely at all times. I want the people working with me to feel comfortable. Look, I've got to trust you for my life if the situation ever arises, so I want you to trust me as well. That's the way I like to do things."

"There is something," Ryah said.

"What is it?"

"I can't place your accent, Envoy Romijn. Where is it from?"

Romijn laughed again. "That's what you need to know? Not the details of your assignment?"

"Yeah. I'm strange like that. It sounds Italian but not quite."

"My mother was half Greek, half Italian. She named me, but my father was Belgian of noble Roman descent, or so the legend goes. They say our ancestor was one of the Caesars. It's a nice tale to tell, but truth be told, it makes no difference to me either way. What occurred a couple thousand years ago is of no consequence to me today. I'm just a guy trying to bring a little peace to this crazy world of ours. Not sure I'll be able to do anything, but I'll do my best. 'I alone cannot change the world, but I can cast a stone that can cast many ripples.' It's one of my favorite quotes, and I tell it to myself every day. Anyway, my mother moved to New York when I was five to stay with my aunt. When I turned ten, my mother left me with my aunt and went back to Europe. I returned to Brussels when I was eighteen to attend university there. After graduating, I went on to Paris to study linguistics and political science for graduate school and traveled back and forth between Rome and New York. I've been at the UN ever since I graduated, working my way up to being an envoy. That was never my intention, though. I kind of stumbled into it, but I found that I could do some good. As long as I find myself useful there, I plan on staying. Sorry for the long story. It was more than you asked for, but I figured it helped explain my accent. Part Italian. Part Dutch Belgian. A dose of the Bronx, some French and Arabic, from my linguistic studies in Paris, and a portion of Southwestern US drawl. I used to try to imitate them when I was a kid. Wanted to be a cowboy in Texas." He smiled. "By the way," he added. "Call me Lucio. I'm not into formalities."

"Alright. Lucio it is," Ryah said.

"That's good," Lucio said. He stopped in front of a door and pressed his badge against the black security receiver. "Here we are."

The door unlocked and Lucio held it open for Ryah to pass through first. The office was almost identical to Ryah's except for the large window in the southeast wall through which the late morning rays shone. A few papers were strewn across the desk, printed out from the computer but with handwritten notes scattered throughout. Standing by the desk at full attention but not in uniform was the person Ryah would supposedly work with. He was not all that impressive physically, other than being slightly taller than average, and had a triathlete's body. He was thin but not gaunt with dark eyes set back into his head which added to his lean appearance. Probably early twenties. No one on the street would see any reason to fear him, at least not by looking at him, but Ryah knew not to underestimate a member of the gamma special forces. Only the elite of the elite were given an offer to go through the training, and there were no more than fifty of them at any one time in the military.

"But why would he be here on a simple bodyguard mission?" Ryah thought. *"Maybe he failed out of the unit. Could be he's being punished for some failure on a mission."* He shook his head. *"No. No. There's another explanation for it. Just adding to the mystery here."*

Lucio made the introductions. "Ryah. This is Sergeant Rogan Silvano. He will be assisting you in this operation. Sergeant Silvano. Major Olmen."

Rogan snapped to attention and saluted Ryah.

"At ease, sergeant," Ryah said. "It's former Major Olmen. I haven't been in the service for years. You can call me Ryah. We should be less formal so that others outside the need to know will be unaware of what we're up to.

Whatever that is," he added. "Do you mind if I call you Rogan?"

Rogan eased up but didn't change the expression on his face. "My squad calls me Rogue, sir."

"Ryah," Ryah repeated.

"Ryah." Rogan looked uncomfortable saying it.

"Now that that's out of the way," Lucio said, "I'll need you two to come with me. I have a meeting with some of your administrators – Klins should be there, maybe Monaco and Azaria – and the Joint Chiefs. Abbad will be there as well. There will be a discussion about what their position is so that I can clearly present it to the UN when I go there, along with any room for negotiation the administrators might allow me. They'll brief you on your mission, but then you'll be dismissed so I and Abbad can speak with them about the classified objectives. I'll fill you in afterwards with the highlights when I see you tonight." He paused and tapped the screen of his portable communication device a few times. "There. I just sent you the flight details. We'll be leaving out of Perrin Air Force Base at 10:30. 22:30 for you military types. Meet me at hangar six at 21:30 hours."

A pair of comms buzzed simultaneously as the information sent by Lucio arrived. "Here you go." He handed Ryah and Rogan a comm and a small apparatus to use in the ear. "These will be the devices you use for our time together. They are already synced to the earpieces if you would prefer to use those instead. And here's my comm number so you can reach me from anywhere. Just remember that if you're not calling from one of these secure comms, anyone can and probably will be listening in. Come to think of it. That may apply even to these." He gave a knowing nod.

Ryah and Rogan took the devices and followed after Lucio, who had already hurried out the door. He led them to the other side of the building where the high-ranking representatives and administrators had their offices. The three passed through the interior security portal without even a cursory inspection thanks to the badge that Lucio carried. Arriving at their meeting room, Lucio entered while Ryah and Rogan waited outside. A minute later, Lucio emerged and waved the two in.

The room was dark. Darker than Ryah expected it to be. It had no windows, and the only light came from an ornate fixture hanging above the middle of a table around which six men sat. The chandelier swayed back and forth in a gentle motion and cast an eerie red glow, which bounced off the table and rose like tongues of flames dancing a demonic waltz. Only Lucio's face could be seen with clarity as he stood in the doorway waiting for Ryah and Rogan to enter.

Lucio took a seat next to Abbad and asked Ryah and Rogan to sit behind him. Ryah found himself obscured by a shadow in the half-light of the room. His eyes strained to adjust to the darkness, peering through it to see what lay in front of him. Across the table were the Joint Chiefs of the land, air, and sea forces respectively. At the head of the table, Klins spoke with Administrator Azaria, the second highest ranking person in the entire Council. It wasn't until Ryah saw him that the severity of the situation began to sink in.

"Thank you for being here," Administrator Azaria began. He addressed Ryah directly. "You come highly recommended by Klins, and I want you to know how much I appreciate your service to the nation. It is an honor to have you here with us."

Azaria turned his attention to the rest of the members of the group and spoke with each one in turn, flattering them like only a seasoned politician knew how to do. He went on for a while and Ryah's head started to nod and fall to his chest. Ryah jerked his head back up and tried to focus on the administrator, but his head began to nod again. Azaria's voice trailed off. Ryah watched his lips moving, but he no longer heard any sounds. He shook his head while rubbing his left ear and looked around the room to see the other's reactions, but none of them seemed to think anything was out of the ordinary. Most of them were bobbing in agreement with something Azaria had said, but Ryah couldn't make any sense of it. It was if he had gone deaf. Or so he thought until he heard his name.

"Ryah."

It was a whisper. A voice muffled as if spoken through a door. "Ryah," it repeated, this time louder, clearer. In the room with him.

"It can't be," Ryah thought. "That was my mother's voice. What is she doing here?"

Ryah looked into the corner of the room where he thought the voice came from. There, standing against the wall was a man he hadn't noticed before. He was staring directly at Ryah, his hands hidden in his pockets, his entire body covered in a long, black gown so that only his eyes showed. They were red. Like the light in the room. Like the reflection of the moonlight in a wild animal's eyes. He rose up, growing larger until he towered above the rest of the room.

"Ryah," he hissed.

His voice changed. It was deep, guttural, no longer feminine. Menacing. Frightening. Again, Ryah's name. This time a howl that pierced Ryah's soul. He covered his ears with both hands and rocked back and forth, trying in vain to block out the sound rushing past with the force of a violent wind. He could feel it blow through his body, threatening to tear him apart. It ripped through his chest and pushed his ribs into his lungs, compressing them, suffocating him. He screamed, but no sound came out. He screamed again as if the scream could save him and wake him from this living nightmare. The storm continued, intensifying each second. Growing. Multiplying. Terrorizing.

And then it stopped. As quickly as it started, the storm disappeared. Ryah looked back towards the corner. There were two men now. They were arguing, speaking in a language Ryah didn't understand. But they were enemies. Ryah was sure of that. Old enemies who couldn't conceal their hatred for each other.

Ryah's head jerked off his chest, and he rubbed his eyes. He was hoping no one had noticed that he had fallen asleep in his chair.

" … by next Friday?" Azaria finished.

Ryah realized Azaria was talking to him and looked back at him. "I'm sorry sir."

"Next Friday. Will that give you enough time?"

"Yes, sir. Of course," Ryah said.

"Great. You and Sergeant Silvano are dismissed." Azaria nodded towards the door.

Ryah stood up to take his leave. He glanced back towards the corner of the room.

"Had a hard time staying awake?" Rogan asked after the door had shut behind them.

"You noticed, huh?" Ryah answered. "You think anyone else did?"

"No. If they had, I would have woken you up. Besides, I was having too good a time watching you. I can't say I blame you. They were droning on for a while."

"So, I didn't miss anything important?" Ryah asked.

"Not much," Rogan said. "I'll fill you in on the details later."

"Alright," Ryah said. He became silent, trying to decide if he should trust Rogan or not. On the one hand, he didn't know Rogan. On the other, Rogan had his back in the meeting. He also seemed like a bit of a wise guy, which Ryah liked. In the end, Ryah took a chance.

"Hey, Rogan. What did you make of those two guys in the corner?"

"I didn't see any guys," Rogan said.

"No? I must've dreamed it," Ryah said.

In his heart, he didn't believe it was a dream. More like something between reality and a dream. Between the world that can be seen when awake and another one that can only be glimpsed when asleep. A world that doesn't exist but that somehow is more real. Ryah had always hoped there was someone else who felt the same thing, saw the same things, who shared his experience and could help him make sense of it. Or perhaps he was just so tired that he had begun to hallucinate. That's what any doctor would have told him. It certainly was the logical option, but for some reason, Ryah couldn't bring himself to believe it.

"Well, I'll see you tonight. 21:30 hours," Rogan said.

"Until then," Ryah replied and headed back to his office to pick up his blood-stained clothes. He figured he would get them and head home. Probably get a few hours of sleep at his house. It took him ten minutes to get back to his office. When he arrived, he sat down on his sofa, and kicked off his shoes.

"Maybe, I'll just sleep here," he told himself.

He lay down on the sofa for a moment. A buzzing sound came from the comm Envoy Romijn had given him. Ryah checked the time. "It's been over two hours," he said to himself, wiping the sleep from his eyes. He touched the screen to reply.

"Yes, sir. How can I help you?" Ryah assumed it was Lucio, but there was no response. "Envoy Romijn. You called? Is there something I can do for you?"

He heard static followed by some voices, distant, muffled. It was Abbad. Or at least it sounded like him. Ryah pressed the comm close to his ear and turned the volume as loud as it would go.

"… guaranteed. Fifty million now. Fifty million later."

Another voice spoke up. Ryah couldn't make out the words.

"Yes, yes," Abbad replied. "For the Kingdom."

Again, the other person, too quiet to hear.

"You'll answer to no one. Except of course …." The static broke up the conversation. Then the voices came back. "To show you our appreciation, we'll send a couple of girls to your home tonight. Let me know how you like them. Maybe they'll help convince you."

A knock on the door startled Ryah. Fumbling to turn off his comm, he walked to the door and opened it.

"Envoy Romijn," Ryah said. "What are you doing here? I thought …." He cut himself off. "What can I do for you?"

"I was hoping you were here. I forgot to give you the identification you'll need to get past the guards at the hangar tonight," Lucio said. "I found Rogan earlier, so he already has his."

"Great. Is there anything else?" Ryah asked.

"No." Lucio studied Ryah's face. "What's going on? You seem preoccupied."

"It's nothing," Ryah answered. "Just … how long ago did your meeting end?"

"I left about thirty minutes ago. Why?" Lucio said.

"Did anyone remain?" Ryah asked.

"Everyone else stayed behind after I went," Lucio said. "Why?"

Ryah didn't respond to the question but asked one of his own. "How well do you know Abbad?"

"I met him a week ago. Can't say I've had the time to form much of an opinion about him." He became serious. "What is it Ryah? What's going on?"

Ryah shook his head. "I don't know. I don't know." His face became ashen. "But I plan on finding out."

Lucio opened his mouth to say something but closed it, his eyes narrowing as if, by doing so, he could read Ryah's thoughts. "Alright, Ryah," he finally said. "Keep me informed. I'll see you tonight."

With that, Lucio shut the door, leaving Ryah alone.

Ryah's mind raced, jumping from thought to thought. *"Was that Abbad on the comm? I can't tell for sure. And who was that person with him? Klins? Azaria? One of the Joint Chiefs? Did someone else enter after everyone else had left? Who called me? Fifty million what? For what? Who's doing the offering? What are they offering? What are they getting in return? Should I tell Rogan?"*

Ryah was overwhelmed with all the questions. None of which he had answers for. One more question came to mind.

"What did I get myself mixed up in?"

Chapter 9

Maryam pulled Kaliya close. The neighborhood where they lived had an air of desperation. Their apartment complex housed the poorest of the poor, the rejects, the outcasts, the addicts, and the prostitutes. Many of them were given a stipend by a government that despised them but didn't have the desire to exterminate them. Yet. The rest fended for themselves.

Prostitutes lined the streets or hooked out of their rooms. Young girls and boys were enticed by handlers who offered riches to go with the promise of sexual freedom, learning, after it was too late to escape, what that freedom would cost them. Old ones, no longer desirable, were jealous of the new arrivals who encroached on their turf. Nauseated by the acts they performed in order to compete with the young, pretty ones. Self-medicating themselves into oblivion. Maryam received a small stipend. It almost covered Kaliya's medicine. The rest of the money she earned by selling her body.

The clock chimed two o'clock as Maryam walked up the stairs leading to her apartment. Clients would start arriving in an hour, and she was in a hurry to get Kaliya fed and out the door to her friend Corinne's apartment. Corinne knew what Maryam did. And why she did it. Corinne was the only person Maryam had ever confided in, but she hadn't told Corinne the entire story. Everything before Kaliya was born, Maryam left out. Maryam swore that would go with her to her grave.

"C'mon Kalli. You've got to go to Aunt Cori's," Maryam said.

"But mommy," Kaliya protested. "I wanted to play with you today."

"I know, Leeya," Maryam said, "but I've got to work. We'll play tomorrow."

"But you say that every day. We never get to play together."

Maryam's heart broke. She never had time for her daugher. But did Kaliya know why she did it? Did Kaliya understand how much she loved her? Everything she did, she did for her daughter. Every missed play date, every skipped meal, every client she entertained. Their fat, sweaty bodies on top of hers. Their breath reeking of garlic, onion, and liquor, if she was lucky. They made her sick. Every one of them. Every time. But what else could she do? It was the only life she knew. The only one she remembered. There would come a day when Kaliya would learn what her mother did. Would Kaliya be disgusted? Would she realize what a sacrifice her mother had made?

Would she follow in her mother's footsteps?

Maryam began to cry. Would her little girl become like her? That was a thought she couldn't bear. She had done everything to bring Kaliya into this world and to give her the life she never had. She couldn't handle the idea that Kaliya would suffer the way she did. The doubts came back and flooded her mind. They were always there, whispering to her, taunting her.

"It would be better to let her die, wouldn't it?" the voices said. *"You should have terminated her before she was born. Can't you see what you've done to her?"*

They were merciless, never letting Maryam forget. Making regret a weapon to be used against her. Waiting for her to be at her lowest point before turning the accusations into ice picks to be plunged deep into her soul.

"I know I'm a failure," she screamed out loud at the voices. "I know what I've done." She sobbed but no tears remained, only a defiance born of rage. "But you can go to hell."

She stopped. Kaliya stood in front of her, scared and confused.

"What are you talking about mommy?" Kaliya asked.

Maryam composed herself. "Nothing, sweetheart. Now go get yourself ready. I promise tomorrow we'll play together. We'll go to the river and throw rocks. We can even play hide and seek if you want."

Kaliya washed up and changed into her other set of clothes. By the time she made it back to the kitchen, Maryam had her food ready. Rice with a little bit of fried egg mixed in. It was their standard meal. On good weeks, Maryam was able to buy some fresh fruit and maybe some bread. If a client tipped her well, they might get meat.

Kaliya devoured the rice and grabbed the panda Allison had given her. When she finished, the two headed down to Aunt Corinne's apartment. Corinne was not her aunt. Maryam had no family, that she knew of anyway, but Kaliya always called her Aunt Cori.

Corinne lived on the ground floor next to the apartment where Beulah Lamieux would tell fortunes. For twenty dollars, she would predict people's futures for them. It was always good news. Optimistic clichés to help them feel good in a world where good could not be found. For fifty dollars, she would tell them the truth.

A faint odor emanated from Beulah's apartment, a mixture of rot and cheap incense. Thick, dark blinds covered the only window so that no one could see in or out. Even with the door open, Maryam could see nothing. It was black, and the light from the outside world seemed to get absorbed in the darkness. Kaliya imagined disembodied faces staring at her through the window, and she would sprint past it whenever she went to Aunt Cori's, being driven by an intangible but overwhelming fear.

"Hi Aunt Cori." Kaliya barged in Corinne's apartment without even knocking. She ran over to Corinne and nearly knocked her over. "Look what I got," she said, holding out her stuffed panda for Corinne to see.

"Hi Kalli. Be careful now. I'm an old woman."

Corinne sounded stern, but Kaliya knew her. Knew her well enough to know that Aunt Cori could never truly be mad at her.

"I got this from a friend," Kaliya said.

"You did? Let me take a closer look." Corinne took the panda that Kaliya offered her and turned it over and over. "Why that is a mighty fine bear you have. You must be a really good girl to have a friend that would give you such a beautiful toy." She looked at Maryam and made a gesture that said, "Where did you get this?"

Maryam responded with one of her own that said, "I'll tell you later."

"So, what time should I expect you," Corinne asked Maryam, "or will Kaliya be spending the night?"

"Probably nine o'clock. I'm tired, and I don't have the energy to deal with much," Maryam answered. "Thanks as always," she added.

"You know," Corinne said before she let Maryam go, "if you ever want to, I mean…. If you ever think you'd rather do something else … well, I'm sure that I … that you …."

"I know," Maryam said. "I know. But not tonight. Tonight, I have to take care of business." She blew Kaliya a kiss and went upstairs to wait.

Maryam's apartment was small but well kept. It had a kitchen, a small living area, and one bedroom where she entertained. She and Kaliya slept on a pullout sofa in the living room. Maryam didn't want her little girl sleeping in that other room.

A knock on the door. Maryam had seen him before. She didn't know his name. She never knew any of their names nor did she want to. She flashed a demure smile and led him to the bedroom.

He acted like he didn't want to be there, which may have been true. His mother had taught him to respect women. "I don't care what they tell you in school," she would say. "Sex is a beautiful thing between a man and a woman that love each other." He repeated that to a teacher when he was in sixth grade. The next day he was removed from her house and placed in a government run group home. But he always remembered her saying that. "Sex is beautiful."

The magazines told him a different story, though. It's how he got started. Playboy, Hustler. He didn't remember which one. It didn't matter. Women were presented as a means to gratify his own desires. It wasn't too long until the magazines were no longer enough. He began frequenting bars, looking for a live body to indulge in. But they placed demands on him, setting limits. He graduated to prostitutes who promised complete freedom, and he was satisfied. At least, temporarily.

And that's when he discovered his truth. Sex was not beautiful. It certainly wasn't love. It was sweaty, unfulfilling, bought and sold after a quick negotiation. He wondered if the prostitutes were told and believed the same lie or if they hurt inside. If they felt trapped like he did. But in the end, he didn't care. He had a desire which demanded to be met, and she was the object by which he would satisfy it.

Maryam understood the battle raging inside. She saw it in his eyes. He didn't really want to be there. He didn't really want to do this. But then he gave in. Like always. Each time, she saw the moment the shadow passed over his eyes, obscuring his vision and blinding him to what he knew to be true. It told him to trade what he needed for what he wanted at that moment. He had a choice. They all had a choice. They were without excuse. She made the same choice every day, just for different reasons. It didn't ease her conscience, though.

She began to let her mind wander. It was how she was able to stomach it. She thought back to when she was a little girl. Did she still have memories of that time? She thought she could picture her father. He had strong hands. That's what she recalled. And her mother. She was beautiful, but ... what was it? Thoughts flashed into her mind of when she was a teenager. She pushed them out.

"*I don't want to think about that now. Just the good times.*"

She concentrated on her childhood, believing that, if she focused hard enough, she could draw them out. What was it about her mother? She wanted to remember. She wanted to go back to that time of innocence, but the other thoughts kept interrupting, reminding her of what happened. Accusing her. Convicting her.

"*It wasn't my fault,*" she insisted.

"*It might not have been, but it is now,*" the voices countered.

Maybe she did remember after all. She just wished she didn't.

He couldn't manage to look Maryam in the eyes when he left the money on the edge of the bed and walked out. She washed herself off and waited for the next one. Fifteen minutes, no more, and the next knock came. Another regular, and Maryam's muscles tensed.

He had no conscience left. Maryam wasn't sure if he ever had one. He was supremely good looking and had no need to buy love. But he did it anyway. She hated what he asked her to do, the kind of things he wanted. These were the clients that made her feel disgusting, like she was nothing more than an animal.

She let her mind wander again. He was a prince, and she was a princess. Her mother used to tell her those stories.

"That was it. I knew I could remember something. She used to sit beside me on the couch and read me a story about a prince who would come and sweep a girl off her feet. Cinderella? I think that was the name. She said daddy was the prince and I was Cinderella. And someday I would find my own prince. He would love me with all his heart like daddy loved her."

The next question, she had pondered many times. *"What is love?"*

"Love? That doesn't exist," the voice answered.

"Yeah, it does. My mother told me that."

"Your mother lied to you. Look what she did to you."

"That wasn't her. She didn't do that."

The voice laughed. It didn't need to continue. She knew what it meant. More than anything else, she wanted to experience the love her mother told her was waiting for her, and she cursed herself for believing the lie, for believing anything her mother had told her. How could her mother have let that happen to her? Love didn't exist. Maryam was sure of that now.

This client left too. Finally. Then a few more. Nameless. Each with his own story. A few women also, but Maryam always told them no. That was a bridge she didn't want to cross.

Eight-thirty, a half an hour since her last client. Maryam was thankful the night had been shorter than normal even if she hadn't earned much. She bathed and removed any indication that anyone had been in her apartment. Only then did she go get Kaliya. Maryam was determined to keep the charade up as long as she could before Kaliya lost her innocence.

She walked past Beulah's apartment. The imitation incense floated out of her room and made her ill. Her supper returned and spilled on the grass.

"Are you OK?" Corinne asked through the open door.

Maryam didn't answer. Corinne walked over and placed her hand on Maryam's back. When Maryam had finished, Corinne helped her up and wiped the vomit off her face.

"Come inside, dear. I'll make you a little tea to ease your stomach."

Maryam wanted to tell her no, to get back to her apartment and fall asleep.

"Sure," Maryam said instead. "I'll take some tea."

Maryam went inside and sat at one of the two chairs around the kitchen table. "Where's Kaliya?" she asked.

"She fell asleep in my bed about an hour ago. She asked me to tell her a story, but she lasted only five minutes." Corinne let out a little laugh. "I'm not sure if she was tired or if it was the way I told the story."

Maryam smiled back at her and watched as Corinne poured boiling water into a small china cup.

"I kept it hot for you, because I knew you would be coming soon," Corinne said.

Maryam took small sips of the tea, letting it warm her body and her spirit. She sat silently while Corinne cleaned the kitchen and poured herself a cup. They chatted about nothing for a few minutes until Maryam finished. Finally, Corinne asked, "How are you doing?"

Maryam knew she wasn't referring to the incident outside the apartment. She wanted to speak, but she couldn't find the words. After a few moments, she said, "I want to stop. I just don't know how."

Corinne rubbed her back. "There's always a way. We'll find a way."

Maryam nodded and thanked Corinne for the tea. She didn't believe her though. There was not a way. Not anymore.

"Do you mind if Kaliya stays here tonight?" Maryam asked. "I don't want to wake her up."

"Of course I don't mind. She's welcome any time. I'll bring her up tomorrow morning after breakfast."

Maryam smiled and got up to leave. "Thank you," she said. "For everything."

She waved as Corinne shut the door and walked towards the rusted staircase which led to her apartment, hesitating as she passed by Beulah's place.

A voice spoke to her. *"Come inside."* It sounded like Corinne's voice, but it came from Beulah's. *"Don't you want to hear the good news?"*

The idea enticed Maryam. She had often wanted to see what Beulah did, and she was intrigued by the thought of knowing what her future held. But she had never succumbed to the temptation. "It's all a bunch of nonsense," she would tell herself. This time was different. She had to know. Was there a way?

"Come inside," it repeated. *"I'll show you the way."*

Maryam hesitated. It didn't feel right. A quiet voice inside of her, different than the first one, whispered to her, but she didn't understand what it said. It seemed to be warning her. She had felt the whisper before and had always heeded the warning, but she didn't care anymore. She went to knock on the door.

A homeless man in the street began to screech. An unearthly shriek which echoed off the buildings in the complex. Maryam turned to watch him as he walked down the block, waving his arms and babbling in an unrecognizable language. The distraction passed, and she turned back to the door. As she did, the apartment opened and a man walked out. There was something about his face. It wasn't really the look, but the face itself that scared her. It was his face, but it belonged to a stranger. She stifled a scream and ran upstairs to her apartment, slamming the door shut and locking it behind her.

Maryam struggled to catch her breath. She waited with her back against the door, holding it shut, her feet dug into the ground for extra leverage. For ten minutes she waited, but the moment never came. "I'm seeing things," she mumbled. Was she losing her mind? Was that what Kaliya talked about?

She waved off the idea and walked down the short hall into the living area. A man sat on her sofa, one she had never seen before. He was nondescript, dressed in clothes from a different era. Nothing remarkable about him at all, one of those types that pass in the background without being noticed. If she had seen him on the street, she wouldn't have given him a second thought.

"I'm sorry, but I'm finished for the night," Maryam said. "You can come back tomorrow." She gave him a sweet but short smile and showed him the door.

"That's not why I'm here," he replied, declining to move.

"Then why are you here?" she asked.

"Allison asked me to visit you."

Chapter 10

"Allison sent you?" Maryam thought back to her visit earlier that day. "I never gave her my address. How did you find me?"

The man looked at her like she should have known the answer. "I'm a little hungry," he said. "Do you have anything to eat? And something to drink, if you don't mind."

"Is there anything in particular you would like?" She didn't try to hide the sarcasm.

"Some bread and honey would do," he answered, "It's been a while since I last ate. And some water," he added.

There was something disconcerting about the man, especially his request. Why would he ask for that? Maybe everyone else kept a cupboard full of honey, but to her, it was a luxury. A treat reserved for special occasions. The last time she had bought some was a year ago. To him, it was a casual demand. No. More of a purposeful demand as if he knew what this simple request meant to her, testing her to see how she would react.

Despite this, Maryam felt compassion for the stranger in her living room. Maybe he was as hungry as he looked. She had known hunger, what it was like to sleep on an empty stomach, trying to keep her mind off the pain but having it intrude into her dreams. Maybe it was his hands and wrists. Scarred, torn like her face. Wounds which had healed but that spoke of the past. A constant reminder of the agony he must have lived through to acquire those scars.

Her tone with him changed. "I can do that." Then, she added, "Are you sure you wouldn't like some tea instead of water? It will only take a few minutes."

"Sure. Thank you," he said.

Maryam stepped into the kitchen. It wasn't a separate room but more of a separate part of the living room from which her guest watched her every move. She placed the teapot on the stove and ignited the flame. The blue tongues wrapped around the sides and held the teapot in a fiery embrace. She opened her cupboard halfway so that her guest couldn't see what was inside and reached for her box of tea bags. She was ashamed of how little she had and didn't want him to know. But she was who she was. She would rather go without herself than let anyone, even a total stranger, be hungry. Three packets of tea remained inside the box. She pulled one out and placed it on the counter next to a brown ceramic cup and a spoon. On a plate, she put two slices of bread and drizzled the remaining honey over them. When the water had finished boiling, she poured it into the cup and brought it all to her guest.

He sat there silently, eating and sipping the tea until he had finished. Maryam examined his face. He had a kind face. Radiant. Honest. Like he was incapable of telling a lie. And his eyes. His eyes penetrated into her, a searchlight scrutinizing her innermost secrets. She became uncomfortable with his stare and turned away.

The stranger broke the silence. "Thank you for the food and the tea." He handed the dishes back to her. "Now, what can I do for you?"

Maryam wasn't sure how to respond. "I don't know," she said. "Maybe you could start by telling me your name."

He smiled at her. "You know who I am and I know you."

She was confused by his statement. "No, I'm sure we've never met before." But she was uncertain. Had she met him? He seemed confident about it. She decided to press forward. "I guess you could help me with my daughter."

"Is that why you asked me here? To help with your daughter?" he said.

"I don't remember asking for you to come here," she said. "I was talking with Allison. Your friend, I assume? And she said she would be sending someone here." Then she remembered what he had said. "I thought you said Allison asked you to visit me."

"Oh, she did. But you did also," he replied. "So, tell me about Kaliya. Where is she now?"

"She's downstairs at my friend's house. She fell asleep, so I left her there."

He listened to her but didn't say a word, so Maryam continued. "Since you seem to know so much about us ..." There was the sarcasm again. She felt embarrassed by her tone. "She's sick. She's very sick." Her voice began to break. "No one knows what's wrong exactly. She has seizures – that's what they call them – but they're just a symptom. The tumors ... there are tumors throughout her body. Her legs. That's where they started. Her lungs. Her heart. They've spread to her brain, and ... and they ... the doctors say there's nothing they can do. The tumors don't respond to any treatment, any medicine. She's ..." Maryam stopped, unable to say anymore.

"What can I do for you?" he asked again. His voice was calm, certain.

"I want you to heal her," she said. "If you can."

"Do you think I can heal her?" he asked.

"I have no idea. I don't even know who you are. I have no reason to think one way or another. Are you some sort of doctor? Some amazing surgeon who just happened to find his way to my house?" she said.

He shook his head.

"A faith healer," she continued. "Like on tv. 'Believe what I say and donate to the cause to prove you believe.' Some slick-talking charlatan who's about to promise me a miracle for whatever I happen to have in my purse?" She looked at him. "I don't have time for that."

He remained silent. That kind face scrutinizing her with those honest, penetrating eyes.

She spoke again, her words no more than a whisper. "I don't know if you can heal her," she said, "but I need you to heal her. I don't have any other hope."

She hung her head and stared at the floor, seeing nothing. Her shoulders slumped forward, and she rested her hands on her lap, stroking one thumb with the other.

He smiled at her again, but she wasn't looking. "You never answered my question, Maryam."

"I'm sure I just did," she said, lifting her head and wiping a tear that ran down her cheek. She wanted to add, 'Weren't you listening?' but she didn't.

"No, Maryam. What can I do for *you*?" he said.

Realizing what he meant, she told him, "I'm not sure there is anything you can do." She watched his reaction. "Unless you have a million dollars you want to give me. Help me get out of this place." She looked around the grim dungeon she called home. "Help me get out of this life."

"Is this the life you chose?" he asked.

Maryam felt her face flush. The question wasn't asking for information. She was sure he already knew the answer. Nor was it meant to embarrass her, although it did.

"My daughter is sick, and I don't have any money. This is my way of keeping her alive. Of keeping us alive," she answered.

"That's not what I asked," he said. "Is this the life you chose for yourself?" he asked.

"No." She tried to stop herself, but the words forced their way out. "No, of course not. What kind of stupid question is that? Of course, I didn't choose it." Her body trembled, and her hands had clenched into fists.

"I need you to tell me the truth," he said.

Maryam said nothing. The words, like an accusation, hit her hard, and she felt her chest constrict. She knew there was more.

"Why do you do this? Why do you stay here?" he asked.

She wanted to repeat her story. Tell him about the money again, but she knew it wasn't true. She felt the mask she hid behind, the mask which held back her fears, her pain, begin to fall away. "I don't know any other way," she said, her voice heavy with guilt. "I've been doing this as long as I can remember ... I don't know any other way."

She wanted to tell him everything, or maybe she just wanted to tell someone. She had kept the truth locked away so long that she didn't know if she could. Her mouth opened as if to speak but no sound came out. Nothing would come out. He reached over and touched her hand.

"Tell me what you need to tell me," he said.

She looked into his eyes, searching for the courage. A shudder traveled through her body.

"I was twelve when I ran away," she said. "I ran to get away. He found me and brought me here. He told me this is what I was." She paused and stared into the darkness, remembering but not wanting to. "There were so many men that he brought. Each day. All day. I just let them do it to me. I could've run away again. But I didn't. I just let them do it. At least I had something to eat. And a place to stay. I couldn't stand the rain. Being out on the streets when it rained. At least I had a place to stay."

The words came out jumbled. A thousand emotions battled inside her.

"I hated myself," she said. "I hated them. I hated him, but I didn't know what else to do. And then ...." She looked down at the floor. "I was fifteen and something was different. I felt sick, but it was a different type of sick. Somehow, I knew. I talked with my friend Leila and she told me. But I already knew. I already knew what it was, and I knew I had to hide it. Had to hide it as long as I could, because if he found out, he would have made me get rid of her. I kept it hidden from him for six months until it was no longer possible. When he found out, he beat me." She winced at the thought as if he were there striking her now. "He beat me, but I told him no. I wasn't getting rid of her. She was my hope, my light. He threw me on the ground and kicked me and beat me some more. Then … then, he gave me this." She stroked the scar on her face with the tips of two fingers in an unconscious motion she had done hundreds of times.

"He left me there bleeding and said no one would want me now. I was back on the streets. This time with a baby inside. I went to the hospital, but when they found out who I was, what I was, they wheeled me back to the operating table. They were going to kill her. Kill her inside me. I pretended to be nauseous and went to the restroom, and then I ran. I ran out of there. I ran until I couldn't run anymore."

She waited, recalling the rest in her mind. "I had Kaliya right there on the street. A week later, I went back. What could I do? I didn't have a choice." Maryam stopped speaking. What she had said wasn't true.

"I did have a choice," she confessed to him. "I could have done something else." The admission added to her guilt. "I tried working in the store, but they didn't … I didn't know how to act with those people. I didn't know how to be anything else but this." The words stung.

"This is not what you are," he said.

She stared at her feet. He took hold of her face and lifted it up so she could look in his eyes. He caressed her cheek. Like a father comforting his daughter. He spoke to her in that quiet voice she heard sometimes, different than all the others.

"This not who you are. I know you, Cate."

She heard it for the first time in almost twenty years. Her name. The secret she swore would die with her. The life too painful to remember. For six years, she endured. Until she ran away. But she ran right back. She grit her teeth and kept her mouth shut, the anger flashing in her eyes. Those fierce, emerald eyes of hers. Beautiful, dark, lost. She wasn't angry at him, though. She was angry at her lost childhood, at the people who stole her innocence, who forced her into the only life she knew. At the man who took her from her home, from her father and mother and their unconditional love. From her brother, who used to pick her up and swing her around in his arms until she was too dizzy to stand. From the joy and peace and happiness she deserved. She was angry at the men who bought her and passed her around. Who used her. She was too young to understand then. She didn't know what they were doing to her. But she knew now. Now she made them pay for it. Now she chose to do it, because she didn't know any other way.

"How did you know?" she asked.

He wept. Silently, tears running down his face. His body shuddered, grief etched across his face. No words came out, only a soft groan as if his soul was breaking.

Finally, he spoke. "I am the way out of this," he said.

"What do you mean?" she asked. She knew, but she didn't know if she believed.

He got up to leave and gave her a hug. "Go find Allison. She'll be expecting you." He walked down the hall but stopped and turned back towards Maryam. "I saw Kaliya today," he said. "She's well."

Chapter 11

Maryam watched him go, looking in his direction long after she could no longer see him. His words lingered in the air, her mind unable to comprehend what he meant.

The cold air shook her body as she stepped outside. She wrapped a sweater around her shoulders and headed down the rusty staircase. Across the street, the light from a coffee shop drifted into the night. Maryam dug in her pocket and pulled out enough change to buy a cup. Finding a stool far away from the door, she dropped the change on the counter.

"Coffee, please," she said. She sat there and waited. And thought. And hoped.

"May I join you?"

A man stood behind her, well over six feet tall with dark hair and dark eyes that hid a secret.

"Not sure I'll be good company, but if you want," she said, offering him the seat.

"My name's Bale," he said.

"Good to meet you, Bale," she replied without looking at him nor meaning what she said.

"I was sitting by the window and noticed you walking down the staircase," he said. "I was hoping you might come over here."

"You did, huh?" Maryam said, getting herself ready for the line she knew was coming.

"Yeah. And I saw the guy come out of your place before you."

"Mm hmm."

"You know him?" he asked.

"I just met him," she said.

"Hmm." He remained silent for a moment. "I know him well. Known him for many years. I could tell you a few stories."

Maryam's ears perked up.

"Yep. I know him well. Wouldn't trust him for the world." He took a sip of coffee and watched Maryam out of the corner of his eye.

"You wouldn't?" she said. "And why's that?"

"I'm sorry. I shouldn't have said anything. Shouldn't have put my nose into your business. But ... well, I just wanted to spare you the pain."

"What are you talking about?"

"Let me ask you a question. What did he offer you?"

"I don't really think that's any of your concern," she said.

"You're right. You're right. I got too personal." He stopped. "Look. I just want what's best for you. Or maybe better said, I want to make sure that guy knows his place. He's got a bit of a god complex, you know. Says he's out to save the world one person at a time. Way I see it though, he just leaves a trail of death and destruction wherever he goes."

Maryam remained silent, contemplating his words.

"Yeah. Death, pain, suffering. It's almost like that's what he wants." He took another sip and let his words simmer. "He wears the mask of a good guy, but inside ... no. I don't believe a word he says."

"He said he was the way out," Maryam said.

"What was that?" Bale asked.

"You asked me what he offered me? He said he was the way out of my mess," she said.

"Is that what he said?" Bale scoffed. "Yeah, I've heard that one before. That's just his way of saying I'm going to get you into a bigger one." His anger rose as he recalled some past incident.

"So, who is he?" she asked.

"Just some guy who wants to trap you with his lies and make you his slave, running around doing his bidding. He even says that. He says that straight out. Not at first of course. He'll sweet talk you and tell you what you want to hear, but before you know it … he got you. You're under his thumb doing what he tells you. Do this. Don't do that. Rules and regulations. Nah, that wasn't for me. I followed him for a while, but I preferred my freedom. Had to fight for it, because he wasn't about to give it to me. That's why I'm here now. Making sure people don't get trapped by him like he tried to trap me. I've made it my mission," he said. "I follow him around, when I can of course, and make sure people don't fall for his propaganda."

He could tell Maryam wasn't convinced, so he added, "Was there anything else he told you?"

Maryam thought for a while. "He said he knew me," she said.

"He did?" He brooded over the words. "He knew you."

Maryam thought back to the stranger's words. How he knew her name. The kindness in the way he spoke to her. "Yes. That's what he said."

He murmured something Maryam didn't understand.

"He knew who I was and everything about me," she continued. "He even knew about…"

"About what?" he asked.

"About how it all started. It seemed … it seemed like he was there."

"Hmm. I wouldn't doubt it. He probably was there. And from the way you're talking, it seems like it was something rather terrible."

Maryam looked away.

"Yeah. I'm sorry," he said and reached out to touch her. A cold shiver ran up her arm. "He probably was there. All along. That's how he operates. He left you alone, didn't he?"

She didn't say anything, but he saw he had touched a nerve.

"Leaves you alone to suffer whatever it was and then comes back and says he's going to take it away." He laughed and shook his head in disbelief. "The audacity of that guy. And he expects you to believe him."

Maryam pushed away from the counter. "Thank you for the information. I'll take it into consideration," she said, her voice trembling.

She walked into the cool night and back across the street. She wanted to believe what the stranger said, wanted to believe in something that could heal her daughter and free herself from her life, but Bale had awoken her insecurities and doubts. His voice intermingled and blended with the other voices until they became one unified chorus, shouting down the quiet stillness of the stranger's words.

"You've got another option," she heard herself say. "You could keep doing what you're doing."

She thought about the people. The stranger with the kind eyes who knew her. Bale, convincing but cold. He didn't ask for anything. But he didn't offer anything either. Following him, she'd still be there, selling herself.

Allison.

'Go see Allison,' the one with the kind eyes said.

But she's one of them. An outlaw. Hiding herself from the Council. "What do I do? Who do I believe?" she asked out loud.

She walked past Corinne's apartment, hoping Corinne would be awake, hoping she could talk with her, hear what she had to say. She hesitated for a moment. Her hand rapped on the door.

"Hi, Maryam," Corinne said. "I thought you would have been asleep. Come on in."

Maryam entered the apartment. The brightness hurt her head. "What's going on Corinne?" she asked as she shielded her eyes.

"I'm not sure. Just a few minutes ago, my lights came on. Bright like you see them. Must be some sort of power surge. I tried to turn them off, but they're not working. Weirdest thing I ever saw. Anyway, I figured I'd get up and do a little cleaning." She pointed down the hall. "Kaliya's awake. There's something ... well, you've got to see for yourself."

Maryam went to the bedroom and opened the door. Kaliya was jumping on the bed. Up and down. Up and down. Like a rabbit on caffeine.

"Hey, momma," she said.

"What are you doing, Kalli?" Maryam asked.

"Nothing. I'm just bouncing," Kaliya said.

"I know that. But why are you bouncing?" Maryam said.

"I don't know. I just feel good."

Maryam grabbed Kaliya by the arm until she stopped jumping. "Let's go Kalli," she said. "Get your bear."

"Ahh, momma."

Maryam gave her the look that meant it wasn't the time to backtalk her. Kaliya followed her down the hall.

"Corinne," Maryam said, "we're going back upstairs. Would you like to spend the night with us seeing as how your lights aren't working?"

"No thanks," Corinne said. "I'll just stay here and tidy up. I'll see you tomorrow, OK?"

"I'm not sure," Maryam said. "I might be going away for a while. Not sure when I'll be back."

Corinne smiled at her. "OK, dear. I'll see you later." She gave her and Kaliya a hug. "Take care of yourself," Corinne said, before adding. "Don't forget about me."

Maryam hugged her back and took her daughter to their apartment, going the long way to avoid Beulah's. When they got home, Maryam put Kaliya to bed and made her promise that she would stop acting so crazy. Kaliya fell asleep almost immediately. Maryam watched for a while and went to put away the dishes. On the counter was the jar of honey, filled to the brim and running over.

Chapter 12

Ryah looked at his watch. 21:20. He waited as a guard checked the identification Envoy Romijn had given him. A few seconds later, the gate slid back along its tracks revealing retractable spikes that disappeared into the ground. The guard handed the badge back and waved him through. Ryah had spent most of the last fifteen years in and around military installations, but this was his first time on Perrin Air Force Base.

"Which way to hangar six?" Ryah asked.

The guard pointed to the northwest. Ryah followed the road hoping there would be a sign to guide him. He didn't have to go far, no more than a quarter mile, and found Rogan standing outside the hangar. Rogan snapped to attention as soon as Ryah stepped off his bike, which earned him a quick rebuke and reminder that they were supposed to hide who they were. Lucio Romijn was already inside, standing by a private jet and going over the flight manifest with the pilot.

"Ryah. Good to see you," Lucio said. "You can park your bike over there," he indicated a corner of the hangar, "and you can pick it up when we get back. Since you're both here and the pilot's ready to go, we'll leave early. Fifteen minutes give or take, so go ahead and board now. Sit where you like."

Ryah slid a backpack off his shoulders and rolled his eyes at Rogan's military duffel bag.

"It's all I had," Rogan fired back. "On my salary, I can't afford to get me a fancy civilian backpack like yours."

Ryah laughed and climbed on board the jet. It had room to hold ten passengers, but the interior had been converted to include a conference table and a separate workstation, leaving only four seats in the back. Ryah threw his backpack on the floor and flopped down. Rogan sat in a seat across the aisle and stared at his comm.

Ryah leaned over to Rogan. "What do you think about this mission?"

"In what sense?" Rogan asked.

"Whatever your impressions are," Ryah said.

"Permission to speak freely?" Rogan said.

"Always."

"Not sure what to make of it," Rogan said. "From what I gather, your background is in intelligence, so I assume we're on a fact-finding mission of sorts. Since Romijn is going to negotiate with the Russians and Chinese on behalf of the Council, I assume the Council wants us to keep tabs on him. Now, both you and I were requested by Ambassador Tanas from the UN, a stranger to both of us, to provide protection for our envoy friend outside. The Council wasn't happy with the request from Tanas but wanted some of their own operatives to go instead of us."

"How do you know about that?" Ryah asked.

"I have my ways." Rogan said and continued. "Tanas insisted on us, so the Council had the option of using us or having no one there at the negotiations representing them. If you were to ask me, I'd say something's off about this entire thing. I'm a nobody, and you're some ex-intelligence officer, who doesn't know any of these players and has a distaste for this line of work."

"You do your homework, I see," Ryah said.

"I also know you always act in the best interests of your men and are a man of character, kind of hard to find in the Council," Rogan said. He realized he crossed the line with that last remark, but Ryah noticed that he didn't seem to care.

"I came to the same conclusions myself," Ryah said. "I get the feeling we're being set up for something, and I don't intend on being anybody's fall guy. I suggest you watch your back, and I'll do the same."

While they were talking, Envoy Romijn boarded the plane carrying some files, and sat down at the table.

"Guys. Come here for a few minutes," he said. "I want to brief you on what we'll be doing. Afterwards, I suggest you two get some rest as we have a long day ahead."

Ryah headed over to where Lucio was and took the file handed to him. He glanced over the contents. Nothing in particular stood out. It all seemed to be typical diplomat nonsense, the kind Ryah tried to avoid whenever possible.

Lucio started. "As you know, I will be representing your country at the UN since you no longer have a presence there. The Council's official position is that they condemn the violation of Russia's national borders by the Chinese. They would like to see an immediate withdrawal and an official apology by the Chinese, and they would like Russia to accept it without prejudice."

"Good luck with that," Ryah said. "I can't see either side agreeing to those conditions, especially when it's coming from us."

"I agree," said Lucio, "which is why I'll need to change the language into something palatable for both sides. That's what I'll be working on. You two will be with me during the negotiations but as my staff. Nobody else needs to know that you're representing the Council. As far as they're concerned, you're part of my usual security detail. What I want you to do is watch for signs of trouble. Buddy up to the guys from Russia and China and see if you can get any inside information. You can handle that, can't you?"

"Of course," Ryah said.

"Great. That's all I have for now."

Lucio buried his head in his papers, which Ryah took as his way of dismissing them. He headed back to his seat and looked over at Rogan.

"I'm going to get some shuteye as soon as we take off," Ryah said. "Wake me if anything interesting happens."

"Will do," Rogan replied and pulled up the news feed on his comm.

Ryah leaned his head back against the seat and felt the rumble of the plane as it bounced along the tarmac. When they reached the end of the runway, the pilot engaged the thrust, and the jet hurtled back down the airstrip towards a grove of trees at the end. The power of the jet, which rivaled that of any military fighter, surprised Ryah as they lifted into the night sky. They reached cruising altitude in a matter of minutes and settled in for the long ride.

Figuring that now was as good a time as any, Ryah reclined the chair until it was almost horizontal and tried to fall asleep. He pushed the button by the side of the overhead light but nothing happened. He pushed it again. It made a barely audible click which seemed like it came from the other room. Sitting up, he smacked the button with the palm of his hand. Without warning, that light, along with all the other ones, shut off, and the plane plunged into total darkness. There was no sound. No hum of the engines. No reply from Rogan when Ryah called out to him. Only silence. And the dark.

Complete and total darkness. He couldn't see his hand when he held it up to his face. He knew it must be there, but he couldn't be sure. It was a strange sensation, not having any of his senses working. He had been on a plane with someone. Or so he thought. It felt like a dream that was fading away. Was it even real? That life in ... what was that place called? Did it even happen? He had the feeling

109

that he had been here for months maybe years, but none of it seemed familiar to him.

He tried to stand up. His bones felt heavy, like they were made of lead, and his muscles didn't seem capable of carrying the weight. He reached out to grab onto something to give himself leverage, but there was nothing around him. He started to crawl in a direction he thought was forward until he ran into a wall made of stones so cold it burned his hand. Screaming, he tried to push off, but his hand had frozen into it. Using all his strength, he ripped his hand off the wall, leaving flesh and muscle attached to the stone. No blood dripped out as if his body had been completely drained of it.

He staggered on, not knowing where he was going or what he hoped to find. A panic set in. A panic that turned to fear. Not a fear he had felt before. It was uncontrollable, indescribable. A terror that gripped his soul and made him want to run. Run away from what? Run away from here? Where was here?

"I have to get out of here. Go. Now! Help! Where am I? Hey! Why don't I hear anything? Help me! Oh, god. Help me."

In the distance, he could see an open door. Outside, a light, actually more of a red glow, crept through the opening. He stumbled towards the exit, hoping he could find someone who could give him an explanation. As he made his approach, he felt the air warm up, slowly at first, but then much more quickly the closer he got towards the door until the point that the heat was almost unbearable. He pushed his way through and tried to take a deep breath, but the air felt like it was on fire and burned his lungs with every gulp. He turned to go back inside but found that the door had locked behind him.

The pain was intense now. In his hand, in his lungs, throughout his whole body. In the red light, he was able to see himself for the first time.

"What happened? This isn't me."

He was naked and grotesque. Like a gargoyle. Scaly almost.

"Scales, or is my flesh burning off? I need to find water to dip myself in. I've got to cool myself off. I feel like I'm on fire here."

He looked down. His knees had broken and had re-healed incorrectly, the legs bending more to the sides than to the front. His arms were different lengths and all out of proportion to his body as if they had been pulled and stretched like a rubber band which had lost its elasticity and refused to return to normal. What he could see of himself was hideous, but he knew that somehow this was his real body. Bizarre visions passed in front of his eyes, and paranoia took a hold of him as his sanity began to slip away.

The path sloped down towards the silhouettes of some figures, and he made his way towards them. The trail, which had started out as wide as a ten-lane road, constricted into a single lane and led into a canyon with steep, stone walls rising up hundreds of meters. Midway through the canyon, a swinging gate, six times his height, stood in his way. Afraid of what had happened before, he tried to turn back, but he lost his footing and slid through the gate only to hear it click shut behind him like the door had done. With no choice but to keep going, he picked himself up and continued his descent, the way widening just a little so that someone, if there was anyone, could walk past him. On the sides of the canyons, creatures with human form hung chained on the walls, unable to move. They screamed, enraged spirits cursing the universe, enveloped in the deepest darkness like he had been just a few moments earlier.

"Or has it been days?"

The path led to a large pit, a mile across at least and with no bottom in sight. The middle of the pit contained a lake where the outlines of people could be seen swimming. Around the edge of the abyss, hundreds of thousands more shadows could be seen. Some of them wandering around aimlessly. Some restrained. Some whipped and tortured by unseen hands. They could have been people.

"Are they people? All I see are their outlines."

Misshapen. Like the night swallowed them and trapped them inside a black veil, their souls screaming to be freed. He thought he recognized some of them. Former enemies. Former friends. It didn't matter. All he felt was contempt for them. For everyone. And hunger. And thirst.

"I've got to eat something. I haven't eaten in months, and I don't know the last time I had something to drink."

His tongue felt swollen, blistered, rotted. His stomach was empty but bloated. And the hate. He knew he hated them, but it didn't give him any pleasure to see them there, whipped by those unseen hands, thin iron bars with hooks on the ends tearing into their flesh. They screamed but no sound came out. And the people in the lake.

"They're not swimming. They're trying to get out, but they can't. There's something in there with them, attacking them, searing off their flesh. How are they still alive?"

He walked closer to the edge of the lake to get a better look. The sight horrified him. But it also drew him in, called to him like a siren song, telling him this was his reward. The lake summoned him to enter and he obeyed. He lost all semblance of self other than the pain. The pain that increased without bound. A pain that did not end, that would not end, that he would be conscious of forever.

"Why can't I die? Why can't I DIE? Oh, god. Kill me!"

Chapter 13

It was bright. So bright that Ryah's head hurt, but the rest of the pain had gone. He squeezed his eyes shut and then opened and closed them one at a time until they had adjusted to the surroundings.

"Let's go. The procession is starting."

Ryah had no idea who had spoken to him. He turned his head around and saw a creature standing there.

"Get up, Ryah," the guide said. "He wants you to see it."

Ryah arose as if from the dead. Fine white linen adorned his body, which had been restored to perfection. He didn't remember this creature that spoke to him, yet he found him strangely familiar.

Ryah followed the creature down the path towards a mountain on top of which there was a palace. There was a festiveness in the air. A joy that filled Ryah's lungs with every breath. Streams of other creatures – some human-like as this one was, others of a form Ryah had never seen before but beautiful and awesome to look at – flooded the plain upon which the two walked. At such a great distance from the palace, their cheers rolled over Ryah like thunder, and he felt himself get caught up in the excitement.

"What's going on?" he asked. "Why are all these people here?"

The guide made a strange look when Ryah said 'people', but he didn't correct him. "The war is over, and we were victorious," he said. "General Chael is leading the armies back into the city and bringing the vanquished captives to the prince so that he can pronounce judgment on them. Everyone has gathered to hear what he will say."

"What will become of them?" Ryah asked.

"Some of them have already been sent to the shadows," the creature said. "The ones that can never be allowed to roam freely again. You saw them there, chained to the walls. There they must remain until the final judgment."

Ryah's stomach turned as the memory of that place swept over him. As soon as he had arrived here, he had forgotten everything he had ever done, that had ever happened to him, as if his past never existed. As if he wasn't supposed to remember. It wasn't until Guriel spoke again that it came back to him.

"*Guriel. His name is Guriel,*" Ryah thought.

The scenes from the battle flashed through his mind. General Chael riding out with a sword in hand, his vast army following and covering the plain. An equally daunting foe, handsome, arrogant, charging out to meet General Chael. It was the challenger, the one who had cursed the prince and the kingdom, that must have been defeated. It was his followers that Ryah must have seen in the world of horrors. That which Guriel called the shadows.

What a contrast to what Ryah saw before him. There was no longer any sign of the clash he had witnessed. No indication that a battle had ever taken place. Everything was perfect, ordered, except for the line of prisoners that made their way towards Ryah.

As Guriel entered the main gate into the city, the crowds parted and allowed Ryah to pass by. He went to the front of the assembly and was escorted to the bottom of a set of steps leading to a courthouse which reminded him of an ancient temple. Throngs of human-like creatures dressed in their finest garments lined the street and sang songs of triumph and praise for the prince. The procession approached. Even from so far, Ryah could make out

114

General Chael, mounted on his brindle horse. Directly behind him were the captives, the sounds of their iron chains clanking with each step they took.

General Chael held up his hand to halt the march and a hush fell over the crowd. Even the captives became quiet. A chorus of trumpets broke the silence. Ryah looked up as the doors at the top of the steps flung open. A brilliant light exploded through the entrance, bursting out like the morning sun and silhouetting a figure as he emerged from inside. The figure walked to the edge of the terrace, his clothes and face radiating the glory of that place. Lightning flashed and thunder shook with each step he took, and Ryah fell to his knees in fear.

A voice rose above the crash of the thunder and resounded in his ears. "Ryah," it said. "There's no need to be afraid. Stand up and take note. I've called you to be a witness."

The figure seemed more like a god to Ryah than a person. His voice was quiet, reassuring, one brother comforting another. Ryah looked towards him and saw that he was looking into the face of the prince.

"Watch, listen, and remember," the prince said to Ryah.

The prince turned towards the prisoners and addressed them. "Stand up and face me." Chains rattled as the captives rose to their feet and confronted the one who had been their sovereign.

"Your crimes are undeniable, and you have no excuse." the prince said. "You have brought evil to a place that never knew it. To a place where it cannot dwell. In your foolishness, you have rebelled against the king, turned your backs on your nation, and brought disgrace to your names. Greed, envy, hatred were found in you where none had been found before. You renounced your citizenship and allegiance to the king to follow a fool on his errand. Liars and murderers you wanted to become. Liars and murderers you will be. And you will receive the reward you have desired."

The prince turned to face the rebel leader to speak to him directly. "And you. You wanted this kingdom for yourself. To exalt yourself over the true ruler and usurp his throne. You believed that you were wiser, better suited to rule, more beautiful and noble than all the rest of the citizens of this land. And you were. But your wisdom became arrogance, and your beauty became treachery, and in your conceit, you failed to see that you were doomed to fail from the start."

The prince looked over the crowd and spoke so that all gathered could hear him. "Their judgment is decided, and their sentence is just."

He said one final word that Ryah didn't understand, then everything fell silent. There was no sound at all, no motion whatsoever. It was as if time froze for everyone except for him. He saw the creatures around him. The prisoners, anger, fear, disbelief etched across their faces. The victors, wonder at what was about to happen, a mix of hate and lament in their eyes. The world began to move again.

From the group of prisoners rose a low moan which grew into a howl. Their chains rattled as they stood and tried to flee, each creature on its own, straining against its bonds in a desperate attempt to break free, to escape their penalty. They screamed and ripped off their clothes to tear at the skin which lay beneath, writhing and flailing as if a fire was burning from within. Deteriorating into a state of insanity, unable to comprehend the terror that was befalling them.

And then they began to change, metamorphose from the beautiful creatures they once were into something hideous. Arms and legs twisted and broke, re-healing into grotesque lumps of flesh which flailed about in unrhythmic spasms. Their chests heaved and their bodies contorted, their faces stretching and elongating, mutating into demonic masks. Ripped off skin replaced by scales. Part human, part reptile, part monster. Their outward appearance reflecting their internal reality.

When the transformations had finished, the prince spoke to General Chael. "They are banished from this land until the appointed time of their final judgment."

A roar went up from the prisoners, begging the prince for mercy, but none was given. Others cried, lashing out in desperation, hoping for any minor reprieve that might be offered. The voice of a rebel captain resounded over the tumult.

"Mighty prince," he said, his words coming out as a plea, "I beg you to spare us. We will do anything you ask. Just don't send us away. Don't consign us to the other realm. We beg you. We implore you. Don't send us away."

The prince didn't say anything. Again and again, the captain pleaded but received no response.

At last, the prince replied, "You will never reside in my kingdom again, and your fate is sealed. You are no longer citizens of this land. No longer my brothers, my people, but slaves to your own depraved minds and wills. You will wander the arid places searching for rest and fulfillment, but you will find none. You will no longer live forever. Instead, you will die forever as the fire burns you from within but never consumes your flesh. Your sentence is pronounced."

He turned to General Chael. "Bring Ant'el to me."

The general grabbed the rebel leader by the arm and led him up the stairs to the side of the prince.

"You were my closest advisor," the prince said. "The one I entrusted with my most important possessions, with my glory. And you betrayed me and my father. If only you had been content with what you had, we would never have come to this. You were called a brother, but from now on you will be called my enemy."

117

Ant'el's eyes brimmed with hate. His voice trembled. "All because of them. It's all because of them. How could you favor them more than me?" His voice rose to a crescendo. "More than me? More than me! I am the one who deserved the glory. Not them. Those weak, pathetic excuses you call your friends, your brothers. Who among them can do what I do? Who watched over your treasure and oversaw your entire kingdom? Who walked with you day after day and counseled you? Which of them has my wisdom? Which of them has my light, my beauty, my glory? And you told me to bow before them? That someday they would rule over me? Those frail, foolish, useless mortals. They should bow before me. I should be their god! You were wrong when you spoke. You disrespected me. You betrayed me, and for that you should have paid with your life and I should have ruled the kingdom. I would have shown them how a true king governs, and I should have received their adoration. Not you. Not him. Me. I deserved to rule the land."

"Ahh, Ant'el," the prince said. "Your mind has begun to turn, I see, already believing your own lies, your pride deceiving yourself into thinking that you are justified, that you had any rights and power beyond that which I gave you. You are a great fool, the greatest that ever lived."

"Then let this fool make one more request," Ant'el said.

The prince didn't respond but exhaled out. A wind began to blow from the top of the mountain, swooping down over the prisoners and stirring up a cloud of dust that obscured Ryah's vision. He could see Ant'el speaking and that the prince made a response, but he couldn't hear it over the wind. The power of the storm grew, and Ryah covered his eyes and ears. When he felt the storm subside, he looked up. He was no longer outside the courts but found himself in a room inside the palace with Chael, Guriel, and the prince.

General Chael spoke up. "Sovereign. You know that Ant'el's word means nothing. May I ask you why you would allow this?"

"His request was not a surprise to me, Chael," the prince said.

"He's too much for them," Chael said.

"I know, my friend," the prince replied.

"And once he gets what he wants, the rest will come," Chael said.

"I'm well aware."

"Most will fall. They will be hopelessly lost," Chael said.

"I have my reasons for allowing it. You will see the wisdom of this … but not now. Until that time, your mission remains the same." With that, the prince ended the conversation.

Ryah waited for more, longing to hear what Chael was referring to, but the prince and Chael disappeared, leaving Ryah alone with Guriel.

"Have you understood?" Guriel asked.

"Understood what?" Ryah replied.

"Have you understood why you were brought here?"

"I don't even know where I am," Ryah said, "and I have no idea what you mean. Where did Ant'el go? Where are his followers?"

"You know where they are." Guriel said.

"In the shadows?" Ryah asked.

"Yes."

"So, they're in the shadow world. What's Chael so worried about?" Ryah asked.

"They're not in the shadow world, Ryah. In the shadows. And Chael asked that for your benefit. The truth is neither he nor I know what the prince's plans are, but we trust him completely."

"I don't understand," Ryah said.

"You will understand when you see her," Guriel said. "And when you do, listen to her. She will help you see that which you see but cannot see. She will help you understand that which you hear but cannot hear."

"What are you talking about? Who is she?" Ryah asked, but there was no one in the room anymore. "Hey! Guriel."

Ryah yelled out his name a few more times with no reply. Each time his voice became more distant as if he was falling into an ever-increasing void. Tumbling through space, watching the light from the palace fade into the expanse. Descending through the emptiness, plummeting through the darkness enveloping him in an infinite tomb. His last thoughts of a woman. Something about her seemed familiar.

Ryah's body jolted and he sat upright. He looked around, but his mind couldn't comprehend what he saw. The artificial light gave everything a strange yellow hue. "Where am I now?" He rubbed his eyes and his head. Another sharp bump and Ryah was thrown out of his seat.

"Hey, Ryah. We've run into some pretty strong turbulence, so I suggest you strap yourself in." The voice was familiar. "Or you might get tossed overboard again," he joked.

Ryah picked himself up and sat back in the seat. The overhead light was still on and shining in his face. He reached up and clicked the off button.

"How long was I out?" he asked.

"Long enough for me to finish a few chapters of my book," Rogan said. "You can sleep through just about anything can't you?"

"Yeah. That's always been a gift of mine," Ryah said. "Until recently," he muttered under his breath, perplexed that he hadn't thought of that before.

"It took me a while to reach that point in my training," Rogan said. "Anyway, you must have had some dream."

"Really?" Ryah said. "I don't remember dreaming."

He didn't remember dreaming. Other than falling through the darkness. "*That must have been my body's reaction to the turbulence,*" he thought.

"Seemed like a nightmare," Rogan said. "Twisting around like you were fighting something off. Then you got calm for a while. You talk in your sleep, you know. Is that what got you removed from active duty? Talking in your sleep? That'll get you killed in the field."

The quizzical look on Ryah's face answered Rogan's question.

"You didn't know, huh?" Rogan said.

"I wasn't aware that I did," Ryah said.

"Well, let's make sure you don't do any more of that," Rogan said. He thought for a moment and got a sly look on his face. "It was kind of fun listening to you, though. When I could understand you, of course. Between the moaning and the mumbling. Captains and princes. Monsters and dragons." A short laugh slipped out. "An officer's nightmare, I suppose."

"*Captains and princes?*" Ryah thought. "*What is he talking about?*"

Vague scenes flashed in front of him. He tried to make out what they were. A room. A wall. No. A canyon. Darkness. Light. Fragments that he tried to piece together but couldn't. Wings. Wind. Some guy talking to him. A couple of guys talking to him. Chains. Dust. He saw the images as if through a veil. His memories, shadows, being snatched away from him as soon as they entered his mind. It didn't matter. It was just a dream. Just some night vision that meant nothing. No point trying to remember. But there was something else. "*Watch,*" someone told him. "*Remember. See. Hear.*" What?

121

"Who's Guriel?" Rogan asked, breaking into Ryah's internal dialogue.

"Who?"

"Guriel. You mentioned his name a few times right before you woke up."

"An old friend," Ryah said.

It wasn't a lie. Guriel was an old friend. He was sure of it. He just couldn't recall who he was.

Chapter 14

They were finally over Rome, preparing to land. Even though Lucio had diverted the plane to Heathrow airport for a reason he didn't divulge to his staff, they were on schedule. Ryah and Rogan remained at the terminal while Lucio took care of some "urgent" business. Thirty minutes into the layover, Lucio reappeared with a worried look on his face, but when Ryah asked him about it, he dismissed it with, "It's nothing." The comment was not reassuring, certainly not in the way he said it. A misgiving began to creep into Ryah's mind. An instinctual unease that he couldn't articulate.

And then there was the dream from last night. He remembered having one, but he couldn't recall what he had seen. He shut his eyes and concentrated, trying to remember what it was about, why it had disturbed him so much, but all he caught was an ephemeral glance like he was looking at a movie screen that would disappear whenever he would turn his head to look at it directly. Was it that which bothered him, or was it something in the way Lucio had described his urgent business as nothing? Was it a combination of the two? Ryah felt they were somehow linked but the connection between the two eluded him.

He had been to Italy once before, flying northwest in a C130X transport over the Tyrrhenian coast before turning northeast at Anzio and heading inland like his countrymen had done over a hundred years earlier. His squadron was inserted just outside of Ciampino and headed towards the Eternal City. They arrived to find the bombed out remains of a once great capital. What hadn't been destroyed in the barrage had been laid waste by the earthquakes, reducing the city to a shell of its former glory. Only the Colosseum remained intact, an irony not lost on Ryah.

What a contrast to what he saw as he flew over the city this morning. Skyscrapers rising out of the ashes, their foundation laid on the earth of a million graves. The iron empire re-establishing itself with a desire to reconquer the world but this time through economic and political domination.

They touched down at Aldo Moro airport. A pair of limousines waited for them at the hangar and took them through security, the guards waving them through without stopping them. Lucio had informed Ryah and Rogan that he would be heading to his office to go to an unrelated meeting and that they would go to their hotel in the Trastevere region. At 2:00 pm, he would send the limousine back for them.

"You probably won't get any other free time," Lucio had told them, "so take advantage of it. Head up to Giolitti's for some gelato. It's about a ten-minute walk if you want to get some fresh air. They're still there by the old parliament building. You can ask anyone. They'll know where it is."

"I'd rather have a nap then some gelato," Ryah told Rogan after Lucio left, "or maybe an espresso. Otherwise, I might not make it through the afternoon."

"This is what I should expect when I get to your age?" Rogan asked. "Naps every afternoon. Maybe a walking stick to help me get around."

Ryah smirked. *Pretty soon, I'm going to have to teach this tough guy a lesson in manners,* he thought.

Ryah leaned his head against the limousine window, watching the scenery pass by, and searched for signs of the ancient fortifications that used to surround the city. He found a single pile of bricks off Via Cristoforo Colombo, all that was left of the Aurelian walls. The limo driver took a detour as he entered the old city, opting to go around the Colosseum instead of heading up the Tiber River without informing his passengers of his intent.

"Where are you headed?" Ryah asked.

The driver answered in a mix of Italian and broken English. "Andiamo al Colosseo. You have to see. They ... how to say ... restaurano ... they restore to the way it was. E stanno costruendo la fondazione per la nuova statua del Colossus Solis."

"Ma che cosa dice?" Ryah asked. "What are you talking about?"

Rogan looked surprised but impressed. Ryah noticed and made a gesture that said, "There's a lot you don't know about me."

The driver continued. "They make the statue again, the Colossus Solis. It's to be big. Quasi cinquanta metri. Fifty meters. Piu grande che la prima. The Vatican pays for it." A smile of pride crossed the driver's face. "Io sono romano. I am roman come i miei genitori, my fathers. Thousands of years we live here. My ancestors, they are always here. In Rome. I never think we rise again, but ... il nostro impero torna."

Ryah turned to Rogan. "The Colossus Solis," Ryah began, "had been built on the northwest side of the Colosseum by Nero in honor of himself and was renamed for the sun god by Emperor Vespasian after Nero's death. When the Romans in the first century said they were going to the Colosseum, they were referring to the statue and not the amphitheatre which now bears the name."

Rogan gave him a strange look, but Ryah didn't notice it as he had already turned back towards the driver.

"The Vatican is paying for it, huh?" Ryah asked.

"Yes," the driver said. "The war. I terremoti. They don't destroy the Vatican. Nothing was damaged. The angels protected them, io lo so. After the war, they give money to build everything, tutto. The people love them. Now they work with l'ONU to make the country great. Like we were. L'impero romano. Maybe I can be the new Caesar." He let out a laugh. "There it is."

The driver pointed to the base constructed from stones stolen from the Arch of Constantine, which lay in shambles on the ground. Ryah stared out the window as the car circled by. He wasn't as impressed by it as the driver was.

"*A man claiming to be god,*" Ryah thought. "*Has that ever turned out well for mankind?*"

It took them another ten minutes to wind their way through the crowded streets and across the Tiber River to their hotel. It was modern, as was everything in that part of the city, but kept its old-world charm. The clerk seemed surprised when both Ryah and Rogan told her they didn't have a chip implanted in their hands and disappeared into the back room. She returned holding a couple of card keys and handed them to Ryah.

"The elevators are back around to your right. Take the one on the far end by the window." She had the slightest of accents. Lovely, almost like Lucio's, but decidedly more European. "Your room is the top floor."

Ryah noticed her grammatical error but didn't correct her, figuring he would find his room when he got there. It was his turn to be surprised when he arrived upstairs. Upon exiting the elevator, he found a short hall at the end of which was a single door. The entry room was enormous, twice as large as Ryah's entire apartment. Italian marble covered the floors, and masterpieces by Caravaggio, Giorgione, and Botticelli lined the walls. Off on one side was a bar stocked with premium liquors and the finest wines. Its top was made of kingwood and the sides were covered in what appeared to be polished silver. In the center of the room, a pair of sofas and four armchairs rested on top of a Persian rug, and a work area was set off to the side.

Six halls branched off from the main room and led down narrow corridors to back bedrooms, an office, a video conference room with giant comms ringing the walls, and a final space which could only be described as an entertainment center.

"So, this is how you officers live," Rogan said.

Ryah played along with his jest. "Only when the good rooms aren't available," he said. Inwardly he marveled at the grandeur of the place.

He threw his pack in the room farthest from the front door, took a shower, and fell asleep. Rogan woke him up at 1:45. Two minutes before two, they arrived downstairs in the lobby.

The limo followed the Tiber as it snaked through the city center and stopped outside the new UN. The building stood on the grounds of the old Castel Sant'Angelo and rose like a majestic cathedral looking down from its mighty spires on the rest of the world. Sculptures of Roman and Greek gods carved into the sides. In a ring above the deities, stained glass windows displayed the visages of the most important figures of the reborn UN – Gramsci, Lukacs, Coudenhove-Kalergi, Juncker, Soros, among others. At the top, visible even from ground level, rested a platform missing whatever it was meant to support.

The limo stopped in the front of the building where Lucio waited outside.

"We've got to go. Follow me," Lucio said.

There was an urgency in his voice, and Ryah fumbled with his badge as he tried to pin it.

"What's going on?" Ryah asked.

"I'll brief you on the details when we get to my office, but then we'll have to hurry off. The negotiations will be starting up soon." Lucio hesitated. "There's been a setback."

Ryah hurried through the foyer modeled after the Pantheon, its circular dome rising hundreds of feet above the ground. He didn't have the chance to marvel at the architecture, nor to observe the thousands of other people who were also oblivious to their surroundings, scuttling off to whatever bureaucratic endeavor occupied their time. If he had looked up, he might have noticed the shadows which traveled across the inside of the dome as if they were tracking each step he took with more than a casual interest.

Lucio maneuvered his way through the maze, twisting and turning through the labyrinthine halls until Ryah was lost in a forest of identical workplaces. After two elevator rides and an untold number of detours, they arrived at Lucio's office. The luxuriousness of the hotel room could not have been in greater contrast to the room where they now found themselves, a nondescript space no larger than Ryah's office at the Council. Lucio pushed a button on the side of his desk, and the comm on the wall lit up. On the screen, a large fire burned. The flames cut into the night sky, burning away the darkness but not illuminating enough for Ryah to make out where it was.

"Vladivostok," Lucio said. "By the Russia-China border. This happened less than an hour ago. The Russians say the Chinese firebombed the city, but we've had no indication on radar that any military aircraft on either side were in the airspace around it. The Chinese have responded that it was Russia's own people tired of living under Moscow's oppressive rule who started the fires in a spontaneous uprising, or some other propaganda nonsense like that. Again, our intelligence implies otherwise. Just when things were starting to go well." He shook his head in frustration.

"Each side had been communicating back to their superiors that we were on the verge of making a deal to end the hostilities. Then this happens. We found out right after lunch recess, while we were in the negotiation room. You've never seen such indignation, finger pointing. Promises and threats to wipe each other off the map. The rhetoric was out of control, so I adjourned for twenty minutes to let everyone cool off and so that I could come get you. Look, I want you two in there with me, but when we're done, I need you to gather whatever information you can about what's happening. So, change of plans. I'm going to introduce you as analysts who are in charge of tracking down the cause of the situation. Expect resistance from both sides. Quite frankly, I have no idea why either one would have done something this stupid. If you ask me, someone or some group is deliberately trying to derail the talks."

Ryah remained calm as he processed all Lucio had told him. His gut reaction was to let the two countries destroy each other, but he had learned long ago that a hated but known enemy was better than one which sprang up in a power vacuum.

"Take a look at your comms," Lucio said. "I just sent you a file with information on each person in the room. The ones with the names in red are the diplomats. The green ones designate their support staff. A black mark means that we don't know much about the person, which usually indicates they're not who they claim to be. Kind of like you two," he added. "There's one that joined the delegation recently that we have no information for, not even a picture. His name is Klokovsky as far as we know. He wasn't there yesterday or today. When I asked General Brostov about him, he said he returned to Russia but that he'd be back later today. I'll speak with you about him after we leave."

Ryah opened the file on his comm and scrolled through the dossiers. He knew who the Russian general in charge of the negotiations was. Everyone in the world of politics knew him. The support staff ... not so much. Two of them looked vaguely familiar. He was sure he had seen them before. Younger versions of them, though. The Chinese on the other hand were more secretive, their diplomats completely unfamiliar to him.

"Alright. Let's go," Lucio said. "While you're with me, I want you to read the room. See what you think. Are there any weak links in the group? If so, follow up with them this evening when we've finished for the day."

He headed out the door, and the three took off at their furious pace again. Rogan bemused but professional. Ryah quiet, pensive, but alert. They came to a large conference room off one of the main hallways, and Lucio scanned the three in. On the left side of the table, the Russians sat with their entourage. Across from them sat the Chinese delegation. At the head, three empty seats separated the two sides. The room was tense. Each side spoke in hushed tones in their native language to members of their own group. As Ryah made his way past the Russians, he overheard a couple words. "Strike tomorrow." That's what it sounded like to him, but he kept walking as if he didn't understand.

"Gentlemen," Lucio said, "thank you for your civility under these trying circumstances and your willingness to continue our talks. These are my two assistants that I told you would be joining us this afternoon," he said motioning towards Ryah and Rogan. "They have been called in to assist our analysts, who have been monitoring the situation since it started, and will be in charge of the investigation."

A member of the Russian delegation broke in, waving his arms in a frenzy. "We don't need their help. The situation is clear. The Chinese have invaded our territory in a deliberate act of war, this time bombing innocent women and children. Criminals. Prestupniki." He pounded the table as he spoke, the vein in the middle of his forehead pulsating with each emphatic gesture.

"It was you, General Brostov," one of the Chinese delegation said. "You have attacked your own people in order to incite your nation against us. We would never attack innocent civilians. The war criminal is you." General Chao remained calm as he spoke, in contrast to the Russian.

"You have forgotten that it was you who disrespected our national sovereignty when you crossed our borders," said Brostov. "You were testing to see if we were weak like the other cowards who trembled in fear when you invaded. I can assure you we are not." He hissed out these last words, threatening but now under control.

"Only because you broke the chemical arms treaty. We know you were developing weapons in Vladivostok in direct violation of our agreement. Our troops were sent there to prevent you from using them against us," said Chao.

"The flaw in your argument is that we do not develop chemical weapons in Vladivostok or anywhere. You used that as a pretext to invade and burn down our city knowing that it was a lie." He leaned over the table as close as he could to the Chinese general. "And now we will make you pay for that lie."

"Gentlemen," Lucio said, "I understand the emotion on both sides, and I can assure you we will get to the bottom of this. But for now, our job is to prevent this incident from becoming an all-out conflagration, so to speak."

Ryah noticed that the two sides remained quiet and gave Lucio their full attention. There was something confident, reassuring in Lucio's voice. This thin man with the presence of Winston Churchill and the demeanor of Mother Theresa. He was trustworthy. But more than that. He made people want to believe him.

Lucio continued. "Have you considered the possibility of a third party? I cannot believe that either of your two great nations would perpetrate such an atrocity. It seems

131

more plausible that outsiders have been playing you off against each other." He paused and his voice grew stern. "But be warned if I find out that it was either of your nations," he said, letting his threat go unfinished.

"Now we need to get back to why we were here in the first place. General Chao," Lucio said looking directly in his eyes, "we are asking you to remove all troops from Russian soil, immediately and unequivocally. Your invasion is against Article 124.31 of the UN code, an article, may I remind you, that you signed personally. Furthermore, we would like an official letter of regret to be sent to the Kremlin." He said this more as a command then a question.

"And General Brostov," he said turning his attention to the Russian, "we are petitioning you to accept this apology without further demand for reparations or any other form of payback."

Both groups murmured their disapproval.

"We all know the alternative if we fail here," Lucio said. "It will not turn out well for either of your countries."

"I'm sorry, Envoy Romijn," said General Chao, "but we cannot accept your proposal as stated."

"And neither can we," added General Brostov. "Reparations are owed us."

General Chao turned to his advisors and muttered in Chinese. Their heads bobbed up and down in submission and approval. General Brostov spoke with his cadre who gesticulated with more intensity than their Chinese counterparts. Lucio took the opportunity to send Ryah and Rogan outside. He joined them a few minutes later.

"That's going well," Lucio said without any sense of irony.

"Really?" Ryah asked.

"Yes. I think we've actually made a breakthrough. It's the first time they didn't curse me and my proposal. I'm going to let them talk it out without me for a while.

Probably go back in a few minutes, but you don't need to be in there with me. I just wanted them to see your faces and for you to get to know the main players. You remember Klokovsky, the Russian I told you about?"

Ryah nodded his head.

"Brostov confirmed he would be returning today. Go tonight to Bar Luciano. He's been there every night except for the last two. It's down a couple of blocks, but you won't find the diplomats there. It's more for locals. I get the feeling he goes there to get away from the rest. I suspect he has something to say and that he wants to talk. As for the Chinese, I can't get a read on them. They're always together. You're going to have to find a way to isolate one of them. Which one? I don't know. But do your best to get any information out of them you can and report back to me."

"Will do," Ryah said.

"Great. I have complete confidence in you," Lucio said. "And what I said about a third party … I'm more and more convinced of that. But who?"

"Who would benefit the most?" Rogan asked as a suggestion.

Lucio nodded his head in agreement. "Who benefits the most? That's exactly what you need to find out."

Chapter 15

It was subtle at first. Barely noticeable. The frenzy of activity masked the feeling in his stomach, but it was there. He hadn't had time to pay attention. It was growing, calling out to him, not letting him ignore it any longer.

"*What is it?*" Ryah thought. "*The look in their eyes maybe. There's no emotion. No feeling. No. That's not it. An emptiness. They look empty, hollow. And this place. From the moment I stepped foot in here, I've wanted to get out.*"

Ryah tried to block out the thoughts, but they persisted, waves of an incoming tide reaching higher and higher until they threatened to drown him.

"*Be careful. All is not what it seems.*"

It wasn't his voice. It was that other one that warned him. A calm but insistent voice, and he took notice.

Ryah and Rogan walked down the main street and took a right into an alley. Two doors down was Bar Luciano, a well kept but small space with one way in and out. The only light came from a pair of overhead fixtures, imitation chandeliers, illuminating the room, swaying back and forth as if rocked by an invisible hand.

Ryah found an open table in the back corner. A few minutes later, Klokovsky entered and ambled up to the bar. The Russian wore a dark blue suit, a matching cap, and a wrinkled white shirt, giving him the appearance of a limo driver who had just finished a long shift. A small red pin rested on the pocket of his shirt.

"What do you think?" Ryah asked.

Rogan shrugged. "Looks like he's trying to blend in with the locals. Not let people know who he really is. Could be nothing."

"Could be," Ryah said.

"How do you think he'll react when he sees us here?" Rogan asked. "Especially, seeing as how he appears to be trying to disguise himself or at least conceal his presence."

"He'd probably be suspicious," Ryah said. "I know I would be. It'd be best if he makes first contact with us." He thought for a moment. "Let me go up to the bar and order a drink. I'll pretend not to see him, but I'll make sure he sees me. If he says something, I'll talk to him. If he says nothing, I'll return. Watch what he does. See if he gets nervous."

"Roger that," Rogan said.

Ryah started to stand up but felt himself being pulled back down by Rogan.

"What's going on?" Ryah asked as he settled into the seat.

"Look," Rogan said, pointing over at Klokovsky.

A man, considerably taller than average with dark, brown hair and a sparse moustache had begun a conversation with him. By their body language, it was apparent they knew each other. Ryah recognized him immediately.

"His name's Abbad," Ryah said.

"You know him?" Rogan asked.

"Met him once," Ryah said. "The day before I met you, back in the states. He said he worked for Ambassador Tanas and tried to engage me in conversation. Acted almost like he wanted to …." Ryah hesitated and decided not to continue on. "That's not important now. What is important is that he may recognize me, so change of plans. I want you to get close to them and listen in on their conversation. There's a seat right by Klokovsky. See how he's got his back to it? You could get over there and he wouldn't notice you, or at least, he wouldn't realize who you were. Keep your comm in transmit mode so I can hear what they're saying."

Rogan obeyed and moved into place, taking the path along the wall. He settled down, pretending to watch the soccer match while keeping his comm in the optimal position to record and transmit the conversation between Klokovsky and Abbad.

"… how are you … finding it well." Abbad's voice came through the comm. Ryah strained to hear, the unexpected static and the loud conversations around him interrupting some of the words. He changed the settings on his device to see if it could cut through the noise.

"The accommodations are in order," Klokovsky said, his voice emotionless.

"Fine. Fine. We had to set you up in a different hotel since we didn't have information you were arriving with the rest of the delegation. I apologize we haven't been able to rectify the situation yet," Abbad said.

Something about the confession sounded insincere to Ryah. Klokovsky waved his hand to dismiss the comment as if he didn't care either way.

"How were the women?" Abbad asked. "Were they to your liking?"

"I prefer brunettes," Klokovsky said.

"Great. I'll remember that," Abbad said. He hesitated before continuing. "Have you decided?" he asked.

"I haven't made up my mind," Klokovsky said.

"You haven't made up your mind?" Abbad asked. "I thought we had given you enough time." He set a file down on the bar. "Look through it. Maybe this will help you decide."

Klokovsky picked up the file and leafed through its contents without saying anything. When he finished, he put it back down for Abbad.

"What do you want me to do?" Klokovsky asked.

"Go back to your superiors and relay the information we discussed. Just make sure you tell them exactly what I told you," Abbad said.

"What does Ambassador Tanas think?" Klokovsky asked.

"He has no idea I'm here," Abbad said. "He has no need to know."

"Why don't you want the ambassador to know?" Klokovsky asked.

"He's trying to prevent a war. That's his mission. That's his character. A man of peace. But I know what would happen if your nation found out about it after negotiations were settled. I'm not willing to take that chance."

"I can't imagine the Ambassador will react well when he finds out you gave me the information. You know he'll find out," Klokovsky said.

"True. But when we accomplish his goal, all will be forgiven. He'll get all the credit and have no choice but to acknowledge the wisdom of my actions. I just need to know you're on board," Abbad said. "You're the key to making this work."

Klokovsky said nothing but held on to his drink, both hands wrapped around the base of the cup, and stared at the bottles which lined the wall in front of him.

"Look. You'll get the rest of the money we promised," Abbad said.

"I can't be bought," Klokovsky said. His voice was cold, insulted.

"I know, I know," Abbad reassured him. "This is simply a reward for doing the right thing."

"I'll think about it," Klokovsky said.

"Great. But I'll need to know by tomorrow morning," Abbad said.

Ryah watched Abbad pick up the file and walk out the door, leaving the Russian alone with his drink. Ryah decided to try the direct approach. He motioned to Rogan to signal his intent and approached Klokovsky, sitting down in the chair Abbad had abandoned.

"Klokovsky is it?" Ryah said.

The Russian jumped a little, surprised by Ryah's presence. He turned to look at Ryah, his eyes widening in fear, then looked back at the wall to hide his momentary panic. "Yeah. Who are you?"

"You know who I am," Ryah said.

The Russian remained silent.

"What was in the file?" Ryah asked.

Klokovsky gripped the glass until his knuckles turned white. He lifted the cup to take a drink, his trembling hands betraying his nervousness. Putting the cup on the bar, he stood up to leave. A hand on his shoulder pushed him back down. Klokovsky looked to his right and saw Rogan standing over him.

"What are you doing here with Abbad?" Ryah asked.

"It's none of your business."

"I think it is," Ryah said. "Now, let's suppose that General Brostov found out you've been speaking with Abbad on the side. What will he think?"

Klokovsky didn't answer.

"What's the punishment in Russia for treason?" Ryah asked. "Were the girls worth it? They weren't even brunettes. How about the money? Is it enough?"

Ryah had seen that look before. Many times. When the person on the other end of the interrogation realized no lie could disentangle himself from the mess.

"What's in the file?" Ryah repeated.

"I can't tell you," Klokovsky said.

"I don't think you have a choice anymore," Ryah said.

138

Klokovsky stared straight ahead, refusing to look at Ryah or Rogan. "I got myself in too deep, and I couldn't find a way out," he said. There was truth in his words, more than even he realized. "Abbad was just reminding me of that."

"What does he have over you?" Ryah asked.

Once again, Klokovsky held his silence, so Ryah decided on a different line of questioning.

"What do you know about Vladivostok?" Ryah asked.

When Ryah mentioned the name of the town, Klokovsky began rubbing his hands together and lowered his gaze. Ryah recognized the signs that Klokovsky had more information than he wanted to share.

"Do you know who did the bombing?" Ryah asked.

Klokovsky raised his hand and scratched the side of his head. Ryah looked at Rogan and gave him a look that said, "Are you seeing what I'm seeing?" Rogan gave a subtle nod.

"Who was it?" Ryah asked. "Who did it? Was it the Chinese?"

Klokovsky gave a subtle shake of his head, barely perceptible.

"No, huh?" Ryah said. "The Russians?"

No again.

"A third party then?" Ryah asked.

Klokovsky stood up unexpectedly and faced Ryah. His eyes expressed a mix of fear and resolve.

"It's time for me to go," he said.

Ryah stared hard, examining every expression from the Russian. He didn't like what he saw.

"Alright. You can go," Ryah said. He took a step backwards to let Klokovsky pass. As he did, Ryah grabbed hold of his arm. "Actually, let me ask you one more question."

Klokovsky shifted back and forth from one foot to the other.

"Why did you do it?" Ryah asked.

"You wouldn't understand." Klokovsky remained silent for a moment. "What are you going to do?"

"I don't know," Ryah said. "I was going to ask you the same thing."

"There's not much I can do," Klokovsky said. "I'll have to disappear for a while. If I somehow survive Brostov's wrath, I know Abbad will send his network after me."

Klokovsky was a dead man, and the look in his eyes told Ryah that Klokovsky knew it as well. Ryah signaled to Rogan that it was time to leave. This time, Klokovsky grabbed him on the forearm.

"Just give me twenty-four hours before you tell the envoy," the Russian said. "Let me have a head start."

Ryah said nothing and stepped into the late evening air. The sun was making its final descent as the last streaks of orange and red hovered above the horizon. A few blocks away, the spires of the UN building swallowed the rays and spit them back out, distorted, irregular. Ryah turned to his partner.

"What do you think?" he asked.

"I don't trust Klokovsky," Rogan said. "Why'd you let him go?"

"I don't actually think he did it," Ryah said. "He wasn't the bomber. He's covering for someone, but I can't tell who. There's something wrong about his story. Something wrong about him."

"What do you mean?" Rogan asked.

"His accent," Ryah said. "It was off. It was very good, but it was off. Sounded like mine when I first came out of linguistic school."

"Is he one of ours?" Rogan asked.

"The thought crossed my mind," Ryah said. "But if he is, is he on an officially sanctioned mission, or has he gone rogue? If he's here with the Council's approval, why didn't they tell us?"

"Maybe he's with a third party," Rogan suggested.

"You think there is another party involved?" Ryah asked. He didn't wait for Rogan to answer. "Or are the Americans the third party?"

"I'm not sure," Rogan said. "I've been hearing reports about an underground network. Not that I believe it, but I wouldn't discount it either. There's always been conspiracy theories about shadow governments, the new world order, that sort of thing. The last time we ignored those rumors, it led to The War. I could see another group trying to learn from the failures of their predecessors. See if they could do it right this time."

"Where'd you hear those reports?" Ryah asked. "And what did you hear?"

"Not much and I'm not sure I'm allowed to divulge that," Rogan said. "All I can tell you is that's what our next mission in the gammas was supposed to be. I got pulled to join you before I got briefed, so even if I wanted to tell you, I wouldn't be of much good."

"You think Abbad could be part of that group?" Ryah asked.

"He's part of something, and he's up to no good. I can tell you that much," Rogan answered. "Are you going to let Lucio know what's going on?"

"Not right away. I want to investigate some more before I say anything to anyone. Besides, our loyalty is to the Council, not the UN." He paused. "That's if the Council is being loyal to us."

They continued down the street and passed the UN building without stopping to get a limo to take them to the hotel.

"Walk back?" Ryah asked.

"I'm up for it," Rogan said. He was glad for some exercise after the last few days.

A man with a kind, gentle appearance, dressed in tattered clothes, came up to Ryah. "Do you have anything you can give me?" he asked.

He stretched out his arms as he asked for the handout. Ryah felt pity for him even before he saw the scars on his wrists.

"I don't have anything on me," Ryah answered, "but if you know where there's a good place to eat around here, you can join me and my friend for a meal."

If Rogan disapproved, he made no mention nor showed any indication of his displeasure.

"Thank you, for your kindness," the man said. "Be careful, Ryah. All is not what it seems," the man said.

Ryah's heart stopped beating. His mind started to spin, and he looked over at Rogan who didn't seem fazed by the encounter. When he turned to look back, the man was gone. He scanned the streets all around him but found no trace of the stranger.

"Are you alright, Ry?" Rogan asked.

Ryah struggled to answer. "Not after that," he said.

"After what?" Rogan asked.

"After what that man said. I can't believe you're not thrown by it," Ryah said.

"Why would I be? Klokovsky just confirmed what we believed," Rogan said.

"I wasn't referring to him," Ryah screamed. "I was referring to that other guy."

"What other guy?" Rogan asked.

"The one …." Ryah stopped. It dawned on him that Rogan had not seen the stranger. Was he hallucinating? Was he losing his mind? Ryah rubbed the back of his head and brought his hand over his face as if he was trying to erase the image. "Nothing," he said. "Nothing important."

But it was important. That voice was the one he had heard his whole life. The one he had learned to trust. He had always thought it was his instinct, perhaps his conscience or a sixth sense, that had guided him. This was the first time he had seen someone speaking to him, and it spoke in that same voice. He had never seen that man before. Or had he? He felt he had. A vision shrouded by a thick veil. A cloudy, distant memory borne by a dream.

They walked in silence the rest of the way. Ryah was so exhausted by the time he reached his room that he forgot about his promise to change hotels and fell asleep as soon as he landed on the bed.

He woke up the next morning as the sun's rays began to infiltrate their way through the curtains and headed to the living area.

"Hey, Ryah," Rogan said. "We need to get going. Lucio sent a message and says there's some big news. He wants us down there right away."

"Did he tell you what it was?" Ryah asked.

"Not exactly. Only that he had been in negotiations for most of the night. I think the two sides have come to an agreement."

Ryah grabbed his comm and headed down with Rogan. A limo waited for them.

"Good morning, guys." Lucio was cheery for having been awake all night. "I've got some great news for you that I want you to take back to your Council."

"What is it?" Ryah asked.

"We were able to broker a peace between the Chinese and the Russians. They've agreed to the original terms that your country asked for," Lucio said. "Quite honestly, it's a shock to me. They'd been arguing like the Hatfields and the McCoys, and then … I'm amazed by that man. A little scared too, I must confess."

"Who?" Ryah asked.

"Ambassador Tanas," Lucio said. "He shows up. Speaks with the two sides for no more than five minutes, and they agree." He spoke with both shock and pleasure. "He told me I wore them down and that he just finished them off, but I can't take credit for that. It was amazing to watch."

"What did he say?"

Ryah was curious. It wasn't the first time he had heard Tanas' name come up, and he hoped he would have the chance to meet him on this mission.

"I'll tell you later," Lucio said. "We're almost at the UN, and we're going to have a press conference on the front steps. The whole world will be watching, and we're going to let them know that there will be peace." He beamed with pride as he said those last words.

The limousine let the three off a block away from the front steps as a crowd of people had already gathered outside, making it impossible to reach their destination by car. As they climbed the stairs, Ryah saw General Chao and General Brostov standing by the podium, their respective entourages behind them. Everyone smiling and shaking hands. Klokovsky nowhere to be found. Lucio took his place in the center of the two generals. Ryah stood off to the side out of sight of the cameras which trained their lenses on the leaders, anticipating the good news they were about to proclaim.

"Welcome."

Lucio's voice rang out. The commotion died down as soon as the crowd heard him speak.

"I am humbled to stand before you to let you know what has recently transpired. As you are aware, tensions between these two mighty nations, these two great peoples, had threatened to escalate into another conflict that neither they nor the world wanted. But they agreed to meet here to negotiate instead of making war."

He paused to the let the suspense grow. Ryah watched the crowd, mesmerized as if in a trance, as they hung on to Lucio's every word.

Lucio continued. "I have the honor of telling you that Russia and China have …"

He stopped speaking. Ryah looked out over the faces in the crowd and saw a wave of horror overtake them. His subconscious told him there was a problem, but his mind had not processed it yet. The next two shots woke Ryah from his state of shock. He looked back in time to see General Chao slumping over and joining Lucio and a Chinese delegate on the ground by the podium. A scarlet spring flowed out of their heads and seeped into the cracks.

Chapter 16

A thousand people scattered, running in random directions. Every man and woman for themselves fleeing the bullets they imagined were continuing to fire down on them. But the barrage had stopped. Only the aftermath, the chaos, ensued. A woman cried out in pain, collapsed in the street with her foot twisted backwards, trying to rearrange it to the way her mind knew it should be. A man stumbled. He put his arm down to cushion the fall, but it snapped on impact as another man fell on him. They both tried to get up but couldn't. An ocean of panic rushed over them, trampling them into the pavement. Their screams were muted. No sound could escape. Their breath trapped inside their lungs as the weight of humanity crushed down on them.

"Move. Get to Lucio."

"Rogan, let's go," but Rogan was already on the move.

"Two deep breaths. In. Out. In. Hold. Out."

Ryah's mind stopped racing. Time slowed down, and his thoughts came into focus. The Chinese had rushed to the aid of their own, four men on each fallen comrade, carrying them off by their arms and their legs to waiting cars. The murdered men's heads hung limp and bobbed up and down like rag dolls with each step their pallbearers took. Russian bodyguards surrounded General Brostov, ducking their heads and searching for the source of the threat. Brostov remained upright, defiant and dared for the assassin to take the next shot as his bodyguards maneuvered him out of the danger zone.

Rogan was by Envoy Romijn's side and had ripped off his shirt to use as a compress stop the flow of blood from

Lucio's temple. Ryah took one last mental snapshot of the scene and stored it with the one which captured where the men had been standing moments before. "No time for that now," he told himself and ran to help Rogan.

"Head shot," Rogan said. "Hit the left side here. Don't see an exit wound yet."

Half of Lucio's face was shredded by the bullet after it fragmented when it struck the skull. The pieces tore through his cheek and jaw, leaving a gaping hole where flesh and teeth had been.

Ryah checked Lucio's pulse. "He's still alive," he said. "I'm going to start CPR. Help me roll him onto his back."

He counted each compression, stopping briefly at thirty. There was no point trying to give breaths, so he checked the pulse and went back to work. Fingers interlaced. Palms down. Push. Release. Push. Release. The rhythm followed the backbeat of the song he sang in his mind to help him keep the correct tempo. Rogan stood up and signaled to the medics who fought their way through the remnants of the crowd, stepping over the dead and wounded on their way to the envoy.

Ryah moved away from the motionless body and looked down at his bloodstained hands. He wiped them on the ground until only a red tinge was left on the tips of a few fingers. The medics finished their cursory examination and whisked the envoy away to a waiting van. Ryah and Rogan watched in silence as the security personnel started to stream out of the building, holding their guns in the air and yelling to each other in some sort of unintelligible UN code.

"*A little late*," Ryah thought.

A man with a submachine gun approached the two. Ryah lifted his arms in submission and held his UN badge in front of him. The guard took one look and ran off to his comrades who continued to secure the perimeter.

"I think we need to get out of here," Rogan said.

"Immediately," Ryah added.

They climbed down the steps and wandered towards the street which led to their hotel.

"As soon as we get away from the scene, I'm going to have to inform the Council of what happened. Although, I'm sure they already know," Ryah said.

"What are you going to tell them?" Rogan asked.

"Not sure at this moment," Ryah said.

"You going to mention Klokovsky?"

"No. That would only bring trouble down on us," Ryah said.

Rogan thought for a moment. "You think he had something to do with this?"

"The thought crossed my mind, but it's too soon to jump to any conclusions."

Ryah's comm vibrated. He reached into his jacket pocket and pulled out one different than the one Rogan had.

"Ryah," he answered. He was silent for a while. "Yes, sir. Yes, sir." Silence again. "We were there, thirty feet away. Yes, sir. Rogan and I. Yes. General Chao and his associate. I'm sure they're dead. How? I saw their eyes as they were carted off. No, I'm sure of it. Envoy Romijn was alive when they took him. I don't think he'll make it. In the temple. I think it came out his jaw. Yes sir. It's pretty bad. The Russians? None of them were hit. Yes. Yes. Could be, but why would they do it? They had just agreed to a deal with the Chinese. Brostov seemed pleased. Mm hmm. Yes sir. Well if they knew about it, their bodyguards didn't. They were panicking. Yes, sir. If I may sir? I agree with Ambassador Tanas, if that's what he told you. I would like permission to stay and investigate. Our travel credentials are sure to be revoked at least for a day or two. We can do this off the record while we wait to be cleared. If we find nothing, we'll leave immediately. If we discover something, do we have permission to remain? Yes, sir. I'll run it past you. Absolutely. I'll send a twice daily report, more often if you need it. Yes, sir. OK. You think so? So how should I contact you? OK."

Ryah put the comm on the ground and stomped on it. He picked up the pieces and threw them away in a trash can on the corner.

"Are our conversations being monitored?" Rogan asked.

Ryah nodded. "That was Administrator Klins. He said he was sure someone was listening in. He's wired cash to the secure location he told us about. We're going to have to leave the hotel and find a place that still accepts currency."

"What was that about Ambassador Tanas?" Rogan asked.

"The ambassador asked us to help out with the investigation," Ryah said. "Report back to him with whatever we find. We'll help, but I'm not sure about reporting to him. Anyone connected to Abbad I can't trust, even if Abbad's working against him."

"How will we contact the Council?" Rogan asked.

"We're not going to be able to," Ryah said. "Klins ordered us to go dark."

"No back up either, I presume?" Rogan said.

"Nope. We're on our own here once we pick up the money," Ryah said. "I'm going to hope that Tanas keeps his mouth shut, and that Abbad doesn't know we're here. If the Russians or Chinese find out we're with the Council, it won't go well for us."

"Do you think we've been made?" Rogan asked.

"Not at this point. As far as anyone besides Lucio and Tanas knows, we're UN analysts called in from a remote location, but the timing of our arrival will appear suspicious to some, especially those inside the UN. Rumors will begin and make their way back to the Russians and Chinese, who'll assume we had something to do with this. I'd say we have a week at most before that happens. Until then, let's fly under the radar, gather what information we can, and get out. The plan is to find a new hotel and then get back to the crime scene to see what's going on. I'd also like to find information on where Lucio has been taken. See if I can drop by and visit. The guy's grown on me. If he somehow survives, I'd like a chance to see if he saw anything." He paused. "Although, I can't imagine that's possible."

"That he saw something or that he survives?" Rogan said.

"Either," Ryah said.

They arrived at the hotel after a short walk. Inside, scores of people had gathered around the pair of screens in the lobby to watch the reports coming out of the UN. Some talking amongst themselves. Most staring in disbelief. War, which had been a possibility, was almost a certainty now, threatening to involve more than just the two nations. Half of the nations in the world were merely serfdoms of the UN and provided it with a standing army which rivaled that of any country. An attack on a UN representative would be viewed as a strike on the member nations.

On one screen, General Brostov was gesticulating in his overblown manner, swearing that Russia had nothing to do with the assassination but refusing to condemn it. Ryah stopped to watch the other screen, where a spokeswoman for the UN, a dark-skinned lady with short brown hair, beautiful and composed, answered questions about Envoy Romijn's condition.

"He's in surgery," she said.

Ryah couldn't hear the question from the journalist.

"No. That's all we know. He's in critical condition with a gunshot wound to the head. We'll let you know as soon as we get updates."

This time he heard it. "Who's responsible?"

"We cannot comment on that," she answered. "All we know …."

She continued to speak but the voice Ryah heard was no longer hers. It was a whispering hiss, asynchronous to the movement of her lips. He looked around to see if anyone noticed, but the room began to blur as if a veil had dropped over his eyes. His head spun as he tried to make sense of what was happening. Apprehension. That's what he felt from the onlookers. Worry, fear. He could hear their thoughts. They spoke to him out loud and all at once so that he couldn't understand. Just a phrase here and there. "*War. Nuclear? I don't want to die.*" A hidden terror grew from within the people, materializing and taking shape until it could be seen, unfolding in front of Ryah like a nightmare.

He closed his eyes for a moment, and when he reopened them, he saw the people trapped as if in a prison cell. Heat rose from beneath their feet and distorted the air around them, causing their bodies to shimmer and sway. Their bodies began to shake. Harder and harder. A rip opened up, starting at the top of their heads and moving down as if they were being unzipped. A rush of wind escaped from each of their torsos, visible, like a mist, and combined into one shadow without definite form. The people screamed in terror, but the shadow laughed with joy. Or was it hate? And pleasure. Pleasure at their fear. Joy at the prospect of conflict and chaos and death. A vine appeared in the middle of the shadow, flowing out and wrapping around the people one by one. As it touched their flesh, the vine changed into a metal chain which interweaved its way through their arms and legs, locking them in a serpentine embrace.

Ryah covered his ears and shook his head, squeezing his eyes shut to block out the vision. He opened his eyes. There were twice as many people or more in the room now, but

151

where did they come from? They didn't look like people anymore, at least some of them didn't. They floated up and into the frescos which covered the ceiling. The painting, a reproduction of a Raphael masterpiece, came alive. Two archangels warred as the people below stumbled around in ignorance, oblivious to the battle which raged above their heads.

The shadow seemed to win the battle and came down from the ceiling to claim the spoils of its victory, grabbing the people below and tearing them limb from limb, ripping out their hearts and drinking the blood which spilled from them. The survivors ran in terror but were overtaken by the shadow. All was lost. There was no hope. Everything was subject to the unrestrained evil which feasted on the souls of the living.

From behind, a hand covered Ryah's face and plunged him into complete darkness. He was frozen, completely immobilized by the fear. A voice whispered in his ear.

"Don't be afraid. See."

The hand disappeared and his eyes were opened. A rope, a leash wrapped around the neck of the shadow.

"Let's go, Ry."

Ryah didn't move. He felt the tug on his arm.

"Ryah. We need to get going."

Ryah turned to his right. Rogan had a hold of his arm, motioning for him to follow.

"Man, you get lost in your thoughts," Rogan said.

"Yeah," Ryah muttered, half his mind still on the vision. He took a deep breath and headed out the door.

Chapter 17

Ryah and Rogan went to their room, collected their belongings, and bypassed the front desk as they left. A sense of relief came over Ryah as soon as he stepped out the hotel door. They went to the predetermined meeting place to pick up the money from the Council contact, enough to last each of them a week, which was more than they planned on staying. Even if their travel documents were revoked, Ryah was sure he could find a way out of the country. He had done that many times under much worse conditions. But why did he agree to stay? He didn't care about the UN nor Russia nor China. If they wanted to destroy themselves, what was that to him? The only answer he could come up with was that he was there for a reason. What the reason was he didn't know.

The contact had given Ryah a few recommendations for hotels, but he and Rogan decided to find something on their own. It took them less than an hour to find three viable locations. Ryah opted for one located just north of the former US embassy, a few minutes by taxi and about twenty minutes on foot from the UN building. Their accommodations consisted of a pair of ten by ten rooms each with a bed, a dresser, and a shared bathroom. The other ten rooms in the hotel, if that was what it could be called, were rented out on an hourly basis as needed. It was the kind of place where no one asked why the occupants were there nor cared to know.

The early afternoon sun warmed this part of the city which had already begun to fall back into its old routine. Politics and international affairs were of no concern to people who didn't know where they would find their next meal. Death was certain for them as it was for everyone else, but they didn't care if it arrived. Nor if it delayed. They lived as if they were disconnected from the source of life. Alive but dead. Awake but in an endless slumber. Flittering about their daily routines until the inevitable end.

Ryah and Rogan walked to the UN building and set up surveillance on the other side of the Tiber River, far enough away to get a picture of the overall scene but close enough to observe the official investigation.

"We'll probably be able to check it out tomorrow," Ryah said in response to a question from Rogan. "I figure the UN guys will be around all afternoon and evening, until they no longer have light to see. I don't see us getting anything major done today. I recommend we go to the hospital to inquire about Lucio and come back tomorrow to finish up our own investigation. I'll make a brief sweep of the perimeter. You see if you can blend in with them over there." Ryah pointed at some of the security personnel to the left of the UN building. "Get details on what they've found. Think you can do that?"

"I've got a problem," Rogan said. "Something's off."

"What is it?" Ryah asked.

"From our vantage point, Lucio would have been facing us," Rogan said.

"Correct."

"He was shot in the left temple," Rogan said.

Ryah knew where he was going.

"They should be looking over on the right side of the building as we see it," Rogan said, "but I don't see anyone over there."

Ryah agreed and scanned the surroundings. On the left of the UN where the investigation was ongoing, there was a wooded area, about an acre in size, with easy access to two main roads. It was reasonable to assume an assassin would

154

strike from there, but the evidence didn't suggest that. On the right, there were three buildings, five to six stories tall, forming a quarter-circle as they followed the bend in the Tiber River. The farthest one was about five hundred meters from the steps of the UN. Ryah looked at the roof.

"That's where I would have set up," he said, pointing towards the farthest building.

"Yep. The angle looks right. Would explain the trajectory of the bullet as well," Rogan said. "I think we should get a closer look."

Ryah nodded in agreement. They started to cross the bridge over the river, but halfway across, Ryah came to a sudden halt. Rogan stopped with him and gazed in the same direction as Ryah.

"Abbad," Ryah said. "What's he doing there?" he murmured more to himself than to Rogan.

"Looks like he's directing the investigation," Rogan answered.

From their position, they could see an exchange between Abbad and someone who seemed to have authority. He pointed off to the other side of the UN and made a move as if to head over there, but Abbad grabbed him and wouldn't let him go. Even though it was too far to hear what was being said, Abbad's body language made it clear that he wanted the investigation to remain where it was.

"Yep. Something's off," Ryah said.

He looked back towards the far building on the right. He thought he saw movement on the roof. Not much. Just a brief glimpse of a shadow which disappeared almost as soon as it appeared.

"I think we need to get over there right away. The answer's up there. I'm sure of it."

The building leased its space to a variety of small businesses – a law firm, an accounting office, two other companies whose name gave no indication of what they did, and a refugee lobbying organization which occupied the two upper floors. No guards were posted in the entrance, and as far as Ryah could tell, there were no security cameras anywhere. Four stairwells, one in each corner, led upstairs, and Ryah was glad to have found the one leading to the roof on only the second try. The door to the roof was shut but unlocked. There were telltale signs it had been forced open, and only a minimal effort was made to disguise the act.

"Either someone was in a hurry, or they knew no one would be looking in this direction," Ryah thought.

He pushed the door open a couple inches and peered through the crack. Seeing nothing, he opened it a little more and looked again, repeating this process until he was sure no one was there. Convinced he and Rogan were alone, Ryah stepped out onto the flat surface. The rays of the sun beat down on his head, the black pitch absorbing the light and radiating it back out as heat. He could feel the soles of his shoes already beginning to melt.

"No more than a few minutes," he told Rogan, "then we need to get off."

Rogan nodded and followed Ryah, both of them bending over a little as they walked, until they arrived at a three-foot-high wall lining the edge of the roof. Rogan took a peek over the wall to see where they were in reference to the street.

"It could have been anywhere around here," Rogan said, "but I suspect twenty feet or so to the right would have given our shooter the best line of fire."

Ryah slid along the wall looking for signs that a weapon of some sort had rested on it. Rogan conducted a search behind him, hoping to find patterns in the gravel where someone had stepped or where they had kneeled down for

156

a long stretch. Up and down, back and forth they went in a checkerboard configuration over the entire quadrant of the roof. Nothing was out of place. Either no one had been there, or they had done a masterful job of covering their tracks.

As they neared the end of their search grid, a light reflected in Rogan's eye. He stepped back and looked down. There it was again. Two steps forward. He stooped over and reached down into the gravel.

"Ryah," he said. "Take a look at this."

Ryah took hold of the tiny, metallic object. "Did you find any more of these?"

"No," Rogan said. "Just the one."

"Are you sure?" Ryah asked.

"I'm taking another look," Rogan said, "but I'm not seeing anything else."

Ryah turned the object over and over, scrutinizing it. Not believing, or possibly not wanting to believe.

"What are you thinking?" Rogan asked.

"6.5 Grendel shell casing," Ryah said. "The only ones that use it as standard issue are the Russians. But I'm having a hard time with it."

Rogan cut in. "Like how nothing else is out of place except that. Everything else is swept clean. Professional. Other than this one casing, sitting right where one would expect to find it."

"Almost as if it had been planted for us to find," Ryah finished.

"My thoughts exactly," Rogan said.

"Right before we came here, I thought I saw a person on the roof. It was just a flash. Just a momentary glimpse," Ryah said.

"You think that's why Abbad was so insistent on having them search the far side? To give a person a chance to plant the evidence?" Rogan asked.

Ryah nodded yes. "That's what my gut is telling me."

"Well, about all we can determine so far is that Russia is not involved," Rogan said. "I'm having my doubts about Klokovsky also."

Ryah said nothing but became lost in quiet contemplation. After a minute, he said, "Let's go." They walked back to the door and entered the stairwell, Rogan first, Ryah shutting the door behind them. As the last light from the outside slipped through the crack, Rogan stopped.

"Open it back up."

Ryah pushed the door back open. "What is it?"

Rogan bent over on the second step. He stood up with a folded piece of paper in his hand. It was slightly wrinkled as if someone had kept it in their pocket, but it was relatively clean, unlike the other trash which littered the stairwell. On the bottom it read *Il Palazzo Imperiale*. He handed the paper to Ryah.

"See if you can interpret this, Google translate," he said.

Ryah looked it over twice, mouthing the words as he went. "My Czech is a little rusty," he said. "It says something along the lines of 'Get to the steps. Twenty minutes. News conference.' There's a symbol at the end of the message which looks familiar." He handed the paper back to Rogan.

It was a small circle with three vertical lines inscribed, the middle line cutting through the center of the circle.

"Yep," Rogan said. "I've seen something like it before, back in America. This one's a little different though. So where to? I assume we're going to Il Palazzo Imperiale. The paper looks like stationery from a hotel, if I had to guess, and if this is what it seems, it's probably where our killer, or the evidence planter, stayed."

"That would be my bet as well," Ryah said. "We'll head there and then get something to eat."

"Sounds like a plan," Rogan said. "We should also drop by the UN. See if we can find out where Lucio is so we can go visit. If we don't, someone might think we're part of the conspiracy."

"Somehow I think we already are," Ryah said.

Rogan gave a slight nod and followed Ryah to the street.

Chapter 18

Ryah vomited as soon as he stepped onto the grounds of Il Palazzo Imperiale. He wiped his mouth with an oak leaf.

"You doing alright?" Rogan asked.

"Yeah. Just haven't eaten for a while," Ryah said, but he knew the truth. His nausea told him all he needed to know about this place.

The hotel stood on the ruins of the Pantheon and filled the plaza that once surrounded the former temple to the gods. As they entered the lobby, a girl, no more than fifteen years old, ran up to Ryah.

"Master, how may I serve you?" she said. She knelt in front of him and kept her eyes fastened on his feet.

"First," Ryah said. "You can stand up and look at me."

His disgust for this place resounded in his words. He looked around the main hall. Everywhere, males and females, dressed as slaves, catered to the needs and whims of the clients. Statues of the most generous patrons lined the edges of the hall and were bowed to in worship. Through a window which looked into a garden, Ryah saw two employees hung from trees by their arms.

"What are they doing there?" Ryah asked, pointing out the window.

"They failed to bow to the statue of a client. The client saw them and demanded punishment," the girls said. "One hour on the tree."

Ryah stepped closer to the window. Above the heads of the employees were signs written in three languages enumerating their crimes. Below, guests mocked them and derived perverse pleasure in their suffering.

"You chose a great day to arrive," the girl said. "On Friday after sundown, we have our weekly feast. Come. Let me show you the rotunda."

Without waiting for a reply, she took Ryah by the hand and led him to the great room. In the middle, a wild boar roasted, the smoke from the fire rising like incense from an altar through the hole in the ceiling.

"Now is the time to let me know what you want," the girl said. "Anything you desire, I can get for you. We have wine from twenty different countries. Pharmaceuticals of all sorts. Females. Males. Any age. They will also be available for you tonight."

A rage consumed Ryah, a desire to set fire to the place and clear the world of this malignancy. He had never grown accustomed to the perversion, nor would he ever accept it. But he had a mission, so he controlled himself before he spoke to her.

"No need for that," he said, his voice calm and certain. "We're here on official business." He motioned to Rogan who showed the stationary to the girl. It was folded over so that the handwritten note could not be seen. "Is this from your hotel?"

The girl looked it over. "Yes, sir," she said. "That's definitely ours."

"I assume it can be found in all the rooms," Ryah said.

"Yes, of course, we have some in every room, but this one is different," she said.

"How so?" Ryah asked.

"It can only be found in our penthouse suites," she said.

Ryah raised an eyebrow. His mind began to connect the dots.

"Any chance you would know who's staying there?" he asked.

"We have six of those suites, so I wouldn't know for sure," she said. "Besides, those clients value their privacy. I'm afraid there's no way I could give you that information."

"Thank you," Ryah said and turned to go. He hesitated. "Just a minute."

The girl turned to face him. Ryah uncovered a little more of the paper, enough to show the symbol of the circle and the three lines.

"Have you seen anybody with this?" he asked.

She studied it closely, taking Ryah by the arm to pull the paper closer to her. Her hand was warm, soft, gentle, and a wave of anger mixed with pity overtook him.

"No, I don't recognize it," she said. "Is it supposed to mean something?"

"That's what I'm trying to find out," he said. "I thought it might be connected to this place somehow."

"I've never seen it before," she said, "but I know someone who might be able to help you."

She ran off, grabbing her toga and holding it to her waist so as not to trip when she ran. Her long, blonde hair swished back and forth with each step. Ryah and Rogan followed her. As they stepped into the lobby, she saw them and motioned for them to join her and some man in a gray suit with whom she was talking.

"These are the men I was mentioning," she said to the man in the gray suit.

As Ryah reached out to shake the man's hand, he turned to thank the girl for her help. For the first time, he noticed the girl's eyes. Dark, emerald eyes. And her features. She was the spitting image of someone he had seen before.

"Thank you …," he said, waiting for her name.

"Laney," she answered. "And you're welcome."

"And my name's Jackson," the man in the gray suit said. "Laney, here, said I might be of some service to you."

"You a regular here?" Ryah asked.

"Whenever I'm in town. And I try to make sure I get here on Fridays," he said with a knowing wink.

Rogan stepped forward as if he was about to lay out the man. Ryah shook his head and Rogan backed down. He took the folded paper and showed the symbol to Jackson.

"Do you recognize this?" Ryah asked.

Jackson didn't look long. "Oh, yeah," he said. "Seen it many times."

"Where?" Ryah asked.

"On my travels around the world. I'm an international trader, you know. Do business on every continent, more than fifty nations. I've seen it in every country I've been to," he said.

"Does it mean something?" Ryah asked.

"Yeah. I mean it's supposed to. It's a bunch of nonsense if you ask me," he said.

"How so?" Ryah asked.

"It's one of those clandestine organizations. Like the illuminati. You know, made up stuff like that. Some underground group that supposedly controls the world or plots to take over the world. I never seem to get the same story twice. What does it matter? Bunch of garbage. Power my friend. That's what rules the world. And money means power." He didn't try to hide his pride or his wealth, stretching out his arm to show off the Patek Philippe on his wrist.

Ryah ignored the gesture. "Do you know the name of this group?" he asked.

"Not really. They go by different names, depending on their location."

Ryah nodded in understanding. "OK. OK. Thank you for your time." He turned and walked off with Rogan following.

"That's it?" Rogan asked.

"I think it's time to check on Lucio," Ryah said as they headed towards the exit of the hotel, offering no other explanation and relieved to be getting out of there. "You hungry?"

"Yeah," Rogan said. "We can grab something on the way to the hospital."

Thirty minutes later, their stomachs satisfied by panini and gelato, they arrived at Hospital Pope John IV. The security guard took one look at their identification and called for an escort.

"Ambassador Tanas let us know we should be expecting you," the guard said. He made another call upstairs saying simply, "They've arrived," and pointed towards the escort who was stepping off the elevator.

"My name's Yohanna," the escort said as she came up to Ryah and Rogan, "and I've been assigned to make sure you get what you need here."

"Any word on Envoy Romijn's condition?" Ryah asked as he followed her towards the bank of elevators.

"He's in a coma," she replied. "Unfortunately, it could go either way. We'll just keep thinking good thoughts."

She pressed the button and waited for the next car, making small talk all the time. Ryah was happy to let his mind wander while Rogan occupied himself with the conversation. The doors opened and a pair of security personnel pushed past Ryah in a hurry to get on. One of them hit the number twelve as Ryah, Rogan, and Yohanna entered.

"Oh. We're going there as well," she said when she saw the twelve light up on the panel. "Make sure we let them off first."

Ryah and Rogan moved to the back to give the others space to get out. Yohanna remained silent while one of the guards let off a steady stream of curses in Italian, shouting alternately into his comm and then at the person beside him. Ryah and Rogan noted the concern in his voice.

"What's he saying?" Rogan whispered to Ryah.

"I can't tell," Ryah said. "I'm not familiar with the dialect. Something about intruder or intrusion."

The elevator chimed and bumped to a stop. The two guards ran out and disappeared around a corner. Yohanna pulled Ryah and Rogan off to the side and asked them to wait for a minute. She bit her lip as she continued to stare down the hall where the security personnel had just gone, saying nothing. But there was no need. The worry carved deep lines in her face.

From their location, Ryah could hear at least five distinct voices yelling, "Fermi! Le sparo!" The crash of a medical cart being overturned and sending the metal instruments clanging to the tile floor echoed through the corridor as the sound of a chase got closer. A man in a partially torn uniform came flying around the corner and straight at Ryah's position. Thirty feet behind him, the security personnel came with their guns drawn, running at full sprint but losing ground on the man. Rogan stepped to the other side of the hall. As the man passed by, Ryah stuck out his foot at the same moment Rogan bumped him in the shoulder, sending him tumbling over Ryah's leg and sliding down the floor into a cement wall. He stood up, dazed but intent on continuing. Ryah ran over and took hold of him, keeping one arm around his throat and pushing his knee into the small of his back.

"Let go, you bastard," he cursed at Ryah. "You don't know what you're doing." He thrashed and twisted, unable to free himself from Ryah's grasp.

"Grazie, signore," one of the guards from the elevator said to Ryah. Turning to another, he said, "How could you let him get away?"

His face was red as he listened to the explanation, clearly unsatisfied with the response. He reached behind him for his handcuffs, and Ryah handed him one of the man's arms. As the guard slipped the manacle on, Ryah saw a symbol he recognized tattooed into the left wrist. A small circle with three vertical lines. One of them going directly through the middle.

Chapter 19

"Hold on," Ryah said as the man was led away. "I want to speak with him."

"You have no authority here," the guard in charge said. "You want to speak with him? You can do it after we're finished with him. If there's anything left." He directed the last statement to the man who cursed and spat as he was dragged onto the elevator.

Yohanna took hold of Ryah's arm. "I'll look into that for you, but we need to get to Envoy Romijn's room right away."

She took them around the corner to a room where the envoy had been recuperating. Inside, two doctors and a team of nurses huddled over Lucio's bed, working in a frenzy while alarms and buzzers sounded their alerts. Yohanna left Ryah and Rogan for a moment to speak with another nurse who was standing off to the side and shaking.

"That man," Yohanna said when she returned, "the one you caught. That nurse saw him sticking a needle into the envoy's arm. When she asked what he was doing, he yelled out, 'For the Kingdom,' and pressed down on the plunger. That's what he said. 'For the Kingdom.' The nurse had no idea what he was talking about. Now, the doctors are trying to counteract whatever he injected, but they don't know what it was."

"For the Kingdom." Rogan's ears perked up when he heard it.

"Yeah. For the Kingdom," Yohanna mumbled to herself.

Ryah turned back to watch the monitors attached to Lucio. The only part he could see was the display indicating Lucio's heartbeat and blood pressure. It hovered at one hundred over sixty, dropped down to ninety over fifty, and then back up. Every few seconds, one of the nurses glanced at the monitors and informed the doctors of what they said.

"Ninety over fifty, again. No. It's staying there. Not going back up. Yes. Still ninety over fifty. Now it's dropping. Eighty over forty. Sixty over forty. He's crashing doctor. Fifty."

A telltale squeal emanated from the heart monitor. The line was flat. No life. One doctor pumped Lucio's chest as a nurse prepared to shock him. She attached the defibrillator pads to his torso and sent a jolt through the lines, causing Lucio's body to bounce off the bed. No luck. Again and again they tried. For ten minutes, the team worked over the still body of the envoy, sweat dripping off their foreheads as they did everything in their power to revive him.

"One more time," a doctor said, "and that's it. One more time. There's nothing else we can do."

The nurse charged the machine and prepared to give Lucio the last burst of electricity. At that moment, Lucio sat straight up in the bed. His eyes were open, wide with terror but seeing nothing. His face dark red, almost purple. His lungs gasping for a breath, but no air was coming in or going out. His body slammed into the bed, and he reached for his chest as if he was trying to remove a weight that was crushing him. His legs flailed and his arms shook. Out of bed again. Then slammed back down. The doctors, who had moments before been by the bedside, were pinned against the wall, powerless to move. Ryah struggled to enter the room, but a rush of wind blasted through his body like a hurricane and pushed him back. He strained with all his might, but he couldn't move, held in place by a force that didn't want him to interfere.

A third time. Lucio's whole body rose out of bed, hovered for a moment, and fell back down. His eyes were blank and rolled back into his head. His mouth foamed, a scream bubbling out but stuck in his throat. This time, Ryah saw it. Dark and formless. Pressing down on Lucio. Laughing at him. Mocking him. Talking to him. Lucio responding with words Ryah couldn't understand. He started to yell at the shadow, trying to save Lucio. Trying anything to get the monstrosity off him. One more scream and the shadow turned its head. Ryah was paralyzed. He saw its face. He knew the face. From a dream. He shouted out its name. The shadow looked past Ryah and lifted off Lucio. It floated into the air and disappeared into the ceiling.

The wind stopped blowing, freeing Ryah from its grip. He ran in to help Lucio but was kept back by a pair of nurses.

"What are you doing here?" a nurse asked, calm as if nothing out of the ordinary had occurred. "The envoy will need some rest before you can speak with him."

"What …?" No other words would come out. He looked at the monitors. One hundred twenty over seventy-five. Pulse of sixty-two. He looked over at Rogan who had a concerned look on his face. He turned to see Yohanna, who was talking to one of the doctors. She finished and walked over to Ryah.

"He's doing much better now," Yohanna said. "Almost a miracle. The doctor says he's out of danger for now, but they'll keep monitoring him. By the way, I got a message from Ambassador Tanas. He asked me to take you down right away to talk with the man you caught. He said they've discovered some important information and for you to get whatever else you can before they … well, you know. Come on. Follow me."

Rogan spoke up. "Would you mind showing me where the restrooms are? I need to make a quick stop."

"Sure," Yohanna said. "They're down that way to your right."

"I think I'll join you," Ryah said.

They walked off together and entered the bathroom. Rogan turned to face Ryah.

"What was that?" he asked.

"What?" Ryah said.

"Something happened there," Rogan said. He stared directly at Ryah, but his mind was elsewhere. After a delay, he focused his thoughts and continued. "This is not the time to play games. I know you saw something."

"What did you see?" Ryah asked.

"I don't know. Nothing. Something," Rogan replied. "Lucio was dead, and then he started bouncing off the bed. Everybody else stood around smiling as if nothing was wrong. The doctors, the nurses. They were congratulating each other. Everyone happy, ecstatic. Except you. You saw something. You said something. 'Ant'el', and then everything went back to normal, Lucio's fine. Never been better. What's going on?"

"I couldn't tell you," Ryah said. "Not that you'd believe me if I could tell you. Not that I believe it myself," he added. "Anyway, we better get back before Yohanna starts thinking things."

Rogan, unsatisfied, decided to wait to pursue the issue. They walked back to Yohanna, who led them to a freight elevator which took them down below ground level. A man wearing a UN security uniform met them, dismissed Yohanna, and walked them down the dimly lit hall.

"I'm Colonel Zidane, intelligence," he said, his French accent showing through. "The Ambassador asked me to personally escort you to our prisoner." He stopped outside a door with no windows and no apparent means of opening it. "We have the man inside. The one who tried to kill Envoy Romijn. He is also the one who the two Chinese gentlemen. When he discovered Romijn was alive, he came here to finish the job."

"How do you know that?" Ryah asked.

"He confessed. Confessed the details," Colonel Zidane said. "Now out of courtesy to the Ambassador, we will let you speak with him." He looked up at a camera in the ceiling and gave a nod. The door clicked and popped open just enough to get a hand in. "We will be able to see you at all times, although I will be the only one who can hear into the room. Just give me an indication if you need anything."

Ryah nodded that he understood and entered the room with Rogan. The door shut behind them, leaving the two alone with the man. He sat in a metal chair with his arms shackled to the wall. His hair was disheveled, and a trickle of blood rolled down his bruised lip. Ryah took the other chair and pulled it up beside him. After the obvious beating, Ryah opted for the soft approach.

"I can't say I'm surprised to see you here," Ryah said.

The man said nothing and looked off to his left, his face calm. Ryah grabbed his chin and moved it so he was forced to look at him.

"Look. I'm not here to hurt you. I simply want to know your name," Ryah said.

The man's jaw quivered and his nostrils flared as he attempted to control his respiration. "You know my name," he said.

"I mean your real name." Ryah let go of the man's face. "They say you shot the envoy. Why did you do that?"

The man didn't answer.

"Who are you with? The Czechs?" Ryah asked. "I know you're not Russian." He leaned down and whispered in the man's ear. "American?"

The man still didn't answer but sat looking straight ahead with a blank look on his face. The only indication he had heard anything was when his left hand twitched at the word 'American'. Ryah could tell the man wouldn't speak, not in his predicament. Not without extreme measures, the likes of which might only cause him to lie.

"What if we make you a little more comfortable?" he said, trying a different tactic. "I'll see if I can get the handcuffs removed. Maybe get you something to drink."

He looked towards the camera in the corner. In less than a minute, the door clicked open. A guard entered to unlock the handcuffs and left a disposable cup with water. He beat a hasty retreat, leaving the three alone again. The man rubbed his wrists, and his eyes softened a little.

"I hope that's better, Klokovsky," Ryah said. He put his arm on his shoulder. "Let's try this again. What's your first name? The real one. Let's start there."

Klokovsky stared straight ahead. "Evan."

For the first time, Ryah believed the man.

"OK, Evan. How about a drink?" he asked.

Ryah handed him the water. Evan took it with both hands and brought it to his lips, taking a small sip but wincing in pain when the water passed over the superficial cut.

"Look, Evan," Ryah said. "I'm not going to lie to you. You know how this is going to end. You're not going to survive this." His voice was compassionate, sincere. "Your only choice is how bad the end is going to be. Tell me something. Something that we can verify, and I'll ask the Colonel out there to make it quick and painless."

Evan opened his mouth as if he were about to say something, but he caught himself and took another drink,

172

putting the cup down on the floor by his feet when he was finished. He took a deep breath and exhaled. His head hung low on his chest, and he stared at Ryah's hands as they took hold of one of his, rubbing the tattoo of the circle and the lines with the thumb of his right hand.

"You're one of them," Ryah said as he pressed on the tattoo. "Are they the people behind it?"

"After what they've done to us … they deserve it," Evan said.

"Who deserves it?" Ryah asked.

"All of them," Evan said. "The Russians. The Chinese. The UN."

His words came out forced as if he had memorized a script.

"Are you doing this on your own, or are there others with you?" Ryah asked.

Evan smirked. "You'd like to know that wouldn't you?"

Ryah bent over and pressed his face close to Evan's, speaking so that only the captive could hear.

"I know you're not who you say you are," Ryah said. "In fact, I know you're an American, probably military intelligence. Or you used to be."

This time Evan didn't make any movements to indicate whether or not Ryah was correct. Ryah continued so that only Evan could hear.

"Are you with the Council?"

"No."

"How'd you get close to the Russians?"

Evan shook his head back and forth and started muttering to himself. His words were barely audible, not meant for Ryah to hear.

"I can't do it," Evan said as if he was arguing with someone. He looked down at the floor and took a deep breath. Then, he looked up, directly in Ryah's eyes. Evan's were cold, distant, impenetrable, like a dark cloud had passed over them.

"I know who you are," Evan said.

The words came out soft but full of hate. He jerked his arm away so Ryah couldn't touch his wrist anymore.

"Who am I?" Ryah asked.

"I know why you're here. You're not who you claim to be," Evan said.

"Why am I here?" Ryah asked, undisturbed by what he just heard.

"I know why you're here. I know who you are. I know what you want." His voice crescendoed with each phrase. "I know who you are. You can't fool me." His eyes became wild. "I know you, Ryah. I know why you're here. You're not who you pretend to be. *You're* the one with the Council." He was screaming by now. "You're with the Council, and you're next. Your people are next. The Kingdom is coming and you can't stop it. There's nothing you can do. The Kingdom is coming to get you too, and we will have our revenge."

He stood up and started to hit Ryah while continuing to berate him. A moment later, the door opened and two guards rushed in. One of them jammed Evan with his taser sending fifty thousand volts into his body. He collapsed to the floor and writhed around. The guard bent over and gave Evan a few more jolts until drool spilled out of his mouth. Colonel Zidane entered and grabbed Ryah to move him outside, allowing the door to shut behind them. He led them back to the lobby and handed them an envelope.

"Here are tickets for your flight back to the US." The Colonel didn't sound surprised to hear they were Americans. "We wanted you to hear it from his own lips so you could let the Council know what's coming." He shook their hands. "The car is waiting for you to take you to the airport now. You will find your belongings in the car already. The Ambassador thanks you for your service."

With that, he turned around and left. Ryah and Rogan walked outside.

"What do you make of that?" Rogan asked.

Ryah shook his head. "I don't know. All I know is that things are not what they seem."

Chapter 20

Maryam had never known that feeling. It was surreal. Her legs carried her body back to her apartment, her mind unaware of what was happening, unable to process what she just heard. She wouldn't have gone to see the doctor that day, but she had made up her mind to leave her home, the city, whatever it took. There was no way she was going back to that life. No more strangers in her bed. No more pretending she didn't care.

She thought back to what had happened the last three weeks.

He was the only doctor who would see her, the one she went to see this morning. The same one who told her to let Kaliya go. Callous, cold, like she was a dying pet. Maybe the doctor was right, though, and she just couldn't bear to hear the truth.

"Don't you dare say that," Maryam had said out loud to herself but as if she was responding to someone else. "Every morning is worth it. Every single morning she wakes up is another memory, for her, for me. No. If there's a chance …."

She knew before she opened the pill bottle. The rattling sound it made when she shook it had diminished each day until it was silent. She looked inside hoping for a miracle, but there was none. She would have to swallow her pride, go back to see that doctor. Beg him for help. It wasn't only the pills that had run out. So had her money. No clients in over three weeks, scraping together what little money she had and selling all her possessions besides the absolute necessities. The old life was over, but she hadn't been able to leave her home yet despite what she had told Corinne.

She was determined to go to Allison, but every time she stepped out to do it, doubts crept into her mind, a nagging voice that told her Allison was a liar, a fraud. This morning, though, she really had no choice, not if she wanted Kaliya to live. She had to go back and plead for her daughter's life.

Maryam arrived as the doctor's office opened. The assistant told her no appointments were available that day.

"All I need is five minutes," Maryam said.

The assistant never understood why the doctor had continued to see her even when she had no money to pay. "*She must pay in other ways,*" she thought and always did her best to run her off. But this day, looking into Kaliya's face, so full of life, so desperately in need of hope, the assistant felt compassion.

"I can't promise you anything," she said to Maryam, "but if you want to have a seat, I'll see what I can do."

"Thank you," Maryam said and sat down with her daughter to wait.

And she waited. So long that she almost gave up. As she was about to leave, the assistant called her over and said, "You can go in now."

Inside the office, a nurse directed Kaliya to the scanning room, a place she had visited many times before. When the session was over, Maryam and Kaliya were taken back to the doctor's office to see the results. He wasn't there, so they stood by the window staring out at the city below.

A few minutes later, the doctor walked in looking disconcerted. "Go wait outside for me," he told her. Maryam sat on the hard metal seat in the waiting area and watched as two more doctors entered the office. She felt sick to her stomach, but she fixed a smile on her face so Kaliya wouldn't get scared. This was the moment she had prepared for, but now that it was here, she wasn't ready for it. Another day. Another week. It couldn't be much more than that. How would she let Kaliya know? What would she

177

do with her final moments with her daughter? What would she do when Kaliya was gone? Would she be able to go on herself?

The doctor called her back in. She heard it, and she sat there. It didn't register. Maryam stared at a poster on the wall over the doctor's right shoulder.

"Did you hear me?" the doctor said. "They're gone."

Maryam stammered out her statement. "I ... I'm not sure what you mean."

"They're gone. The tumors. I don't understand. I mean, I can't explain it. But they're gone. My colleagues agree. And not only gone, but there's no trace they were ever there. In all my years of medicine, I've never seen anything like this."

Maryam remembered what the stranger had said. "She's well." And then he left. How did he know? He must have been a physician after all. But when did he give Kaliya the medicine? While she was with the other men? But how?

Maryam walked back to her apartment in a stupor. Kaliya ran up and down the street beside her, talking with everyone she met, dancing and singing and not knowing why.

That night, after they both had fallen asleep, Maryam dreamed of two men arguing outside her window. She didn't understand what they were saying, but she could tell they were angry. The contest soon turned physical, and amidst the shouting, Maryam heard the distinct sound of metal on metal, like two swords striking each other.

A bang on the door made her jump. Another one. Again, louder each time as if someone were being thrown into it with greater and greater force. The window frame shook with each thud, the pounding intensifying, threatening to break down the door. And then she heard it. A loud crack. The door frame splintered and the barrier which kept her safe destroyed. The battle was in her home. Two unknown men fighting for life. Wrestling. Groaning.

Yelling unknown words in a language she couldn't understand. Out of the darkness came a voice, loud and clear. "Maryam." There was no mistaking it. She heard her name being called out deep and melodic, like it was spoken by a chorus of trumpets.

Maryam woke up at the sound of her name. All was quiet except for the pounding of her heart. She grabbed a short, metal pipe she kept by her side, and tiptoed to the bedroom door. She slipped it open, holding it tight against the hinges so they wouldn't squeak, and peered outside. It was dark except for the rays of light shining through the edge of the blinds. The front door she was expecting to find shattered on the floor remained bolted shut, completely intact. Everything was orderly, and there was no sign a struggle had taken place.

"I'm out of here," she told herself. "Tomorrow morning, no more excuses."

She made good on her promise. That morning as soon as she woke up, she and Kaliya headed out of the apartment for the last time. An hour later, they found themselves back at Riverplace, relieved that they hadn't been attacked on the transit and trying to recall how to get to Allison's house.

The sun warmed the air as it climbed above the horizon. The gray mist which enveloped the place each morning had burned off, and the light from the source of life illuminated the decay and disease which had been hidden in the fog on Maryam's first visit. The junkies and prostitutes, happy to have been hidden by the night, fled the sunlight as it chased away the shadows on its slow journey across the street. They retreated to their makeshift shelters. Vampires safe in their coffins, cursing the light and waiting for the darkness to return.

Maryam entered the plaza. The broken statue of Poseidon lay in the middle with its face to the ground like a deposed ruler bowing before a greater power. Around the

179

edge of the plaza, a shanty town of cardboard huts and impromptu lean-tos had sprung up. Remnants of previous homes were strewn across the area, blown to and fro by the wind, a reminder that nothing was permanent here. To her left about fifty yards from where she stood, Maryam saw Allison outside a tent, stooped over and speaking with someone inside. Not wanting to disturb her, Maryam waited while Kaliya chased after a raven which sat by a crushed dolphin. The bird flew off when Kaliya approached and settled on the statue, watching with interest as Kaliya turned her attention to a flock of pigeons bobbing their way across the stones. The whoosh of air as the birds lifted off the ground caught Allison's attention. Turning, she saw Maryam.

"Maryam," Allison called out. There was joy in her voice, no mistaking it. She hurried over and gave Maryam a hug. "I'm glad to see you. What brings you by? Kaliya is looking great," she added.

Maryam didn't know what to say. She didn't know why she was there nor what Allison would think, although, she had the feeling Allison knew the reasons better than she did. Before Maryam could think of something, Allison spoke again.

"Come with me. I'm making my rounds this morning, and I'd like you to see what we do here."

Allison hooked her arm under Maryam's elbow and took her back to the tent where a black bag lay on the ground. Allison picked it up and walked next door where the smell of urine and decaying flesh washed over Maryam in an overwhelming, repulsive wave. Allison seemed oblivious to the odor and called out to the person inside.

"Marcus. It's Allison. How are you doing today?"

Marcus mumbled something unintelligible back at her.

"Can you step outside so I can see you?" she asked.

A man in his early thirties but with the appearance of a sixty-year-old exited the tent. A mixture of open sores and old scars lined his forearms, needle tracks which bore evidence of his chosen addiction. He wore a t-shirt and a torn pair of sweatpants that hadn't been washed since he first put them on over a year ago. Maryam looked in his eyes expecting to see pain or sadness or something. But there was nothing.

Allison had him sit down and pushed up the pant leg above the right knee. Maryam jerked her head and looked away, nauseated by what she saw. Allison touched his right calf with her gloved hands, pressing around an open wound which oozed a dark green liquid that smelled of death.

"Marcus. Have you been taking the medicine I gave you?" Allison asked as she pulled some gauze out of her bag.

He shook his head.

"You know you have no chance of getting better if you don't do it. We're going to have to take that leg soon." She placed her arm on his shoulder and looked directly in his eyes as she said it.

A tear formed in Marcus' eye but he said nothing. Allison reached up to wipe the tear away. She drew her hand down his face, caressing his cheek. She smiled at him, and for the first time, Maryam saw some emotion on his face.

Allison handed him a pill. "I want you to take this while I'm here. It looks like I'm going to have to drop by every few hours to make sure you do what you're supposed to," Allison scolded.

Marcus swallowed the pill. "Yes, Ms. Allison," he said. "Thank you."

He reached up and squeezed Allison's hand before heading back into the tent. Allison grabbed her bag and motioned for Maryam to follow.

"Kaliya," Allison yelled out. "Come over here. See what I got for you."

Kaliya ran over to them and bounced into Allison's arms.

"Hi, Ms. Allison," she said, her voice bubbling with excitement.

"Reach into my coat pocket," Allison ordered.

Kaliya did and pulled out two pieces of candy. She put her hand back to leave one of them there.

"No, dear," Allison said. "Save that for later."

Kaliya squealed with delight and ran after a pigeon that got too close.

"This is what you do?" Maryam asked. "You give medicine to these people."

"It's one of my jobs," Allison said.

"Why do you do it?" Maryam asked.

"Someone needs to," Allison said. "It's not like the Council is going to do anything."

She looked at Maryam who seemed distressed.

"That's not what you mean, huh?" Allison paused as if she didn't want to continue. "It's a bit of a long story. Not one I'm proud of," she admitted. The regret showed on her face.

Chapter 21

They walked together across the plaza. Allison's happy demeanor disappeared as the memories flooded her mind.

"I used to be a doctor, a researcher, at New Carmel Medical Center," she said. She placed her hands over her mouth and stopped speaking, unable to continue until the thought passed. "My job was to work on these people."

Maryam didn't know what she meant by 'work on', but she was afraid to ask.

"We wanted to see the effects of addiction on the human body, so we rounded them up and brought them in. We tried to help some … but that wasn't really the goal of our experiments." She shuddered at the thought. "They weren't people to me. Just bodies. Animals really. They didn't care about themselves, so why should we? Darwinism. Sacrifice of the weak for the benefit of the strong. Virtue through science to accelerate our evolution. I gained a lot of knowledge, much of which I use here. Not that it makes up for it."

Allison stopped right in the middle of the plaza by the old fountain. Her face grew dim and her eyes narrowed as they peered into the darkness of her past, staring at the ghosts and shadows which haunted her mind, wondering if she should tell all. In the end, Allison decided that full honesty was the only policy.

"That wasn't the worst," Allison said. "The prostitutes that would come in, the females, of course, that were pregnant." The words failed her. "We would remove them."

Maryam didn't ask what she meant. She knew this time.

"We would use the parts to make medications. Some for healing. Some for beauty creams to remove wrinkles. The tiny hands and feet, we would throw away. There was no use for them."

"I understand," Maryam said as she wrapped her arm around Allison's shoulder, holding her as she sobbed and surprised at her own compassion towards Allison. "You do this to make up for what you did."

"There's nothing I can do to atone for what I did," Allison said and wiped the last tear away. "But I don't need to."

The statement seemed out of place for someone who had just expressed so much remorse.

"How about that guy you sent to see me? Why doesn't he come here and help these people?" Maryam asked.

"They can only be healed if they want his help," she answered. "He offers his services to anyone who wants them, but most people are so blind to their condition that they don't realize they even have a problem. I think that's the saddest part of it. I can treat the symptoms. Make them a little more comfortable and maybe help them see that they need more help than I can give."

"He's a physician, I assume," Maryam said.

"The best I've ever met," Allison said.

They walked across the plaza and down the street for over a mile, Kaliya tagging along behind them. Allison stopped every time she saw someone she knew to talk with them and listen to them. The farther away from the plaza they got, the more infrequent her stops became until there was no one left that she recognized. As they turned to go back, Allison grabbed Maryam's arm and dragged her down a small flight of stairs into a basement entrance, calling for Kaliya to join them. The door was locked, and Allison jammed herself into a corner in an attempt to hide, her head peeking above street level.

"What is it?" Maryam asked.

Allison put her finger to her lips to quiet Maryam and Kaliya and pointed to the other side of the street where an armored vehicle had pulled up. Twenty soldiers in full gear and carrying rifles piled out of the back and started grabbing people who were too slow or too stoned to escape. Two of the soldiers brought a man back to an officer who had exited out the front of the truck. With a quick smack of his baton, the officer brought the captive to his knees. He removed a folded piece of paper from his pocket and showed it to the man kneeled in front of him. Maryam could hear every word he said.

"Have you seen any of these people?" the officer asked, shoving the paper in front of the man's eyes. The man shook his head. "Look closer. Are you sure you've never seen any of them."

The man peered at the photos. "N ... no, I haven't," he stammered.

"How about this?" The officer showed him another piece of paper. "They wear it on their wrist."

The man either didn't know or was too scared to recall and shook his head again.

"You're no use to me then," the officer said as he removed a pistol from his holster.

One shot rang out and the man collapsed to the ground.

"How about you?" he asked another person the soldiers had carried to him. "Do you know any of these people?"

Allison made a move towards the steps, but Maryam grabbed her and held her back.

"What are you doing?" Maryam whispered.

"They're looking for me," Allison said.

"You can't go," Maryam said. "Look what they did to that guy. What do you think they'll do to you?"

"I can't let them hurt these people," Allison said.

Before she could pull away from Maryam, they saw the soldiers run back and climb on board the truck, which took off in a hurry down the street in a direction opposite the plaza. Maryam let out a deep breath and walked up the stairs to the sidewalk with Allison, wondering what had caused them to leave like they did. From behind them and off to their left, she heard a deep, masculine voice.

"Don't worry," the voice said. "I had your back."

"Thank you, Jason," Allison said without turning around, "but I don't want you to do anything. If I decide to go, let me go."

Maryam wheeled around to see who was there. Her eyes grew wide in terror. Without being conscious of it, she took hold of her daughter and hid herself behind Allison. A face she had only seen once appeared before her now. The face of a man who had beaten and stabbed a man to death in front of her eyes. A man who had threatened to rape her and her daughter but who was left bleeding and as good as dead by another stranger on the transit.

"Kane." She mouthed the words to herself and stared at those once lifeless eyes, which looked back without seeming to recognize her.

Jason or Kane, whatever his name was now, replied to Allison. "I'm here to take care of you, to make sure nothing bad happens to you. I could easily take out most if not all of them before any of them got close to you."

Maryam couldn't tell if it was bravado or if he was telling the truth.

"We don't do that here, Jason," she said. "We let him take care of us. We don't resort to using weapons to advance our cause. You've only been with us a couple months. There's a lot you have yet to learn."

"With all due respect, Allison," Jason said. "He told us to keep our weapons on us at all times. I'm sure it wasn't just for show."

186

"He was speaking metaphorically," Allison said. "We fight in a different way."

"Well, I may be new, but I know what I heard. Maybe he told you something different, so I guess we'll have to agree to disagree." He stretched out his hand to Maryam. "My name's Jason," he said. "It's good to meet you. I assume you're a friend of Allison's."

Maryam refused to take his hand.

"I believe we've met before," she said, her voice cold and full of anger.

Jason's face fell as he felt the hate. "If we did, then I wouldn't remember. I barely remember anything from my previous life. Or perhaps, I don't want to, but if you say we met, then I know I owe you an apology." He dropped to his knees in front of Maryam. "I can only imagine what I did, but from the bottom of my heart, I am truly sorry. I hope you can forgive me."

Maryam marveled at the change but said nothing as he rose back to his feet and faced Allison.

"The patrols are coming more often," Jason said. "And they're getting closer. It's just a matter of time."

Allison didn't reply.

Sensing her hesitation, Jason said, "You know we're going to have to leave. Sooner would be better."

"What about these people?" Allison said, her voice cracking as she spoke.

"We take the ones we can. The ones who want to go," Jason said. He touched Allison's hand. "There are others. Everywhere you go, there will be others. You've done all you can here. It's just not safe anymore."

"What are you talking about?" Maryam asked her. "Why would anyone want to hurt you?" She could not comprehend what vile act Allison had committed to warrant the attention of an elimination squad.

"Italy," Allison said. "They blame it on us."

187

"What happened in Italy?" Maryam asked. She didn't make it a habit to follow the news, especially international events. But then she realized what Allison was talking about. Everyone, including herself, knew about Italy. "You mean at the UN?"

Allison nodded her head. "The Chinese delegates that were assassinated on the steps. And the guy from the UN … Envoy Romijn. Somehow they linked it to us."

"Did you have something to do with it?" Maryam asked.

"No. Heavens no," Allison said. "I would never do anything of the sort. I can't even comprehend how someone could bring themselves to do it."

"Do you think it was one of our member groups in Europe?" Jason asked.

"I don't know," Allison said. "I certainly hope not. We don't kill in the name of our cause. We fight back but in our own way, against the real enemy. I am afraid, though, of the possibility that it was one of us."

"Who is 'us'?" Maryam asked. "What cause are you referring to?"

Allison pulled the sleeve of her right shirt back, revealing her wrist. Maryam recoiled again like she had done the first time. She saw it there. A circle with the number one written three times, looking like lines. The middle one stretching across the diameter.

"I've read about you," Maryam said, unsure of whether or not she should continue, her emotions a mix of fear and curiosity. "They call your movement 'The Kingdom.' Say your goal is to destroy the nations and set up your own kingdom that rules over the world. Is that what you're really all about?"

"Look around," Allison said. "What do you see? This is my mission."

Jason stood silently and watched Maryam's expression. After a while, he turned to Allison.

"You know they'll kill you if they find you," Jason said.

"They might," Allison said, "if he lets them. But not before it's time. Besides, don't you think it's better to die than to live like the people who hunt us?"

Jason nodded his head. "I do now," he said.

Allison smiled at him. "Well, enough of this. I'll go back and talk to the others. See about an evacuation plan. But not yet. I have some more patients to tend to. You going to join me?" she asked Jason.

"Absolutely," he said.

"Great. You're a quick learner. Would have made a fantastic doctor."

Jason beamed with pride.

"Do me a favor first," Allison said. "I need you to take Maryam and her daughter to the safe house."

Maryam looked terrified. Whether it was because of the Council searching for Allison and her people or because of being alone with Jason, Maryam wasn't sure.

Allison touched her arm. "Don't be afraid. The place where you're going has no connection to us as far as the Council is concerned. And only I and a few other people know about it anyway. You'll love it there. And so will Kaliya. I'm sure she'll make a few friends." She winked at Kaliya. "Jason will make sure you get there safely," she added.

Allison squeezed Jason's arm, letting him know to watch out for their welfare.

"I'll take care of them," Jason assured her. "No harm will come to them."

He bent over and kissed Allison on each cheek, then walked off with Maryam following. Kaliya ran up to Jason and placed her tiny, frail hand in his giant, calloused paw. They went down the street laughing and playing some childhood game Jason was teaching her. Maryam pondered all she had heard and seen that day, surprised by Jason's

189

tenderness but afraid of the monster she was sure lurked inside.

Chapter 22

Jason took them to a three-story brick building which had survived the earthquakes, the only damage a crack running in a zigzag up the front stairs. He climbed to the top and knocked on the door. The person inside asked who it was. Jason let out a howl, which delighted Kaliya but froze Maryam on the inside. The door opened and revealed a fifty something year old lady in a long white lab coat which covered a gray t-shirt and a pair of jeans.

"Hi Jason," she said, looking at Maryam and Kaliya. "It looks like you're making a delivery."

"Yes, ma'am," Jason said. "Allison asked me to bring them over."

"Let's stop with the ma'am thing, shall we," the lady said.

"It's just that … well, you remind me of my mother."

The lady threw a rag at Jason, pretending to be unhappy with the compliment. She turned to Maryam.

"Welcome," she said. "My name's Caroline, but everybody here calls me Carol. Come on inside with me." She walked them up the stairs. "What are your names?" she asked.

"I'm Kaliya," Kaliya said, jumping in without concern for proper manners.

"Kaliya. How beautiful," Carol said.

"And I'm Maryam."

"Kaliya and Maryam. It is so nice to have you here. Normally, the ladies that come here have to share a room, but since you have your daughter with you… she is your daughter, right? I assumed because she has your eyes."

Maryam nodded.

"Good. You and your daughter will get a room together on the second floor where we keep families if we ever have any. I'll introduce you to the people that live here a little later." They began climbing the stairs to the second floor as Carol continued talking. "But I want you to meet the person that lives across the hall from you. She arrived a little over a year ago and decided to stay. Kind of our official welcome wagon, make you feel comfortable person. She'll help you get settled in."

Carol stopped in front of a partially open door and knocked.

"Hey, Selena," she called out. "I've got a couple of people I'd like you to meet."

A tall, slender woman with jet black hair and skin the color of mocha came out of the room. She had a smile that could melt the heart of a gorgon and dark eyes that twinkled as she talked.

"Awesome. I've got new house mates," she sang out. "And one of them is a beautiful young lady." She gave Kaliya a hug and looked up at Maryam. "I see where she gets her stunning looks. Come on down the hall with me. I'll show you where you'll be staying."

At the end of the hall, Selena pointed inside a room. "Here's where you'll stay as long as you need."

"What exactly is this place?" Maryam asked.

"It's where ladies who are trying to escape the life come to be safe and to make a new life for themselves," Selena said. "We call ourselves the House of Hope."

"What do the women do here?" Maryam asked.

Selena sat down on the edge of the bed, anticipating a lengthy conversation, one she had had many times. "We all have responsibilities to help maintain the house. We usually rotate them every month or so. Also, Carol and another lady you'll meet, Jackie, teach skills that will help you get a job and become self-sufficient. Carol, she's a doctor at New

Carmel Medical, an old friend of Allison's. Jackie's an entrepreneur who owns two very successful businesses, a jewelry store and a deli. I know, crazy combo. She's just really good at running things. If you're interested, she'll show you how to design necklaces, rings, all that. She went to France to study art and somehow ended up being a jewelry designer. I'm not sure how she got into the deli business. She has one of the graduates from here running that place and spends most of her time at the jewelry store. We usually give the newcomers a couple of weeks to get settled in. Then, we ask you to make a choice. You can always change your mind you know, but you'll have to choose something to get started. Making sandwiches or making necklaces. Every once in a while, there's an opening at the hospital, if you're interested in that sort of thing. Me. I could never get used to the blood."

Maryam hadn't been around anyone who talked so much. Even her friend, Corinne, was more reserved. But Maryam didn't mind. It would be nice to have someone she could talk to.

Selena continued. "After a month, they'll start paying you a stipend. It's not much, but you get to keep all of it. Room and board, they're free here. As long as you follow the rules."

Maryam raised her eyebrow and thought, "*Rules?*"

Selena must have read her expression. "Don't worry. They're not extensive. Lights out by midnight. Don't tell anyone about this place. A couple other ones that I don't want to bore you with now. You'll catch on. They're all about keeping everyone safe." She looked at the clock on the wall. "I bet you two are hungry. If you want, I'll take you to the kitchen where you can get something to eat. Do you like to cook?"

"I do," Maryam said.

"Great," Selena said. "We also need someone to work in the kitchen if you're interested. Saida works there now but she doesn't like it." Selena lowered her voice to a whisper. "And her food's not that great, sorry to say. Don't tell her I said that, though."

"I won't," Maryam said.

Selena looked at Kaliya. Her face was stern, but the twinkle remained in her eyes.

"I won't either," Kaliya said. "I promise."

Chapter 23

It took a couple months for Maryam and Kaliya to get into a routine. Things weren't perfect, far from it in fact, but Maryam was happy to have escaped her old life. Selena had become her best friend almost overnight, and they would spend most of their free time together talking about everything or nothing. A few times, Maryam had mentioned the Kingdom in an attempt to see what Selena knew about it.

"This is the Kingdom," Selena would say.

Maryam would press for more information, but Selena's explanations never made sense to her. One thing Maryam was sure of, though, was that these people were not capable of an assassination, elaborate or otherwise. Since news was not allowed in the house – one of the other rules Selena didn't mention that first day – it was hard to know what was going on in the world.

The only indication Maryam had that there was trouble was when she overheard Carol talking with Jackie about some matter. Maryam couldn't hear much of the conversation as she walked down the hall towards Carol's office, something about a round-up. The dialogue stopped as soon as Maryam entered. She saw them put on their happy faces but knew there was an anxiety underneath the façade. There was no doubt in Maryam's mind that the Council was closer to finding out about Allison. The only hope being that Allison had taken the advice to leave.

Carol found an open position in the radiology department, so Maryam decided to go to the hospital and learn how to be a tech, something which turned out to suit her personality perfectly. She would walk the four blocks to the hospital in the morning, arriving around eight o'clock and leaving at six in the evening. The only break she had was an hour for lunch, which she would take at a café in the main lobby.

It was her third week at New Carmel Medical, on a Wednesday during her lunch break. She ordered a coffee and croissant and sat alone in a booth, rolling balls of bread between her fingers.

"What a coincidence to meet you here," a voice said to her. "I assume by your uniform this is where you work now."

Maryam looked up at the tall man with dark hair and dark eyes.

"Bale," he said and extended his hand. "We met in a coffee shop on the other side of town one night, if I remember correctly. I don't remember what we talked about, but I remember meeting you. How could I ever forget those lovely, green eyes?"

He seemed pleasant, not like the first time Maryam met him.

"Do you mind if I join you?" he asked. "I'm here to see an old friend who's really sick. I don't think he's going to make it, and I needed to get away. I'd love to sit and chat, if that's OK with you. Stop thinking about him for a few minutes. But please, if I'm intruding, just tell me to be on my way. It won't offend me."

"Sure," she said. "I'm just sitting here, lost in my thoughts. I wouldn't mind a little company."

Bale sat down across from her and called the waiter over. "A coffee please. Black. And a chicken salad sandwich." He looked at Maryam. "Anything for you?"

She shook her head. "No thank you."

The waiter left and Bale turned his attention to her. "Lost in thought, huh? Anything in particular? I've been told I'm a good listener."

"Nothing really," Maryam said. "Just things that are going on."

"Like what?"

"This job. The Kingdom," she said.

Bale's eyes seemed to burn when he heard those last words. "How are you liking your job?" he asked.

"It's good. I'm enjoying it. Much more than my last line of work. The house, though, is another story."

"The house?" he said.

Maryam realized she had let slip out something she should not have. "Nothing. Just where I'm living."

"Where are you living?" he asked.

Maryam couldn't tell if he was interested in her or the information she had. She decided not to give him any indication of where she was staying. "I live with a couple of other girls in a house at the end of the blue line." She lied, hoping it would throw him off track.

"With all due respect and no offense meant," he said, "I bet it's a little hard living with all women. Gets a little catty, I imagine."

"Yeah. I suppose it does," she said. "My daughter's beginning to get on my nerves, too. She had been so happy when we first moved, but now she's been complaining about every little thing. I'm not sure what got into her."

"Your daughter. I don't remember you mentioning you had a daughter. What's her name?" he asked.

"Kaliya," she said. "She just turned eleven. I didn't think she was going to make it."

"Oh," Bale said, his eyebrows raised in surprise. "What was wrong with her?"

"She was sick. Dying if I must be honest," she said.

"But she's better now?" Bale asked. "Hmm. How'd that happen?"

"She had these tumors that gave her seizures, but really they were everywhere in her body. This guy, a friend of a friend dropped by and gave her some medicine. At least, I think he did, because after he left, she got better. Remember? It was the night we met."

Bale's mood took a turn for the worse. He looked past Maryam and shook his head.

"It was that guy. I can't believe he would do that," he said. "Giving you false hope like that. Does he have no shame?"

"What are you talking about?" Maryam asked.

"I bet he said he was going to heal her, make her completely well, didn't he?" Bale said.

"Actually, not," Maryam replied.

"How do you know she's better then?" Bale asked.

"My doctor told me. They did a CAT scan and found that the tumors had completely disappeared," she said. "It was right after he came to visit."

Bale no longer tried to conceal his anger. "I knew it. I knew he would pull something like this." His voice rose in pitch and his face turned red. "What a con artist? How dare he do something like that to someone as wonderful as you."

"I'm confused," Maryam said. "He healed my daughter. What's wrong with that?"

"You're not giving him credit for that are you? That charlatan. That peddler of fake cures," Bale said.

"In my book, it was a miracle," Maryam said.

"A miracle? You believe in miracles? That must be why he chose you," Bale said. "You're not superstitious, are you? Next, you'll be believing in ghosts. Oh, and a devil with a pitchfork and horns who runs around trying to get you to do bad things." He laughed but became serious again, reaching out to touch Maryam's arm. "I hate to be the bearer of bad news, but the tumors will be back. I've seen it before. He found some sort of homeopathic medicine that 'cures' people's tumors for a few months, but then they come back stronger than ever. And this time it's worse. The pain they endure ... they'll wish they had died."

Maryam was visibly upset. "I think it's time for you to go now," she said.

"I'm sorry," he said. "I just ... never mind. I'll leave."

The waiter came over with his order.

"Can you make that to go?" he asked. As the waiter walked off, Bale turned to Maryam. "I apologize for troubling you," he said. "I wish you the best and hope I am wrong."

The conversation bothered Maryam the rest of the day and into the night. She didn't touch her food at dinner and went to bed as the last rays of sunlight were being swallowed by the night. She lay awake for hours staring at the ceiling and listening to Kaliya's gentle breathing on the bed next to her. When she did fall asleep, it was to a dream that wouldn't let her rest. Kingdoms and devils and pitchforks fighting over Kaliya's body which could have been alive or which could have been dead.

The dream changed, and Maryam found herself standing in front of a mirror, stroking the scar on the left side of her face. Behind her was the man who gave it to her, she looked at him and then back at her own face. It was his hand stroking her face. She turned away for a second and looked back again. Now it was Bale's face that stared at her while she stood there and enjoyed his caress.

A huge wind blew against Maryam, tearing her away from the room. When the gale stopped, she found herself in a courtroom with Allison, Selena, Carol, and Jackie. The judge banged his gavel. Unseen hands grabbed the women and chained them to a pole sitting atop a pile of wood in the center of the courtroom. The judge brought the gavel down once more, and a fire was set beneath them.

Maryam tried to scream as smoke poured out of her mouth. The heat got closer and singed her skin. A pair of hands shook her.

"Maryam, get up."

Maryam blinked a couple times and stared into the darkness. She felt herself being shaken again.

"Fire, Maryam! Wake up!"

Through the window, flames licked the side of the building, their glow silhouetting the figures of Selena and Kaliya.

"Maryam, get up now!"

She jumped out of bed, grabbed her shoes, and headed towards the fire escape. Selena took hold of her arm.

"That side of the building is on fire," Selena said. "We need to get out a different way."

The three girls ran towards the stairs, Selena in the lead. Carol had worked late and decided to stay on a cot she kept in the office. She was at the front door, guiding the girls to safety.

As the first few girls exited the building, Maryam heard what sounded like fireworks. She figured that something must be exploding outside, perhaps a transformer or maybe the streetlights, but the sound was distinct. Time slowed down for her, and she stopped to watch the scene as if she were a casual observer.

She saw Delia and Emma push past Carol who grabbed at their arms, trying to pull them back. They disappeared outside and she heard the fireworks again. Carol moved in slow motion, her mouth wide open, but making no sound. More fireworks and Carol's body started a strange, jerky dance like a marionette being controlled by shaky hands, her arms and legs flailing, her torso pinned to the door. Tiny red streams sprayed out of small holes in her body. She collapsed to the ground. Her body bent sideways, her head flopping backwards so that she stared at the ceiling.

Maryam stood still, frozen by fear and instinct. She barely heard when Selena ordered her to follow and didn't move until her friend pulled on her arm.

Selena dragged Maryam and Kaliya through the kitchen and down a hall. At the end was a door which could only be opened from the inside. Selena cracked it open and peeked outside, looking up and down the alley behind the house. She opened it a little more and took one step but retrieved her foot back inside. Whispering something quietly to herself, she looked back at Maryam.

"I need you to listen carefully to me," Selena said.

Maryam nodded her head to let Selena know she was paying attention.

"I'm going to leave and run off to the left," Selena said. "I want you to count to ten and then take Kaliya and go off to the right. Run and don't look back. Do you hear me? Don't look back. At the end of the block, there's an abandoned office building. It's locked up so you can't get inside, but you can hide in the steps that lead to the basement. Just go down them. You'll see what I mean when you get there. Don't stay on the street. They'll be taking everyone they see. Do you understand? Everything? OK. Count to ten and go to your right."

"Yes." Maryam nodded. "To ten."

"Good," Selena said and slipped out the door.

Maryam waited inside and counted. When she reached ten, she took hold of Kaliya's hand and ran as fast as she could to her right. Over her shoulder, she heard shouting. Only once did she dare to look back. In the windows on the second and third floors of the house, shadows ran through the flames.

Reaching the office building, Maryam climbed down the stairs and found a little cubby dug into the cement where they could look out into the street without being seen. Across the street, a security vehicle stared back at her.

She watched and waited, listening to the roar of the fire, smelling the smoke as it drifted towards her hiding place. Through the haze, a pair of men appeared, bringing along with them a third person struggling to break free. Maryam's legs gave out, and she crashed to the ground.

Where is she?" A security officer's deep voice boomed over the commotion.

Maryam heard a loud crack and then a dull thud.

"Pick her up," the officer said.

In spite of her fear, Maryam stood up to watch.

"I'm going to ask you again," he said. "Where is she?"

"I told you. I don't know what you're talking about," a woman said.

Even in the darkness, Maryam recognized the jet-black hair and mocha skin. The officer took hold of her friend's wrist and wrapped her arm behind her back, placing his baton between the elbow and the shoulder and using it to increase the leverage on the bent arm. Selena let out a scream. The officer pulled back the sleeve on Selena's right arm, twisting it a few times to increase her pain, and pointed at the tattoo.

"She has one of these doesn't she?" he said. "Just like yours."

Selena whimpered but said nothing.

"I guess you're going to have to learn the hard way."

Two soldiers grabbed Selena's arms and held her upright while the officer went around the side of the truck. He returned with a club, a sabat which looked more like a thick cricket bat, and stood in front of Selena. Maryam stood there, powerless. Afraid to watch. Afraid to turn away. She pulled Kaliya into her chest and held her hands over her daughter's ears so Kaliya couldn't hear the wooden club as it struck over and over.

When he had finished, the officer leaned into the remnants of Selena's face.

"Just tell me what I want to know," he said, "and I'll end this."

Selena cried but still wouldn't give the officer the information he desired.

"Well. If that's the way you want it," he said.

The officer made a signal, and the two soldiers dragged Selena to the back of the truck. Just before she was thrown inside, she turned her head to look at the hidden cubby under the stairs. With her final gesture, she mouthed three words. Maryam was certain of what she said, but she didn't understand why. There was no doubt. "I love you." And then she was taken from Maryam's sight.

"Let's go."

A voice came from the top of the stairs.

"If you want to live, let's go."

Maryam knew the voice and hesitated. A large man ran down, picked up Kaliya, and grabbed Maryam's hand. She followed him up the stairs and down a side street away from the death. Four blocks away, they ducked into an abandoned building.

"You're safe here," Jason said. "You two can stay until morning. Sleep if you can, because you're going to have a long journey." He handed Maryam a slip of paper. "Find this place. Allison will be waiting for you."

Without another word, he ducked out the door. Maryam rocked Kaliya in her arms. The doubts echoed in her mind. *You made a mistake. What did you get yourself into? This is too big for you to handle. There's no way you'll get out of this.*

Maryam looked at the paper. She looked at Kaliya. In her mind, she saw herself in the mirror as Bale stroked her face.

203

Chapter 24

"I can keep this up as long as you want," he said.

The woman tied to the chair cowered in a vain attempt to protect herself from the next blow. It didn't come. She wasn't going to break and he knew it, not using that method anyway. He brushed the blonde hair out of her face. She winced as he touched the bruises that had formed over her eyes.

"Truth is. I don't want to hurt you."

He lied. It didn't matter to him whether the torture would get the result he wanted or not. His delight was in the pain he inflicted. Information was just the icing.

"Tell me. Who is this leader that you told me about?" he said. "The one who's going to come back and crush us all. What was his name again?" He moved behind the chair. "And how is he going to accomplish this? Where's his army? Where does he keep his supplies? How does he communicate? Tell me something."

"I don't know." Tears flowed out and stung her cheeks.

Her chair crashed to the ground, her head jerking back and hitting the floor. She struggled to breathe, to inhale and extend her miserable life. He calculated how much longer she could continue. Another four or five hours at least. He smiled.

"Look. I didn't want to do this, but you've left me no choice," he said.

He made a motion through the one-way mirror. A minute later, the door buzzed as the electronic lock disengaged. A soldier entered with a young girl, no more than twelve, certainly not a teenager yet, whose hands were bound behind her back. She tried to run over to the woman in the chair.

"Mommy!" she cried.

The soldier held her back as the girl kicked and struggled to break free. When he got the nod from his commander, he laid the girl on a metal table and strapped her down so her head hung off the edge. The commander set the woman upright so she could see what was about to happen. The soldier filled a pitcher with water and stretched a thin layer of film over the girl's mouth.

"That's enough. You're dismissed."

The commander began to protest. "She was ready to break. I just need another few minutes."

"Thank you, but this is my interrogation."

The commander left the room, shooting Ryah a look as he passed by.

Ryah knew the woman wasn't going to break, no matter what they did to her daughter. She was at the point where she would have said anything to get the abuse to stop, and he wouldn't have been able to tell if it was true or not. He knew the signs. This wasn't his first interrogation. Hardened criminals, foreign spies, detained soldiers, they all fell under his control at one time or another. His expertise, though, was with high value targets. His covert insertion and extraction team would capture the targets and bring them to secure locations for the interviews. If they had time, that is. Otherwise, Ryah would work his magic on site and dispose of them when he finished. It's not that he hadn't used the same techniques the commander had. It's just that he found they weren't necessarily effective. And he never used them on kids. Only on enemies of the state.

All the information Ryah had found concerning the assassination attempt pointed to the underground network of individuals called the Kingdom. There were a few loose threads he wanted to follow up on and had requested to stay in Italy for a while longer. His request was denied. Evan's admission along with other clues gave the Council enough to go on. For the last few months, the Council had engaged in a systematic round-up of anyone they thought might be connected to the network. Ryah had taken the lead role in the investigation, if that's what it could be called. *"More of a witch hunt,"* he thought, but he kept his mouth shut, telling his opinions to no one except for Rogan who he had kept as his number two.

Ryah untied the woman and her daughter. The girl ran to her mother, and they both cried as they hugged each other. Ryah signaled that it was time, and Rogan put his arm around the girl to take her outside. She fought as hard as a twelve-year-old could.

"It's OK, dear," Ryah said. "I'll take care of her."

His words seemed to bring comfort to the girl. She calmed down, gave her mom one last hug, and left the room with Rogan. Ryah went up to the woman and untied her.

"What's your name?" His voice was relaxed, sincere, like he really wanted to know.

"Priscilla," she said.

"Priscilla," Ryah said. "You're in a bad situation that you're not going to get out of. I think you know that."

Priscilla nodded her head.

"You know what they're doing to your people," he said as a half question. Ryah's stomach roiled at the thought.

"Yes," she said.

"You're going to end up in the same place. I would give you the opportunity to publicly reject the group, condemn them, but I don't think it would make a difference."

Fear rolled over her face for a moment, but then a sense of tranquility replaced it.

"I wouldn't renounce them regardless. Do what you want with me. If he allows it, so be it, but I will not deny them."

206

"I have no doubt of that," Ryah said. "I don't doubt your character or your determination for a moment." He paused. "But it's not you I'm thinking about." He waited for the realization to come over her. "It's your daughter that concerns me. What those animals outside will do to her ... I don't want to think about it. They'll make sure she lives through it, of course, but only so she can meet the same fate as you. I don't want to see that happen."

The woman moaned and whispered softly to herself but didn't answer Ryah.

"I know you've considered this," Ryah said. "Why would you let her go through that? Is this leader you're following worth it? What does he have to offer? I have to admit I don't get it."

"I can see that you don't," she whispered. The way she said it struck a nerve. There was no anger. It was more pity, compassion.

"No. No I don't understand at all," Ryah admitted. "Especially why you're allowing your daughter to go through this." He waited for a moment. "That's why I'm here. To offer you a deal." He stared at her downturned face. "Tell me something I want to know, and I'll make sure your daughter goes free."

Priscilla looked into Ryah's eyes. If he was lying, she couldn't tell. She lowered her head and spoke to him.

"What do you want to know?" she asked.

"I want to know who the leader is," he said. "Not the local guy, but the one calling the shots."

"He goes by many names," she said.

"Like what?" he asked.

"The One."

"You're going to have to tell me something I don't already know," Ryah said. "If you want your girl to be OK."

"That's what we call him."

"Have you ever met him?" he asked. "Do you know where he stays?"

"No. I haven't met him, and he doesn't have a home when he's here. He just travels around staying with different people. The same in every country he visits."

Ryah was going to ask if she could be more specific, but he knew the answer to that. He decided to change the line of questioning.

"How long have you belonged to the … what do you call yourselves again?" he said.

"Some people call us the Kingdom," she said.

"Right, right. The Kingdom."

"But that's kind of a mistake," she said.

"How so?" Ryah asked.

"There's not a kingdom," she said.

"What do you mean?"

"There are two kingdoms. We are one and they are the other."

"Who are they?" Ryah asked. "Who is the other? Russia? China?"

The woman smiled for the first time. "No, my dear man. You have no idea, do you?" She looked at Ryah's face and saw something that intrigued her. Her eyes narrowed and her brow furrowed. "Or do you?"

The way she asked that unsettled Ryah. They stared at each other for a minute until Priscilla lowered her gaze.

"I'm ready to go now," she said.

"I'm afraid you're not getting out of here," Ryah said.

"I know. I mean, I'm ready to go."

Ryah understood and realized he wouldn't be getting any more information out of her. The piece about the two kingdoms was new, though. The first real new thing since Italy. He looked up and signaled at the camera, and two soldiers entered to take Priscilla away. Ryah knew he wouldn't see her again. No one who entered that room was seen again, but he was determined to make an exception. Ryah called in the commander who had been watching the interrogation in an adjacent room.

"Let the girl go," Ryah said. "She doesn't know anything."

"What do you mean, let her go?" the commander asked.

"I promised the mother if she gave me something that I'd let her daughter go," Ryah said.

The commander looked at Ryah to see if he was serious. "I thought you were just saying that to get her to speak," he said. "That's certainly what I would do." He laughed at his own cunning.

"Do as I say," Ryah ordered.

"But ...." The commander stopped when he saw the look in his eyes. "Yes, sir. I will have to report this to the Council, you know."

"By all means," Ryah said. "It will be in my official report as well. Rogan, make sure the girl gets to her grandparents. I hear they're waiting somewhere upstairs. Meet me in my office when you're done."

Rogan nodded. The commander fumed, swearing under his breath that he would make Ryah pay.

Chapter 25

Ryah returned to his office and waited for Rogan to meet him there. A knock on the door let Ryah know Rogan had returned.

"Everything go OK?" Ryah asked.

"As well as could be expected under the circumstances," Rogan said. He looked around the room as if he was searching for something suspicious. "Can I still speak freely?" he asked.

It wasn't a question of what he could say to Ryah but whether or not the Council had fixed the camera in his office yet.

"By all means," Ryah answered, letting him know they were still unmonitored. It was the only reason he kept that old dingy office even after being offered a corner room with a window. Administrator Klins thought it a bit strange until Ryah told him that a luxury office would be a distraction and that he preferred the isolation because it helped him focus.

"That was interesting," Rogan said. "The part about the second kingdom."

Ryah nodded his head. "Finally, a different lead to pursue. All we've been doing is chasing down people that might have some tenuous connection with that group, that movement. Whatever you want to call it. Every once in a while, we actually find someone who does belong. Not that it matters to the Council. If you're accused, you're guilty." He looked over at Rogan. "You can tell pretty quickly who's a part and who's not."

"Yep," Rogan said.

"The ones who give it up right away are not," Ryah said. "They think they'll find mercy somehow. I guess they do, if you consider a bullet to the head merciful."

Rogan pondered the comment but let Ryah continue.

"I wonder what Lucio thinks about all this," Ryah said. "Whenever I bring up the subject of the Kingdom, he gets upset. About what, I can't tell. It might be he thinks it's a dead end, but I could be way off base. Truth is, I can't get a feel for the man."

"You keep in touch with Romijn?" Rogan asked.

"Once a week, with Klins' permission of course," Ryah said. "To keep him informed. Klins says he may lend us out to Lucio again. Sooner than later, so be prepared for another short notice trip."

Rogan sat silently and stared at the wall in front of him.

"What are you thinking?" Ryah asked.

Rogan scrunched up his face before responding. "I'm not sure we're going after the right people," he said. "Think about it. Who's been accused? Women. Children. A couple of old men. I mean there's been others, but none of them strikes me as the revolutionary type. I think they're involved somehow, but they're the fringe. The grunts that do the bidding of the leaders, to throw us off track to protect the main guys. We haven't been able to crack their core, to see their structure or who's calling the shots. Any of that. We don't have any idea of their purpose or their goals. What's their end game? What's their cause? What are they trying to accomplish?"

"Yeah," Ryah said but didn't elaborate. He looked at his comm. A grunt slipped out. "It's time to get going. It's Friday and they're going to get started in about an hour and a half. This is one part of the assignment that I could do without."

Rogan nodded in agreement.

"You know you don't have to be there," Ryah said.

211

"Nor do I want to," Rogan said, "but where my commanding officer goes, I go. Even to this."

It took them thirty minutes to get to the stadium on the other side of the Carmel River. Another forty-five and they were inside. The traffic was always terrible on these days. More people wanted to go to these events than any other ones. The scalpers lined up outside and had no problem selling their tickets for double the face value. Front row seats would go for as much as five-thousand, and that was for a regular one of these. Today, the Council had promised something special.

Ryah and Rogan entered the VIP box and found their seats a few rows behind Administrator Klins. They looked around at the tens of thousands of people in the stadium. Camera crews were stationed all around to make sure the live broadcast covered every angle and so that the hundreds of millions of worldwide viewers wound not miss a moment of the action. The stands were electric. Vendors walked up and down the aisles, hawking food, alcohol, t-shirts, and other memorabilia. Security details broke up fights, the guilty parties getting tased and thrown down the steps. Each time this happened, a roar of excitement would go up from the crowd. A preview to the main attraction.

Klins' arrival would mean the start of the show as he would call it. He was the highest-ranking official that would come on a regular basis. It was part of his responsibility. On occasion, the High Administrator would show up, but the lone empty seat in the front row of the box let Ryah know it would only be Administrator Klins today.

Ryah took a brief look at the setting sun. It had been a gorgeous day and promised to be a beautiful night, so they had left the roof open.

"A few more minutes," he thought. *"They like to wait until twilight to get started."*

As the last rays of light disappeared, a hush fell over the crowd. They waited for a minute. Then two. Then a few more. The anticipation building with each passing moment. Finally, a single spotlight turned on, directed at the VIP box. The stadium erupted as Administrator Klins made his way to his seat. He stopped at a podium on the right end of the row and tested the microphone.

"Ladies and gentlemen," he said. "Welcome to New Carmel Stadium, and welcome to the Friday night executions!"

The cheers were deafening. People stomped on the cement floors, their feet alternating over and over, until it sounded like thunder. Klins held up his hand and the tumult died down.

"Tonight, you will be witnesses to what happens when you commit treason against the United States," Klins said. "You will testify to your friends and neighbors, letting them know the horror that awaits those who dare challenge the legitimate authority of the Council. You will see with your own eyes what befalls those who want to disrupt orderly rule in order to bring chaos and destruction to our nation. Who follow 'The One' and not the High Administrator. Let the treacherous know we will find them, whether they owe allegiance to a kingdom or to a foreign land. We will find them. And this … this will be their fate."

In the darkness, ten people had been led into the arena. Upon hearing Klins' last word, the floor of the stadium flooded with light. Blood curdling screams, threats, and curses rained down on the people in the middle. Executioners dressed in long, black gowns strode up behind two of the prisoners and forced them to lie on their stomachs with their hands tied behind their backs. The cameras zoomed in on the death squad with their knives in hand as they slashed the throats of the condemned. When they had finished, the cameras turned their attention to the next three prisoners. One corner of each screen remained dedicated to the first two so the crowd could watch their death throes.

A son, a mother, and a father were next, going in that order so the man would have to watch his family die. Ryah shut his eyes. He didn't want to see anymore. Many people had died in front of his eyes. But in war, it was different. This was gratuitous, meant to dissuade others from following their example, but it seemed less of a deterrent than a way for the thirsty to satisfy their bloodlust. When he saw the apparatus in front of them, he knew how they would die, long before the screams began. He would have covered his ears as well, but if he had, he would have shared the fate of those below.

The first two had already died when Ryah opened his eyes. There was no need to execute the man whose heart gave out long before they finished with his wife. A chorus of boos cascaded down from the stands. They wouldn't be disappointed for long.

The cameras turned their attention to a statue in the middle of the arena. Towering over the field, it had the face and wings of an eagle and the body of a man with its arms stretched out as if it were waiting to receive a gift. The statue was made of brass, hollowed out with a hole in the chest at a height slightly below the outstretched arms, which sloped gently down towards the hole. Shadows made by flames could be seen flickering through the opening.

As the crowd watched in hushed anticipation, a single drum started to sound. It was soon accompanied by another and another until the arena filled with a thunderous pounding, drowning out all other sounds, constraining the hearts of the listeners to beat along with it in a rapturous orgy of rhythm and ecstasy.

When the perverse symphony reached its climax, the next five prisoners, chained at the wrists and ankles, marched towards the statue, guarded by two men on either side. One at a time, the people, beaten so badly they could barely remain upright, walked up a set of stairs that led to the arms of the statue. The four guards lifted the condemned person onto the outstretched arms and pushed him towards the hole and the fire which waited inside. Five times, the violent sacrifice repeated as the drums continued their cruel cacophony and the crowd swayed and pulsated with the beat.

Administrator Klins held up his hand one more time, and the drumming ceased. He gave another speech which lasted over ten minutes, but Ryah no longer paid attention. His head swam as his stomach churned. His only hope was that he would get out of there without throwing up. When Klins finished, he turned back and motioned for Ryah and Rogan to follow him while the soldiers escorted the next set of prisoners onto the stage. Outside on the private mezzanine, Klins pulled Ryah and Rogan aside.

"Any new information?" he asked them.

"We think we might have a lead," Ryah said, thankful to be out of the arena and that he hadn't eaten dinner. "But I don't know if it will pan out." He paused. "Administrator Klins, I'm not sure we're on the correct path." He didn't elaborate. "And I'm unsure why we're still pursuing it anyway. This really isn't our problem. What do we care if the Russians, Chinese, and UN loyalists destroy each other?"

Klins nodded his head in agreement. "True, Ryah. The issue is the United States is rumored to be behind this group, the Kingdom. We have to show the world, unequivocally, that we are not allied with them. If not, the Russians and or the Chinese might decide that we're the true enemy and come after us. Trust me, we're preparing for the eventuality, but the goal for now is prevention. Let them keep their attention on each other. Destroy each other

215

as you said." He smiled. "Just keep me apprised of what you find. And let Romijn know if you learn anything. He says he'll be in town soon to discuss the situation. Remarkable, he's alive, don't you think?"

"Yes, sir," Ryah said.

"Well, my part here is done," Klins said. "I'm going back to the Council for a meeting. Feel free to stay or take off. It's up to you."

Klins walked off with his contingent of guards and assistants, and Ryah turned to Rogan.

"Feel like getting something to eat?" Ryah asked.

"Thought you'd want to go back and sit down," Rogan said.

"Not my thing," Ryah said.

Rogan smiled and followed Ryah downstairs to where their motorcycles waited. They rode away from the stadium, looking for a restaurant far enough from the arena so they wouldn't be caught in the exiting traffic. After driving around for ten minutes without finding a place that interested them, they decided to head north of the city where Ryah lived.

Rogan was the first to notice.

"Hey, Ryah," he said through the comm connected in his helmet. "I think we're being followed again."

"Who?"

"You see that car, the black sedan with the tinted windows. They've been trading places with a tan sports car for the last couple of miles. Typical recon. They probably have another vehicle or two, but I haven't been able to make them yet."

Ryah looked at the sedan in his mirror. "Yeah. Got 'em. Any idea who they are?"

"Not a clue," Rogan said.

"Let them follow us," Ryah said. "Just watch your back."

"Roger that," Rogan said.

A half mile from Ryah's place, they stopped at a steak house. They found a seat near the front window, so they could be seen and so they could see as well.

"Up the road a hundred meters," Ryah indicated with a subtle shift of his head while looking out the window through the corner of his eye. "Is that the tan car?"

Rogan used the reflection off a polished, oversized steak knife. "Yep. That's it."

"I think I found a van that's with them," Ryah said. "Can't see any drivers or passengers, though. Bet they're trying to get ears on us. Make sure to watch everyone that enters."

"Whoever they are, they better not mess with my steak," Rogan said in such a way that Ryah couldn't tell if he was joking.

Ryah tried to relax but couldn't. He had the uncomfortable feeling he was being watched. And not by the people outside.

Thirty minutes and two beers later, the steaks came. Ribeyes somewhere between medium and medium rare, a pat of butter with salt and pepper the only seasonings. They ate and talked. Joking mainly. Tall tales of their respective military exploits. Each one trying to outdo the other. When Ryah finished, he wiped his knife clean – an unconscious habit he picked up in the field – and set it down on the table. He never looked at the knife again. If he had, he might have seen the reflection in it. The reflection of a man, but not really a man. The formless figure of a shadow hovering overhead and observing his every move.

Chapter 26

"One more and I'm out of here," Ryah said.

"Sounds good. I'll wait until you leave. See if anyone follows you," Rogan replied.

Ryah ordered a final beer, gulped it down, and left the steak house just after 11:00. His head began to buzz, and he regretted having that last round. Even though he was only a minute from his apartment, he decided to take the circuitous route in order to throw anyone that might be following him off his track. After making several stops and sneaking through a couple pedestrian alleyways, he was sure he had lost his tail, and he arrived home just after midnight. Rogan sent him a message saying that the van had remained in place but the tan car had gone after him only to return fifteen minutes later, convincing Ryah that the surveillance team, whoever they were, hadn't followed him home.

A quick shower and he was under the covers. His mind flashed back to the events of the day. A meeting with Representative Jherel. Working in his office with Rogan. Priscilla and her daughter. He skipped over his time in the stadium, preferring not to see those images again. The steak house and the ride home. Not an atypical day other than, perhaps, the surveillance teams, which were becoming more frequent or more obvious. Rogan had spotted the team first, so Ryah had to buy dinner. That was their deal. It didn't really matter, though. Since they were on call twenty-four seven, everything Ryah ate got charged to the Council. Drinks too. Pretty much anything else he felt like putting on their tab, not that he had passed on this tidbit of information to Rogan. The first month, the accountants called Ryah into their office to explain the more 'unusual' charges, but one message from an annoyed Administrator Klins changed their attitude. After that, they paid Ryah's bills without asking any questions.

Ryah looked at the clock. 12:30. His head hurt a little but not enough to keep him from falling asleep. It was a restful sleep, washing over him and refreshing him, healing his body and his spirit.

A nudge on his shoulder woke Ryah.

"Get up, Ryah. It's time for you to see."

His body jolted upright. He looked around the room to find who had shaken him. From beneath the door, he observed shadows passing back and forth, illuminated by the faint light from the other side. Voices blended together into a whirlwind, indistinguishable from the others, flowing through the walls and around him.

Ryah felt his body being lifted out of bed and his feet set on the floor. He moved straight ahead, pushed towards the other room by an unseen hand. The door didn't open for him, but he found himself on the other side anyway, staring down a hallway that was at least a quarter mile long with the width of a two-lane road. On the left side of the hall hung a series of mirrors with people in front of all of them except for the last one. Some faced their mirrors. Others looked away, none of them aware of Ryah's presence.

He wandered down the hall, now under his own power, curious as to who these people were. In front of the first mirror, a woman sat in a chair and stroked her curly, auburn hair. The collar on her shirt hung low so that the top part of her chest was bare except for a pendant inlaid with diamonds and emeralds held by a gold choker. She laid the brush down beside a photo of a blond man who had his arm wrapped around her. Picking up three pairs of diamond

219

studs, she inserted them into the holes that climbed up the outside of her ears.

As Ryah passed behind the woman, he stopped to look at her reflection. Her cheeks, covered with just enough blush to hide the imperfections on the surface, glowed a warm crimson which accentuated the deep ruby red of her lips. Her eyes were soft, seductive, yearning for the encounter that was soon to come.

She took hold of the brush again and began to run it back over her head, pausing on occasion to admire herself in the mirror, unaware that with each stroke a pile of hair had begun to build up on the floor around her. Ryah watched as she repeated the movement over and over, patches of her scalp starting to show and the mound of hair growing larger. He took his eyes off the reflection for a moment and looked directly at her. Her brown hair hung off her head in long, wavy strands as if nothing had happened. When he looked back in the mirror, her head was bare, the delusion broken for him but not for her.

Ryah moved in front of the woman and stared into her eyes. He could see the image in the mirror reflected in her irises, showing her as he first found her, smiling, beautiful, the long, brown curls hanging down and bouncing as she twisted her head back and forth to admire herself. As he continued to observe, her skin began to stretch. It was subtle, barely noticeable. Ryah stooped down to take a closer look. Beneath the exterior, he saw it. Another face looking back at him, hidden just beneath the surface. A dark, nearly formless figure looking out through the woman's face had replaced her eyes with its own.

He heard a noise as a door in the hall opened behind him. A man with dark hair ran up to the woman and wrapped his arms around her as she laughed in delight. The man bent over to kiss her. She jumped up and melted in his embrace, neither of them taking notice of the woman's glory that lay strewn across the floor.

Ryah continued down the corridor, taking no notice of the next two people. He hesitated as he came upon the third one, a man dressed in gray-blue fatigues, his collar bearing the insignia of a captain in the infantry. Ribbons adorned his breast pocket and the Medal of Honor hung around his neck. Ryah recognized him the moment he laid eyes on him. Anyone in the United States would have.

The voice spoke again to Ryah.

"See what he sees."

Ryah peered into the mirror. A chaotic night scene stared back, the dark pierced by flares as they made their slow descent to earth. The momentary light shined on bodies surrounding the captain. Charred remains. Shattered arms and legs. Pleas for mercy, cries to be healed poured out from the wounded, but none would come.

In the soft flicker of a flare, the captain checked his weapon for the last time. One partial magazine remained. He surveyed what he could of the scene. Boxed in with his back to the raging river, the bridge behind him lay in pieces, removing any chance of escape. A full regiment bore down on the remnant of his company, the last hope of a country unable to survive another loss on the battlefield.

"Hold the line. All is lost if you don't hold the line." The desperate command echoed in his mind. On him rested the fate of the nation.

The captain barked out orders, but no one heard him or no one had the will to fight any longer. Turning to his company, he forced them out of their stupor and compelled them to follow as he raced across the plain to the death that awaited. But it was not death that he found. Triumph instead. Glory. A hundred men fighting with the fury of a thousand overpowered the enemy which surrounded them, inspiring the nation to believe that victory was possible.

In the mirror, nighttime turned to day. Confetti fell down all around a convertible in which the captain rode. Throngs of people shoved each other to get to the front of the sidewalk so they could see the captain as he drove by and offer him praise. Patriotic songs blared from each building he passed. All this in his honor. The one who saved his country as the world watched. The one who changed the course of history. The hero of a nation.

The mirror fogged over and erased the scene of the parade. Ryah looked back at the captain whose face beamed with pride.

"Now see, Ryah," the voice said.

Returning his gaze to the mirror, Ryah found himself staring at a much younger man, wearing a crooked smile and the bars of a lieutenant. He was with three other men on the edge of a field surrounded by oak and beech trees as night began to fall. Movement out of the corner of Ryah's eye caught his attention. A young girl with blonde hair and green eyes, no more than six years old, danced around the outside of a house while her mother watched, both unaware of the four men who spied on them in the twilight.

"I'm going to get a drink, Cate," Ryah heard the woman say as she disappeared inside.

The lieutenant made his move, sneaking up behind the girl and placing his hand over her mouth so she couldn't scream. He dragged her off to the woods, where the sounds of depravity were muffled by the impotent trees that stood guard, powerless to come to her aid. In the background, Ryah heard the woman calling for the girl, her voice becoming more frantic each time her daughter didn't answer. She turned towards the rumble of a motor and ran in that direction. A doll lay on the ground beside the fresh tire tracks that headed off the farm.

Ryah looked away from the mirror. A sword swept through the air and cut off the captain's head. In its place grew two more. One laughing, proud, sure. The other grim, melancholy.

Ryah moved down the hall. Up ahead was another person he recognized. He got closer, not sure if it was true. He had seen the man only once, on a transit ride that ended with the man in a bloody mess, he and his two partners more dead than alive, the work of Ryah's own hands. Ryah thought of the woman and the little girl who had been the victims of this monster that disgraced his presence now. He approached the worthless creature that knelt on the ground in front of the mirror to see what illusion clouded its vile mind.

The man looked at his reflection, groaning in agony and tearing at tumors that sprouted out of his skin. Each time he ripped one off, another would replace it, larger, more grotesque, growing from the death which reigned inside him. He looked at his face and dipped his head in shame. Ryah walked around in front and reached down to take hold of the man's chin. The man raised his head. His face was dark. Thick petals, like scales, covered his lifeless eyes. A long, slender tongue darted in and out of his mouth.

Ryah dropped the man's head and stood back. As he did, a flash of lightning struck the man, who fell to the ground. A terrible scream came from deep inside. His body shook and trembled as foam built up around his lips. Darkness overtook him, except that the darkness came from within, flowing out his mouth and taking shape above his head. Ryah protected his ears from the shadow's final violent screech before it floated off, disappearing into the ceiling.

A gentle wind started to blow and swirled around the man lying on the ground. Ryah saw the wind enter the man's mouth as if it were trying to resuscitate him. It lifted the man up and stood him on his feet. When Ryah looked in the mirror again, the man was staring back, his face and body restored to normal.

"*No, not normal*," Ryah thought. "*Better. Perfect almost.*"

Ryah continued down the corridor, passing by the rest of the people, until he arrived at the last mirror, the only one in the entire hall which stood unoccupied. Placing himself in front, he looked at the reflection, but there was no trace of his image. Only the likeness of the wall behind him.

Chapter 27

The wall opened up, exposing the world outside. The same force, which had lifted him out of bed, picked him up again and set him down in the middle of a city with cobblestone streets. Buildings made of brick that looked like they would have been at home in the ancient world rose up high on either side of the road so that Ryah could only see the path which lay directly in front of him. It was hot and dusty. His mouth was dry, and he licked his lips to moisten them a little. From up ahead, an uproar caught his attention. Curious, he headed towards the commotion.

As he walked down the narrow road, a few people passed him going in the opposite direction. They looked straight ahead with looks of joy on their faces as if a great treasure waited for them at the end of the road. The way was wide enough for no more than two people to walk shoulder to shoulder, so when a pair of men came towards Ryah, he leaned against a wall to let them pass.

"We found it," Ryah heard one man say.

"I didn't think we would," the other one said, laughing and hugging his companion. He turned to Ryah and smiled at him. "Friend, you're going the wrong way. We've finally found the way out. Come with us. We'll show you."

Ryah ignored them and kept moving towards the excitement which lay just up ahead.

The narrow path opened into a giant square, more than a kilometer on each side, surrounded by towering walls. At each corner, a ten-lane road carried thousands of people, all on foot, flowing into the plaza. No one left the square, not that Ryah could tell anyway, and he wondered how so many people could fit, especially with the long lines of humanity that kept pouring in. At the edges of the square, a few people stumbled around, feeling their way along the fortifications as if they were trying to find a door. Ryah turned to look back where he had come from, but everything was obscured, almost like a thick, black veil lay behind him, preventing him from seeing the exit. He began to panic and shouted into the darkness. An emaciated, balding man with a thin moustache and a noticeable limp took hold of Ryah's arm.

"Don't worry. I'll take you up front," he said.

Ryah didn't want to go to the front. He didn't even know what the front was. He only wanted to get away from this place. He tried to escape from the man's grasp, but the man was much stronger than he appeared, dragging Ryah through the gauntlet of people until he reached a platform in the middle of the square.

"Here you go," the man said. "Just be patient and wait your turn. It'll come soon."

With that, the man vanished into the ever-increasing crowd which pressed down on Ryah, hemming him in on every side. He struggled to breathe. The swarm of humanity crushed his lungs. The small gasps of hot, stagnant air he could sip were not enough to sustain him. He buried his face in his hands to stave off the nausea and covered his ears at the same time to silence the clamor. All the while, the crowd pushed him forward, step by step, towards a set of stairs on the left side of the platform. Through the crowd, he saw snippets of the scene around him and heard fragments of the conversations on the stage but couldn't tell what was going on.

Ryah felt a tap on his shoulder and turned around.

"How long you been here?" a man with brown hair asked Ryah. He didn't give Ryah a chance to answer. "I've been waiting for the longest time. I came from the other side of the world, figuratively speaking." He smiled at Ryah as if they were sharing an inside joke. "I kept hearing about this place, how great it was. I had to get here as soon as I could. They weren't kidding. Man. Look around here. I'd say they undersold it. Did you see the people coming out of the line? No? You've got to go see them. I'm going to have that exact same look on my face after I cross the stage. This is going to be incredible. And after they find out what I'm selling them." He laughed out loud. "I'm getting the best of this deal. No doubt about it. No one can outsmart this guy," he said as he pointed at himself with both thumbs.

Ryah cut him off. "Where exactly am I? And what are you selling?" he asked.

The man, who carried nothing with him, gave Ryah a strange stare but ignored the questions, continuing on with his own.

"How much are you going to ask for?" he asked Ryah. "I'm going to hold out. They always offer you something that sounds great, but they're trying to undercut you. Lowball you. They're not going to do that to me. No way. I'm going to make them pay me a fair price. You watch. In fact, let me cut in front of you. I'll show you how to do it right. Just watch what I do and follow my lead."

He didn't give Ryah a choice but stepped in front of him, proceeding to tap on the shoulder of the person in front and start his spiel over again.

The line of people marched forward. Ryah looked around for a gap in the crowd, for any chance to get out of his predicament, but there was none. The man with brown hair, who had been unable to move up any more spaces, turned back towards him.

"Last chance," he said. "Once you pass that post right there, there's no turning back." He laughed again. "Of course, you're not going back. No one makes that choice." He stopped speaking and had a look of wonder on his face.

227

"Actually, I think I heard a story of one person who didn't cross the stage. They offered him everything. The world, in fact. He turned it down flat. I'd hate to see what happened to him. They don't like that." He nodded his head in agreement with himself. "Yeah, don't cross the line when you're bargaining with them. You get too greedy and you'll get nothing." He thought a little more. "Not sure if I believe that story, though. Always seemed like a fairy tale to me."

It felt like hours before Ryah got close to the steps leading to the stage. The more the man in front of him described what was about to happen, the more curious Ryah became, the interest increased by not being able to see onto the platform because of its height above the ground. Every few minutes he heard a name called, then a discussion followed by what sounded like a hammer striking wood. Ryah had long ago passed the 'post of no return' as he had begun to call it but no longer cared whether it had any significance or not. The desire to see what awaited overpowered any sense of fear or awareness of danger.

Finally. Only three people before Ryah got his turn. The man in front of him was anxious, giddy, like a kid on his birthday waiting to open his presents. Ryah climbed the stairs. When he reached the sixth step, he could see, for the first time, the action on the stage. In the middle, a man in a black robe and a black hood stood at a podium. Behind him sat another man, dressed in the same manner, sitting at a desk with a large book in front of him. An extremely beautiful woman stood by the man at the podium and looked all around her, smiling but clearly a little nervous. Ryah strained to see the crowd, but lights shining down from some scaffolding on the far side prevented him from seeing beyond the edge of the platform.

The man in the black hood turned towards Ryah. There was no face underneath the dark robes, none that Ryah could see anyway, and a cold shiver raced through his body.

228

The man stretched out his hands to give a gift to the woman. She reached out to accept his offer and turned to walk off the stage. He looked at her and noticed a change. Her features were still beautiful, but her skin had become translucent. As Ryah stared, he saw a new face just below the surface begin to emerge.

The sound of a gavel hitting the podium rang out, followed by complete silence, breaking Ryah's concentration. He looked back at the woman one last time and noticed that her appearance had returned to normal. The man in front turned around and mouthed something at Ryah. Again, the man said something. Ryah reached up and rubbed his ears. The man jabbered on, his mouth opening and closing, a look of extreme excitement in his eyes, but Ryah couldn't hear a word the man was saying. Ryah spoke back to him, but no sound came out. He yelled. But there was nothing. No noise, no clamor. Nothing. He had fallen completely deaf.

Ryah turned back to the stage. The man behind the desk wrote in his book as the next person moved into position by the podium. Images from beyond the edge of the stage began to emerge. Figures, forms cloaked in shadows. Human-like but somehow different, each of them holding something in their outstretched hands. The person looked back and forth, listening to offers that Ryah couldn't hear. After deliberating for a few minutes, the person pointed to his right. The man in black reached into the crowd and took hold of an envelope. He opened it and dumped the contents into the person's hands. Jewels of every kind spilled all over the stage. The person dove onto the floor and scooped them up to put them back into the envelope. The man in black made a gesture at the person, who acknowledged him with a nod of the head. The gavel came down onto the podium but made no sound. The man behind the desk scribbled in his book as the recipient of the gift limped off the stage. Ryah looked down at the recipient's feet. A chain had been fastened around one leg, the other end of the chain extending into the crowd and held onto by the one who offered the riches.

Only one more person before Ryah got his turn. The excitable, talkative man ran onto the stage. Pointing. Jumping up and down. He lasted less than a minute.

"*So much for holding out,*" Ryah thought.

His prize was brought to him. Young, innocent, naked. Right there on the platform in front of everyone, the man took what was given him. When he had finished, he discarded the boy, and another one was brought as a replacement for later use. They turned to walk off the stage together, but the man stumbled and fell. As he rose to his feet, he turned towards Ryah. The man was still smiling as a thin, murky film began to grow over his eyes. He tripped again and stretched out his hand so the boy could help him off the stage. A dark, amorphous figure reached back and lifted the man up, leading him off into the shadows on the right, the man still grinning from ear to ear.

The gavel struck and Ryah's hearing was restored as quickly as it had been removed. A thin line now was all that separated him from the stage. His turn had come, and he had a choice to make. Had he really passed the point of no return, or was this line the true one? A deep, ominous voice spoke up and echoed in his ears.

"Ryah Olmen."

The man in black at the podium called out to him.

He sat up in his bed and looked around the dimly lit room. Had he dreamt it? It had felt so real. In his heart, though, he was glad it had been a dream. "But what would I have sold myself for?" he thought. Ryah lay back down and tried to go to sleep, hoping to see how the story would end.

It was cool. Not the kind of cool where a jacket was needed, and Ryah wished he had at least brought a sweater. He stood on the side of a mountain which overlooked a large valley cut in two by a river. In the distance, the lights from a city at the top of a hill shone into the darkness, barely visible but growing brighter. Ryah looked into the sky. The moon was not out, and there were no stars whatsoever. It wasn't cloudy. They just weren't shining on this night. In the river basin, a tiny dot sprung up against the backdrop of the city on the hill.

As Ryah watched, the dot grew, expanding until it filled the entire valley. Another city had sprung up before his eyes. It was great in size and strength, but no light emanated from it, completely dark as if in a blackout. The city was rectangular in shape and was surrounded by high walls with one gate at each corner. The gate closest to Ryah began to open and shut as if it were a mouth, and he realized that it was speaking. He listened, intent on hearing its words. It took a while, but the sound from the city made its way across the plain, arriving like a peal of thunder to where Ryah stood. Profane boasts and curses resounded in his ears. The promise of total destruction to its most hated of enemies. Moments later, a flood of men in armored vehicles poured out of the mouth and flew up the hill towards their goal, driving around the city of light looking for a weak point in the wall.

A sudden gale blew through the valley and up the slope of the mountain. Ryah squinted and leaned into the current as it buffeted against him, trying not to be swept away, but to no avail. Losing his footing, the wind carried him into the sky and held him aloft, far above the earth and the battle that raged below. He watched as the wall of the city on the hill was torn down, brick by brick. Men, women, and children ran out to escape the onslaught, only to be caught by soldiers lying in ambush and executed where they stood.

The sound of hooves thundering through the sky startled Ryah. He looked up and saw two massive armies riding towards each other at top speed with him in the middle of their path. He tried to run, but his feet fluttered helplessly in the air. He watched and waited, wide-eyed in terror. Powerless to move, unable to save himself.

The riders came closer and closer until he could see the horses' faces, their eyes glowing red with hate. He felt the air shake around him and his heart fell.

"Save me," he cried to no one in particular.

It was too late. They were on him now, no more than a hundred feet before he they would trample him. He shut his eyes and prepared to accept his fate.

"Make your choice, Ryah," the voice said.

Ryah kept his eyes closed, but he knew it was Guriel. Like everything else Guriel had told him, this was wrapped in a mystery that he was only now realizing he needed to decipher. A sense of peace washed over Ryah and he no longer feared. If Guriel was indeed here, he would be OK.

"If I'm wrong," he said, "this is gonna hurt."

Chapter 28

Ryah stared at the wall across from his bed. The dreams had troubled him before, but they had always been dreams. This one seemed real, like someone was speaking to him, trying to get him to understand a deeper truth in a language that he could understand.

"Make your choice."

That was the last thing he remembered, and there it remained in his mind.

The bedroom was dark save for the light peeking through the blinds. He saw the outlines of feet at the foot of his bed and wiggled his toes to make sure they were his. In his mind, he replayed the dream and found he could recall a significant portion of it. Some of the people he saw intrigued him more than others, especially the two that addressed him as he entered the city square. And the warriors in the sky. What was their significance? He had seen the battle in which General Chael had crushed his opponent. He had seen the fate of the vanquished, but there they were again, riding through the night sky and fighting as if they had been victorious. What did this have to do with Russia and China and Lucio and this mysterious group he had been investigating?

"It must be my subconscious speaking to me," Ryah thought. *"Some clue that I've seen or heard but don't recognize, and my brain has made up this world of flying horsemen and shadows and who knows what else to explain it to me. I read about this once in an article. Or was it a book? 'A psychological phenomenon where your mind speaks in symbols.' I remember that phrase exactly. But what is my mind trying to tell me?"*

Ryah pondered the mystery for over an hour, but a troubling suspicion kept interrupting his deliberations. "What if it *is* real?" Every time the thought entered his mind, he would push it down and dismiss it as the talk of a man losing his sanity.

"*They're just dreams,*" Ryah thought.

"*But what about Rome? I was awake when I saw that,*" his mind countered.

"*Hallucinations. From sleep deprivation I'm sure. And why is it that I am the only one who seems to be able to see these things? No. They don't exist.*"

Ryah made up his mind and looked at the clock. 4:12 am. A few hours of sleep would do him good. He pulled the blanket over his shoulders as he lay on his back looking at the ceiling. The words spoken by Guriel echoed around the room as if the walls were whispering to him.

"*Guriel.*"

If only he existed.

"*If Guriel was here, I could ask him what was going on,*" Ryah thought.

"Guriel," Ryah said out loud. The name rolled off his tongue and left a bittersweet taste in his mouth.

"Yes, Ryah."

The blanket got tangled in Ryah's legs in his haste to jump out of bed. He felt himself tumbling face first towards a pair of shoes he had left by the bedside, and he stretched out his arms to break his fall. His hands slid as they hit the floor, and his shoulder took a sharp jolt as the rest of his body came crashing down. He stumbled to one knee and checked to see if he was OK.

"Get your clothes on. It's time for you to go."

The pain had made him forget for a moment the reason he had fallen, but the sound of the voice brought him back. In the corner of the room, he stood. Dressed all in white like the first time Ryah saw him. Ryah felt himself being lifted up and placed on his feet.

"Go where?" Ryah asked.

Before he could finish asking his question, the vision disappeared, leaving Ryah alone in his room. He rubbed his eyes trying to determine if what he saw was real or just another illusion.

There was no point trying to sleep now, so he dressed himself and headed out the front door not really sure where to go. A cool breeze swept down the street and stirred up some leaves which lay in the gutter. Ryah watched as a single leaf twirled around, caught in an updraft, and floated through the air before landing on a windowsill. He wrapped his jacket tight against his chest and held it shut with one hand, his other hand remaining in his pocket to keep it warm. The wind picked up its pace as if it was determined to oppose his progress, so when the lights from an all-night café showed themselves, he decided to step inside for a cup of coffee and to wait out the brewing storm.

Inside he found three people, not counting the cook and the waitress. Two burly, hardened men sat at the counter, eating their meals before they made their way to their early shifts.

"Construction workers, probably," Ryah thought since they were the type he encountered whenever he made it here this early.

A woman was seated by herself at a table in the corner and watched with keen interest as Ryah made his way to the front. Ryah noticed the woman scrutinizing him, wary, almost afraid.

"*Don't worry,*" Ryah thought. "*I'm not going to hurt you. You should know better than to be alone out here at night, though, especially in this neighborhood.*" He turned to the waitress. "Coffee. Black with one sugar."

"Anything else, darling," she said. "Maybe something to eat?"

"Sure. If you've got a breakfast special, I'll take one of those," he said.

"You got it, hon. I'll bring it to you when it's ready."

Ryah moved to one of the tables and sat with his back to the woman so she wouldn't think he was a threat. He stared out the window, watching the wind play games with the leaves and litter and let his mind wander.

"What was the name?" he mumbled to himself. "I'm sure I've seen her before. Cate. That was it. She has a strange resemblance to that little girl. That one on the transit. Could it be her? If so, then who was that other woman with her on the train. Her mother? No. I saw her mother in the dream and that wasn't her." He paused for a moment. "That's it. I saw that girl on the transit and then had a dream about her. Nothing more. Nothing less."

He had himself convinced. Almost.

"*And Guriel?*" he thought. "*Psychosis. Sleep deprivation,*" he listed off a couple of potential answers and then a couple more. "*I was still asleep. I'm seeing what I want to see. Who knows? Who cares? All it means is I should take a little time off. Maybe go off to the mountains for some R and R. Clear my head for a while.*"

He felt the presence of someone standing behind him and turned, expecting to see the waitress with his order.

"May I join you?" the woman said.

Ryah examined her. She was older, maybe late fifties, early sixties. Her face was kind, but worried, the stress showing in her eyes.

"I'm not in the mood for company," he said. He wore the frozen stare that he used when he interrogated an enemy combatant.

The woman shifted her feet in a nervous dance but remained where she was. Ryah could tell she wasn't going to leave him in peace. He made a gesture with his hand to offer her a seat but made it clear that it wouldn't be a long conversation nor one that he had any interest in.

"Thank you," she said and sat down.

Her eyes darted back and forth between Ryah's face and the table in front of her. The long-sleeve blouse she wore covered her arms all the way to the base of her thumbs, hiding her wrists from view. Her graying hair dangled over an ear. She reached up to brush it aside, exposing the edge of a tattoo on her right wrist. Ryah glanced at the blue arc of the circle and looked back at the woman's face. His jaw was set as he prepared himself for what he was about to do.

"I've been waiting for you to arrive," she said.

The words caught Ryah off guard. "You've been waiting for me? I didn't even know where I was going ten minutes ago."

"I was told you would be here," she insisted.

"I see," Ryah said. He was skeptical but decided to play along. "You were told I would be here. By whom?"

"I was told to come find you here," she repeated but gave no more information.

The waitress came over with the order and placed his food on the table. Ryah thanked her and pushed the food to the side but kept the coffee in front of him. He found himself slipping into interrogator mode.

"Alright. Then let's start with some simple information. What's your name?"

"My name's Allison," she said.

"OK, Allison. Good to meet you," he said and stretched his hand across the table. She reached back to shake his hand. He took hold of it and wouldn't let go. With his left hand, he rolled back her right sleeve. "What's this here?" he asked, knowing what the answer was.

The tattoo of the circle with the three ones that looked like lines seemed to glow on her wrist.

"You know," she said. She withdrew her arm and hid it under the table.

Ryah took a sip of coffee and watched her face. The fear remained but so did a calm determination. He had seen it many times over the last few months. But this one was different. He said nothing in order to let the tension increase. The woman was the one to break the silence.

"I've come to ask a favor," she said.

"A favor?" he said. "What kind of favor? It doesn't seem to me that you're in a position to be requesting anything of me."

"You've got a kind heart," she said. "I know you do. I also know what you're capable of."

Her words hung in the air, half admiration, half condemnation. But it wasn't flattery and it wasn't said to gain an advantage. Simply an acknowledgment of the truth.

"The little girl you let go, Priscilla's daughter, her grandparents brought her to my clinic. She told me about you, what she could anyway. She recognized your face from a magazine, the picture with you giving CPR to that diplomat they tried to assassinate outside the UN. She told me you were the one who saved her. The one who last saw her mother." Her voice began to shake. "What happened …?" She was incapable of finishing her question.

"She's not feeling any more pain," he answered.

Allison bowed her head and wept silently.

"About that favor," Ryah said. He paused. "Since you know who I am, you must know that I could have you arrested right now. You know the fate that would await you."

Her speech became bold. Bolder than someone in her position should have been.

"You can only do what he permits you to do. If my life is what he requires of me, then so be it, but you are under his authority and cannot do anything that he won't allow," she said.

Ryah was confused. Was she referring to Klins? Was she implying that he was a part of their movement? He noted the possibility but denied that it had much chance of being true.

"I want you to stop persecuting us," she said. "You're doing the wrong thing."

"The wrong thing, huh?" he said. "Aren't you the ones who tried to assassinate the envoy? Your group anyway."

"No. Absolutely not." She hesitated. "At least ... I hope not. That's not our way. I can't believe any of our people would do such a thing." She buried her face in her hands but kept looking straight at Ryah.

"You're not into violence? That's not what they've been telling me in the interviews," Ryah said. "Stories about a kingdom that's trying to take over the nations, depose all lawful government and set up some guy that will rule the whole world. That sounds like a group bent on violence to me."

"The interviews. Quite the euphemism." Her tone betrayed her bitterness. "You misunderstand what they're saying."

"So, you don't deny it," he said. "I just somehow 'misunderstand.' Well, tell me what I'm not understanding. Who is this king? How do you plan on taking over the world? From what I can tell, you're a rather weak group with no capabilities of defeating a small police force much less the armies of an entire nation. I'm not mocking you. It's simply been my observation. Is there something else I don't know? Do you have a secret military that we're not aware of?"

"There is a battle," she said, "and we are in a war, but it's not against you."

"Against whom then?" he asked.

239

"You know," she said.

"I do?"

"You've seen them," she said. "In your dreams."

Ryah's whole body tensed and his eyes narrowed. Her comments unnerved him and sent a shiver through his chest.

"What do you know about my dreams?" he asked, his voice barely more than a whisper.

She seemed surprised by his response. "It *is* you."

Ryah said nothing, not knowing what to say.

Allison continued. "We've been told that a man of visions and dreams would come to us. That he had the answers. When I was told to come see you, I had no idea why other than a feeling I get deep down sometimes that maybe …." Her conversation was more with herself than with Ryah. "Why else would he tell me to? It didn't make sense. Although, much of what he says doesn't make sense until long after he says it." She returned her focus towards Ryah. "When I saw you come in … somehow I knew it was you. I wished it wasn't, because I know what you can do. But your reaction confirmed it. You've had the dreams, haven't you? What have you seen?"

The way she asked it confused Ryah. "Don't you know?" he asked. "You seem to know so much about me."

"I have no idea what's in your dreams," she confessed. "All I know is that you've been given the privilege of knowing. And that is why I came to seek you out. To find the answers."

"I have no answers for you," Ryah said.

The two sat in silence for a few minutes until Allison made a move as if she were leaving.

"What are you going to do?" she asked.

Ryah knew what she meant. "I don't know," he said. "But you're safe for now, although, I recommend you leave before I change my mind."

Allison hurried out the front door, happy to have made it out of the café in one piece and unaware that Ryah had decided to follow her.

Chapter 29

Sticking to the main streets made it harder for Ryah to keep a tail on Allison than he would have liked. It was also the safest thing for her to do.

She traveled down the sidewalk guided by the streetlights while Ryah hung in the shadows a block back and darted between cars and the doorways of buildings. Every once in a while, Allison would glance over her shoulder as if expecting to be followed. By the direction she headed, Ryah was certain she was making for the transit station. He worked on a plan to keep himself from being spotted, a difficult task for someone as large as he was.

As expected, Allison entered the transit station and headed to the lower platform. Ryah stayed at the top of escalators and waited for the train to pull into the station before hurrying down to jump into one of the last cars. At each stop, he would stand in the doorway and wait to see if she would get off, which she did at the third one.

Back up the stairs and onto the street. They arrived at a section on the very edge of the city. It was a part of town Ryah didn't know very well, but he recognized it as being one where the wealthy but not fabulously wealthy stayed.

"It seems they've moved their base of operation out here," Ryah thought, knowing the security operations in and around Riverplace had uncovered the former headquarters of the group and had sent the remnant scattering throughout the city. *"Allison doesn't seem like she belongs out here, so I wonder if she has a benefactor that's helping to finance and hide them."* A logical conclusion but not one Ryah was dogmatic about.

A couple left turns and one back to the right and Allison stopped in front of a house surrounded by a ten-foot wall.

She punched a code into the front gate. It swung outward allowing her to pass. Ryah waited a minute and walked down the other side of the street. One camera watched the entrance, but no other devices protected the property, giving the occupants a false sense of security. The house was on a corner lot. At the end of the block just outside the reach of the streetlight, Ryah jumped up and grasped the top of the wall. With the ease of a gymnast, he pulled himself up and over, landing quietly in the grass beside a tree.

He crouched down and listened. No sign of dogs. No indication of internal security. He got up and stuck to the wall as he made his way towards a car by the gate and waited again.

"Meet me at these coordinates. As soon as you can."

Ryah sent the message to Rogan and placed his comm underneath the car, jamming it into a spot where it wouldn't fall out.

"*Low battery indicator was on,*" he thought, regretting he hadn't charged the comm overnight.

Ryah retraced his steps to the end of the wall and climbed back over. Across the street, there was a park, no more than a small clearing in the trees with a single bench and a path that cut through the middle. He sat down and waited for his partner's arrival. A cold blast from the northwest hit the park and bent the trees. He shivered and pulled his jacket tighter, huddling to keep himself warm.

Ryah looked up in time to see the gate from the house swing open. The car pulled out and drove by. He peered into the window but couldn't tell if Allison was inside. Not that it mattered. With his comm used as a tracking device, he could follow them as long as the signal lasted. Even if she wasn't in the car, he would at least be able to gather information about where the car traveled. Somehow the people at this house were connected to the movement, and Ryah was going to let the clues take him wherever they led.

The sun started to show itself on the horizon and warmed the air as it ascended into the morning sky. A few minutes later, Rogan arrived on his motorcycle and looked up and down the street, searching for Ryah. Finding him sitting on the bench, he rolled up to the park and took off his helmet.

"I've been trying to call you," Rogan said. "Got your message and came right away. I was going to the coordinates you sent, but then the GPS started showing that you were on the move. I wasn't sure if I should come here directly or follow your signal. Guess I made the right choice. So, what's going on? What are you doing out here?"

"I followed a member of the group, the Kingdom, to this house. I get the feeling she's higher up in the organization," Ryah said. "I slipped my comm under a car when she entered that house, but then they took off. I have no idea if she went with them or not, but I figure we should follow them either way. Give me a ride back to my place so I can get my bike, and then I'll follow you to find them. We need to get a move on. The battery on the comm is low."

Rogan knew Ryah was holding back. He failed to mention how he found her or how he knew she belonged to the Kingdom. Rogan figured he had his reasons.

"Any idea where we're heading?"

"They made out to the Kinset Valley," Rogan answered. "The signal stopped there for about thirty minutes and then shut off. I think your comm finally died."

Ryah and Rogan spoke through their helmet comms as they rode Northeast on Highway 10, which paralleled the Carmel River back towards its source.

"You ever been here before?" Rogan asked.

"Yeah. A long time ago. Back when I was still in intelligence. There were rumors a foreign power had inserted some operatives and were using the valley as a base to launch their operations. I came out with my supervisor and a couple other people in the unit, but it turned out to be nothing, at least as far as we could tell. You?"

"Never."

"There's not too much out there," Ryah said. "The valley is the oldest in the region and used to be a rather fertile place before all the earthquakes. Lots of farms at the bottom of the valley, vineyards along the slopes of the mountains. They cleared a bunch of oak trees to make room for them. I remember some environmental group getting all up in arms about that, back when that was a thing. Long ago, there were four rivers that converged just north of the Kinset and came together to form one large tributary which flowed into the Carmel River. A bunch of natural springs rose out of the rocks, so even when the four rivers dried up, there was still plenty of water for the entire region. I once had a bottle of wine from this area. Best I ever tasted. Once in a while, I try to find another bottle of that vintage. No luck yet."

As they approached a big bend in the river, the road took a sharp left as it mimicked the path of the water. Rogan put on his brakes a little late, and his bike started to slide out from under him.

Ryah laughed when he saw the look on Rogan's face. "That almost got you." It was the first time he had seen any signs of emotion from his partner, and he couldn't help but think it might have been fear. "You ride much?"

"Most of my life," Rogan said. "Enough to have dumped my bike a few times."

Ryah laughed again and continued driving. After another hour, they reached Kinset Road, which crossed over the river towards the Northwest. It had been at least twenty years since the last farm had closed and the settlers had left the area, leaving the road to fall into disrepair. Ryah and Rogan slowed their pace as they maneuvered around the potholes and fallen boulders which littered the path in front of them.

"These large rocks indicate that we're entering the Kinset Valley, so start looking for anything that might catch your attention."

Rogan nodded and observed the scene. Remnants of working farms dotted the landscape. A few pieces of old machinery stood on the side of the road like rusted ghosts from a more prosperous time. Nothing seemed out of place as the two edged their way into the basin. A weathered hut with a rotting wooden frame and aluminum sheeting for a roof jutted onto the road, perhaps displaced by one of the minor tremors which occurred along a fault which ran through the middle of the valley.

At the hut, they got off their bikes to stretch their legs. A well-worn foot path encircled the shack and extended down a gentle slope towards a brook which bubbled up out of the ground. All along the path, stretching out hundreds of yards in each direction, the grass had been flattened, rectangular and circular patches of yellowed grass surrounded by green but trampled plots of land, as if a great army of people had camped there.

"The signal stopped a couple of miles beyond this point," Rogan said. "It looks like they might have used this as a temporary base."

Ryah nodded his head.

Rogan added. "And by the looks of it, there could easily have been a thousand people out here. How were they not detected by intelligence?"

"Our satellites are no longer set up to monitor this area. Somebody must know that," Ryah said.

The sun had passed its zenith and was descending to its resting place. Ryah walked to the bike with Rogan following.

"If we keep going any farther on our bikes," Rogan said, "they'll likely hear us."

Ryah nodded. "I guess we're hoofing it from here."

They rolled their motorcycles down the busted road towards the far end of the Kinset Valley, steering around rocks and avoiding the potholes. At the base of a large hill and off the side of the road a little way, Ryah spotted a spring bubbling out of the ground and stopped to get a drink. Wild blueberries grew all around the area, and Ryah and Rogan ate their fill.

"Good a place as any to wait," Ryah said.

Rogan lay down in the green grass by the brook and fell asleep, signifying his complete and total agreement. Ryah took the time to move the motorcycles back into the tree line and covered them with branches. When he finished, he joined Rogan in some much needed sleep.

The sun had almost gone down when Rogan woke Ryah. He pointed to the north to focus Ryah's attention.

"You see that," Rogan said.

A steady but barely visible stream of smoke rose into the evening sky, the source of the fire blocked from view. They walked up a hill until they came to the crest, arriving as the final rays from the sun disappeared out of sight. It was a cloudless night, yet the moon and stars were not visible as if they didn't exist out here. A half mile away at the top of the next hill, lights from hundreds of indistinguishable fires and a few buildings chased away the darkness which hovered over the valley.

Ryah surveyed the scene and pointed to the western side of the camp.

"Let's make our approach from there," he said. "Most of the fires are concentrated on the other side. Plus, the tree line goes right up to the edge. We'll be able to get close without being seen."

"Any chance they have sentries posted over there?" Rogan asked.

"I doubt it," Ryah said. "They're not hiding their fires at all, so they must feel comfortable. We'll go into stealth mode, though, just to be sure."

Twenty minutes later, they were in position on a ridge overlooking the 'tent city' as Rogan had christened it. There was a lot of activity in the middle where the buildings, which turned out to be an old farmhouse and barn, were located. A meeting of sorts was taking place inside the barn, and only a few stragglers walked through the nearly deserted outer ring of tents. It didn't take long for Ryah to locate the car. A minute later, he had retrieved his comm.

A man who had not gone to the meeting stood by the side of a house. In the half light of the fire, Ryah saw him. He signaled for Rogan to come down and crept closer to get a better look. The man picked up a few pieces of wood and threw them on top of a fire, causing a chain of sparks to fly upwards. He looked around for another piece. Not finding any, he went to the edge of the woods.

He didn't know what hit him. One moment he was stooped over to grab a log for tinder, and the next he was semi-conscious and being dragged into the woods by his arms.

His first thought was that one of the wild animals, a bear most likely, was dragging him to the woods. He tried to yell, but his mouth had been stuffed with some sort of material. After the cobwebs cleared, it became apparent two men were hauling him through the underbrush. Fifty paces from the edge of the clearing, they stopped.

"Call for help," Ryah said as he removed the muffle from the man's mouth, "and it will be the last sound you make."

Rogan shone a flashlight into the man's eyes so he couldn't see their faces but so that the man's face was clear to them. As clear as the moment Ryah ran into him on the transit and beat him within an inch of his life.

"*What is he doing out here?*" Ryah thought. In his heart, he believed he had found the connection he had been looking for.

"I've seen this one before," Ryah said. He pulled out his own flashlight so that his face was illuminated. "Do you recognize me?" he asked. "I know you. If I remember correctly, your name is Kevin or Clown or something like that."

Even in the soft light, Ryah could see the man's face turn pale. Drops of sweat trickled down his forehead, but if it was from fear or from the struggle, Ryah couldn't tell.

"Th ... they used to call me Kane," he stuttered, in an irony that didn't escape Ryah. "But now I go by Jason."

Rogan remained off to the side, a passive observer, but ready to jump in at a moment's notice.

"Jason, huh? You don't look like a Jason to me. More like a Fido. Maybe a Rover." Ryah didn't try to hide his contempt, something he did only when he despised the captive whose fate was predetermined. "What are you doing out here? Who are these people?"

"I think you know who these people are," Jason said. He waited for a moment before he spoke up again. "What are you going to do to them?"

"I think your bigger concern should be what I'm about to do to you," Ryah said.

He gave a nod to Rogan who put the gag back in Jason's mouth. The two dragged Jason against a small tree and pulled his hands behind him so that they wrapped around the trunk. Stripping Jason's shirt off his shoulders, Ryah used the sleeves to tie him up.

"What information do you want from him?" Rogan asked so Jason couldn't hear.

"I doubt he has anything useful for us," Ryah said out loud. "My only question is should I take him back to the Council or just finish him off here. If I had to decide now, it would be the latter."

Rogan wasn't sure if Ryah was using an interrogation technique to get Jason to talk. His bet was no. He had never seen Ryah this full of anger and for an unknown reason. Rogan's hunch was confirmed when Ryah pulled out his knife and jammed it into the man's thigh. The man moaned in pain as the blood began to drip down his leg, leaving a small pool on a pile of dry leaves underneath. Ryah twisted the knife and held it there for a few seconds before pulling it out and causing a wider gash. Rogan placed his hand on Ryah's shoulder to get his attention. The look on Ryah's face let Rogan know he should let Ryah continue undisturbed.

As Ryah raised the knife to deliver the next blow, the sound of a twig snapping caused him to break off the assault.

"Please stop," a soft voice called out to them. "Please don't hurt him anymore," she said.

"Show yourself," Ryah ordered.

As she stepped into the light, Ryah was transported to another place and time. He saw her again on the transit. The scar down her cheek. The blonde hair and fierce green eyes. Beautiful, strong. He felt her hands as they caressed his face. Often, she was on his mind. Wondering what had become of her. Wondering what might be, if only things were different.

"What are you doing here?" he asked.

"Please don't hurt him," she repeated. "He's with me."

"I don't understand," Ryah said. "I don't understand why you're trying to save this filth."

Rogan noticed the change in Ryah's tone. It was nervous, gentle. Maryam walked up to Ryah and touched his face.

"I've thought about you often. Hoping you thought of me," she said touching his heart.

"You're one of them," Ryah said without removing her hand from his chest. It was neither disappointment nor surprise. More a jumble of confused emotions. "What are you doing with these people?" he managed to ask. "You don't strike me as the type." He grabbed her arm and exposed her right wrist. There were no markings on her wrist. "I don't see the symbol here either. Are you some sort of undercover operative?"

Maryam flashed a sad smile. "My dear man. You have no idea, do you?"

"What I don't know is why you're protecting him … after what he did," Ryah said. *"Unless you've always been in league with him,"* he thought.

"People change," Maryam replied.

Ryah's mind flashed back to the dream, but he pushed the thought aside. "He's gotta go with me, you know. And I'll have to report back about this."

Maryam's expression changed. "Please don't," she said. "Please don't. I'm begging you." She held onto his arm. "We just moved out here. There's no way we can move everyone so quickly. They'll find us and kill us. Kill me. My daughter." Tears rolled down in a silent plea for mercy.

Ryah thought about the young girl and took a chance.

"You mean Cate," he said.

"How do you know m…?"

Maryam stopped herself. Her mind began to spin. She had overheard Allison talking about the man who saw visions. Could it be true? Could he be the one?

"Her name's Kaliya," she said. "And I'm Maryam."

"Kaliya," he repeated out loud but to himself. He stared off into the distance for a minute. Silent. Brooding.

Turning to Rogan, he said, "Let's go."

Without another word, Ryah walked off. Rogan didn't say anything until they made it back to the motorcycles, but he knew the reason they left. He saw it in the way he looked at her. The way she looked at him.

"You have to tell the Council," Rogan said.

Ryah didn't respond.

"If you don't," Rogan continued, "it'll be you in the stadium along with them."

"I know," Ryah said. "I know."

Chapter 30

The ride back was silent except for the hum of the engines, both lost in their thoughts and trying to make sense of what happened from their own perspective. As they approached the Carmel city limits, Rogan spoke up.

"What are you going to do?" he asked.

"I'm not sure yet. Nothing for now," Ryah said.

"With all due respect," Rogan said, "why not? They're not worth your life. She's not worth your life."

Ryah shot Rogan a look.

"It's not what you think," Ryah said. "I've only met her once and under adverse circumstances."

"Then what is it?" Rogan asked.

Ryah sensed Rogan's skepticism. He wasn't altogether sure that Rogan was wrong.

"There's something …," Ryah began. "It's … I don't think it's them," he confessed. "There's something else going on, and I'm not sure how to explain it to you. Not sure if I can explain it to myself at this point. It's as if our meetings have not been a coincidence. She was there to tell me something, to prevent me from making a mistake." He paused for a while. "I don't want to act on this until I know what's going on."

"I hope you're right," Rogan said. "I've got your back. At least until I think you're not acting in the nation's best interest."

Ryah looked at his friend. "Always a gamma." He smiled. "I wouldn't expect anything less of you. Anyway, it's time to get some sleep. Only a few hours before we've got to be back at work. Meet me in my office at 0800 so we can plan out a strategy for the next few weeks."

"Roger that," Rogan said and rode off.

Ryah arrived home and lay down in bed. His mind raced as it tried to organize all the details of the case. From the attempt on Lucio's life and the events in Rome right afterward. The unexpected encounter with Allison and the reunion with Maryam. The interrogations. The Kingdom. The One. The answer was in there, somewhere, but it was as if there was a deliberate attempt, a concerted effort to prevent him from finding it.

The dreams. The answer was in the dreams. Ryah was sure of that.

"Tonight, I'll get more answers," he said.

Ryah's comm lit up and a voice started speaking. He looked at the clock and realized he had been asleep for hours. His sleep had been dreamless. The disappointment overcame him, and he wondered how long the answer would continue to elude him. The voice spoke up again.

"Ryah." It was Administrator Klins' assistant. "I need you down here immediately."

"Yes, ma'am," he said. "Do I need to contact Rogan?"

"No, I already got in touch with him," she said. "How long until you can get here?"

"Thirty minutes at the most," Ryah said.

"I'll let the administrator know," she said and disconnected from Ryah.

He got dressed as quickly as he could and headed down to the Council building. The first lights of dawn had still not appeared when he arrived to find Rogan waiting for him in the parking garage.

"Any idea what we're doing here?" Rogan asked.

"No," Ryah said. "They didn't give me any details."

The reason for the call became clearer when they saw the visitor in the administrator's office. Lucio Romijn stood by the window lost in conversation with Klins. Ryah knocked on the door and Lucio turned to face them.

"Ryah, Rogan. Good to see you again," Lucio said.

"Welcome back," Ryah said and looked over Lucio's face. "*The doctors did a great job,*" he thought. "*You can tell he had an accident, but the scar is minimal. I'd never know how much trauma he went through if I wasn't there to witness it.*"

Lucio seemed to read Ryah's thoughts. "It's healing nicely. Much better than I had hoped." His smile was jovial, and he didn't take offense at the stares. "How are things going on your end?"

"Not much more than what I told you the last time we spoke. We found a couple centers run by members of the Kingdom. They had connections to New Carmel Medical Center. Ran a couple of businesses around that area and around Riverplace. That's a part of downtown near the old docks in case you're not familiar with it. We were able to round up a few hundred people and got a couple of what we suspect are mid-level leaders. A number of them escaped our dragnet, but we have some leads to where they might have gone."

Rogan noticed the purposeful omission.

Ryah continued. "I've got to tell you, though. I'm not sure they were involved in the assassination plot. At least not the members of the Kingdom from here. They don't strike me as being capable."

Klins looked displeased.

"There's a possibility they have a separate military wing we haven't been able to infiltrate yet," Ryah said, "so that's where we're going to concentrate our efforts next."

Klins relaxed, the scowl disappearing from his face.

"You can see," Klins said to Lucio. "We're holding up our end of the bargain."

Lucio's expression didn't change, but he started to pace across the room.

"What brings you back?" Ryah asked Lucio. "I heard the talks were going well."

"No. No they're not," Lucio said. He rubbed his jaw and thought for a moment. "No, they're not. And I, for the life of me, can't figure out why. Every time we make headway, things fall apart. The first few times I chalked it up to national pride. Ego. Make a big scene for the constituents at home about how 'they won't bow before any foreign power.' 'Our nation will rise up and drown yours in a river of blood' type thing. You know how it is. But we offered a way for both sides to save face. A legitimate opportunity for peace where both nations would come out a winner. I thought they were going to take it. I truly thought they were going to take it. They didn't." He looked surprised, almost disgusted. "It's as if …." He paused. "It's as if, there's someone purposefully sabotaging the negotiations."

"Any idea who?" Ryah asked.

"The same ones who attempted to kill me," Lucio suggested. "The people who call themselves the Kingdom." He didn't seem convinced by his own statement. "I don't get it really. We at the UN have the same goals as they do. I guess they have a military solution in mind as opposed to us. As you alluded to, we don't think they have any real military capability, none we know of anyway. Certainly nothing that could stand against the combined forces of the nations."

"That's their game then," Ryah said, "whoever they are."

"What do you mean?" Lucio asked.

"Pit one nation against the other in order to create chaos and ensure mutual destruction," Ryah said. "That would be my bet."

Ryah's comment made Lucio visibly uncomfortable. He pondered for a while before he responded to Ryah.

"I'll need to make a call, but I think you may be right. Yep, you may be right." He nodded in agreement with whatever was going on inside his mind and turned to Klins. "Do you have a secure line and somewhere I can speak in private?"

"You can use my office," Klins said. "We'll step outside."

Administrator Klins, Ryah, and Rogan left the room to give the envoy some privacy. After a few minutes, Lucio returned and asked for them to step back inside.

"Administrator Klins. Do I have your permission to borrow these two again?" Lucio asked. "I'd like them to come back to Rome with me."

Ryah spoke up. "May I ask why you need us? They'll figure we're there to sabotage the talks and that you're in it with us."

"I told him the same thing," Lucio said, "but he insisted."

"Who's he?" Ryah asked.

"Karhan Abbad," Lucio said. "He's the assistant to Ambassador Tanas."

Ryah's stomach froze. He didn't trust Abbad and had long suspected him of being involved. By Klins' expression, it seemed like he had an issue with Abbad as well.

"Why does he want us?" Ryah said.

"You're a bit of a hero over there," Lucio said, "how you saved my life and all. But also because of your experience interrogating the Kingdom members. The administrator tells me you know what to look for. You know how they act. Their secret signs to each other. The way they phrase things. Whatever it is. He says you understand their subtleties better than anyone, that there's no one more qualified than you to root them out."

"I don't think it's a good idea," Ryah said. "One little slip and we'll have a mess we won't be able to clean up."

"I don't like it either," Klins interjected, "but if I do decide to let someone go, it needs to be you, Ryah. You have more experience with this type of mission than any of our operatives."

"With all due respect, sir," Ryah said, "I don't see how this benefits us at all."

Lucio answered him. "We've discovered that the Kingdom is plotting a similar assassination attempt against someone in the Council. We have no idea who, though. We do know the people in Rome are calling the shots."

"Won't those people know who I am, then?" Ryah asked.

"No. Only the people in this room know who you are," Lucio said.

"Besides Abbad," Ryah said, "and that colonel. Colonel Zidane, right? There have got to be others as well."

"You have no need to worry about Abbad," Lucio said. "I'd trust him with my life."

Ryah felt the irony of his statement.

"As for the colonel," Lucio said, "he had a heart attack last month and passed away. No one else has any idea about your true identity. We've kept that hidden per Ambassador Tanas' orders, seeing how we presumed we'd be asking for your assistance again."

"You must have people on your end who are investigating the conspiracy," Ryah said, searching for any way to extricate himself and Rogan from the looming disaster. "I'm still not sure why you need us."

"We do have a team, but I've got the feeling one of them is the problem," Lucio admitted. "That's why I'm asking for your help."

"When would you need them?" Klins asked.

"Now," Lucio said. "My plane's taking off within the hour. On the flight over, we'll work on the story of where you've been the last few months."

Klins thought about it for a minute, the internal debate showing in his body language.

"Alright. Make it so," Klins said to Lucio. "You have the Council's permission to borrow these two again." He looked over at Ryah. "You've got your things ready to go?" he joked. He smiled and added, "Just get what you need when you land. Charge it to the UN." He looked over at Lucio who nodded back. "Great. I'll walk you two out."

The four men left, and Lucio went down the hall to use the restroom, leaving Klins alone with Ryah and Rogan.

"Ryah, Rogan," Klins said. His appearance became somber. "I know what you're thinking. This is not an ideal situation, but the fact is I need you on the inside. Abbad's in on it, I'm sure, but I can't let him know I'm on to him. If I turned down his request, he would get suspicious. Be careful. Be extremely careful with what you say, especially when you're around him. He obviously knows who you are and why you're there. He won't give you up, though. Not directly anyway. If he does, he'll out himself in the process. Your job is to find out what he's up to and report directly to me. Do not let Lucio know about this. He's naïve to trust Abbad, but Lucio's one of the few good men I've met at the UN. So, protect Lucio from himself."

Klins took his leave and gave Ryah a chance to talk to Rogan.

"Rogue," Ryah said, "there's something else going on here. Something behind the scenes that I can't make sense of."

"Yeah, I know," Rogan said. "I don't like where this is going. I feel like we're being set up."

"I agree," Ryah said. "Abbad's using Lucio's friendship with us and the Council to get close to us. But why? That's the part that I can't wrap my mind around. Abbad asked me to be personally involved in the initial negotiations even though I'd never met him before or even heard of him. He wanted us to take the fall. I have no doubt of that. Deflect the attention from the real group who was behind the assassination, which he's clearly a part of. But why go after Lucio? Another expendable person in his quest for power? When Lucio survived, that must have thrown a wrench into Abbad's plans, and he had to find a scapegoat to divert suspicion from himself. Is Abbad with the Kingdom group or is he using them as a distraction? What's his end game? We need to figure that out without him becoming aware of what we're doing. Having said that, that's not what I was talking about when I said there was something else going on behind the scenes."

"What do you mean?" Rogan asked.

"I'm not sure I can explain. You probably wouldn't believe me if I could," Ryah said. "It's just … there are other things going on that we can't see, like we're living in an alternate reality that keeps us blinded to what's actually going on."

"A Plato's Cave type thing? Matrix movie red pill, blue pill?" Rogan asked without seeming to be put off by the sudden change in the conversation.

"No. No, they had it wrong. The irony is they had an inkling of the truth, but they completely missed it."

"What then?" Rogan asked.

"That, I don't know," Ryah said.

"Where's this coming from?" Rogan asked. "Does this have something to do with what happened in Lucio's operating room?"

"It could, in part. But I can't say for sure. Even if it does, I don't know how it all ties in," Ryah said. He stared off into the distance as if the answer was somewhere out there. "Even if it does, I'm not sure I believe it."

Chapter 31

Lucio's jet arrived just before 8:00 pm local time. Ryah refused to go back to the hotel he stayed in last time. He didn't give Lucio a reason. The envoy insisted that they stay with him, then, as he had a couple of spare rooms.

"It's not much," Lucio told them. "Nothing luxurious anyway. That's not my style."

His comments were an understatement. Lucio's home was a three-bedroom flat a half mile away from the UN building. A stack of boxes occupied most of the space in one bedroom, the one he offered Ryah. The other one, where Rogan would sleep, had been converted into a home gym of sorts with a rowing machine and a few kettlebells. The rest of the apartment was clinical, empty, definitely in need of a woman's touch. A few photos decorated the kitchen counter, and a painting of New York as it appeared in the late 1700's adorned one wall. The living area held a small table as well a sofa which had been constructed sometime during the Italian Renaissance, the only sign of opulence in the place.

Two rented tuxedos arrived soon after they did, along with some polished black shoes. Lucio indicated that Ryah and Rogan should change immediately.

"Sorry," Lucio said. "In all our talk on the flight, I failed to mention that we would be going to a cocktail party tonight. It starts at ten and I need to get there on time to do the meet and greet. It's an informal gathering the UN likes to throw for our constituent nations. Politicians, businesspeople, a who's who of celebrities will be there. We've invited the Russian and Chinese delegations, but there's no guarantee they'll show. You can go with me when I do, or you can come later when the fun starts." Lucio rolled his eyes when he said fun. "I'll probably slip out when it does. Not my cup of tea, but I'd like you to be there. The more they drink, the looser their lips get, and I bet you'll hear some interesting stories if nothing else."

"Will Abbad be there?" Ryah asked.

"No," Lucio said. "He avoids those things like the plague. Has a strong distaste for these events. Ambassador Tanas might make an appearance, but he's been out of the city since Sunday. I'm not sure if he'll make it back tonight."

Lucio handed Ryah and Rogan a pair of cards used to make purchases.

"These are for any incidentals you might run across. I know you two don't have the hand implants yet," he said. "Me neither. I must be the last person in Rome not to get it. Something unsettling about it. Not that I need it seeing as how I'm on official business twenty-four seven or so it seems, and the only outside places I go to know me so well that they automatically send my charges to the UN. I'm a creature of habit, I suppose. The ambassador keeps riding me to get the implant, so I guess I'll have to break down some day and get it." He smiled a toothy grin. "But not today. Anyway, there's enough currency on your cards to last a few days. It'll automatically refill to a preset limit at the end of each day, as long as the global chip is working. It'll keep track of your purchases and link up to our banking network, so get whatever you need. I figure you'll be here at least a couple of weeks, but who knows what will happen."

Lucio left for the party at a quarter to ten and decided to dismiss his security detail so he could walk to the UN building alone. When Ryah chastised him for taking such a risk, Lucio dismissed it with, "When it's my time to go, it's my time to go." Ryah watched him through the window as he made his way down the sidewalk, stepping lightly as if he didn't have a care in the world. The more time Ryah spent with the envoy, the more he grew to admire him.

"If only there were more men in the world like him," Ryah told Rogan.

Rogan nodded in agreement and went off to take a shower, leaving Ryah to contemplate what the world would be like if Lucio was in charge instead of men like Klins or General Brostov. If kindness and duty and selflessness were the driving forces of the men who led nations, instead of power and greed and lust. When Rogan had finished, they went down to wait for the limo.

The United Nations building was alive with activity when they arrived. Ryah showed his credentials to the guard at the entrance who let him pass without going through the scanners. Their guide led them down a long hallway. They went by rows of locked rooms each with an identical door and a window which looked out into the hallway. All of the blinds were closed, and in the dim light, Ryah saw a distorted likeness of himself each time he passed in front of one of the shuttered windows. The hall came to a dead end, and the guard who accompanied Ryah and Rogan pressed his badge against an invisible portal. The sound of an electronic lock disengaging broke the silence, and a hidden door started to slide open. Ryah turned to adjust his bowtie in the window mirror to his left.

"Please enter gentlemen," the guard said.

As Ryah and Rogan passed through, the door slid shut and closed with an audible click. Ryah looked behind him, but there was no sign that a door was there or had ever been. It was dark inside, not completely but enough that it took a while for his eyes to adjust. While he waited, he groped along the wall trying to find the exit. Rogan walked off into the crowd searching for Lucio, seemingly unfazed by the dark.

After a minute, Ryah finally saw the flurry of activity he had only been able to hear a moment before. He found himself in the middle of a large room beneath the basement of the UN building, which had been built for the express purpose of holding large gatherings such as this. A few hundred people were already there. Three other doors besides the one Ryah came through allowed a steady stream of new guests to enter and join the festivities. Off on one side, a string quartet played an etude by Chopin. The music drifted over the participants and mingled with their conversations in a delicate counter melody. Slight curls of smoke wafted throughout the room and brought the sweet, mildly pungent odor of designer hash to Ryah's nose. Waiters glided in and out of the dignitaries, politicians, and business people, presenting their delicacies collected from around the world. Women in slim dresses and male models in tailored tuxedos hung on the arms of the guests, eye candy willing to serve and service every need for whatever trinket would be thrown their way.

A young girl with brown hair sauntered over to Ryah and took hold of his left arm. Her soft, brown eyes and warm, red lips smiled at him, enticing him to partake in her unspoken offer. Ryah removed her hand from his arm and directed her away.

"No thank you," he said.

Without saying a word, the girl bounced off to the next person and wrapped herself around him, this time accomplishing her goal. The man handed her something Ryah couldn't see and proceeded to unbutton his pants. Ryah walked up behind the man. A quick, unseen elbow to the back of his head knocked him out while still on his feet. He caught the man as he fell and lowered him to the ground, propping him against the wall in the corner next to another man who was already too stoned to stay upright.

No one besides the girl paid attention, too concerned with their own affairs to care.

As Ryah descended into the immense room, he felt the heat intensify and looked for a waiter carrying a cold beer. Finding none, he grabbed a waitress and asked her to bring him water in a wine glass. As he waited, he felt a tap on his shoulder.

"Hey friend. What brings you here?" a man with a distinct American accent asked him.

He was average looking, slightly rotund and in the first stage of losing his hair but dressed in a handmade suit from a high-end Italian designer. The scent of his cologne masked his body odor but couldn't conceal it, and Ryah took a half step back to give himself a little space to breathe. The man extended a chubby, warm, moist hand towards Ryah.

"My name's Terrence Howard III. No relation to that actor from a while back."

His white jowls shook as he laughed at his own joke, the smell of marijuana spilling from his mouth. His eyes were bloodshot and his speech slurred, indicating that he had arrived at the intersection of buzzed and stoned.

"Ryah."

"Good to meet you Ryah," Terrence said, although it seemed like he already knew who Ryah was, at least to some degree. "From the looks of it, you're one of the politicians. No offense meant. I've been coming to these parties for the last ten years, so I've learned to distinguish your type from the businesspeople who really run the show." He laughed again, although Ryah wasn't sure why. "I'm a businessman. A good one if I say so myself. That's why I'm here. Always good to stay in touch with my clients … and make new ones, of course. What better place to meet the movers and the shakers?"

Terrence slapped him on the chest with the back of his hand, annoying Ryah more than he let on.

"I'm not a politician," Ryah said. "Just a man trying to make a few bucks."

"An American, huh? I can tell by the way you talk. You know, old man," Terrence said, "if you ever want to get out of your line of work and make some real money, I can show you the ropes."

"What do you do?" Ryah asked not actually interested in the answer.

"I'm a broker of sorts. I get people what they want," Terrence said. "Help them connect with those who have it. For a small fee of course. I'm surprised you don't know me or at least know of me."

"What sort of things?" Ryah asked hoping that Terrence would let slip something in his drug induced state. He wasn't disappointed.

"Whatever. Weapons, pharmaceuticals, women, men, information. It doesn't matter what you need, I'm your guy. And everybody here knows it." Terrence beamed with pride. "When the Russians need something from the Chinese, they go through me. If the Israelis got something the Arabs want, the Arabs'll ask me to get it. To help them save face, you know. A Saudi sheik needs to add to his harem collection. That's me. Nothing too big or too small. And all this talk about war now, it's good for business. It's not like I need to do anything to encourage it. People are happy to hate each other, and I'm happy to take advantage of it. Look, there's winners and losers in everything, right? Those with power and those destined to serve those in power. That's just the way of the world." His voice became hushed. "I've got a shipment of blacks going to North Africa right now. The strong ones and pretty ones will be kept there. The rest will be shipped over to the continent. If a storm comes along and sinks the leftovers, then that's too bad, eh?" He gave Ryah a knowing wink. "The UN here. They got all sorts of commissions 'fighting against' what I do, so they say. But the governments of their constituent nations rely on the money and goods I broker, so the UN looks the other way. They bluster on about human rights and dignity and all that. 'The conscience of the world.' Isn't that what they call themselves? But they're more than happy with what I provide. Look. You know, everyone here's on the take. Every single one. Except Ambassador Tanas and Envoy Romijn. They're apparently incorruptible. As for the rest of the people here at the UN, they let me do what I want, because I provide the services that keep the leaders of the nations happy. Without me being the intermediary between the UN and their constituent nations, providing each side what they want from the other one, the countries would turn on the UN and it'd be just another dog with no bite. The UN wouldn't have an army to enforce their decrees. A delicate balance between subservience and rebellion, and I'm the one who maintains it. If you ask me, though, I don't think the UN'll be happy until the Russians, the Chinese, and the US come under their umbrella. Personally, I hope that doesn't happen. Not in my lifetime anyway. There's nothing in that for me."

"*This guy's a sleaze,*" Ryah thought, "*but he's not who I'm looking for.*"

The waitress returned with water and left as Terrence invited another man over. He spoke with him briefly before the man left.

"That was Omar Muhammed," Terrence said. "Direct Representative of the Turkish-Persian Supreme Assembly. You'll never see him on the news, but he's the one who gets things done. He wanted to know if his shipment of missiles is on the way. I told him once the money hits my bank, they'll be moving."

267

"What are they for?" Ryah asked.

"Who knows?" Terrence said. "Blowing up Jews. Shooting down planes. Killing other Muslims who aren't 'pure Muslims'. What do I care? Just as long as the check clears." He paused for a moment. "You should come join me. You look like someone I could trust. Someone who knows his way around."

"It doesn't look like you need me," Ryah said.

"I've got too much business. I've been looking for a right-hand man to help me out," Terrence said. "Besides, it wasn't at random that I came up to you."

"What do you mean?" Ryah asked.

"Your name was whispered in my ear," Terrence said.

Ryah couldn't tell if Terrence was being sincere or if he was just a slick talker.

"How much are we talking?" He asked.

"Ten million. A month that is. Easy," Terrence said. "I'm making double that. You'd have to make your own territory, but I'd give you some cash and some leads to get you started. You just give me a cut. Fifty percent the first year. Ten percent less each year. You'll be rich beyond your dreams. Get yourself anything you want. You can never have too much." He smiled again. "What d'ya say?"

"Tempting," Ryah said. "I'll think about it."

"Don't think too long," Terrence said. "You're not the only person I've got my eye on."

Terrence extended his fleshy hand again and left to start another conversation. Ryah looked for the nearest restroom to wash the stench off his hands. As he did the room began to spin. The lights flickered on and off, creating a strobe effect, but no one seemed to notice.

In the pulsating light, faces without bodies appeared and disappeared, swirling in and around the people like a haunted chorus, dancing an otherworldly ballet. Mesmerizing. Inviting. Everyone joined in, swaying along

268

in rhythm. Above the hall, a giant crystal chandelier swung gently back and forth. Ryah looked up and saw thousands of reflections of the people below bouncing off the individual pieces of glass as though he was looking through the eyes of a fly. And then he saw them. Everywhere. In the air above the people and all around. Shadows fighting each other in order to gain control of the people. Bargaining. Bartering with each other. Grasping shadowy chains which snaked through the room and entangled people in their links.

Ryah fled, running over people in his haste to escape. Fear overcoming conscience thought. He saw the people's eyes as he ran. Lifeless but unaware they were.

He busted through a door and found himself in the restroom, alone except for a man who was on his way out. Ryah splashed some cold water on his face and wiped it off with a handful of paper towels.

He looked in the mirror. His own face stared back. The piercing eyes. The strong jawline. As he gazed into the mirror, a mist behind him began to form. A dark churning shadow transforming into a pair of hands that came behind Ryah and covered his ears. He screamed but heard nothing.

Chapter 32

"Hey Ryah," Rogan said. "I've been looking all over for you. Where've you been?"

Ryah didn't respond. His eyes were open wide as if he had seen a ghost. He looked over at Rogan. "Tell Lucio I'm feeling ill," he said, "and that I need to go."

"Alright," Rogan said. "Give me a minute. I'll find him and go with you."

A minute later Rogan returned and walked Ryah down a different corridor back to Lucio's apartment. By then, Ryah had calmed down, and Rogan figured it would be OK to ask him questions now.

"What happened?" Rogan asked.

"Don't know," Ryah said. "Must be something I ate. I'm going to try to sleep."

Ryah went back to the room and moved a few boxes out of the way to get to the bed. He lay down, waiting for the adrenaline to wear off, and drifted into a restless sleep. It only felt like a few minutes when Lucio came and knocked on his door.

"Hey Ryah," Lucio said. "I've got a meeting in thirty minutes and I'd like you to be there."

Ryah looked at his watch. It was almost ten in the morning. He took a quick shower and joined Lucio on his walk to the office. Lucio briefed Ryah and Rogan on who and what to expect but made no mention of last night other than to ask Ryah if he was feeling better. At ten thirty, they were seated in a conference room with General Brostov and his associates along with Vice Premier Xiao who had taken over the negotiations for the Chinese.

Ryah sat beside Lucio at the head of the table this time, while Rogan remained behind and to the right. The discussion began again with each side reminding the other of where they stood. Ryah stared across the table at General Brostov as something in the shadows behind the general leaned forward and whispered in his ear. Ryah heard it speak.

"General, we are prepared to meet the request of the Vice Premier. Let him know that it is acceptable," it said.

"Your request is acceptable," General Brostov echoed.

Ryah rubbed his eyes. "*Not now.*"

It leaned forward and whispered in the general's ear again.

"But only if …," it said.

"But only if," the general repeated.

"You meet our demands," it said.

"You meet our demands," the general said.

"Which demands are those?" Vice Premier Xiao asked.

"About them," the shadow whispered. Its black face pressed up against the neck of General Brostov, a tongue flickering in and out of his ear.

"About them," Brostov said.

"They are the ones that created this mess. We want you to bring the traitors to us," the shadow said and Brostov repeated.

Xiao spoke up. "That we can do, and we will do."

The Chinese Vice Premier leaned back and whispered to his associates. Ryah sat on the edge of the chair, his fingers digging into the table until they started to bleed. He wanted to run, but a force like an invisible hand held him in place.

The shadow continued to talk to the Russian. "You can't trust Xiao. Everything he tells you is a lie. The Chinese have sided with them and want to rule with them."

The Chinese Vice Premier stared at the Russian from across the table. A second figure, black and formless, went up to Xiao.

"But we demand you turn over the Russian murderers that helped in the assassination of General Chao," the second shadow whispered to the Vice Premier.

The Vice Premier obediently repeated it out loud. General Brostov's face turned deep red.

"We had no part in that," Brostov insisted, upset by the implication.

"I told you they were liars," the shadow whispered in Brostov's ear.

"I told you they were involved," the other shadow whispered in Xiao's ear. "They're with them and want to rule with them."

The negotiations devolved as the parties shouted back and forth at each other. Distracted by the argument, Ryah didn't notice the shadows staring directly at him.

While Ryah watched, his attention diverted, a third shadow appeared and whispered in Lucio's ear. "Look at who you're dealing with. It's hopeless."

Lucio spoke up. "Gentlemen. I know you have concerns, but there's always a way. Let's concentrate on what we can agree on first and then work through each of the other issues separately."

"It's hopeless," the shadow repeated. "Peace is no longer possible until the kingdom is restored."

"We've got to continue working together," Lucio told the Russians and the Chinese. "The world needs you to reconcile."

"NO!" the shadow screamed in Lucio's ear. "War is what we need."

Lucio kept speaking as if he was oblivious to the shadow, as if it had no influence over him.

The shadow became furious, its face transforming into a raging fire ready to consume Lucio. Ryah's arms twitched and his body began to shake. The shadow turned towards Ryah. It studied him and watched his expressions. It slid back and forth, left and right. Ryah's eyes followed. Back and forth, left and right, tracking the shadow in its movement. The shadow moved on top of General Brostov and raised an arm. A long knife appeared at the end. It lowered the arm over the general's head as if it were going to impale him.

"No!" Ryah screamed out.

The shadows froze for a moment and then converged on Ryah. He jumped out of his seat before they could reach him and fled the room, oblivious to the stares of the delegates. When he got outside, he ran down the hall, past security, and out of the building, not stopping until he reached Lucio's apartment. There, he huddled in a corner and felt the fear overcome him. It hadn't been long before he heard a voice say, *"Don't stay here. They're coming. Go now."*

Ryah obeyed without question and tore out of the apartment. The sound of a gunshot echoed in the stairwell. A bullet whistled past Ryah's head. His brain shut down and instinct took over.

"The fire escape."

Ryah opened the window and jumped through, sliding down the handrails to each level until he reached the ground.

"Keep going. They're behind you."

He heard their shouts. Six. Seven distinct voices. Maybe more. Others with them that didn't say anything.

"You've got a decent head start."

His feet pounded on the pavement as he darted down an alley, knocking over a trash can and almost falling. His heart raced, the adrenaline pushing him forward in a blind rush. A turn to the left and down another alley. Over a wooden fence, his shirt catching on a loose nail and holding him up for a second. The footsteps and the shouting ever closer. Surrounding him. Boxing him in. Down another alley.

Ryah stopped. He had run into a dead end. With nowhere left to go he turned and faced his pursuers. At least ten of them. Knives and batons came out. Ryah looked around for something to defend himself with.

His pursuers came at him in waves. Darting in and out. Slashing. Swinging. Ryah felt a knife cut through his arm. He fought back. Picking up one of the attackers and throwing him into the wall. It was only enough to stun him for a moment, and the man was back in the fight.

A baton flew through the air, but Ryah ducked just in time. A trailing knife thrust was blocked. He struck back with a well-timed punched to the man's nose. It cracked, sending a spray of blood through the air. Another blow from a baton. This one landed on his shoulder. It hurt but didn't do permanent damage. Ryah spun around in time to receive a punch just below the ribs from an attacker who had been behind him. Ryah doubled over in pain as the strike smashed into his liver.

"Don't give up."

But there were too many of them, and Ryah's strength waned with each blow. One on the back of his knee buckled him. He stood back up and took another crack to his temple. He shook his head. Everything was foggy. The air spun and time seemed to freeze. He staggered like a man who was drunk. Hopeless. Desperate to hang on to life. One more strike and Ryah crashed to the ground, his face smashing into the stones in the alley. He couldn't move but could only look straight out at the feet and legs of his attackers who moved towards him.

They could take their time now and they knew it. There was nothing Ryah could do anymore. No way to prevent them from completing their mission. Ryah felt the knee in the small of his back. Felt his head being lifted up and the cold of the blade touch his throat. He didn't have any time left. This was it.

Ryah sensed the weight being lifted off his back. He was at complete peace. He moved his head and looked around, wondering if this was what the afterlife was like. Wondering if he had been wrong his whole life about there being one. A body flew through the air and crashed against the wall. It didn't get up. Another one. Arms and legs flailed. Curses spewed out of unseen mouths. The sound of a battle raging above him, but Ryah didn't care. He no longer felt any pain and didn't care what waited for him. Whether it was Heaven or Hell. Valhalla or Sheol. It was all the same to him.

For what seemed like an eternity, the fight continued, the din diminishing with each passing minute until it was silent. Ryah lay there and watched. A shadow approached him, gliding up in front of him and blocking the light streaming through the alley. An arm reached down and lifted him up.

"Ryah, are you alright? Ryah."

Ryah's mind began to clear and his vision came into focus.

"Ryah. Wake up buddy."

It was Rogan.

"Ryah," he said. "We gotta get the hell out of here."

Chapter 33

"What happened?" Ryah asked. He felt the effects of a concussion and a temporary loss of memory.

"We'll deal with that later," Rogan said. "Right now, we need to go."

Rogan helped Ryah to his feet and held on to him as they staggered past the bodies strewn throughout the alley. None of them wearing a uniform to let Ryah know which group they belonged to. None of them alive to tell him what they knew. The wound on Ryah's arm was superficial and needed only a little pressure to stop the blood flow. The bigger problem was the throbbing in Ryah's head caused by at least three solid baton strikes as well as the blow when he landed on the ground. It would take more than a couple aspirin to silence the pounding, but he had been in this situation before and knew how to keep from being incapacitated while he waited for full recovery.

They went back to the main road and found a small shop which hadn't closed for lunch yet. Inside, a woman at the counter watched as they entered, nervous as she saw the bruise on Ryah's forehead.

"My friend fell," Rogan said. "Wasn't watching where he was going and hit his head on a bench. Do you have a restroom we could borrow so I could clean him up? It won't take a minute."

The clerk, who had a limited command of English, understood enough to lead them to the bathroom located in the back.

"Hai bisogno di aiuto?" she asked. "Chiamo l'ambulanza?"

"No, grazie," Ryah said. "I'll be OK. Sto bene."

He washed himself off, while Rogan pretended to look at the leather goods that were on display, spending most of his time taking glances out the window to make sure no one had followed them. When Ryah came out of the storeroom area, Rogan asked the clerk if there was a space in the back where Ryah could sit for a few minutes to recuperate.

"I have to leave my friend here for a moment, if you don't mind," Rogan told the clerk. "He dropped his wallet, and I need to look for it." After Ryah translated, Rogan said to him, "I'm going back to the alley to see if I can find any clues as to who those people are. It shouldn't take more than thirty minutes, but I don't want you getting in my way in your condition. Play nice with the lady. I think she's taken a liking to you."

He nodded towards the woman with his chin. Ryah looked at her and saw the concern on her face as if he were a hurt puppy she needed to nurse back to health. He gave the woman his best smile, which came out as more of a grimace, something she found adorable and turned back to Rogan. His eyes said it all. "*Please hurry back.*" It seemed Ryah was more afraid of being alone with this woman doting on him than going back and facing an army of strangers.

His worries were unfounded, though. The woman, Giulia, tended to him, cleaning the wound on his arm and placing a balm on it before wrapping it in some gauze. She poured a clear, viscous liquid, a kind of oil, on his forehead and temple, which had an immediate, soothing effect on the pain. After she finished, she made him an espresso, rich, dark, perfect like only the Italians can make.

Thirty minutes later, Rogan returned. Ryah thanked Giulia and left with Rogan who seemed anxious to speak with him in private. They stuck to the alleys, avoiding the main streets as much as possible, and kept a vigil for vehicles or people that looked suspicious.

"We need to get you a change of clothes," Rogan said. "You stick out even more so than normal. Lucio's apartment is off limits. They'll be looking for you there."

"Who are they?" Ryah asked, pretty sure of the answer but wanting to know what Rogan thought.

"I can't say for sure," Rogan said, "but I know Abbad's involved."

Ryah's fears had been realized. It seems that Lucio's faith in Abbad was misplaced after all, not that it surprised Ryah.

"I suspect that, too," Ryah said.

"It's not a suspicion," Rogan said. "There's no doubt about the connection."

Ryah understood that Rogan had found something.

Rogan continued. "When the assassin took off, or I should say attempted assassin, there was a lot of chaos in the room at first, as you can imagine."

Ryah had no idea what Rogan was talking about.

"You're going to have to back up a bit," Ryah said. "For some reason, there's a big gap in my memory. I recall going to the meeting room and seeing Lucio, the Russians, and the Chinese, and then my mind goes blank until you helped me to my feet. It must be the concussion. Do me a favor and help me fill in the holes."

"You don't remember chasing after the assassin?" Rogan asked.

Ryah shook his head. "I don't really remember anything."

"You yelled and everyone in the room looked," Rogan said. "It was just enough to get Brostov to turn and move his head out of the way. The bullet shattered the window and skimmed his jaw. By the looks of the hole in the far wall, the projectile came from a rifle. It was definitely high powered, but I don't know how they got a weapon in there. I didn't see it, so I imagine it was a bull pup of some sort

278

with a short barrel. The guy was wearing a cloak. I saw that. And to get the weapon past all the security, he had to have had inside help."

Ryah nodded in agreement but let Rogan talk. Ryah was sure none of that had happened, at least not in the way it was described. The concussion had not affected his memory at all, and every detail remained perfectly clear. It was as if he saw one thing happen while everyone else saw something else. Two worlds colliding. One seen. One unseen, hidden behind a veil that hung over the eyes of unsuspecting men, blinding them to a truth they didn't want to discover. Two realms entangled. Humans and shadows chained to each other in a single destiny. But for Ryah, the curtain had been pulled back. Just a little. Enough to see but not enough to understand. Enough to know someone was speaking to him but not enough to hear what he was saying.

"And then you took off," Rogan said. "I stayed behind to make sure Lucio was fine. He told me to go after you. You had a couple minute head start by the time I made it out of there, so I didn't know where you had gone. I headed out the front and saw a group of people, the ones that attacked you in the alley, running down the street towards Lucio's place. I assumed they were security going after the assassin, trying to help you, so I followed. But I had a funny feeling. They weren't in uniform. I didn't see any weapons at first. I saw one of them, one of the last ones out, sending the uniformed security in the opposite direction. When they disappeared, he took off towards your position, or what turned out to be your position. I decided to tail him. He bypassed Lucio's apartment and ran down some alleys in the back, probably a mile or more, finally reaching the one where you were. He slowed up, so I did the same, and I heard the sounds of a fight just beyond him. I got as close as I could without being noticed, and when I saw what was happening, I took him out and came in to help you. You held your own. I was impressed, but they were too much."

"How'd you manage to take all of them out?" Ryah asked.

"I'm a gamma," Rogan said without arrogance. "Anyway, as I was helping you up, I saw him come into the alley, size up the situation, and slip out. He didn't know I saw him, I don't think."

"Who?" Ryah asked.

"Abbad," Rogan said. "It was him. There is no doubt it was him and that he's involved."

Ryah thought for a moment. "Did you find anything when you went back just now?" he asked.

"That's the strange thing," Rogan said. "It couldn't have been more than fifteen maybe twenty minutes between the time we left and the time I made it back to the alley. But there was nothing there. The whole scene had been sanitized. I didn't find a single clue or indication that anything had happened. Either Abbad is more powerful than we thought, or the conspiracy is greater than we realized, because it would have taken a lot to clean up all those bodies. There was one thing, though. When I was helping you out, I remember seeing the tattoo. The one that so many people in the Kingdom wear. However, it was on their left wrists, the ones who had it. I'm not sure of the significance of that, seeing how everyone in the states had it on their right wrist. Different branch? Is that how they distinguish themselves over here?"

Ryah shrugged and kept walking along as best he could. After a short time, they found themselves across the street from one of the ubiquitous coffee bars which dotted the streets of Rome. Rogan left in search of a change of clothes and an ATM to get currency off their cards, figuring it would be harder for whoever was after them to track their movements if they used cash. Rogan returned having found

280

what he needed as well as a cheap hotel where they could hole up until they could plan out their next move.

"I received a message from Lucio while I was gone," Rogan said. "He wanted us to meet him right away. Sounded urgent. I didn't answer and took out the GPS card so they couldn't trace us through my comm. Went to the subway and threw it on a train. Not that I don't trust Lucio. I just don't trust anybody."

"Smart move," Ryah said. He reached for his comm but couldn't find it.

"You dropped it in the alley," Rogan said. "I was going to go back for it, but it was gone, along with everything else there."

"I'm going to need to contact Lucio," Ryah said. "If he's in on this, I'm going to want to know what he knows. See if I can get him to let some information slip. If he's not, then he probably has information that he'll give willingly. Let me go 'borrow' a comm, so I can give him a call. Follow me in a few minutes but make sure no one sees you. If I don't make it out this time, I want you to leave me and get back to the US. Let the Council know what's happening."

Rogan followed Ryah's command and watched as he entered the bar across the street. A few minutes later, Ryah gave a quick, barely perceptible signal to Rogan and left. Ryah kept walking for another twenty minutes until he came to a park beyond the old Borghese Gallery, where he switched on the comm he borrowed from someone's coat pocket and called Lucio.

"Lucio. It's Ryah."

"Ryah. I'm glad to hear from you," Lucio said. "Been trying to reach you all day. Where's Rogan? Is he with you?"

"Rogan's fine," Ryah said. "Both our comms got lost in the pursuit, so I had to procure this one. How are things over there?"

"That's what I've got to talk to you about," Lucio said.

"What is it?"

"I can't tell you now," Lucio said. "I'll need to meet you in person. Where and when can I find you?"

Ryah hesitated. Was this a trap? It didn't sound like one. Lucio's voice trembled, like he was afraid he was about to be discovered.

"It's urgent," Lucio said. "I can't tell you now, but … wait, I've got to go. Call me back in five minutes."

He disconnected, leaving Ryah wondering what was happening. Ryah knew he needed to move, so he took off jogging down the road to get as far away from his previous position as he could in five minutes. He waited an extra few and then called Lucio back.

"Ryah," Lucio said. "Something's going on. Give me an hour and meet me at the place I showed you that one time. The Piazza."

Ryah knew what Lucio meant. The Piazza was a public area with many escape routes. The kind of place to meet if Lucio had no desire to trap him. An intentional decision to make him feel safe.

"Will Rogan be there with you?" Lucio asked.

"No," Ryah lied, still not sure of Lucio's motives. "He's off following a clue we found, but I'll let him know what we talk about."

Ryah tossed the comm behind a tree, not bothering to shut it off, and found a place where he could survey the scene without being spotted. He stayed in his hiding place for thirty minutes, giving him enough time to make it to the meeting location and scout it out. No one came in search of the comm. There was no other unusual activity either, providing him a measure of confidence that Lucio could be trusted.

As Ryah headed to the Piazza, Rogan appeared by his side.

"I saw you toss the comm," Rogan said. "What's the plan now?"

"I'm headed to meet Lucio in half an hour at the Piazza del Popolo," Ryah said. "He says he has information for me. I'll get there and scope it out for a while. See if Lucio shows up and if anyone's following and then make him wait on me. I'll find another pair of comms so we can communicate."

"I'm two steps ahead of you," Rogan said and handed a comm to Ryah.

"Where'd you get these?" Ryah asked. "Never mind," he said when he saw the look on Rogan's face.

"I've already figured out their identification numbers and have them on auto call," Rogan said. "Just say 'Contact Rogue'."

"Got it," Ryah said and moved away from Rogan to make his approach solo.

Across the street from the Piazza del Popolo, there was a mini mall where Ryah decided to wait. A large window looked out over Via del Corso and gave him a clear view when Lucio entered the plaza. He walked to the obelisk in the center and looked around, trying to remain inconspicuous but not doing a good job. He had nothing with him that Ryah could see except for a folder. Lucio leaned against the gate that surrounded the obelisk and waited. And waited. The sun began its descent and Lucio grew more impatient. He finally decided to leave and headed towards Via del Corso.

"Lucio," Ryah called out.

Lucio turned his head. The aggravation was etched in his face.

"Where have you been?" Lucio asked. "I asked you to meet me an hour ago."

"I was watching you," Ryah asked. "Making sure you weren't followed."

Lucio took a deep sigh and let out his frustration. "I forgot your background. I would have done the same in your place." He waited for a moment to calm himself down. "Alright. Now that you're here, I need you to see this." He handed Ryah the folder. "I don't know how to tell you this, except to be straight forward." He took a deep breath. "I was wrong. Very wrong. Deceived by him. But not anymore."

Ryah looked through the folder. There was a long series of communications, at least six times back and forth with a contact in the US. The words were cryptic, but the overall meaning was clear. Accompanying it were two pictures. He stared at them, then looked away, lost in contemplation.

"How'd you get this?" Ryah asked.

"After you ran out, I went up to report to him, but he wasn't in his office," Lucio said. "I went to his desk to write him a note, and while I was doing this, his screen came on displaying the latest message you saw there. For some reason, I thought he knew I was there and that he was trying to contact me, so I looked at it. I wished I hadn't read it, but I know now I needed to." He scratched his eyebrow with his left hand, a nervous tic Ryah had picked up on. "I downloaded it, went back to my office, and printed it out, after disconnecting from the server, of course."

Ryah processed everything Lucio said. Every word. Every inflection of his voice. Every wrinkle on his face.

"Why are you coming to me with this?" Ryah asked. "You need to turn it in to the authorities."

"You don't understand," Lucio said. "If I try to send this out electronically, he'll intercept the communication. He has too many friends in all the right places. I thought about going directly to Ambassador Tanas, but he's not around, and when he is around, the other one's tied to his hip. There's no one else to go to in the UN. No one I can trust at this moment. Just you and Rogan."

"What am I supposed to do with this?" Ryah asked.

"Take it back to your Council," Lucio said. "It involves you as much as it does the Russians and the Chinese. Get it out of here tonight. I'll make an excuse, saying you got called back by Klins. Take my plane. I'll have it ready for you in an hour."

"That won't work," Ryah said. "If everything is as you say, I don't want this getting tied back to you. We need to make it look like we acquired the information on our own and are trying to get it back surreptitiously. Not sure how to do it though."

"Greece," Lucio said.

"Greece?"

"They're a part of the UN, but they act rather independently. If you can get across the border without being caught, you can find a flight back to the US. They're going to step up the timetable, I'm sure, especially if they think you have the information, so you have to get back and warn the Council before this happens."

"Why can't I just call the Council?" Ryah asked.

Lucio hesitated. "It's because … well, I don't know how to say it … we have your entire network under surveillance. Every communication that comes out, we have the ability to intercept it. Cancel it. Change it. Whatever we want before it gets to you."

"For how long?"

"Six months," Lucio said. "I argued against it and have never used it, but Abbad never had qualms about it. Actually, he was the one who pushed for it and led the project. I guess I know the full reason why now."

"Greece." Ryah said it as sort of a question. "How about resources?"

"Use your card," Lucio said. "I took the liberty of refunding it in full. If they're tracking you, they'll be able to follow, but there'll be a delay. When you get to Greece, be creative."

"Can't I just turn it to currency?" Ryah asked.

"Yes. But the card won't allow you to withdraw enough for what you need, and I didn't have any on me," Lucio said. "Sooner or later, you're going to have to make an electronic purchase."

"OK," Ryah said. "Are these copies for me?"

"Yes. Yes, of course," Lucio said. "Take them."

Ryah turned to go but he stopped. "Why are you helping us? If he finds out …"

"I know," Lucio interrupted. "But I need to do what I can to stop this from happening. Even if it means my life."

Ryah headed down Via del Corso and was soon joined by Rogan.

"Did you hear everything?" Ryah asked.

"Yeah, my comm was open," Rogan said.

"What do you think?" Ryah asked.

"I think Lucio was being sincere," Rogan said. "That is, I couldn't detect any deception."

"That was my impression too," Ryah said.

"What was in the communication?" Rogan asked.

"It was between Abbad and a contact in the states," Ryah said. He handed Rogan the file. "I know her. I met with her once. She came to me and asked me to back off her group. She was the one we tracked out to the Kinset Valley."

In the photo, Abbad was seen with Allison. The picture was grainy, but it was clear who the two were. It wasn't a casual meeting. That was for sure. Not with the communication between the two.

"So that's their plan," Rogan said when he finished reading. "Make it look like the Chinese are going to do it."

"Yep," Ryah said. "To draw us into the war against them."

"But it's really the Russians?" Rogan asked.

"No," Ryah said. "It's the Kingdom. They're just waiting for Abbad's orders, but they've put a back door in so that if anyone digs a little deeper, they'll think it's the Russians. Either way, the Council will be dragged into the war, and the only group that will come out a winner is the Kingdom."

"It's clever … what they're doing," Rogan said. "I mean how they plan to spread the virus. By the time people figure out what's happening, half of the people will be infected. We'll be weakened and we'll have no choice but to align ourselves with some other nation for self-preservation. Them or perhaps the UN."

"Using the prostitutes and the homeless to carry the disease," Ryah said. "That's why they had their headquarters down there." He paused for a while. "I can't believe I fell for her lies. I won't make the same mistake again."

Chapter 34

Termini Station was crowded, giving Ryah and Rogan the cover they needed. They had already spotted a team of four set up to do roaming surveillance, but the station was too large for them to be effective. It was clear this location was an afterthought, more of a cover all the bases thing than it was a serious belief the two would come here. The team spent most of their time covering the subway line that led to the airport, which is where the rest of Abbad's goon squad, as Rogan called them, had gone, expecting that the two would fly to the US as soon as they could. In that respect, Lucio's advice had been good, and Ryah was starting to have more faith in the envoy. But his recommendation of Abbad had almost proved fatal, so Ryah wasn't in a hurry to put his full trust in him.

Through it all, Ryah had the uncomfortable sensation something was amiss. His stomach was churning – the signal that things weren't what they seemed, that danger waited around each corner. He scanned the crowds, looking for the telltale signs of a trained operative. They moved in a certain way, looked at people, looked through people, spoke, and even ate and drank in a manner that betrayed their training. The only one he had ever seen that didn't act like that was Rogan. He could fit in with a group of tourists one minute then interact with a cluster of nuns the next, and no one would think anything of it. There was a lot about his young friend that he didn't know, but what he did know was that when all hell broke loose, Rogan was one he wanted by his side.

"How you doing, Ry?" Rogan asked.

"Good. I haven't found any trouble up here," Ryah said. "The last time I saw the goon squad was twenty minutes ago. They're sending out a pair regular as clockwork. One more round before we get on the train."

"Remind me of our route again," Rogan said.

"The frecciarossa to Brindisi. Hop a ferry to Patras. Bus to Athens and then fly home. With any luck we'll be there the day after tomorrow," Ryah said.

"Do you think we've got the time?" Rogan asked.

"We don't have much of a choice," Ryah said. "The communication said the attack was for next month. I'm sure they'll move up the timetable now, if they can't capture us, but they'll spend a few days trying to find us before they make any changes." It was more wishful thinking than fact, and Ryah knew it.

The surveillance team passed by, and Ryah and Rogan boarded the train which had just pulled into the berth. They found their seats in car seven across from a pair of college students backpacking their way across the continent. The two girls began flirting with them as soon as they sat down, bringing unwanted attention when all Ryah wanted was to remain inconspicuous. When the train started rolling, he found an empty booth in the back of the car and went there for some privacy while Rogan kept the girls occupied.

"Five hours," he thought. "That's plenty of time to get some sleep."

He shut his eyes and tried to ignore the thoughts that kept creeping into his mind. The intercepted communications between Abbad and Allison. The talk in the café. The woman with those fierce, green eyes which had mesmerized him, made him believe. Made him a fool. And to think, he had saved her on the transit.

"*Still,*" Ryah thought, "*I get the feeling I'm missing something. Maybe she's innocent in all this. Caught up in the conspiracy without wanting to be a part. I can't believe she's involved.*"

But there she was in the picture. Standing in the background behind Abbad and Allison. There was no denying what he saw. He just wished it wasn't true.

Ryah took off the sweater covering the wound on his arm and rolled it under his head.

"I'll deal with her when the time comes," he thought and drifted off to sleep.

His dreams were restless. Thoughts of people and shadows chained to each other and chasing him.

He tried to run but his legs were buried in mud. A storm raged overhead. Lightning strikes illuminated faces, a different one with each flash, laughing at him as he tried to pull himself along the ground in a desperate attempt to allude his pursuers who inched ever closer. A soft voice whispered to him, but he couldn't hear it. He strained his whole body to listen. It spoke truth to him. He knew it, but the words fell on deaf ears. If only he could find the source, get close to it, make sense of it.

Without warning, the muck and mire disappeared, and he found himself on a vast, empty plain. The smell of disease and decay filled the air. Whichever way he turned, the stench grew stronger, sinking down into his airway and saturating his lungs. The sickness seeped into his blood stream and corrupted him from the inside. His flesh began to decompose, the odor of death reeking from his corpse-like body.

The earth around him fell away and exposed a field of coffins. The lids opened, releasing their dead, raised up to exact revenge on the one who had sent them to their graves. Ryah shut his eyes in a futile attempt to blind himself to his own guilt and covered his ears to protect himself from the wailing charges which fell from the lips of his accusers. Their screams became a rush of wind that blew through his body and threatened to rip him apart.

A man came up beside Ryah. He stared straight ahead without seeing Ryah, looking into a darkness that surrounded him. His lips opened and closed as if he was repeatedly mouthing a single word. Ryah peered at the face. He knew the face. "Evan?" Ryah asked out loud but the man didn't answer.

As he watched, a young woman with deep, emerald eyes walked past the man, brushing by him as she headed towards a distant light. The man reached out to get her attention, but she ignored him and continued on. He tried to run after her. A large metal shackle around his waist tightened, digging into his ribs and causing him to cry out in pain. Ryah followed a chain attached to the shackle as it winded its way back into the darkness. At the end of the chain, a grotesque, disfigured shadow stood, laughing as it pulled the man away from the young woman with deep, emerald eyes and a scar down her cheek. The man called out a name Ryah didn't understand. The man yelled again, this time a screech that seemed to emanate from the shadow and not from him. The young woman stopped for a moment, turned, and gave him a smile before disappearing from their sight.

The man's eyes grew wide. He fell to his knees and began to sob. A dark cloud appeared above his head and a powerful wind began to blow. Lightning arced through the sky and touched the ground all around, setting off a fire that engulfed him. He didn't move, didn't try to escape as the inferno grew. Through the roar of the flames, Ryah heard the man scream out, "You promised. You promised." Ryah looked to see who he was talking to, but the shadow had disappeared as well. With a sickening sizzle, the man's face caught on fire and began to melt, starting with the forehead and traveling downwards until only the mouth remained, repeating the words over and over. "You promised." Ryah shut his eyes in order to block out the horror and covered his ears so he wouldn't have to hear him anymore, but still the words came through, rising above the exploding thunder.

A touch on his shoulder. Ryah opened his eyes. All was calm. He stood on an ancient mountain worn down by wind and rain until it was barely more than a hill. New blades of grass sprung to life between the rocks that jutted out of the surface. White flowers dotted the valley below, gleaming in the rays of the glorious light that shone down from above and giving it the illusion of a white river flowing in a gentle breeze. He was on the outskirts of a city, but he only saw one man, frail in body but strong in spirit, who walked along the edge of a cliff, guiding his herd of sheep from one patch of grass to the next.

"Go to him."

Ryah jerked around.

"He will tell you."

"Who is he?" Ryah asked. "Tell me what?"

"Go to him."

"How do I find him?" Ryah asked.

"Look around. You know."

Ryah looked around. He had been here before, and he knew what he had to do. When he turned back, Guriel had disappeared.

Ryah woke up as the train pulled into Brindisi and went to find Rogan who was sitting alone. "Change of plans," Ryah said. "I'm going somewhere else first."

"Where to?" Rogan asked.

"Jerusalem."

Rogan scrunched his face.

"You don't have to go if you don't want," Ryah said, annoyed more out of exhaustion than by Rogan's expression. "Feel free to head back. Let the Council know I'll follow in a few days."

"It's not that," Rogan said. He pulled a couple of tickets out of his pocket and handed them to Ryah. "I was talking to the girls that sat across from us. Said they had plans to travel to Israel but changed their minds at the last minute. I guess they took a liking to me and asked if I could use their tickets. I took them to not be rude – and because one of them was kind of cute – but I was going to throw them out when we left the train. Crazy coincidence, huh?"

"Yeah," Ryah said. "Crazy coincidence."

Chapter 35

Ryah traded in the cards for the remaining currency just before they boarded the plane. He knew that Abbad would be alerted in a matter of minutes to their location, but he wouldn't have any idea where they had gone, at least for a while. Even if Abbad did find out, he would be powerless to stop them. Israel had withdrawn from the UN at the same time the United States did and refused to maintain any official ties with the international organization. The tiny nation had been slowly cut off from the rest of the world and the lone semi-formal relationship they retained was with the Council.

Ryah had been included as an attaché on more than one joint military mission with the Israelis, so at the airline counter after the clerk denied Ryah access to the flight, one call to his contact in Israeli intelligence got him on the plane. Not a single operative from any other foreign power, besides a few Americans, could be found within the walls that Israel had constructed around its entire border, and Ryah knew he would have nothing to worry about from Abbad. Once the plane took off and entered international airspace, he switched back to his US credentials.

After making a mental check of the remaining currency, Ryah calculated he could make it last for three days, assuming he would be able to catch a military transport back to the US. When they landed, he hailed a taxi and sent Rogan off to get a hotel.

"Make it for two nights," Ryah told him, "but only pay for the first night, just in case."

As he sat in the taxi looking out the window, the old city came into view. The earthquakes had leveled much of Jerusalem two years ago, but because of outside pressure and the nation's isolation, the Israelis had been struggling to rebuild. He passed near the summit of Mount Moriah and caught a glimpse of the ruins of the Dome of the Rock and the Western Wall which lay scattered across the old temple mount, structures unable to be rebuilt. Government funds were reserved for necessities, and those relics of an ancient past were considered luxuries, a reminder of a time when religion had meaning. Now survival was all that mattered, for the Israelis and for Ryah.

The driver neared Har ha-Zeitim and dropped Ryah off at the foot of the old, weathered mountain.

"You sure I drop you off here?" the driver asked in a thick accent.

"Yeah," was all Ryah said.

The sun beat down on him. They were in the middle of a rainy season where the clouds would roll in like clockwork just before noon and unleash their fury for an hour. Right after the deluge finished, the sun would come out and dry up the land so that a few hours later there would be no sign that it had rained except for the new grass on the hillside and the fresh flowers in the valley below. Ryah looked at his watch. Off in the distance, the sky grew dark. He climbed to the remains of a house that stood halfway up the mountain. Another few minutes, give or take, and he would be caught in the downpour.

He looked around. This was the correct place. He knew it the moment he saw it, but why was he here? The first drops started to hit the roof, creating a dull plink as they ricocheted off the tiles. The rain intensified, slowly at first and then increasing to a torrent, until it flowed over the windows like a river of liquid glass and drowned out the world outside. He found a dry corner of the house, sat down against the wall, and breathed in the strange combination of dust and mildew. The warped floorboards bowed under his weight and creaked their disapproval.

It was dark inside the house. The electricity had long been cut off, and what little ambient light there was had a difficult time penetrating the windows. A slight breeze churned the curtains. Ryah watched their outlines trembling in the half-light like spirits dancing a ghastly waltz. Dark shadows raced up and down the entranceway hall as the front door swung open and closed, battered by the elements outside. Despite the conditions, he felt at peace, shutting his eyes and listening to the rain. He stayed there for a few minutes. Alone. Secure.

A chill traveling down his spine alerted him and woke him from his trance. Ryah perceived the presence of something approaching and peered into the darkness. He saw nothing. But he felt it. Coming for him. He waited and watched. His muscles tense. His senses awake. Then he saw it. A shadow moving down the hall. Heading towards him. A silhouette appeared in the doorway, and he jumped up, knocking over a lamp stand and sending it to the floor with a crash.

"Who's there?" The accent was a mixture of British and Middle Eastern.

"Who are you?" Ryah asked, his heart thundering. "What are you doing here?"

"I'm just looking for a place to get out of the rain," the voice said. "Looks like you're doing the same thing. Do you mind if I join you?"

He didn't wait for an answer but limped into the room and picked up an overturned chair. Ryah couldn't see him well, but by his voice, he appeared to be well-advanced in age.

"My name's Yehosha," the man said.

"Ryah."

"Ryah. Hmm. American right?"

"Yes."

"Strange place to meet an American," Yehosha said. "In a broken-down shack in the rain on an abandoned mountain." The thought amused him, and he let out a chuckle. "What brings you here? To this area, I mean?"

"I'm looking for something," Ryah said.

"Looking for something," Yehosha repeated. "What did you expect to find out here?"

"I don't know," Ryah said.

"Hmm. So, you're looking for something, but you don't know what you're going to find," Yehosha said.

"That about sums it up," Ryah said.

"A regular mystery, I see," Yehosha said. "Well, maybe I could be of help. I've lived in this area my entire life, if you don't count the four years I spent in London when I was in my twenties. I went there to see the world, experience some adventure. A young man's dream, you know. Life in the big city, surrounded by anything you could desire, but I found that what my heart really wanted was to be home. Here in the hills. Squeezing out a living. Never was a rich man but I never wanted either." He paused for a moment. "You sound like a young man. Are you on your own adventure?"

"In a sense, I suppose," Ryah said.

"Tell me about it," Yehosha said. "It looks like we got some time."

"I'm not sure I know how to explain it," Ryah said. "You probably wouldn't believe it anyway."

"I'm not so sure about that," Yehosha said. "I've seen a lot of things. Heard a lot of things most people wouldn't believe. Doesn't mean they're not true though. I've learned a lot living on these hills."

"Like what?" Ryah asked.

"Oh, sometimes at night, when I'm lying underneath the stars. I like to do that. Come out when everyone else is gone away and the city lights get cut low and just sleep under the stars. They speak to me. Tell me things sometimes."

"You're an astrologer?" Ryah asked.

"No." Yehosha laughed at the thought. "No, nothing like that." He hesitated. "Although, it probably sounds just as crazy. No, it's more like messengers that come and speak to me."

"Aliens?" Ryah asked.

"No." This time Yehosha got serious. "It's not that either. Like you said, it's hard to explain."

"Tell me about it," Ryah said. "I've got a pretty open mind." He smiled but doubted that Yehosha could see it.

"Alright. But don't say I didn't warn you. I haven't told anyone about this. Not for a long time anyway. The last time I did, they tried to lock me up. My family I mean. They thought I had gone mad. I can't blame them. I was beginning to think the same thing. But …." The silence lasted a while. "But I came to believe it was true. I have no doubt." He paused again and seemed to struggle with himself. "No. No doubt … OK, maybe a little … No. None."

"Whatever it is, it sounds like an interesting story," Ryah said. "And I'd like to hear it."

"OK. Here goes. It started years ago. Long before I was born. Long before anyone walked the earth. There was a war. A war between a king and one of his former subjects. A war in which the rebel was defeated. The king banished him and the other rebels from his kingdom, although, one or a few, I'm not sure which, were allowed to go back and petition the king."

"For what?" Ryah asked, anxious to hear what Yehosha had to say.

298

"I don't know exactly," Yehosha said. "I guess I should have told you up front that there are a lot of parts of the story I don't know. Lots of questions for which I don't have satisfactory answers. For various things, I suppose would be the best response to your question. I know some of the requests have to do with us."

"Us?" Ryah asked. "I thought you said this happened a long time ago."

"For us, yes," Yehosha said. "It's that they don't live in our world, nor do they live in what we call time."

"Another dimension?" Ryah asked.

"I don't think so," Yehosha said. "That would imply they are material in some sense. But they're not. They're … hmm … I don't know. Sorry, there I go again."

"That's alright," Ryah said. "Please continue."

"Well, the worst of the rebels were sent to a prison of sorts. Really a shadow world where they are held in chains in darkness and await their final sentence. Others were allowed to roam freely, for a while, until their appointed time comes." Yehosha paused. "Sounds crazy, doesn't it?" he asked, talking to himself as much as he was Ryah.

Ryah remembered his dream about the shadow world. The nightmare that continued to terrify him even when he was awake.

"These others, the ones that are allowed temporary freedom," Ryah said, "where are they now? Where do they live?"

"That I don't know. Where they live, that is. I know they roam the earth, but where they live … I couldn't tell you," Yehosha said.

"If they roam the earth, where are they?" Ryah asked. "Are they all around us? Why can't we see them?"

"We can sometimes," Yehosha said. "Some of us anyway. Those who have the eyes to see. Most of the time, we're blinded to their presence. They want it that way. But when they appear, it's usually as a shadow. We're kept from seeing their true nature."

"Why is that?" Ryah asked.

"If we saw them for what they truly were," Yehosha said, "I suppose we'd run away in terror. But the better answer is it helps them accomplish their purpose more easily, hiding in the shadows like they do."

"What are they doing here?" Ryah asked. "I mean, what are they trying to accomplish?"

"They want us," Yehosha said.

"What do you mean they want us?" Ryah asked.

"They want us," Yehosha repeated. "Us. Our very selves."

"I don't understand," Ryah said.

"They want to enslave us," Yehosha said. "Or more precisely, they want us to sell ourselves to them. You see, we have to choose to sell ourselves. They can't take anything we don't give them. That's part of the deal. They offer us what we want in exchange for our freedom."

"What could they possibly offer that we would trade for our freedom?" Ryah asked.

"You'd be surprised what people are willing to sell themselves for," Yehosha said.

"Quite frankly," Ryah said. "I don't know of anyone who would willingly sell themselves. I mean, who would? Would you?"

"Everyone would," Yehosha said. "In fact, everyone has. Every single person. You. Me. Everyone. But you see, it's more than that. When you sell yourself, what you're really doing is renouncing your citizenship and pledging allegiance to the shadows. And when you do it, it's forever. No turning back and no way to repay the king. No way to get out of the contract either. The shadows tell you the contract is only valid while you're alive, but it's just a lie, like everything else that comes out of their mouths. The debt is still on the books after you die."

"So, I have to repay this king, the same one who was at war with the shadows. He's the one I owe the debt to. Am I getting this right?" Ryah asked.

Yehosha nodded.

"What exactly do I owe him?" Ryah asked. "I've never met this guy. Never seen him. Never been a part of his kingdom as far as I can tell, so I can't imagine that I owe him anything. But for the sake of argument, let's say I am indebted to him. When I die, it's all over. No way to pay. No reason to pay. Who really cares what I owe?"

"You're seeing things wrong, my young friend," Yehosha replied. "and I don't even think you really believe that. The truth is, you belong to the king. Or did. You were his subject and you willingly sold yourself to his enemy for a few trinkets and an empty promise. But you still owe him everything. You see, this life is just the prelude. The next one, the real one, it lasts forever, and what you do now determines who and where you'll serve."

"I don't know about you," Ryah said, "but I'm nobody's servant and definitely nobody's slave. Not to this king. Not to these shadows. I've never sold myself to anyone, and I don't do anybody's bidding. Certainly not the bidding of some mythical shadow creatures from a different world." Even though he tried to appear confident, his words came out uncertain as if he were fighting against an inner voice, one that told him what Yehosha said was true.

"But you are a slave and you do serve them," Yehosha said. "You just don't know it. You've been blinded to the truth. Just how they want it. How the shadows want it, that is." He paused and waited for Ryah, who said nothing. "I can see you don't believe me. I'm not offended and not surprised. I told you you'd think I was crazy."

Ryah paused and looked up at the ceiling. "Maybe I do believe," he said. "Maybe I've even seen them."

"Oh?" Yehosha's ears perked up. "You've seen them."

"Perhaps." Ryah hesitated, the rain pouring on the roof the only sound in the room. "Maybe ... in my dreams ... sometimes when I'm awake."

Ryah became quiet. He thought about his dreams. They were just like what Yehosha said. Another crazy coincidence? Shared psychosis? Lies? But to what purpose? Those were the only logical explanations he could come up with. Unless Yehosha was right, but that was too unbelievable. Except ... Ryah pressed on.

"Why are they here?" Ryah asked. "Why do they want to enslave us?"

"Pride. Ego. A sick need to be worshiped. Who knows? They know that, if we do, if we choose to sell ourselves to them, we'll be their slaves in this life whether we acknowledge it or not, although they would prefer that we did acknowledge it. But worse, when we die, we'll suffer the same fate as they will. Their desire is to drag us into the abyss with them."

"Why?"

"Spite," Yehosha said. "Hatred. I've tried to find a better answer, but it always seems to boil down to that."

"Why do they hate us?" Ryah asked. "What did we do to them?"

"It's not us they hate," Yehosha said. "Well, I guess they do, but we're really just a proxy for the king. It's him they hate. And because of him, they hate us."

"But why?" Ryah asked.

"Because the king wants us back in his kingdom," Yehosha said. "To give us a second chance. He wants us to rejoin him. He doesn't want the shadows back, though. They don't get that opportunity."

"This king you're talking about," Ryah said, "have you ever seen him?"

"No. No one has," Yehosha said.

"Then how do you know he exists?" Ryah asked.

"That's a good question," Yehosha said. "For starters, look all around you."

Ryah wasn't sure what he meant and sat still waiting for more. When it didn't come, he broke the silence. "For the sake of argument, and I'm not saying I believe any of this, but how do we buy back our freedom? Who do we pay?"

"The king, of course," Yehosha said. "We're his subjects. Or were until we sold out to the shadows. When you belong to the shadows, you're theirs until you can pay the king all we owe. The problem is, we can never pay the king back."

Yehosha had just finished telling him that the king wanted him back but that there was nothing that could be done. At least that's the way it sounded to him. Ryah was confused and a hopelessness began to creep into his heart.

"Is there any way to stop the shadows?" Ryah asked.

"Depends what you mean," Yehosha said. "They're way too powerful for you. If it wasn't for the king putting restrictions on them, we'd all be in a world of trouble." He paused. "Well, I guess we are … but it'd be much worse."

"Why don't these shadows just take over then, if they're so much more powerful than us? If there's nothing we can do."

"I didn't say there was nothing we could do. But to answer your question, they're held back by the king," Yehosha said. "They can only go so far as he will allow them. Unless, of course, we choose to let them do more. One day, though, when the chosen leave this place, the shadows will be free to run things as they see fit. They will control the entire world for a short while and be permitted to show themselves. That's their goal you know. Of course, they think that somehow they can change their fate. They're as deluded as we are."

"I thought you said everyone had already sold out to them," Ryah said. "Aren't we already under their control according to you?"

"No. We're not truly under their control, not if we don't want to be, in that our freedom has been paid for," Yehosha said.

Ryah was becoming aggravated at the double talk and the lack of a firm answer. Deep down, he felt like there was truth to what Yehosha was saying. He had seen too much not to believe, but it was beyond what he was able to comprehend. It was as if he was listening but not really hearing. In his frustration, he lashed out at Yehosha.

"You just said that everyone is a slave to them and that we could never pay the king back. You're not making sense, old man. I think you're as crazy as they say you are."

Yehosha didn't take offense. "No, we can never pay the king back, but he has already paid the price for us, the ransom so to speak," he said.

"So this king, who is our king, that we owe everything even though we don't know him, allows these shadows to be here and lets them make us their slaves," Ryah said, "meaning we are fated to a veritable hell. And then he says we have to pay him back, but we can't pay him back. But it doesn't matter, because he's already bought us back, yet we still owe him. Is that it? Does any of that actually make sense to you?"

Ryah waited for Yehosha to answer but he didn't.

"Look, just answer this," Ryah said. "Why aren't we all free if he's already paid?"

"It's really quite simple," Yehosha said. "People don't want their freedom, and they have to want it to get it. And to get it, they have to accept the king's offer, which, after we accept it, requires that we sacrifice all we have for his

304

sake. Most people would rather live in the shadows, though, than accept his offer."

"Why?" Ryah asked.

"They don't understand the offer," Yehosha said. "Or they don't know about it. Even when they know about it and understand, they don't believe. I mean, it sounds pretty crazy when it's said out loud. Besides, the shadows' offer seems beautiful in comparison, doesn't it? We get everything we've always wanted. Every desire fulfilled. No strings attached. That's the way they put it, don't they?" He seemed to be talking more to himself than to Ryah. "But it's all a lie. A lie to drag us down with them. The irony is the lie is more believable than the truth."

"How many people accept the offer?" Ryah asked. "The king's offer, I mean."

"Very few," Yehosha said. "Very few. Almost nobody really."

"And the rest … the rest are …"

"I'm afraid so," Yehosha said.

"Is anyone else aware of the shadows?" Ryah asked.

"Just a handful," Yehosha said. "Even many of those in the Kingdom are ignorant of their existence. But there are some who know. Some who can help explain to you better than I can. Go to them and ask them. But beware. There is a counterfeit kingdom that has risen which mimics the real one. They often look alike and talk alike, but there is a difference. One leads to life. The other to death."

"How do you tell them apart?" Ryah said.

"The members of the counterfeit kingdom are liars and murderers just like the shadows. They have sworn loyalty to the evil ones and willingly do their bidding, doing that which the shadows cannot do themselves and hastening the arrival of their day. The day of the shadows." Yehosha shuddered as he said it. He looked directly at Ryah, his eyes piercing through the darkness. "I repeat. Be careful. The humans that serve them may appear to be angels of light and mercy, but in the end, you'll know them by their deeds. And by their allegiance."

Ryah sat back and contemplated what he had heard. Whether it was true or not, he didn't know, but one thing he knew for sure was that the shadows existed. The only alternative explanation for what he had experienced was that he had gone crazy, and he knew that wasn't the case. But what should he do with this information? He couldn't tell anyone else, because they wouldn't believe him, yet he couldn't just sit back and pretend they didn't exist, not with what he had seen and felt and heard. Not if Yehosha was correct about what they wanted.

A beam of light entered the window and fell by Ryah's feet. He looked up and realized for the first time that the rain had stopped. Yehosha rose from the chair to leave.

"Well, I've got to get going," he said. "I hope you find what you're looking for."

Ryah didn't answer but thought some more. He had so many questions left, so many more things he wanted to know. But there was one question that disturbed him. One thing out of all the incredible things he was just told that he couldn't reconcile.

"Why would the king allow the shadows to come here in the first place if he cares about us so much?" Ryah asked.

"That's one of the great mysteries that I don't have an answer for," Yehosha said. He turned and walked down the hall. When he got to the door, he turned around once more. "Best of luck on your quest," he said and disappeared from sight.

Chapter 36

Ryah stepped outside the house. There was no sign of Yehosha nor of anyone else. The ground was already beginning to dry up under the hot Middle Eastern sun, and the mud on Ryah's shoes transformed into dust as he walked down the mountain towards the main road. Waiting in the partial shade of an olive tree for a taxi to pass by, he contemplated his next step. It's not that he didn't know what he had to do. He did, although his stomach churned at the thought. Hadn't the old man said it? "They appear as angels of mercy and light, but in the end their deeds are evil." They murdered General Chao and his associate. Tried to assassinate Lucio and Brostov. Pretended to help the homeless only to use them as biological weapons to destroy those who stood in their way. Liars and murderers. That described them well.

And the attack on the transit? Were they so deluded that they were willing to die to facilitate their scheme? Was it all an elaborate setup to introduce Maryam to him? The way she looked at him. The way she spoke. More lies?

Those eyes told a different story. They seemed so full of hurt but also of love. But not what passes for love. Real love. Sacrificial love. Love that asks for nothing in return. Was she part of the true kingdom?

"No," it whispered in his ear. "*Don't fall for it. They knew who you were. Somehow, they knew, and they used you to further their agenda. I don't know how or why they involved you in their scheme, but they did.*"

"*But the way she touched me. I felt it. And how she asked me to spare Jason's life. There's something wrong here. This can't be true.*"

"They played you," it whispered. *"They knew how to get to you. The shadows have been watching you. They know your need to protect the weak. They used it against you. Brought her to you on purpose and gave you that story. Set you up to take the fall. What do you think Klins will do when he finds out you let them slip away? You think she will save your life? Fool. It was all part of the plan. You are nothing but a pawn in her twisted game, and you're too blind to see it."*

"No. No! That can't be true."

"Oh no?" it whispered. *"The photos don't lie. You saw her with Abbad, didn't you? Are you going to deny what you saw with your own two eyes? You know Abbad's behind everything and she's with him. They're part of the false kingdom. The one that wants to destroy the world and rebuild it in their image."*

Ryah shut his eyes and thought about the photo. Not the one with Allison and Abbad. The one he held on to. The one he hadn't shown Rogan. It was her. The woman with the fierce green eyes. Sitting with Abbad in a coffee shop. She was with them. He hadn't wanted to believe it. He wanted to believe it was some kind of mistake. But it wasn't. She was a traitor. A collaborator in the kingdom of shadows, and she was deserving of death. Ryah had made up his mind. He walked to the main road, determined to carry out his plan, oblivious to the cold hands of the shadow that wrapped around his face and covered his ears.

The taxi dropped Ryah off in the middle of the old city. Rogan waited in the designated spot and waved Ryah over to the table where he had already begun to eat his meal.

"Hey, Ryah. You ready to order?"

"Take it to go," Ryah said. "I've booked us seats on a military transport flight that leaves in less than two hours. We'll be home before nightfall."

Rogan wrapped up his food and followed Ryah, who walked with resolve down the street. "What did you find?" he asked.

"I found what I needed to," Ryah said.

He was unusually sullen, Rogan noted, but he didn't push Ryah for more information. There was no change in his mood the entire flight back. Rogan sat in silence and watched him. A few minutes before landing, Ryah finally spoke up.

"I'm going in to see Klins alone. Stay away from the Council, but get ready to move should I need you."

"What's going on?" Rogan asked.

"I need to tell Klins about the Kingdom. How I found them but let them go. He's not going to take it well, and I don't blame him. I don't want you around when that happens. I'm going to take the heat for it and tell him you didn't know anything about it. If I make it out of there with my skin intact, I'm going to hunt them down and exterminate them. And for that, I'm going to need your help."

"Whatever you say, Ryah," Rogan said, "but I don't need you to cover for me."

"That's an order, sergeant," Ryah commanded and said no more.

There was no point delaying it. No reason to wait until the next day. Time was of the essence, or so he told himself. Truth was that, in his anger and hurt, he wasn't thinking as clearly as he thought he was.

Klins waited in his office for Ryah. His smile disappeared as soon as he saw the look on Ryah's face.

"Welcome back, Ryah. You said you wanted to speak with me right away. I assume you've found some information that you needed to share."

"I have, sir," Ryah said. "I've got a lot to tell you."

"Proceed."

Ryah pulled out the communication files Lucio had given him and placed them on Klins' desk. "Please read these," he said and waited for Klins to do so.

When Klins had finished, he looked up at Ryah. "How long ago did you get these?" he asked.

"A couple of days," Ryah said.

"Why didn't Lucio send these to me personally, and why didn't you contact me as soon as you got it?" he asked.

"There was no way to do it," Ryah said. "Abbad has much greater control than we realized. And he has the Council under surveillance. Any communication in and out of here, they can listen to."

Klins' face turned red but he maintained his calm. Ryah had always been impressed with his ability to do that.

"Who is that woman in the picture with Abbad?" Klins asked. "Did Lucio tell you who she was?"

"I do know her," Ryah said. "I trailed her one day when I thought she might have had something to do with the Kingdom. Turns out she did, but I let her go."

Klins no longer kept his cool. "You knew about her, but you did nothing?" he yelled at Ryah. "You deliberately withheld this information from me? What the hell were you thinking? Who are you to make that decision? My orders were clear, were they not? Tell me everything you find. I'm sure those were the words that came out of my mouth. And because of your insubordination, we lost the opportunity to take out the head of a terrorist organization whose goal is to destroy our nation. That sounds a lot like treason to me, don't you think?"

"Yes, sir," Ryah said. "I take full responsibility for my actions."

Klins brooded and Ryah knew his fate was being decided right there.

"Where was Rogan when all this was happening?" Klins asked.

"In the dark," Ryah said. "He had no need to know. He would have come to tell you."

"Then, your intention was to deceive me?" Klins asked.

"No, sir," Ryah said. "I thought it was a mistake. That is, I didn't think they were involved, just that they were the scapegoats for someone else."

"Don't you think that's a decision that I needed to make?"

"Yes, sir. I have no excuse. I just ask that you let me make up for it. Let me hunt these people down and take them out for you."

Klins said nothing but stared off beyond Ryah. Finally, he spoke up.

"Tell me where to find them," Klins said.

"Out in the Kinset, past the old wineries," Ryah answered.

"Wait for me here," Klins said and walked out of the office.

A few minutes later, two security personnel came in and escorted Ryah to an interrogation cell in the basement. Minutes turned to hours while Ryah sat on the cold metal chair that his captives had often sat in, waiting, wondering. When Klins returned, he was alone.

"We sent a reconnaissance flight to the location you gave us," Klins said. "There was no one there."

"They were," Ryah said. "I swear to you."

"There was evidence that they were," Klins said. "You are correct in that, but they had moved their base. Any idea where they might have gone?"

"No, sir. I don't," Ryah said. "But I can track them down. Even though I don't deserve it, I'm asking you to give me another chance. I won't fail again. That I can guarantee."

Klins deliberated for a while. "If you do fail," he said, "it will be your head. And that I can guarantee."

"Thank you, sir," Ryah said.

The electronic lock clicked, and the door to the holding room cracked open.

"You have a day. Two at most," Klins said and motioned for Ryah to leave.

Ryah had been in the interrogation room for much longer than he thought, so when he was finally allowed out, dawn was starting to break. His first stop that morning would be Riverplace, where he knew the Kingdom used to recruit their new members. He hoped they would still be following the same pattern or, at least, that someone there had information which might lead him to their new location. After exiting the transit station, he walked down the main road towards the plaza where the homeless would congregate. There was no one out that day. Not a single prostitute to proposition him. No one to beg him for spare change to get their daily fix. It was deserted, with no signs of life, like a ghost town that had been long abandoned.

He went through the back alleys but found nothing. Not until he made it back to the main street ready to give up did he see a couple people, one of them he recognized. He crossed the street and went up to the two.

"Jason, right?" Ryah said.

Jason turned around. The fear ran down his face when he realized who it was, and he sent the person with him on her way.

"Yeah," Jason said. "It's a surprise to see you here. What brings you down this way?"

"I was looking for you," Ryah said, "or one of your associates." Ryah acted as if he was nervous. "I have information that I need to get back to your group. It's urgent. Is there any way to put me in contact with your leader?"

"Which leader?" Jason asked.

"That lady, I don't remember her name," Ryah said. "The one who came to visit me."

"You mean Allison," Jason said.

"Allison. Right. I need to see her. To speak with her."

"You can tell me, and I'll make sure she gets the message," Jason said.

"No ... no, I can't do that. I need to speak with her in person," Ryah said. "I know I can trust her."

Jason hesitated and Ryah noticed his uncertainty.

"Look. It's imperative that I see her," Ryah said. "Just tell her I need to see her and get back to me. Can you do that?"

"Yeah. Yeah, I guess I can," Jason said. "Where can I meet you?"

"There's a café across from the hospital. The one that sells those fried pies. You know the one, right?"

Jason nodded his head.

"I'll be waiting there for you," Ryah said. "How long until you know?"

"No more than an hour," Jason said and took off down the street.

Ryah hoped this would work out as he didn't really have a backup plan. He made his way towards New Carmel Medical Center, stopping briefly to buy a change of clothes. As he walked out of the store in his new outfit, he felt refreshed. But the exhaustion was overwhelming, blocking out his instincts that were trying to warn him. When he arrived at the café, Jason was already waiting.

"What's the word?" Ryah asked.

"Allison wants to meet," Jason said. "She says to bring you right away. Would that be alright?"

"That'll work," Ryah said. "Is she close by?"

"No. I'll have to take you to her," Jason said. He was the one who looked nervous now.

"OK. Would you mind if I got something to eat first?" Ryah said. "I haven't eaten in a couple days, and I feel like I'm ready to pass out."

"Sure. Of course. Tell you what. Let me know what you want, and I'll get it for you," Jason said.

"I appreciate it. Just a breakfast sandwich and a coffee. Black. One sugar," Ryah said. "I'm going to wash up."

Ryah went to the restroom and pulled out his comm. "Being taken to Kingdom group," he wrote Rogan. "Notify Klins and track my signal. Send backup. Make sure they're well-armed. We're not taking prisoners." He pocketed his comm and then pulled it back out. "Plenty of backup. Recommend at least a battalion."

As he walked back to the counter where Jason was collecting the order, Rogan returned his communication. "Told Klins. Bringing gamma squad and a battalion. Are you sure about this?"

"Yes," was Ryah's simple response.

Ryah and Jason walked out of the café together and found a car waiting for them.

"Go ahead and take the front seat," Jason said.

The driver was a man Ryah had never met before. He was unshaven, a couple days growth, and the stubble on his beard was a mixture of brown and gray. He said nothing but accelerated as soon as Ryah closed the car door.

The ride into the countryside was quiet. Ryah didn't feel like talking and was happy the others felt the same way. His mind ran over the details like it always did on a mission. The process. The order. The cleanup. But this time there were a couple problems. He hadn't had time to plan or talk it out with Rogan, and there was no way to communicate with him now without seeming suspicious. He would have to play this one by ear and hope that Rogan would follow his lead. But the larger issue was the emotion which clouded his reasoning. Revenge, hate, fear. Maybe a mix of those and a few others. He was going into the shadow stronghold unarmed to face a foe against which he suspected weapons were useless anyway.

"*At least I'll die in battle,*" he thought, "*and not as some lowly criminal in the Council's killing field. And I'll do it fighting for the correct side.*" He was consoled knowing that whether or not he made it out neither would Jason nor the woman with the fierce green eyes. He would make sure of that.

Judging by the sun in the sky, it was around noon when they arrived at their destination, a camp in the mountains surrounding the Kinset Valley Basin. It was no more than two miles from the kingdom's previous encampment, but it was located in a much better strategic position. In and among the trees and near the top of a mountain that overlooked the entire valley, the site was well hidden, and their lookouts would be able to see anyone approaching along the river and the road that ran beside it. Their only exposure came from their rear flank, which would not be an issue unless someone was aware of their base. And that would be their undoing.

The car came to a stop in front of an abandoned hunting cabin. Ryah exited and walked up to it with Jason. Three knocks and the door opened. Allison came out while removing a white lab coat and handed it to her assistant. Before the door could shut, Ryah was able to get a glimpse of what was inside. At least two people were being treated, receiving injections of some sort, and Ryah made a mental note that this was most likely their lab. Allison grabbed Ryah by the arm and led him away down a path towards the main section of the base.

"I'm so glad to see you again," Allison said. "I never got the chance to thank you for what you did. Without you, we never would have been able to move everyone in time. I'm pretty sure I saw a surveillance flight this morning. If they had seen us ... Look, I can't thank you enough for giving us a chance. For believing me. For believing in us." She squeezed Ryah's arm. "What did you need to speak with me about?"

"It involves you and Maryam as well," Ryah said. "Is she around? Is there any way I can see her?"

"Of course," Allison said. "I'll go find her and bring her to you so we can talk. She might be out of the camp. I don't know. Sometimes she and Kaliya go play by the river. Do me a favor and wait for me by the large tree over there. The one all alone in the clearing. You'll find some logs to sit on while you wait. We use that when we want to have large meetings."

She ran off to look for Maryam, and Ryah went to the clearing to wait. He pulled out his comm to contact Rogan. Even without satellite coverage of the valley, at this elevation he was able to get a faint signal. He looked at the screen and saw a simple message. "In position."

After a while when Allison didn't return, Ryah started to walk around, pacing the clearing at first and then branching out to get a feel for the rest of the camp but never losing sight of the clearing just in case Allison came back. Over an hour later, Allison returned. She, Maryam, and Kaliya came up a trail that led through the oaks and beeches and straight to Ryah.

When Maryam saw Ryah, she ran up to him and threw her arms around him. His arms remained by his side as she stretched up to kiss him on the cheek. She felt his coldness and looked into his face. She saw his eyes. Indifferent. Distant. Determined. Her instinct caused her to push back. Something was wrong, but she didn't know what. A voice inside her told her to run. To get out of there as fast as she could, but her feet were frozen in place. She was afraid. More than she had ever been. More than when the Council burned down her home and stole her friend off the street.

"What's going on, Ryah?" she asked.

"Why did you lie to me?" he said.

"What do you mean?" There was panic in her voice. Her heart began to pound. "I've never lied to you."

He said nothing but he didn't have to. She read it on his face.

"Oh no, Ryah," she said. "What have you done?"

Chapter 37

The sound of automatic rifle fire split open the trees from two sides of the camp. Maryam tried to run, but Ryah had a tight grip on her arm. She looked up and saw the hate in his face. From where it came, she couldn't understand, but it was plain to see. Using all her might, she pushed free and grabbed Kaliya who stood petrified and immobile by her side. Together they took off down the path towards the river away from the explosions of the percussion grenades that came from the same direction as the rifle bursts. Ryah didn't pursue them, knowing the soldiers were using the detonations to drive them towards a trap. Basic artillery. If he had been the target, he would have run towards the artillery position and then down a line off and around to the side. Sort of like swimming out of a rip current. These people ran on survival instinct, away from the danger and right into the snares that awaited them.

Ryah headed towards the tree line in the back, ducking down so as not to get caught in the friendly fire that whizzed over his head. A hundred meters back he found Rogan who pulled him off to the side to brief him on the plan.

"Who've you brought to the party?" Ryah asked.

"We've got one gamma squad," Rogan said, "and a battalion of the Council guard. As requested."

"Great," Ryah said. "What's the battle plan? I assume you're driving them towards the river. Did you set up a position down there?"

"The gammas made a semi-circle around this site," Rogan said. "Their job is to force the enemy down into the plain to make it easier to see them. The soldiers from the Council guard will be cutting off their escape routes and channeling them towards the river. There's no way they're making it across during flood season, but if a few happen to, there's a platoon stationed on the other side with orders to shoot anyone that's wet."

"It's the way I would have done it," Ryah said. "Did you bring an extra weapon for me?"

"Of course. Take your pick," Rogan said. He stared at Ryah. "Are you sure?"

Ryah knew what Rogan was talking about. "Yes," he answered, but he didn't mean it. There was a small part of him that said no. A quiet voice that couldn't be heard above the sounds of the battle. He picked up a .22 handgun and a fixed blade knife, weapons of torture more than weapons of war, and headed down the hill towards the sound of the fight. As he walked out of the tree line, he saw scores of people looking like dots below, some sprinting in random directions, many of them lying where they had fallen. The gammas above maintained their position while the Council guard encircled the rest of the base and closed in like a lasso slowly being cinched around the neck of its prey. There was no escape from this trap. Not a single person broke through the lines. One person flung himself in the river in a desperate bid to swim across. But the undertow dragged him down and he didn't surface again.

As Ryah approached the main body of survivors huddled together in the middle of the encroaching army, he heard their cries.

"*Good,*" he thought as he surveyed the damage already done and heard their terror. "*Where's the army that's going to save you now? I guess you'll be joining them in their shadow world soon.*"

Rogan ran ahead to a field commander and hurried back to Ryah.

"The fight's over and you're in charge now," Rogan said. "Let us know what you want."

Ryah nodded. "Find Allison and any others that look like leaders and bring them to me."

Rogan turned to carry out the orders, but Ryah stopped him.

"And Maryam. I want her and her daughter alive. They'll be the last to go," Ryah said.

It took no more than thirty minutes to round up the survivors and bring them to the clearing where the Kingdom held their meetings. One of the soldiers came up to Ryah.

"Sir," the soldier said. "We've brought all the survivors back here, but we haven't been able to locate the woman you requested. Our captain is over there interrogating one of the prisoners now to see what information he can get out of him."

Ryah followed the soldier back to watch the proceedings up close. The captain had propped up a log on two chairs to use as his torture device. The prisoner had been tied to the log so that he hung in the air like a pig on a barbecue spit. He hung there upside down with the weight of his body supported on his shattered joints, his face a foot off the ground.

"I'll ask you again," the captain said, stooping down and holding the photo of Allison in front of his face. "Where can I find her?"

Between the screams of agony, the prisoner managed to murmur a soft, "I don't know. Please, I don't know."

The captain nodded and a corporal next to him kicked him with the point of his steel-toed boots. The rib made a snapping sound as it cracked. A few seconds later, a red stream started to flow out of the helpless man's mouth. He tried to scream, but the sound came out as a gagging cough as saliva mixed with blood in his throat.

"*Punctured a lung,*" Ryah thought. "*He'll be coming to a painful end soon.*"

He watched as the man turned deep red, then purple. His whole body started to twitch in a spasm. His chest jerked up and down, his head banging off the wood behind him. Even in such pain, the instinct to survive was great, but futile. It took a full minute for it to stop. For the next two, the body would tremble as the unconscious man's brain stem slowly shut down until he moved no more.

"I guess we're not getting any more information out of this one," the captain said. "Who's next?" He looked into the sea of faces in front of him. "Ah, how about this one." He pointed to a young woman, barely twenty years old, with cream-colored skin and jet-black hair.

Two soldiers dragged her in front of him and tied her to a tree. Ryah looked away. He didn't want to see this, even though he knew she deserved it. She and all the filth she associated with. The shrieks lasted longer than Ryah thought he could stomach. When they stopped, he looked back. A red pool had formed on the ground by her feet as blood spurted out in bursts. Her cream-colored skin turned the palest white Ryah could imagine, and her life drained away, one heartbeat at a time.

"You know people," the captain shouted. "I can keep this up all afternoon. Or I can make it stop. All I need is the whereabouts of this one woman. You know her." He held the picture high over his head. "Her name's Allison. C'mon now. Somebody here knows her. These men here," he said, pointing to the soldiers. "They haven't been fed in weeks. They're hungry and I can't hold them back much longer. The first person, who lets me know where she is, lives. The rest will go to the dogs."

With that, the soldiers in the unit and most of the gammas started to howl like wolves commemorating their latest kill. In the midst of their celebration, a couple of

321

soldiers walked into the clearing dragging a woman with them. They stopped in front of the captain and threw her down in front of him.

"Well, it's about time you made an appearance," the captain said, smiling at his captive. "You know, you could have saved a couple of lives if you weren't such a coward."

"You would have killed them anyway," Allison said.

"True," the captain replied. "But it might have ended more quickly for them." His tone was arrogant, mocking, condescending.

"What do you want from me?" Allison asked.

The captain removed his knife from its sheath and stroked it down Allison's face. "First, I'd like to make you look like that one over there," he said, pointing the blade towards a woman at the edge of the crowd. "Then, who knows? And after that we can talk."

Allison remained still, resigned and unafraid.

"If you're looking for me, then why do you need the rest of these people?" she asked.

"Bargaining chips," he said. "Target practice. Let's see … what else?"

While the captain spoke, a flash shot out of the woods and landed on top of him before he or any of the soldiers could react. A man growling with the ferocity and rage of a wounded bear locked his arms around the captain's head and twisted it in such a way that any minute move would shatter his spine.

"Jason," Allison said. "We don't do that here. That's not our way."

Jason held on, refusing to let go. Spit flew from his mouth as he cursed the captain. Allison walked up to Jason and placed a hand on his shoulder. Ryah's stomach tightened more.

"Let go, Jason," she whispered. "Let go. It's alright. I've got this."

Jason released his grip and was immediately seized by a squad of soldiers. The captain brushed himself off and walked over to Jason. Without saying a word, he raised his pistol. A shot rang out. Jason fell and his body made a thud like a sack of feed when it hit the ground.

"NO!" Allison screamed. "Why did you do that?"

He turned and slapped her across the face, dropping her to her knees.

"I'll take it from here."

The captain looked behind him.

"You're dismissed," Ryah said.

The captain wore a look of disgust. "As you wish sir," he said and stepped aside, muttering under his breath.

"As you're well aware," Ryah said to Allison. "You're not getting out of here, so you might as well just tell us what you know. I'll make sure it's as quick as possible."

"Whether we get out of here or not," Allison said, "is not for you to decide. There are more here with us than against us. And if you kill us, it's because he let you. Nothing more."

Ryah sized up the crowd. "You may be right," he said, "but I think you're missing the fact that we're holding all the weapons." He paused and looked in her eyes. "I'll give you one more chance. Where are they?"

"Who?" Allison asked.

"The prostitutes. The homeless," Ryah said.

"They're spread throughout the camp," Allison said. "Why?" Her brow furrowed in confusion.

"And where is your lab? The one you're using to create the virus," Ryah said.

"What?" Allison said. "What lab? What virus? What are you talking about?"

"Spare me your lies, Allison," Ryah said. "We have the communications between you and Abbad. We have a picture of you with him. We know all about your plan. It's too late. Just let us know where it is. We're going to find it anyway. So just tell me where it is."

"Ryah, dear," Allison said. "I have no idea what you're talking about." She touched his face with her right hand, the sleeve slipping down and revealing the tattoo. "What have they done to you?" She shook her head slightly, but it wasn't anger. It was compassion.

He brushed her arm away and called behind him. "Bring them to me."

The gammas escorted two people, one a young girl, not even a teenager, with blonde hair and beautiful green eyes, the spitting image of her mother who walked beside her.

"No, Ryah," Allison pleaded. "Please. You don't know what you're doing."

"Tell me where it is, Allison," Ryah said. "Don't make me do this."

Allison cried and whispered to herself but didn't answer him. He raised the .22 and put it to Maryam's head.

"Tell me, Allison." His finger pulled back on the trigger, squeezing gently to give Allison time to reconsider.

"Stop. Stop now." The voice wasn't a command. It was an appeal. "Please stop. I can't let you do this."

A man pushed his way through the crowd wearing the uniform of a gamma officer. Ryah knew the man. Everyone in America knew this man. He was older now and wore the insignia of a lieutenant colonel. His face showed the signs of his alcoholism, a vice which would have had him kicked out of the military long ago if he wasn't America's greatest war hero. The one who changed the course of history. The one who saved a nation.

"Please stop," he repeated. "I know this one." He turned to Maryam. "Do you remember me?"

Maryam shook her head.

"I remember you," he said. "They told me you would be here." He paused as his lips began to tremble. "I came here to destroy you. To remove you from my nightmares."

There was an emptiness in his eyes. Looking into them was like looking into a mirror, where all that is seen is an image without substance.

"I still see it. Your face. At night when I sleep. You come to me and you curse me." He looked into the distance as he remembered. "You scream at me to stop. Your face. So young. So afraid. And you curse me."

He hesitated. "Look at me. Look at what your curses have done to me. Look at what I've done to myself."

Maryam began to sob. His face was familiar, older. She thought hard. Back to a time when all was childlike and simple.

"I think about you every day. I think about what I did to you. What we did to you."

He wanted to reach out, but he was afraid to touch her.

"Do you remember me, Cate? Do you know who I am?"

Ryah watched Maryam's eyes grow wide. And he understood. Just like she did.

"Do you remember me now, Cate?" Ryah heard the colonel ask. "You were six years old, and I took your innocence. Me and those other three. We took it in the woods not far from here, while your mom called your name. We could have left you, left you to live with your shame, but we made it worse. We sold you. We sold you so others could do the same to you that we did."

Tears flowed down Maryam's cheek, but her face displayed no emotion.

"The regret," he said. "The guilt. I can't live with it. I don't deserve to live. Not after what I did." He fell to his knees in front of Maryam. "Forgive me, Cate, if you can. If it's even possible, forgive me."

The colonel's body quivered and his hands shook. His face was tortured. He had lived with it for twenty years. That was why he drank. To cover up the guilt. To ease the pain, so he wouldn't remember, at least for a little while. But the whiskey could only mask the sound of the screams in his mind which multiplied with each passing year. That was why he ran into battle brazen and unafraid. It wasn't courage that drove him. It was self-hate. Loathsome self-destruction. And every time he survived a mission, his guilt increased. So, he killed and tortured and taught others to do the same. With every blow, with every slice, he was killing himself, trying to kill the evil inside. But the evil only laughed at him and grew stronger. He was no longer a man. Just a shadow. An empty shell, more dead than alive.

Out there in the middle of the woods, surrounded by his soldiers, he reached out to grab hold of Maryam's leg, begging for a silent mercy. Ryah understood her betrayal, felt her anger. He knew the hate borne of revenge. It's what he would have felt. It's how he felt towards her.

But what he witnessed changed everything. Maryam didn't hesitate anymore. Reaching down, she took hold of the colonel's chin. A lone tear rolled down her face and landed on the top of his head. Bending over, she kissed him. Mercy offered. The unpardonable forgiven.

As she did, a bolt of lightning shattered the silence, striking the colonel in his chest. His body shook as though a battle raged inside. One last shudder and the shadow that lived inside the colonel, the evil that laughed and caused him to hate the world and hate himself, the darkness he had sold himself to, threw him to the ground. Ryah heard it curse, those same vile words he had heard in a dream, as it drifted away into the sky. He looked at the colonel again. The man was transformed, radiant, a light from within but not of him glowing and chasing away the darkness.

A gentle but powerful wind began to flow around Ryah, whispering but as if it were a voice speaking a command. At its sound, a hard substance like scales fell from his eyes and ears. The black air around him ripped open, a dark veil torn by unseen hands, and a light shone through the fissure. Ryah saw it all. For the first time he knew the truth. And he believed it.

He looked around at the people who called themselves the Kingdom. The true Kingdom. It was a kingdom full of the weak, the frail, the forgotten, and unwanted. But there was a strength in them. A light that couldn't be extinguished. A light that could chase away the darkness inside mankind and free them from the shadows. It wasn't their own light, though, but a gift from the king purchased with a ransom that only he could pay, a portion of himself that they were allowed to possess, if they were to accept it. A gift they were commanded to share with others.

The breeze transported him into the sky above the plain, and time disappeared for Ryah. Memories and visions flooded his mind, past and present, the seen and the unseen mixing together as one, the truth unfolding like simultaneous movies on a screen that only he could witness.

A black cloud in the form of a great dragon bellowed over the plain, shadows spilling from its mouth and diving into the valley. Swords and bows in their hands, their hate, their very nature, spurring them on. The weapons they held became humans – the captain, the gammas, and the soldiers, obeying the voice of their grim masters – earthly instruments of destruction in the celestial war against the Kingdom.

Shots rang out, the captain shouting orders, and Kingdom members fell. Ryah looked down on Allison and saw a red stain on her white shirt. She stood, not daring to move, aware but as if in a dream. Her body began to sway, and her eyes rolled into her head. Her knees buckled and she collapsed to the ground, her torso tumbling over backwards onto her legs, her arms dangling at her sides. She lay staring up at the sky, at the stars that were just beginning to show themselves as the day faded. She had a smile on her face. And the stars smiled back at her.

A sound echoed through the valley, like the rolling of a distant thunder, except that it didn't dissipate but grew louder and louder, filling the whole basin with the roar of an onrushing wind, drowning out all other noise and reverberating in Ryah's heart. He looked to his left to watch. A glorious army approached, illuminating the sky with a brilliant, white light as if the stars had descended from the heavens to make their home on earth and now rushed through the valley to do battle with the shadows.

The host of warriors descended through the clouds. Thousands of horses charged through the valley, running down the banks of the river, along the slopes of the hills, and galloping on top of the water as they flung themselves in a fearless dash to be the first to reach their enemy. On the back of each horse, a man, but more than a man, rode with fury, carrying a flaming sword held high above his head and screaming a war cry that could make the fiercest warrior tremble in fear. The earth itself recognized the authority of the king's army as trees bowed and rocks split in an attempt to get out of its way.

At the head of the line was the great General Chael. His uniform was bright white, an orange fire emanating from his clothes, but he was not consumed in the flames. His face was set forward, and he spurred his horse onward, shouting oaths to defend his people and destroy his enemy underfoot. The two armies met with a loud clash, like a clap of thunder, locked together in a violent struggle. Light against shadow. Good versus evil. Neither one gaining an advantage until the set time.

The war faded into the background, and Ryah saw the kingdoms of the world. The men, their people, whose hearts were united with the shadows, fighting for power, for gold, for treasures that were fleeting. Believing the lie. Desiring freedom but living as slaves.

The past came into focus, and he saw Klins taking money from Abbad, storing it in his own treasure house in betrayal of his people. He saw photos being doctored to make Allison and Maryam appear guilty, subtle deception with a treacherous, deadly motive. He saw Evan as he sat on the rooftop in New Carmel and placed a bullet through Giordan's lungs to shut him up and then as he fired again on the rooftop in Rome, aiming in just the perfect spot to make it look like Lucio would die but knowing he wouldn't. He saw Evan's love for his sister Cate used against him, a lie that bound him instead of freeing him, and he knew the truth that could have set him free. He saw Lucio, an angel of light and peace and mercy, the self-declared savior of mankind, orchestrating it all. Paying off Evan and Jackson, feeding them the lines to deliver to Ryah. Directing the attackers in the alley, not caring whether Ryah lived or died, only that the Kingdom would be blamed. Orchestrating everything so that Ryah and Rogan would be deceived into believing it was the Kingdom who wanted to rule the world when it was Lucio all along. And he saw the one shadow that lived inside each of them. The one who dared reign in place of the king. The one whose army was defeated and banished forever.

Ryah looked down once more on the battle in the valley and saw her there. The woman with the fierce green eyes. Screaming, crying, dragging on the arm of someone who had fallen. Rogan ran to her and took hold, but she wouldn't move. He shouted at her and pulled her against her will. They ran back through the trees and away from the death which surrounded them, Rogan grasping Maryam with his left hand and Kaliya with the other. They fled towards the river as bullets flew past them. And Ryah saw the army of light surrounding them and holding them in their protective embrace, preventing both human and shadow from touching a hair on their heads.

His eyes returned once more to the place where Maryam had kneeled. A man lay there, his breathing labored as he stared into the sky. He saw him there. Saw himself there, torn apart by a hail of bullets, his life spilling onto the ground.

Ryah heard a voice from behind and turned around. He was there like he had been so many times before, dressed in white and calling to Ryah, beckoning for him to follow.

"Come, Ryah," Guriel said.

Ryah noticed his clothes covered in blood. "I can't," he said. "Look at me. I can't come. Not like this. Tell my lord, my king, I can't. After what I've done to his people. I know where I belong."

"It was always a part of his plan, Ryah."

Ryah stared at Guriel, searching for answers to questions he couldn't formulate. Guriel seemed to know what Ryah was thinking.

"So they, too, might know and believe," Guriel said.

"Who?"

Guriel smiled. "Come, Ryah," he repeated. "It's time for you to see."

Chapter 38

Ryah looked up at the sky. It was blue … but different. A shade of blue he had never seen before. He was on a hillside, lying in grass that made him feel like he was on a bed of the finest silk. All around were plants of a kind he had never seen before. They danced and swayed in the wind as if they wanted to speak to him. In the distance, a city rose above the plain, glimmering like a diamond and casting rainbows of diverse colors, none of which he even knew existed. There was a smell in the air that was indescribably pleasant, and the wind held him in its warm embrace.

He stood up to walk towards the city, and as he did, he strode on top of those impossibly thin blades of silk as if he were weightless. He heard a voice calling to him, and he felt at peace. Not just relaxed, but at peace. And happy. Like that day he spent with his best friend at the lake, fishing and laughing, long before he grew up and knew what the world was really like. He understood that the happiness, this time, would last forever, and he knew he would never get tired of it.

On his journey, he passed by a waterfall which fell straight down and whose waters were as smooth as glass. He stopped at the pool at the base of the waterfall and bent over to take a drink. It was the most refreshing thing he had ever tasted, and he felt the life in its waters. When he bent over for another drink, he saw a creature looking back at him. The creature was magnificent, perfect, and he knew it was him, what he was truly meant to be.

The voice spoke again, and a wind grabbed onto him. It took him into the city in a matter of moments, carrying him through a gate cut out of a single large gemstone that was both perfectly clear and the deepest green at the same time. The breeze on which he traveled made him pass over translucent streets made of precious metals and gently dropped him off in front of a house. He hesitated, not knowing what to do, but there was no fear and no anxiety, only wonder and awe at this magnificent place he had been transported to.

He opened the door without knocking, somehow knowing that this was where he belonged. From inside, he heard some voices. Familiar voices of people he used to know. Of someone who used to be his enemy and of someone who helped him see the truth. And one more voice. The one he had heard his whole life if he was listening carefully.

"Welcome home, son," the prince said. "I've been waiting for you."

Made in the USA
Las Vegas, NV
29 October 2022

58409824R00194